Parting the Veil

PARTING THE VEIL

Jay Davis

TOR®

A TOM DOHERTY ASSOCIATES BOOK
NEW YORK

This is a work of fiction. All the characters and events portrayed in this book are either products of the author's imagination or are used fictitiously.

PARTING THE VEIL

Chapter illustration by Michael Marino

A Tor Book
Published by Tom Doherty Associates, LLC
175 Fifth Avenue
New York, NY 10010

www.tor.com

Tor® is a registered trademark of Tom Doherty Associates, LLC.

ISBN 0-765-34836-5
EAN 978-0-765-34836-4

First edition: July 2004
First mass market edition: July 2005

Printed in the United States of America

0 9 8 7 6 5 4 3 2 1

For my father, James D. Davis,
who returned to the Light before this book
was completed and who watches over me still.
I miss you, Pop, and I love you.

For four precious friends who also went home:
Patrick Kusman, Bruce Mikel, Sharon Owens and Paul Bingaman.

And with heartfelt gratitude and love to my Creator
for parting the veil and illuminating the path.

ACKNOWLEDGMENTS

I am profoundly grateful to:

Don Williams for sharing his gentle spirit and loving smile, and for his patience and encouragement.

One of my guardian angels, John Diamond, for his kindness, diligence and unwavering faith in this book. No one could ask for a better agent.

Betty and Dwayne Brown, Don and Cheri Davis, Nadine Davis, Sue and John Steiniger, Vicki Operschall, Mary Elizabeth and Albert Diemert, Barbara Wilson and the rest of my family for their constant love and support.

Dottie Kime, Bobbi Smith, Anne Zafian, Glory Roseman, Bryan Fenton, Peter Orullian, Penny and Diana Bingaman, Pete Chandler, Toni Lake and Brad Vaught for their friendship and enthusiasm.

My extraordinary friend Roy Mills, who made more contributions than he knows.

Terrence M. Rohen, who pointed out the path to rediscovering meaning; Shari Cohen, M.D., for her expertise, healing touch and encouragement; and to Detective James Presson for his technical advice.

Three friends and colleagues: George Martin, George Fisher and Don "Moose" Parish for standing by me at the beginning.

And Michael Marino—teacher, artist, hoopster and friend—for his artistic contributions.

I am also indebted to all Near-Death Experiencers for sharing their experiences; to James Redfield, Marianne Williamson, Neale Donald Walsch, Betty Eadie and Melvin Morse for courageously sharing their insights; and to the unknown messengers who always brought me inspiration, strength and peace when I needed it the most. Thank you.

Parting the Veil

ONE

The Light at the End of the Tunnel

LIFE IS A HIT-AND-RUN driver that smashes, upends, uproots, and confuses before moving on with seeming indifference. It is an act of terror that in one dark moment reshapes the whole world . . . or a single dreaded phone call in the middle of the night. It is a sudden, spreading pressure deep in the chest . . . a lump that appears where none was before . . . or awakening to discover that the previous night together was the last one as lovers. Sometimes, it is a stretch of road that turns out to be treacherous, unforgiving and deadly. Life is the split second in which everything changes, and the path that is chosen to make sense of those changes. Life—in all its perplexing glory—is what awaits John Creed a few miles up the road.

Friday's classes had ended half an hour earlier, and the thirty-year-old teacher was on his way home from McQueen High School in

Reno, where he had taught psychology for the last four years. He was seated behind the leather-padded wheel of his sporty red convertible, a car that he cherished, especially on days when the northern Nevada weather made driving a convertible the only sensible thing to do. Today was such a day: the temperature was perfect, with a warm, steady breeze, and the sky was cloudless, unbroken by anything except the snow-covered Sierra Nevadas to the west. The road, like the weather, was also perfect, practically deserted now that the students were gone. It was an auspicious combination—a wide-open road and a wide-open sky—and John found himself wishing that the five miles home were five or ten times that.

Smiling, he reached for the black case on the seat beside him, flipped it open and scanned three rows of neatly alphabetized CDs. The selection was eclectic: classical, New Age, a smattering of jazz, and some pop and rock his students also liked. This being the first night of the weekend, rock seemed more appropriate than anything else, so he selected a CD that contained the tune already playing in his head. As the first few notes rang out from speakers in front and back, he smiled to himself, glanced up at the road, and waved at the approaching school bus heading back to McQueen after delivering its load.

The driver of the bus was Ruby Mazzoni, the mother of one of John's favorite students. As she raised her hand to wave back, John smiled at the face behind the broad dusty windshield. To his surprise, Ruby's smile suddenly faltered and changed into an ugly, hateful scowl. The hand that had been raised to return his greeting abruptly slammed down hard on the top of the steering wheel and wrenched it to the left with a violent jerk. As John's bewilderment skidded toward dawning horror, the bus gained speed, crossed out of its lane and slammed into his car.

The last thing he saw was Ruby's tortured grin.

~

As THE PARAMEDICS handed over John's faltering body to the emergency room team at Washoe Medical Center, a grimness supplanted their professional stoicism. "There's no way that one's going to make it," one of them observed as John was whisked away.

The other paramedic stared at the stretcher as it disappeared down the hall. "Shut up, Gordy!" he snapped. Privately, he shared his partner's sentiment, but he was superstitious enough to believe that if he actually voiced the fear, it was more likely to come true. "What if he hears you?" he whispered, knowing full well that the odds were against it. "Voices carry, you know."

Gordy thought of the still, bloodied form of the high school teacher and shook his head. "Don't worry," he replied in a sad voice. "The only thing that one's going to hear is the soft, sweet sound of the heavenly choir. All the doctors are going to do is buy them some time to warm up."

❧

"GET TO IT, people! We've got to work faster!" The doctor in charge of the trauma center emergency room frowned, more from frustration than any real concern about the efforts of his staff, who were already working up to capacity. The exhortation was superfluous, yet at the same time completely necessary, an ER ritual meant more to vent tension than to urge the troops on.

John Creed was awash in brilliant white light, lying on a table surrounded by people and beeping machines, the center of a frenzied medical exercise that had been going on continuously for forty-two minutes. Yet nowhere in his mind did any of it register. Except for a broken arm and leg, the air bag in his car had initially saved him from serious injury, but the double flip-and-roll the convertible had done after being smashed off the road had given fate a second chance. The broken limbs were of no immediate concern to the medical team, but the injuries to his head and his weak, erratic heartbeat and faltering blood pressure were sounding the alarm bells of impending death. The ER staff heard them, even if John didn't, and they were trying like crazy to head off an outcome that they all thought inevitable.

"Come on, people," the doctor said again, but with less emphasis this time. Even as he spoke, something began to change: the patient's heartbeat stayed erratic but grew frighteningly fast, his respiration remained shallow but grew more rapid than before, and his open, sightless eyes narrowed in pain. The nurse who noticed it first said, "Something's going on here," a fraction of a second before the monitors confirmed it, and then things rapidly fell apart as John's blood pressure plunged, his breathing abruptly stopped, and the beating of his heart grew more erratic, then ceased.

IT TOOK JOHN a full minute to realize that the tall, blond-haired man lying on the table five feet below was actually himself. He was floating, like a bird or a cloud (or a ghost, perhaps), hovering above his bruised and battered body, watching as the medical team scrambled to save him. Despite his feelings of disorientation, he wasn't greatly upset by what he was seeing. Instead, the longer he watched, the more at peace he felt with his strange state, as if some atavistic coping mechanism had come into play, buffering his mind against the shock and fear that he should have felt. It was a strange sensation, but not an unpleasant one.

Even as his body jerked when electricity shot through its chest, he felt none of the panic or urgency or frustration that played on the faces of the medical team. Instead, he felt a serene detachment, as if the whole scene involved someone other than himself. And then he realized that in a sense it did: what he was now—*who* he was now and always had been—no longer was confined to flesh and blood. Evidently, that part of his life was coming to a close, and he was being allowed to linger at the scene of his death, perhaps to understand and accept the transition.

The question, of course, was the transition to *what*.

For John Creed, death had always been the ultimate bogeyman, the greatest and most private uncertainty in his life. He thought about it often because there were so many reminders: the news, which was filled with death from horrific terrorist attacks, wars, natural disasters or disease; the memories of funerals, especially his grandmother's; the lingering demise of a valued colleague who had developed AIDS; even trips to the doctor, which were constant reminders that the body was vulnerable and subject to the whims and laws of mortality. It was fair to say that at times he was almost obsessed with death, because of the great, blazing question of what came after. *What then?* he couldn't help but wonder. *What really happens when we die?*

It wasn't as if he didn't believe in an afterlife. Down deep, he did. But there was always that small, persistent doubt that he could never dismiss. It didn't haunt his days or keep him up at night, and he lived each day like most people: pragmatically oblivious to the possibility of death, making plans for tomorrow, sometimes squandering today. But what he had come to think of as the Question was always lurking somewhere in his mind, waiting for something to call it to the fore. And when that happened, as it often did, he wondered about death with a hint of fear, felt guilty for doing so and wondered some more. Even though he had long ago resigned himself to never knowing the answer until the Question was moot, it didn't stop him from asking.

And now, he realized with much curiosity and a little trepidation, it was about to be answered.

He glanced back down at the room, as if expecting the answer to come from there. But there was nothing left to see; it was all but over. State-of-the-art devices had been used, injections given, and prayers and curses had intermingled in the air. Now that none of it had worked, the team simply stared at one another or found other things to do, each of them asking himself his own version of the Question, and on some level feeling cheated because he hadn't found the answer this time either. As one of the nurses slowly drew the sheet up over the body's head and turned away with brimming eyes, John Creed felt a sympathetic twinge of sadness, and suddenly found himself floating upward, away from his body and up through the ceiling.

The air around him turned gray and fuzzy, and he felt a surge of anticipation as chimes began to tinkle and ring in the distance, like a windblown serenade of crystal and steel. Then the wind—perhaps the one that stirred the chimes—grew stronger and louder until his ears were overwhelmed with a great rushing sound, a sound of power that probably should have scared him but, surprisingly, didn't. He glanced around with curious eyes to see what was approaching, half expecting a train or a roaring rocket. Instead, the air began to darken in front of him and swiftly coalesced into great whirling clouds, like the top of a tornado or some gigantic portal. The chimes beneath the wind slowly faded and died, and he was drawn into the center of the swirling mass.

Soon, the rushing sound was also a thing of the past, and he sailed into a void that was blacker and emptier than he thought was possible. He couldn't see where he was going, but he knew that he was moving—faster and faster, if his senses were correct—and after a short while, his anticipation and wonder began to be tempered by a creeping uncertainty. *What is happening? Where am I going?* There were no answers, of course, but before the endless darkness gave old doubts and fears an open avenue to conscious thought, he realized that he was no longer alone. He sensed shapes in the distance on either side of him—people and animals, he was fairly certain—glowing so faintly that he had almost missed them; some appeared to be moving as fast as he was, while others seemed aimless and drifting in the void. None gave any indication of seeing him, though, and instead of being comforting, their silent presence seemed eerie and perplexing, and John began to wonder, in spite of his faith, whether the afterlife might be eternal limbo after all.

But at the exact moment when he was tempted to despair, he felt a sense of utter tranquillity and harmony wash over him, and everything around him began to change. The wind that had borne him altered its direction and slowed to a gentle, guiding breeze, and a pinpoint of light appeared in the distance, growing larger and brighter as he floated in its direction. In the next moment, the spectral figures were gone and the darkness around him was no longer impenetrable, and he could dimly make out the circular walls of a long, gray tunnel. Soon, he found himself being set down lightly on his feet, and he began walking, as if in a dream, toward the source of the light. His fear was long gone, and in its place came a sense of excitement and anticipation that grew stronger and deeper with each step he took.

The farther he went into the tunnel, the brighter it got, until he saw that the walls were pillowy, like clouds, and gleaming softly with a bluish light. Soon the twinkle in the distance was no longer a pinpoint, but a growing beacon of brilliant light, a light that drew him forward and warmed his being with indescribable feelings he had never known. Up ahead in the distance, he could make out figures standing in the light, a lone form bathed in the bluish glow and two smaller ones behind it and off to one side. Although their faces were indistinguishable from so far away, he felt instinctively reassured and excited by their presence, and he quickened his pace and hurried toward them. . . .

T W O

Déjà Vu

ELEVEN-YEAR-OLD MATT DANDRIDGE wasn't particularly surprised when his father came home that night and announced that his boss had fired him from his job as an electronics engineer at Boeing. "That arrogant jerk just swaggered up to my desk and tossed this in the middle of my schematics without so much as a word," Elliot Dandridge fumed to his wife as they sat at the kitchen table staring down at a pink piece of paper. A large vein throbbed visibly down the middle of his forehead; Matt had seen that before, and knew it meant trouble.

"No 'Good-bye, see ya,' or 'I've got some bad news for you, Elliot,'" his father continued. "Not even a 'Don't let the door hit you in the back on the way out!' Nothing! He just threw this at me and walked away. I cornered him in the washroom after I read it, and all he could say was something about the boys upstairs had decided it was time for some downsizing." Elliot grabbed the termination notice and angrily crumpled it into a tiny pink ball. Standing in the doorway between the kitchen and the dining room, Matt flinched at the gesture. "Downsizing—bull!" his father went on. "Nobody else got fired! Who ever heard of a company as big as Boeing downsizing by one lousy employee?"

"Maybe the others are getting their notices tomorrow," Kate Dandridge offered soberly. "It seems like Boeing's been letting people go ever since the World Trade Center disaster. This is probably just the start of the next wave of layoffs." She looked at Elliot with almost hopeful eyes, eyes that were accustomed to looking for silver linings in every situation, no matter how thin the lining or how dark the cloud.

At the mention of the infamous terrorist attacks, a darker cloud passed over Elliot's already dark thoughts. When it passed, he glanced down at the wadded paper in his hand and said nothing, as if considering the possibility that Kate was right. In the end, he was doubtful. "I don't think so, Kate. That's not how they do it. Everybody gets them at the same time, or at least they come in bunches." He shook his head angrily from side to side and stared through the kitchen window at the incongruously sunny Missouri spring day. "No, it's the same old story. You do a good job—*too* good a job—and the bosses can't stand it, because it shows them up!" With an oath, he tossed the pink slip into the trash. "Now what are we going to do?"

Matt wondered the same thing. The last time this happened, they'd almost lost their house and had to move in with his grandmother; his parents had tried to hide that from him, but he'd known it anyway. And the same thing had happened the time before that. Elliot Dandridge was always getting fired, and always for the same reason: everybody felt threatened by his superior abilities.

Now it had happened again. The only difference was that this time it had taken almost three years to happen, which, as far as Matt knew, was some kind of a record. Preferring not to hang around and hear the same old story, Matt decided to make himself scarce. As soon as he was sure his dad wasn't looking, he caught his mother's eye, gave her a small wave and slipped outside.

The Dandridges' house was an old, white, two-story structure that sat on a big corner lot surrounded by a black wrought-iron fence. It was in an older section of St. Charles and had been built at least thirty years prior to the onslaught of frenzied developers who had turned the quiet Missouri River town (along with neighboring St. Peters) into St. Louis's fastest-growing suburb in the 1970s. Most of the houses in the surrounding blocks were similar to Matt's in that they were predominantly two- or three-story structures, with tall, big-paned windows and even taller trees, but that was about as far as the similarities went; this was no subdivision, with hundreds of houses constructed from only four basic plans, as was the rest of the city. Instead, each brick or clapboard home had a charm and uniqueness all its own. Within a four-block radius were schools and churches, the first state capitol, Lindenwood University, and a funeral home, all of which had been there for years and years. Matt's house hadn't been there quite that long, but to a boy his age it might as well have been. With its hardwood floors, high ceilings and wide wooden staircases, it was nothing like the newer houses most of his friends lived in, but Matt liked it anyway.

His favorite part of the house was the porch—or veranda, as his mother liked to call it—which ran along the entire front of the house. It was a great place to read or play, or just sit in the swing and think about stuff—if his older sister, Lori, hadn't already claimed it. And sometimes, when he could sneak beneath the porch without being seen, it made a great place to hide, as long as he didn't think about what else might be under there. This time, however—even though he was tempted to hide and not come out until his dad found another job—he plopped down at the top of the wide wooden stairs that led down to the walk, and put his elbows on his knees and his chin in his hands, and thought.

Matt knew from experience there'd be rough times ahead. His dad would be pretty mad for a while and crabbier than usual. And he'd yell at Matt more often than usual, too, but he wouldn't really mean anything by it, wouldn't really be mad at *him*—at least that's what his mother always said. When Matt was younger he hadn't been able to make that distinction, but now that he was older, he sort of understood and did his best to cope, and even to help. He was still five years away from being old enough to do anything other than run a paper route, but he could see how getting fired from a job would make you mad.

Still, he knew it wasn't going to be easy. Sometimes his father was so unpredictable. Matt thought about the funny Jewish lawyer on *Picket Fences,* the TV show he had seen once or twice when his mother played her old videotapes. The lawyer was always doing outrageous things and then explaining them away by grinning and saying, "Sometimes, I'm a character." Elliot Dandridge was like that, only the things he did weren't always funny, and they didn't always turn out like they did on TV. Matt loved his father, and knew without a doubt that his father loved him, but he never knew what his dad would do next. A little more than a year ago, Matt had come to the painful conclusion that his dad was different from other adults and didn't quite fit in with the people around him, which was probably the reason he kept losing his jobs. The realization made it easier to deal with his father—but it also made Matt wonder sometimes if he might grow up to be just like him.

Had his mother or teachers or the neighbors who knew him been asked if they thought Matt would grow up to be like Elliot Dandridge, they would have shaken their heads no and smiled with relief. On appearances alone, it seemed unlikely. Elliot had a fringe of dark curly hair around a widening bald spot, muddy brown eyes that were completely unremarkable except when he was angry, and an equally unremarkable face and physique, with the notable exceptions of a charming smile and ears that stood out just a tad too much. Matt had inherited the same endearing smile and too-large ears, but the rest of his father's genes had been lost in the shuffle. Whereas Elliot was no taller than five feet ten (although he claimed five-eleven, and sometimes six feet), Matt was unquestionably tall for his age, as his mother and all of her family had been. Like most of Kate's family, he was also freckle-faced and blond, with emerald green eyes like an Irish imp harboring an amusing secret. And he had his mother's personality: he was thoughtful, friendly and quick to laugh. In short, he was a sweet kid, and everybody liked him. Matt, in turn, tried to like everybody else.

As he sat on the porch step and stared into space, wondering if his dad would find another job, the voices carrying from inside the house did little, if anything, to allay his fears. His father was going on about the aerospace industry, how cutthroat it was and how tough it would be to land another job with the world in an uproar and so many other people out of work, and complaining bitterly about their failure to save for a day such as this; his voice was getting anxious, and louder by the moment. His mother's voice was getting louder, too, as she simultaneously tried to shout Elliot down and calm his fears, but the anger in her voice was better hidden. Trying to inject some hope into the discussion, Kate pointed out that she could upgrade her job with the local school district to a full-time position, which would bring in more money.

"The difference won't be enough to pay the bills," Elliot lamented. "Secretaries don't get paid crap."

"That's true," Kate conceded, "but it'll help stretch your severance pay until you find another job."

Elliot looked away and stared guiltily out the back window. He took a deep breath and said in a defensive voice, "There won't be any severance."

"*What?*" Kate reacted. "How can they get away with that? You're entitled to at least three weeks severance—and probably a lot more, if they're downsizing." A panicked note crept into her voice. "They can't just cut you off without a penny!" She grabbed her husband's wrist and forced him to look at her. "You've got to go back in there tomorrow and straighten this out, Elliot. There has to be a mistake."

Elliot shook his head glumly from side to side. "There's no mistake. I'll get paid for this week, but that's it."

"But they have to give you—"

Elliot lunged to his feet, shaking off her hand. "No, they *don't*," he shouted. "When they told me I was being fired, I quit instead! All right?" He glared down at his shocked wife, knowing he'd made a horrendous mistake but determined to defend it, nonetheless. "If they don't want me, I'm not going to give them the satisfaction of firing me! They can have that lousy job!"

Kate covered her mouth in shock and dismay, and stared at her husband, speechless. A moment later, her shoulders started trembling and she began sobbing quietly while Elliot looked on.

Outside, Matt flinched at the sound of his father's voice, and began fidgeting as his mother's crying drifted through the house and out onto the porch. He wished that his sister was home from track practice so she could sit and talk with him and he wouldn't have to hear his parents fight. But Lori wouldn't be home for another half hour. He dropped his hands to the edge of the step and started to get up, then sat back down and stared at his sneakers. He shook his head, wishing there was some way he could comfort his mother—and some way his dad could undo what he'd done.

But there wasn't, at least for now, and as Kate's crying grew louder and more troubled, and as Elliot's attempts to console her grew more inept by the minute, Matt's anxiety grew until he could hardly stand it. He knew that for the next several hours the house would be a two-story bomb just waiting for someone to light the fuse; the last time he had been the one who set it off, and the scene that ensued still haunted him sometimes in his dreams. This time, he vowed, he wouldn't be the one who pushed his dad over the edge.

The emotional atmosphere in the house climbed another notch. Elliot gave up on excuses and was soon angry again; Kate's crying quickly hitched and climbed its way to exasperation, then a matching anger. Matt winced at the sound; their voices were like a grating ball of white noise in his brain. Still shaking his head, he got to his feet and glanced around the yard, then up and down the block, searching for sanctuary. Finally, his gaze settled on his bike, and he crept to where it leaned against the porch, quietly walked it out to the corner, and jumped on the seat and headed across the street.

When he got to the other side, he turned right and pedaled up the sidewalk, heading for his friend Tommy's house. As he passed his own house he saw his father through the open window, pacing in the kitchen, his voice carrying easily to Matt's side of the street. Matt frowned and pedaled faster, hoping Tommy couldn't hear the argument two short blocks away.

Three houses later, he could still hear their voices, but he was beginning to have difficulty making out the words. Matt leaned forward and pumped his legs harder, straining to reach the magical spot where he would no longer hear them. As he reached the middle of the block, the sounds were barely audible. As he approached its end, he thought maybe he'd finally gotten out of range, but he wasn't sure; the voices still buzzed in his head, and he couldn't decide if they were real or remembered. He listened harder, closing his eyes and focusing every ounce of his rattled attention. He pedaled faster, as fast as the bike would allow him to go. When he reached the corner, he sailed off the curb and into the cross street. His eyes flew open as his tires hit the pavement with a jarring thud, and went wider still as he skidded into the path of an oncoming car. There was a screeching crash of metal on metal, and Matt sailed through the air and landed in a heap in the middle of the street, where his head hit the pavement with a sickening *smack*. He felt a bright burst of pain explode in his brain and envelope his body, then the merciful release of a numbing darkness. As people came running and the driver of the car began screaming hysterically, a strange sensation intruded on his darkness and he felt a tingling, then a tugging from deep inside. A moment later, he was free of it all.

THREE

Return to the World

UNTIL RECENTLY, the comatose man in Room 203 of the intensive care unit had been in the peak of health. Tall and tan, with an athletic build, piercing blue eyes and thick blond hair, John Creed at age thirty had the look of a stereotypical surfer—which was ironic, considering he had grown up in St. Louis and never surfed in his life. Whereas some of his friends had begun to let themselves go, John had worked to keep himself in shape by running, playing basketball and going to the gym. But none of that had saved him from Ruby Mazzoni's bus, and his usually impressive physical presence was now striking not for its good looks and attractive build, but because of the bandages and casts that covered his body, and the vacant blue eyes that stared into space.

On this particular morning, however, those eyes finally focused and John Creed gradually emerged from the coma feeling exhausted, confused and more than a little bit sore. The presence of a nurse and the beeping machines with multicolored readouts that surrounded his bed didn't immediately fit in with the last thing he remembered, namely, driving home from school on a bright, sunny day. That image was still fresh and had happened, it seemed, only moments ago. The hospital room was totally unexpected, and hinted of time lost and events unremembered.

The nurse waited only long enough to hear John mutter, "Where am I?" before running back to the nurses' station to summon the doctor and inform the staff. The other nurses looked up from their work in disbelief, and Dr. Henry Tolar, one of the surgeons who had attended John Creed when he'd been brought to the hospital, actually scowled at Nurse McGowan as if she'd just told a particularly gruesome joke. The last thing Dr. Tolar expected was that his patient would wake up. As it was, he was still dealing with John's unexpected return to life after being given up for dead that night in the ER. So much time had elapsed after the flatline that he'd been convinced that John had suffered massive, irreversible cerebral damage, and Tolar had considered—however briefly—letting nature take its course. Having been trained to cheat death at whatever the cost, he ordered full medical support for the patient instead, and hoped he wasn't making a terrible mistake. Privately, he had expected John to merely linger for a while—a few days, weeks, maybe a few months—and slip away quietly, much less dramatically than he had the first time. He certainly never expected him to come back from the coma. But a second look at Nurse McGowan's face made him wonder if the man had proved him wrong once again.

As the doctor entered the room, John's eyes followed his hurried steps to the bedside. "Where am I?" he whispered. His lips were dry, his voice weak and rusty from disuse.

"Washoe Med," Tolar replied absently, thoroughly amazed. "You had an accident."

John stared uncomprehendingly. His head felt heavy, and the muscles in his neck were unyieldingly stiff, as if he'd slept all night in an awkward position. "What kind of an accident?"

The doctor frowned slightly and answered, "A car accident. A bus driver—from your school, I believe—more or less ran you off the road." He looked at John with questioning eyes, as if the explanation might have jogged his memory. When he saw no signs that it had, he added bluntly, "Actually, she rammed you with her bus and knocked you off the road."

John was stunned. He stared at the doctor, wide-eyed. After a few moments, his expression clouded. "I don't remember any of that. . . ."

"Well, I'm not surprised. You've been through a lot."

John searched his memory again, but came up empty. He remembered starting the drive home from school, but everything after that was a blank—up until a few minutes ago. He looked at the doctor again. When he spoke, his voice was unsteady: "Are you saying someone tried to kill me?"

"Evidently," Tolar replied, growing uncomfortable with his unexpected role as the bearer of bad news. "But don't worry," he added hastily, groping for something more positive, "the bus driver's in jail. She won't bother you here."

John kept staring at the doctor, his mind numb with retroactive shock. *One of the bus drivers tried to kill me? Why?* he wondered. On that score his mind was as blank as it was on the accident. "Who?" he finally asked.

"I couldn't tell you," Tolar replied, happy to have finally run out of information. "You'll have to ask the police. I'm sure they'll want to talk to you now that you're awake." Having said all he intended to say on the subject, the doctor bent over the bed and removed a small penlight from his breast pocket and shone it into John's right eye, then his left. He nodded, satisfied with the pupillary reactions, and hastily checked a few other things. When he was done, he straightened up and met his patient's troubled gaze. "How do you feel?" he asked. The question clearly addressed John's physical, not emotional, condition.

"Maybe you should tell me," John answered in a distracted voice. "I don't even know what I'm being treated for."

The doctor smiled tentatively. "I'd say you're feeling better. A little banged up, perhaps, but certainly better than when they brought you in." He glanced at the monitor readouts above the bed and added, "As a matter of fact, you're doing remarkably well for someone who was in a coma for as long as you were."

John's eyes narrowed. When he spoke, the words came slowly. "And how long was that?"

Tolar hesitated before answering. "Ten days," he said softly.

John's eyes went wide as he processed the answer. "Ten days?"

Tolar nodded nervously and busied himself checking the bandages on the side of John's head; he'd always felt awkward telling coma patients just how long they'd been out.

After several moments of uneasy silence, John suddenly asked, "Could you raise the head of the bed up a little? I want to see what's happened to me."

Nurse McGowan looked at Tolar, who nodded assent. "I don't see why not," he replied, happy to deal with an easier question. "You've got a couple of broken ribs, but it shouldn't put too much pressure on them. If it does, just say so."

John said nothing as the nurse adjusted the bed. He settled gingerly into the new position, wincing when the broken ribs made themselves known, then stared in dismay at what he saw. His left arm was in a cast. So was his left leg. There were bandages taped around his chest. And although he couldn't see them, he could feel additional dressings on the left side of his head.

"Rest assured we're doing our best to put you back together," Dr. Tolar said in response to the look on John's face. He stepped back, did his own head-to-toe survey and nodded. "Not bad for a man we almost lost on the operating table."

John's eyes narrowed. "What do you mean?" he whispered.

Tolar's smile abruptly faded, and he mentally kicked himself for making a second slip in as many minutes. He hesitated, then admitted, "Technically, you were clinically dead . . . for a brief time." He smiled nervously and added, "But obviously we were able to bring you back."

"How long is a 'brief time'?" John shot back.

Disconcerted, Dr. Tolar and Nurse McGowan averted their eyes. Glancing down at his chart, the doctor said softly, "Ten minutes or so . . ."

John's eyes went wide, and he felt as if he had just fallen into a deep, dark pit. "*Ten minutes or so!*"

"Something like that," the doctor dissembled. He looked up from the chart and tried to calm his patient with a reassuring smile. "Don't worry, you're going to be all right. The hard part's over, and we're taking good care of you, trust me." He flipped the chart closed, replaced the pen in his pocket and said cheerily, "Now try to get some rest. I'll be back in a while to check on you again." With Nurse McGowan in tow, he left the room as quickly as he could, shaking his head almost imperceptibly from side to side, with an expression that was part triumph, part mystification. Had he been inclined to think in nonclinical terms, Dr. Tolar would have described John's amazing recovery as nothing less than a miracle; as it was, all he could think of were the tests he could run to pinpoint the damage he was sure had occurred. The thought that he might have unduly stressed his patient with his blunt revelations about the cause of his condition was already forgotten.

Feeling overwhelmed, John watched them leave. Or rather his eyes tracked their movement as his mind groped around the edges of Tolar's stunning news. He was shocked and sobered by the thought that someone had tried to kill him, and wondered if the doctor was misinformed. And the news that the would-be killer had actually succeeded—if only temporarily—was like being blindsided all over again. To have been dead, even for a moment, was profoundly upsetting, in spite of being brought back. Then there was the matter of the last ten days—ten lost days, he corrected himself—and he couldn't help wondering what had happened to his mind as well as his body as a result of the coma. That was unsettling and shook him almost as badly as the attempt on his life.

But what scared him the most, on several different levels, was the thought that he had died but remembered nothing. . . .

Finding it too traumatic to pursue for the time being, John glanced outside his room. Dr. Tolar and Nurse McGowan were just joining the knot of other staff who had gathered around the nurses' station to hear what was going on. The group were out of earshot, but when they all turned in unison to stare at John's room, it became painfully obvious that his emergence from the coma was the Surprise of the Month. What he didn't know was that virtually all of the staff had given up hope that he would ever recover, and the decision had been made only an hour earlier to move him out of the ICU and into a room where the care he'd receive would be more in line with his dwindling chances of recovery.

The intensive care ward was a circle of glass-fronted rooms with a nurses' station in the center; from his bed John could see into most of the other units. Unsettled by the stares of the nurses and doctors, he averted his gaze and glanced around the ward, one room at a time. With each successive person, he grew less and less preoccupied with his own situation, speculating instead on everyone else's condition, wondering if they would recover, and wondering what their families would do if for some reason they didn't. And while he was wondering, his body eventually decided it had done enough for one day, and put him quietly to sleep.

Not long after, the dreams began.

FOUR

Will Gibson Drops By

"GOOD MORNING, Mr. Creed. I'm Will Gibson, the hospital's social worker."

John glanced up with mild surprise from the breakfast he was eating; he hadn't been aware that hospitals had social workers. The man at the foot of the bed was a few inches shorter than John, slim, and appeared to be in his midtwenties. He had dark brown skin, a clean-shaven head and large, dark brown eyes that seemed to light up when he flashed a smile. Instead of the traditional hospital lab coat, he was dressed in a pair of casual slacks, with a blue long-sleeve shirt and matching tie.

Having just taken a large bite of scrambled eggs, John waved his hand in an apologetic greeting. After three days of tests that had failed to show even the slightest hint of cerebral damage, he had finally been moved out of the ICU and into a regular room where he could be kept for observation. This was his first real meal in almost two weeks, and he was enjoying it immensely; it was with great reluctance that he put down his fork and pushed away the tray. He swallowed and gave his visitor a slightly embarrassed smile. "Excuse me," he muttered, then coughed. He took a sip of orange juice to clear his throat, coughed once more, put down the glass and gingerly laid his hand on his broken ribs. "Please," he replied in a watery but friendly voice, "my students might call me Mr. Creed, but I insist that anyone over the age of eighteen call me John."

Gibson grinned and extended his hand. "John, then. I guess that makes me just plain Will."

The two shook hands while Will apologized for interrupting his meal, and John settled back in the bed, smiling. He decided Will Gibson was one of those rare people you automatically liked on sight; the social worker exuded a warmth and genuineness that was not always obvious in the other hospital staff. "What brings you up here?" John asked. "I wasn't aware that a visit from the social worker was part of the package."

"Well, it is kind of standard," Gibson replied. He added delicately, "Especially when a patient might need some, uh, nonmedical support."

A wry look settled on Creed's face. "So Tolar's still worried I might flip out."

Gibson looked embarrassed but made the best of it. "Well, not exactly. But you've been through a pretty rough time, and he thought I should stop by and see if you needed anything."

"Like someone to talk to?" John considered the last person to offer himself in that role—a police detective who had shown up at his bedside after he had awakened from the coma. John had been unable to tell him anything, so the cop had filled him in on all the gruesome details instead. By the time he'd left, John knew that the bus driver was Ruby Mazzoni, and he knew without a doubt that she had meant to kill him. The only piece missing was the reason why.

Will smiled. "I *am* a good listener. If you'd like to talk about the accident, or if you have some lingering concerns about being in a coma—"

John shook his head. "Thanks. But I'm fine."

Will smiled uncertainly. "Okay." He glanced down momentarily at the clipboard he was carrying. "It says here that you're single. Is there anyone who can take care of you until you're back on your feet?"

"Hmm . . . That's a good question. I live alone, except for Alex, my golden retriever—my friend Bobbi is taking care of her right now. Alex is pretty good at fetching, but I doubt that she can cook."

Will grinned. "Then I better start the ball rolling with Social Services so we can get someone to help out after you're released. Do you know if your insurance covers in-home care?"

"I don't know," John replied. "I haven't really thought that far ahead." The truth was that he had thought a lot about going home, but up until this moment, he hadn't stopped to consider how he would manage until the casts came off. Now he realized he wouldn't be able to fix his own meals or walk the dog or do any number of things he had always taken for granted, and it was dismaying to realize how helpless he would be. Chalk up another reason why living alone is getting old, he thought to himself. "I just talked my mother into going back home with my dad yesterday, because I didn't know how much longer I'd be stuck in here," he said, frowning. "Maybe I should have taken her up on her offer to stay. Are they letting me go pretty soon?"

"I don't know," Will replied. "But we might as well get the paperwork started. If you make other arrangements in the meantime, we can always cancel."

"Okay."

Will nodded, smiling. He made a notation on the clipboard and glanced up again. "Is there anything else I can do for you?"

John thought about it. It was obvious the social worker was trying to get him to talk about the accident, and John was tempted but decided against it. "No, I don't think so," he finally said.

"Are you sure?"

"Well, don't lose my file just because I can't think of anything at the moment," John replied affably. "I appreciate you coming in. It's nice to see someone who doesn't want to take my temperature or steal my blood, for a change. . . ." He glanced out the window and let his gaze fall on the mountains that lined what little he could see of the horizon. "Right now," he said softly, "I'm just happy to be alive, I guess. . . . Everything else seems kind of unimportant." He looked back at Will and forced a smile. Perhaps because of the jumbled dreams that had troubled his sleep for the last few nights, and partly because he sensed that Will wanted to help, he added, "I can't think of anything I need right now, but you never can tell when I might change my mind. Come back by when you get the time, and ask me again."

OVER THE NEXT WEEK, while John remained in Washoe Medical Center for further observation and tests, Will Gibson came by several times. As often happens with people who are thrown together by a chance meeting under unusual circumstances, the two men were quickly becoming friends. As the pain decreased a little more with each passing day, and the tests grew fewer and farther between, John had grown restless and increasingly lonely. The initial steady stream of visitors had predictably dwindled to little more than a trickle, and Will's daily visits were just about the only thing keeping him sane.

"You must be a masochist," John greeted him one dark and gloomy afternoon.

"Why is that?" Will asked, pulling a chair over to the bedside.

"You keep coming back to listen to me whine."

Will smiled. "Just doing my job."

John returned the smile, shaking his head. "I doubt that listening to people complain is in your job description."

"You'd be surprised. Besides, my job description's pretty vague."

John laughed. "That makes sense," he said, grinning good-naturedly. "You sociologists are a pretty vague bunch, anyway. You know what we said about sociology majors in college, don't you? A sociology major is just a frustrated psych major who can't handle the science."

Gibson rolled his eyes and grinned, in spite of himself. Like John, he had come to enjoy their friendly sparring. "Well, at least you can get a job with a BA in sociology. The only thing a bachelor's degree in psych is good for is to wipe—"

"Hey!" John cut him off, laughing for the first time that day. "That's not entirely true. You may need a Ph.D. to be a real psychologist, but my lowly bachelor's degree does qualify me to teach at the high school level." He smiled and added, "And that's exactly what I wanted to do."

Will ran a hand over his clean-shaven scalp, an unconscious gesture that John had noted the first time they met. "I know," Will replied in a voice that was suddenly thoughtful. "Sometimes I'm a little envious of you. . . . But, for the most part, I like what I do—even if it isn't exactly the world-changing career that naive undergraduates dream about. If I thought I wasn't making some kind of a difference, I'd quit in a minute."

"Ever think about doing something else?" John asked.

"Once or twice. I almost joined the army after the first terrorist attacks, but I realized I could probably do more good by staying at the hospital." Will shook off a frown, then smiled. "And I do volunteer work on the side, over at St. Timothy's—that's the homeless shelter over on Donovan. Sometimes I stop off on my way home from work to help out, and I usually work in the food pantry on Saturdays."

"I'm impressed," John said. "That must make for some long days."

"Well, don't be too impressed. I get something out of it too—it makes me feel useful."

John nodded. "I'd like to see your shelter sometime. I'm ashamed to admit it, but I wasn't even aware it existed until you told me."

"Unfortunately, most people aren't," Will replied as his beeper went off. He frowned and stood up to leave. "I'll tell you what," he said, "once you're out of here and feel up to it, I'll take you myself. We can always use another pair of hands—assuming that's what you meant."

"That's exactly what I meant."

Will smiled warmly, then reached out and shook John's hand. "See you tomorrow?"

John made a face. "Yeah, I guess I'll still be here." He watched his friend leave, and continued staring at the doorway after he'd gone, thinking about their conversation. After a few minutes, he turned his gaze to the window, and his thoughts to other matters. A rare summer storm was approaching, and the overcast, lowering sky had obscured the mountains, making a perfect backdrop for the foreboding thoughts that had gripped his mood for the last few days.

It seemed as if his whole world had been turned upside down, as if having come so close to the thing he feared most had pried loose the underpinnings of his constructed reality. Nothing felt the same as it had before, or looked quite the same or had the same meaning. He had heard that people who had a brush with death often reevaluated their lives, and now he knew why. Caught unawares once, he was keenly aware that it could happen again—*would* happen again—and he wanted to make sure that the time he had left wasn't squandered.

He even began to question his move to Nevada. He had been born in St. Louis and lived his whole life there, and except for moments of fanciful what-ifs, he had never really wanted to live anyplace else. He liked the Midwest, and his family was there. He had even gone to school at Lindenwood University in the St. Louis suburbs, because he had felt no need to get away from his parents. But a few years later, a failed relationship had driven him to make a new start out West. Now, looking out at the dark and brooding sky, he couldn't help but wonder if he'd done the right thing. At times like this, the last thing a man wanted was to be alone.

He continued to stare out the window for almost an hour,

remembering and evaluating and planning what to do with his life in the post-Ruby era. Eventually his thoughts turned to other enigmas, like his unresolved questions and fears about death, and the incomprehensible dreams that had started last week. He explored those thoughts for a while, completely ensconced in his interior world, until a fit of yawning finally broke the spell. Realizing he was suddenly incredibly sleepy, he reached for a book, hoping to escape from the encroaching drowsiness; the last thing he wanted was an afternoon nap and a matinee session of fragmentary dreams that made no sense.

Ten minutes later, he got them anyway.

FIVE

Holly Mandylor
Declines an Invitation

"I NEVER KNEW MY DADDY."

The man dressed like a cowboy half leered at Holly, then moved closer and slid a hand onto her thigh. "I'll be your daddy," he said, giving her leg a squeeze.

Holly Mandylor pursed her lips reprovingly, and firmly removed his hand. The only people who were worse than tourists about coming on to cocktail waitresses in Las Vegas were the locals, and the third-rate casino where she worked seemed to attract more than its share. This one, she began to suspect, was worse than most.

Holly was twenty-seven and pretty, with reddish-brown hair and striking green eyes, and a figure that was athletic but distinctly feminine. Most men found her particularly appealing, and the fact that she was also six feet tall discouraged only the ones whose height insecurities were stronger than their hormones. She was also very friendly, not in a way that was calculated to boost her tips, but with a warmth and genuineness that made most people smile when she brought their drinks. Holly liked people—unlike some of her coworkers, who would smile at the customers but scowl and complain when they left the floor—and for that reason her tips usually ran higher than anyone else's. And even though she often took longer than most of the waitresses to deliver her drinks, very few customers ever complained.

This particular customer—whom she had not been serving—had been sitting at the bar since shortly after Holly came on duty. Every time she had returned to get a drink order filled, the man had given her an engaging, almost sheepish smile, then nodded and touched his finger to the brim of his hat. Holly knew better than to do any serious socializing with customers, but the man's routine was so irresistibly charming that she had decided to take her break at the bar. That his engaging smile had changed so quickly into a commonplace leer was a surprise to Holly, and a big disappointment. And his offer to be her "daddy"—with its obvious connotations—was simply insulting.

"That's not what I meant," she replied to the come-on. Her tone was polite, but with a definite edge to it. "You said your mom and dad still lived here in Vegas," she reminded him, "and I said my mom died when I was a girl, but that I never knew my dad, so I don't know where he lives—or if he's even alive." She stared at the cowboy with unwavering eyes. Her ire had been triggered, but she held it in check and offered the stranger a chance to recant: "I wasn't asking you to be my daddy. Maybe you misunderstood."

The cowboy set down his beer and grinned. His hand, which had never retreated more than a few inches from her thigh after Holly removed it, now boldly returned to its former berth. The man's grin grew wider. His fingers began moving in slow, lazy circles up the skin of her leg as Holly's eyes grew wide with irritated disbelief and then narrowed in anger. "No, little lady," the man replied, his voice low and smugly provocative, "I think I understand exactly what you mean."

This time Holly slapped him before removing his hand. She slapped him so hard that people at the nearby blackjack tables turned around at the sound; even some of the dealers—normally so stoic, with their house faces on—paused to watch. "I think I misjudged you," Holly said stiffly, barely able to hide the betrayal she felt. "Now, if you'll excuse me, my break's over." And with that she turned her back and prepared to retreat while she still had some dignity.

The cowboy angrily rubbed his reddening cheek. His eyes had lost their lust and predatory smugness, and seethed instead with frustrated rage; the hand that had recently caressed Holly's thigh now hung at his waist in a tight white fist; and his expensive hat was unceremoniously parked on the sticky tile floor, knocked from his head by the force of Holly's blow. The cowboy stared down at it, then back up at Holly. "Look what you did to my hat!" he hissed.

Holly glanced over her shoulder with a smirk, and the man grabbed her wrist and spun her around. "I think I'm the one who misjudged the situation," he spat, squeezing her arm until it began to ache. "I didn't know whores could afford to be so picky." He loosened his grip and shoved her away.

Holly stumbled into a table, then regained her balance and spun around. Before she realized what she was doing, she charged the cowboy with a shriek of rage—but then made herself stop just short of where he stood. She glared at him hotly with a Medusa's stare, privately chiding herself for being so naive. She stood there for a moment, chest heaving and arms trembling, her hand bunched tight into a bloodless fist as she tried to decide whether to cry or attack. Instead of doing either, she glanced at the spot where the cowboy hat lay, pursed her lips and nodded once, then took a single step forward and ground her high heel through its brown felt crown. The man's eyes flashed with surprise and outrage, and Holly boldly met his stare with a vindictive smile. Then she stepped on the hat's brim with her other shoe, extricated the heel that had done the damage, and turned and walked away with a satisfied smile. As she moved out of earshot, she heard a plaintive howl of childish dismay.

FIVE MINUTES LATER, Holly saw the cowboy emerge from the men's room with his ruined hat in his hand. He gave her an inscrutable look as he left. Ten minutes later, he returned with Gil Turner, the day-shift manager. Turner's face wore its customary frown, and he was shaking his balding head from side to side. After making their way to the bar, Turner and the cowboy pulled out two stools and sat down.

When she saw them watching her, Holly knew she was in trouble. She and Turner were hardly the best of friends, nor was he liked by anyone else in the place, as far as she knew. He was an unpredictable boss, given to irrational screaming fits, whose managerial style was best described as management by intimidation. He badgered, belittled, insulted and threatened his employees, especially those who weren't sufficiently demure in his commanding presence. He was a grade-A tyrant, a bully with a title who could make people quail, which was somewhat ironic considering his tame appearance and whiny voice.

Holly averted her eyes and put off returning to the bar for as long as she could, until she finally ran out of drinks and friendly conversation. Smiling nervously, she approached the service area, still looking away and holding her serving tray in front of her like a protective shield. Right up until the moment she heard her name, she kept hoping Turner's presence was only a coincidence.

"Miss Mandylor," Turner began, "we need to talk." His tone was soft, but Holly had learned long ago not to be fooled; that was how his tirades began, and in a matter of seconds he could be red-faced and screaming, looking for all the world like an overgrown child who was throwing a fit—the only difference being that he was a man, not a child, and a man who could make her life miserable, at that. The presence of a hundred or so customers within earshot would make no difference, either, she knew; oblivious to just how silly he looked when he pitched a fit, Gil Turner would plow ahead, audience or not. Standing slightly behind him, the cowboy still looked angry, but with a smirk taking shape in his eyes and mouth.

Trying not to betray her anxiety, Holly met her boss's eyes, which were as hard as flint. "Yes, Mr. Turner?"

"I'd like to know what went on here a few minutes ago."

Holly stalled. She couldn't believe the cowboy had been stupid enough to report her after what he'd done. "Pardon me?"

Turner snatched the ruined cowboy hat from the customer's hand and waved it in front of Holly's face. "Don't 'pardon me,'" he said, raising his voice. "Why the hell did you ruin this man's hat?"

Against her will, Holly lowered her eyes. After having had a little time to think about her encounter with the alleged victim, she wasn't exactly proud of what she'd done, but she certainly didn't regret it either; the man had been wrong, and instead of apologizing, had only made things worse. In retrospect, he was lucky she hadn't planted her high heel somewhere else. Recalling the slimy feel of his fingers circling her thigh, Holly looked back up and glared at the cowboy. Then she met Turner's eyes. "He wouldn't leave me alone."

"Let me give you a little hint, Miss Mandylor," Turner retorted. "The customers aren't supposed to leave you alone. That's why they come here: to win money and have a few drinks. Your job is to smile and bring them those drinks."

"I wasn't even waiting on him," Holly replied defensively. "He was sitting at the bar."

"Then why'd you even bother him?"

"I didn't bother him. I was just trying to be friendly."

Gil Turner's eyes narrowed. A sarcastic smile came to his lips. "Maybe you were a little too friendly."

Holly was immediately indignant. Turner had never made it

a secret that he thought she was a woman of questionable virtue; he gossiped about it behind her back, and routinely warned her against fraternizing with the customers, telling her not to be "too friendly" in a tone that was as lecherous as it was condescending. That he was wrong about her had always galled Holly, but that he should actually accuse her of it now, when this customer was the one who had come on to her, was almost more than she could stand. When she answered the charge, she chose her words carefully and delivered them as evenly as humanly possible. "I was on my break, and all I did was stop and say hello. We talked for a few minutes, but I didn't say *anything* to lead him on. *He* was the one who started making advances." She glanced at the cowboy with angry eyes. "I did what I had to because he wouldn't take no for an answer."

Gil Turner smirked, glanced at the cowboy and looked back at Holly. "That's an interesting scenario, Miss Mandylor. Let me get this straight. . . . You were carrying on an innocent conversation with Mr. Billings here—did I mention that I've known Mr. Billings for ten years and that our wives went to high school together?"

Holly said nothing. A knot began to grow in the pit of her stomach.

Turner smiled knowingly and continued. "Anyway, you were having a *friendly* conversation with Mr. Billings, and he suddenly started coming on to you."

Holly nodded, but still said nothing.

"So you slapped him in the face—"

"Yes."

"And ruined his hat—"

"Yes . . . After he wouldn't take his hands off of me."

"Then you went back to work, as if nothing had happened."

Holly hesitated before answering, wondering what kind of lie Billings had told him, and angry because it would be just like Turner to take the wrong side. When she finally spoke, her voice was quavering but quickly grew stronger, girded by the truth and righteous indignation: "That's pretty much how it happened. I tried to walk away when things started going wrong, but he wouldn't let me. Then he shoved me, and I stepped on his hat and walked away."

Turner shook his head and snorted derisively. "Your version differs significantly from Mr. Billings's."

"I bet it does," Holly replied sarcastically.

"According to Mr. Billings, *you* came on to *him*," Turner explained. "And considering what kind of woman you are, I have no reason to doubt his story."

Holly's face colored slightly. That was the thing she detested the most about Gil Turner: his ability to make you feel stupid or cheap even when you knew you weren't. She answered him with as much poise as she could muster under the circumstances. "That's a lie," she replied, then glared at Billings. "And you know it."

The cowboy smugly returned her stare. "What I told him was the sad but simple truth: I was sitting here having a drink and minding my own business when you sat down and started flirting with me. I told you I was married and didn't do that kind of thing, but the next thing I knew, you were trying to get into my pants!" He frowned elaborately, as if pained by the tale, and concluded, "When I had to push you off of me, you just went nuts."

Holly stared at her accuser and at the man who believed him, momentarily speechless. Her mind was a blur of white-hot fire, and without thinking, she moved the serving tray away from her chest, as if she were considering using it as the hammer of truth on their smirking faces. In the end, she lowered the tray and just shook her head. "That isn't how it happened," she said softly. "That's not how it happened at all."

For a few moments, Turner and Billings feigned regret, as if caught up in a tragedy that was not of their making. Then the manager said, "I wish I could believe you, Holly. But I don't see how I can."

Holly glanced down at the other end of the bar, where the bartender was trying to look busy. Knowing he'd back her up if given the chance, she turned back to Turner. "Did you ask Tom what happened?"

she asked hopefully. Without waiting for a reply, she started to call him over, but Turner stopped her.

"Of course I asked Tom. But he didn't really say anything to change my mind."

Holly narrowed her eyes and clenched her jaw, realizing she was fighting a losing battle. But she couldn't give up without trying again. "Then ask the people at those blackjack tables," she said, gesturing behind her. "Somebody had to see what happened."

"I'm not going to bother those people with a personnel problem," Turner responded. "I can't just go around interrogating customers like they were federal witnesses. This is a casino, Miss Mandylor, not a crime scene."

"So you don't believe me," Holly replied, deflated, "and you're not going to give me a chance to prove he's lying. Is that it?"

Turner looked at Billings. "I think I've heard everything I need to hear." He turned back to Holly. "More than I wanted to hear, as a matter of fact."

"And?" Holly asked, already knowing the answer.

Turner gave her a stern, almost regretful look; at its edges, however, was a measure of sadistic glee. "You know where the front doors are, don't you, Miss Mandylor?"

Holly shook her head bitterly. Her mouth was a straight, hard line of resignation and anger. "Yes."

"Good. Then I suggest you use them and leave the casino. In the future, you'll have to pick up men on someone else's time. As of now, you're fired."

Holly glared at her accusers for a long, hard time, casting about for something that would grant her release, wanting to strike out and draw blood in place of justice. In the end, she settled for merely saving face. "Don't bother with the pink slip—I quit!" she hissed. Then, with hands that were quivering from pent-up emotion, she flung the serving tray as hard as she could at their smiling faces, turned on her heel and stormed out of the casino.

SIX

Home Again,
Perchance to Dream

AFTER THREE WEEKS in Washoe Medical Center, John Creed finally went home. It was a sunny spring day, much like the day when Ruby Mazzoni had sent him to the hospital with her school bus version of demolition derby, and it felt good to be outside with the sun on his face. More than anything else, it felt good to be free and on his own again, free to sleep through the night without being awakened by a nurse with a shot or a question, and free of the doctors' almost obsessive suspicions that there had to be something the tests hadn't found. His bruises were long gone, his cuts only scars, and his broken bones were mended or at least healing nicely; were it not for the fiberglass casts on his arm and leg, there was nothing to indicate he had ever been injured, much less clinically dead for a period of time. The only persistent legacy of his brush with death were questions about the accident, and the dreams that had started when he emerged from the coma. Those would take longer to put behind him.

Margie Mullin, a friend and English teacher at McQueen High, drove him home from the hospital. Margie was a pretty, red-haired woman of fifty whose most striking attributes were her unflagging generosity and a delightful naivete that sometimes caused her to blush bright red at the drop of a hat. She was also prone to planning surprises, and when they stepped through the door of John's house, they were greeted by giant banners, a three-tiered cake that Margie had baked and a throng of students and teachers from school. Will Gibson, the social worker from Washoe Medical Center, was also there, as was Bobbi Smith, John's longtime friend and next-door neighbor. Alex, John's seven-month-old golden retriever, was first in line with a toothy puppy grin and a tail that was wagging about a hundred miles an hour.

"Welcome home!" his friends shouted in unison as Alex danced around John in frantic circles. He bent down and hugged the dog as best he could, grinning with delight as she licked his face to say hello. Then he straightened up and stared in amazement at the group of friends who crowded around to welcome him back.

"Whoa! Easy, people," Margie intervened. "Remember, this man just got out of the hospital and the last thing he needs is more broken bones." She cleared a path and motioned John to his favorite chair. "Let's get you off your feet. You don't want to overdo it." Moving slowly because of the walking cast, John made his way to a big, overstuffed chair and sat down awkwardly. Margie fluffed a pillow and wedged it behind his back. "You can hold court right here," she said, smiling.

John grinned and shook his head. "You're too much, you know it? If my mother were here, she'd be jealous."

"Well, you'll just have to put up with me instead," she said with mock sternness. "Now sit back and relax." She smiled and added with genuine warmth, "And welcome home. I'm really glad to see you."

The next hour resembled a condensed version of Old Home Week. Colleagues filled him in on what had happened at the school, and asked how he was feeling and when he was coming back. Students filled him in on how boring the substitute was, and asked how he was feeling and when he was coming back. One even asked how it felt to be dead, but before John could reply, Will and Margie shooed the boy off.

It was Bobbi who finally suggested that it was time to end the party because John was looking tired. Margie and Will agreed, and within fifteen minutes they had successfully managed to make everyone say their good-byes and take their leave. Once Mary Mayhall, one of John's fellow teachers, had left, the living room was empty except for John, Margie and Will Gibson.

"I better be going, too," Will said, having just returned from helping load Margie's car. "Are you feeling okay? This wasn't too much for you, was it?"

John smiled. "No. I feel fine. And thanks for coming. You really didn't have to, you know."

Will glanced at Margie, whom he'd gotten to know a little over the last few weeks, and said, "When Margie told me about it, I thought it was a great idea. And I never could resist an invitation to a party from a pretty lady." Margie blushed as the men laughed, and Will went on, "Besides, I wanted to make sure you got settled in okay." He looked at John thoughtfully. "You know, it's good to talk to you somewhere besides a hospital room. Seeing you in your home makes you a real person and not just somebody who magically appears on my rounds one day and then disappears later. People who work in a hospital sometimes forget that." He smiled and added, "Maybe everybody ought to go home with a patient now and then just to remind them, you know?"

"Sounds like a good idea to me," John replied.

"As long as they don't charge you for a house call!" Margie added.

Everybody laughed at that, and the sudden noise brought Alex running back into the room. They laughed again as the dog ran from one person to the next, smiling and excitedly wagging her tail. Will bent down to stroke her head. "Now you look after your master, Alex," he admonished the dog. "He's going to need some help." He looked up at John and asked, "Are you sure you don't want me to get someone to stay with you, at least for a couple of days?"

"Don't worry, Will," Margie interjected. "Everything's covered. Bobbi will check on him during the day, and I'll come by after work to bring him some dinner and make sure he isn't doing anything he isn't supposed to."

John gave Will a look and laughed. "Give it up, Will. Once Margie makes up her mind, there's no stopping her. I already tried." His voice grew serious. "Thank you both for taking such good care of me. This whole thing would have been a lot tougher without you."

"We didn't do anything anyone else wouldn't do," Margie replied.

"You know better than that," John disagreed, shaking his head slightly.

"Hey," Will reminded him, "friends are supposed to look out for each other, aren't they?" He grinned and added, "Maybe Margie and I have ulterior motives. We might expect you to return the favor someday."

"Don't worry," John replied earnestly, staring at his friends—one old, one new—with heartfelt gratitude, "if that day ever comes—and God forbid that it does—I hope I can do even half as much as you've done for me."

"It's a deal," Will said, and Margie agreed. John kissed Margie's cheek and shook Will's hand, and they went on their way, leaving him alone for the first time in weeks.

~

THE DAY'S EVENTS had tired him out, and John headed for bed at nine o'clock, three hours earlier than usual. During the last week of his hospital stay he had found it increasingly difficult to sleep, partly because of the uncomfortable bed, partly due to the dreams he had when he finally fell asleep, but mainly because he had grown restless and anxious to go home. As he pulled back the covers and slid between the sheets, he felt like a man who had truly come home. His bed had a deliciously distinctive feel, a comforting and relaxing aura about it that no other bed could ever quite duplicate—especially if it had been used by a succession of people who were sick or dying. With the opportunity to once again sleep at home, he expected a good night's rest, something he hadn't experienced in a long, long time. And he did drop off almost as soon as his head hit the pillow, falling easily and quickly into a welcoming sleep.

It wasn't long, however, before the dreams began. They started with a little boy who was sitting on the porch steps of a house, staring disconsolately at his white high-top sneakers. He looked about ten or eleven but tall for his age, all arms and legs, with a mop of shaggy blond hair that fell down over his forehead and into his eyes. The boy looked strangely familiar, and at first, John—or rather that part of the brain that tethers the sleeper to waking reality—assumed he was looking at himself as a boy, so alike were the two of them in appearance and build. But soon the boy stood up and glanced around the yard as shouts of anger drifted from the house, and John (or his locus of reality control) realized that the child was someone else. He also saw that the boy was troubled, with a look of near-panic twitching in his eyes.

After a few moments, the boy seemed to make a decision and went to a bike that was leaning against a corner of the house. He glanced up surreptitiously at the window above him, shook his head sadly, grabbed the bike's handlebars and quietly walked it out of the yard. Once he reached the sidewalk, he hopped on the seat and pedaled across the street.

John was suddenly overwhelmed by an unshakable conviction that the boy was in danger. He tried to call out and stop him from leaving, but when he opened his mouth, no sound came out. He tried again, and again nothing happened. Frustrated, he waved his arms, but the boy didn't see him, either. By this time the boy had crossed the street and was starting to pedal faster on his way down the block, and John suddenly knew that the danger was imminent—at the end of the block, or the one after that. Realizing it would be impossible to catch him on foot, he fought back a surge of panic, and raced to a van that was parked nearby. Miraculously, the keys were in the ignition and the door was unlocked, and with no thought other than to head off the boy, he flung open the door, jumped inside—

And found himself behind the wheel of his bright red convertible, driving away from school on a bright spring day. The boy on the bike—and the house with the porch, the tree-lined streets and the unseen danger at the end of the block—had suddenly disappeared, replaced by the familiar Nevada countryside, with its nearby mountains and open sky. John's initial reaction was one of confusion and supreme frustration, but in only a short while, the memories of the boy and the danger he faced became elusive and faded, as if they never existed.

As he sat behind the wheel, the long, straight stretch of highway called out reassuringly, leading him home after a hard day's work. It felt good to be on the open road in an open car, with the warm spring air rushing past all around him, blowing through his hair and gently buffeting his face; he could almost forget he was riding in a car; it was as if he were racing through the countryside under his own special powers, floating comfortably but with speed through the buoyant air.

For the first few miles he had the road to himself, and he yielded by degrees to a fresh sense of freedom; all his worries and concerns simply blew away, as if chased from the convertible by an obliging wind. John smiled as a line from a song began playing in his head, and he reached for his CDs and slipped one in the stereo. His smile grew wider as the first few bars rang out above the wind, and he was about to join in when he noticed a school bus coming down the highway from the other direction.

He knew most of the drivers, so he automatically lifted his hand from the steering wheel, ready to wave. As the bus came closer he saw that the driver was Ruby Mazzoni, the mother of one of his favorite students, a bright girl who had inexplicably begun having problems this semester. John's smile faltered for a second as he recalled the girl's recent haunted look, then he shook it off and waved at the bus. Mrs. Mazzoni raised her hand to return the greeting and started to smile. Then she suddenly scowled instead, slammed down her hand on the top of the steering wheel and aimed the bus straight at John's car.

The unexpectedness of it all robbed him of time to avoid the collision. Even as the bus crossed the yellow line, its engine roaring and gaining speed, a part of John's mind refused to believe she would actually hit him. But hit him she did, at the very same instant when John finally reacted and wrenched the wheel hard and fast to the right. There was a jarring crash, the screeching sound of crunching metal and pain that suddenly flooded his brain. The last thing he saw was Ruby's tortured grin. . . .

JARRED FROM THE NIGHTMARE, John bolted upright in bed and gasped. His heart was racing, slamming against the walls of his heaving chest like a frenzied animal throwing itself against the bars of an iron cage. His body and the sheets were soaked with sweat. His arm and leg, his ribs, his head, so recently mended or almost so, throbbed with pain or the memory of it. His eyes were open but his mind was numb, and the gradient darkness of his bedroom registered only as a solid, smothering blackness, a shroud of nonexistence, the lightless, textureless embrace of death.

It took several excruciatingly long minutes before he began to realize that he had only been dreaming and hadn't died after all, and several minutes more before the panic subsided. Gradually, the familiar security of his bedroom—almost forgotten after weeks in the hospital—exerted its comforting influence, and as it did, John's breathing slowed almost to normal, his heart grew calmer, his forehead cooled and the pain subsided. But the shock of the nightmare lingered on. Whereas previously his knowledge of that fateful crash had only been constructed from the bits and pieces others had told him, now, for the first time, he finally understood what had happened that day. And the price of remembering after repressing it so long was shock and pain and roaring outrage that secondhand information could never exact.

John rubbed his forehead and slid his legs over the side of the bed. He turned on the light and sat there awhile, getting his bearings, then decided that the bedroom was far too close to the scene of the crime, its darkness too likely to lull him back into a dreaming sleep. He struggled to his feet, wincing as his walking cast thumped on the floor, then slipped on his robe and went to the living room, where he settled his shaky body into his favorite chair. For the next three hours, he thought about the dream, which had remained with him even after he woke, each part as vivid as if he'd actually lived it.

Who was the boy who had jumped on the bike, and why did he look so familiar? And what did the dream mean? Was it some long-forgotten scene or unresolved business from his own childhood, a concern he harbored for one of his students or was it simply a meaningless sketch of a boy jumping on a bike and riding away? There was no way to be sure.

Whereas the child in danger could reasonably be attributed to the stuff of dreams, the episode with Ruby wasn't so easy to dismiss. No matter how hard he tried, he couldn't shake the image of her hate-filled face as she deliberately steered the bus in the path of his car. At first he tried to convince himself that that was one of the dream's embellishments and not reality at all; even if the crash sequence mirrored what actually happened, it was still a dream and therefore some of it had to be fiction. But in the end, he realized he was only kidding himself. He'd had a dream, yes, but he knew in his heart it was more memory than concoction, an overdue epiphany, at the very least; after weeks of being trapped in his unconscious, it had finally broken through in the guise of a nightmare. Ruby Mazzoni *had* tried to kill him, and the look he had seen was also real, as dark and ugly as the act itself. The only question remaining was one of motive.

Why, he asked himself for the hundredth time. *Why did she do it? What did I do to set Ruby off?*

No matter how hard he tried, he couldn't find an answer. Even with all the gaps filled in, he still couldn't fathom what had driven her to it. And unless everyone else was lying—which wasn't likely—no one else knew either. Only Ruby Mazzoni could answer that question, and, by all accounts, she had steadfastly refused to do just that, despite the best efforts of everyone involved.

But she hasn't been asked by me yet, John mused, suddenly realizing what he had to do to get back his peace of mind. *The least she can do is tell me why. She owes me that much—and a lot more!*

Of course, the more would have to wait until later. Right now, all he needed was a simple *why.* Since the only logical way to bring that about was to talk to the woman face-to-face, it took him less than a minute to make his decision: first thing tomorrow, he would go to see Ruby and get some answers.

SEVEN

John Creed Goes to Jail

"ARE YOU SURE you want to go through with this?" Will Gibson asked as they pulled into the parking lot of the county jail. He understood why John needed to confront the woman who had almost ended his life—it was a crucial step in putting the matter behind him—but it felt risky; Will didn't want to see his friend go through any more pain than he already had. Because John's car had been totaled in the wreck, Will had agreed to drive him to see Ruby Mazzoni only because he hoped to talk him out of it before they arrived at the jail. The drive had taken twenty minutes, and they'd breakfasted at Denny's for an hour before that, but Will hadn't even made a dent in John's resolve.

"I appreciate your concern, Will," John said with a slight edge in his voice. "But this is something I have to do. When somebody tries to kill you, it isn't enough to escape with your life. You need some answers, too." He reached for the door latch and added grimly, "And now I intend to get some."

"Okay," Will replied, letting it go. "Would you like me to come in with you?"

"You might as well wait here."

"Are you sure?"

"Don't worry," Creed replied with a sardonic grin, "I'm not going to attack her or anything." He held up his left arm, which was in a fiberglass cast that was due to be removed the following week, along with the one he wore on his leg. "About the only thing I could do is smack her with this, and I don't want to risk breaking anything again. All I want to do is talk."

"All right," Will answered. "I'll wait out here." He flashed what he hoped was a supportive smile and added, "Take as long as you need— and good luck."

"Thanks. I'll probably need it." John opened the door, climbed awkwardly out of the car and disappeared into the building.

He had called the police station that morning to let them know he was coming to see Ruby. Unlike Will, Margie and Bobbi, the sergeant to whom he had spoken had not been the least bit appalled at the thought of John confronting the woman who tried to kill him. "Come on down any time you want," he had replied laconically. "She isn't going anywhere. Just ask for Sergeant Marino."

The same sergeant was at the front desk when John walked inside. He was a handsome man, with dark, curly hair and dark brown eyes; even seated, he looked considerably taller than average. "Hi, I'm John Creed," John said, extending a hand, which the policeman shook belatedly; few, if any, of the people who found themselves on the other side of the sergeant's desk offered their hands in a friendly gesture. "I spoke to you on the phone this morning. I'm here to see Ruby Mazzoni."

Marino nodded and made a notation on the clipboard in front of him. "Just have a seat over there," he said, gesturing with his pen at a row of plastic chairs against the wall. "Her lawyer almost had a stroke when he heard you were coming. He's with her now, probably trying to talk her out of seeing you."

A worried look crossed John's face. "Can he do that?"

"Yep," the policeman replied. "There's no law that says she has to see you if she doesn't want to."

"Great," John replied sarcastically. He hobbled over to a chair and sat down to wait.

Ten minutes later, a short, middle-aged man in a rumpled suit burst through the door that led from the cells. He stormed up to the desk and announced in an exasperated voice, "My client insists on going ahead with the meeting."

"Tough break, Counselor," Marino answered wryly.

"Spare me the sarcasm," the lawyer shot back. He pointed at John. "Is that him?"

Marino nodded yes.

The lawyer stalked over to John, who stood up as he approached. "I'm Barry Teitlebaum," he said, pointedly making no effort to offer his hand. "I'm Mrs. Mazzoni's attorney. I think you should know that I strongly advised my client against this meeting, but she insists on going through with it—without my presence, I might add." He paused and added, "I think you should know that Mrs. Mazzoni is a troubled woman. . . . I'm not sure what she expects to accomplish from this meeting, or what you expect to get out of it, either, for that matter—"

"I just want some answers," John replied simply.

"Well, the answers you get might not necessarily reflect the truth," Teitlebaum cautioned. "As I said, my client is confused and troubled. Bear that in mind." With that he turned and walked away, leaving John speechless and more than a little bit angry.

∽

RUBY MAZZONI HAD BEEN in the county jail since the day she attempted to kill John Creed, but it probably wouldn't have worked out that way were it not for her dogged insistence on telling the truth.

The entire affair could easily have been labeled a simple but tragic vehicular accident in which Ruby had lost control of the bus—which is the version Ruby's lawyer favored—because John Creed, as the only witness, had been completely unable to recall what happened when he talked to the police. But from the very first moment when a passing policeman discovered the wreck, Ruby had proclaimed that she had deliberately rammed her bus into Creed's car. Not once since that time had she recanted her story. She freely—almost boastfully—admitted her guilt. What she hadn't told a soul was *why* she had done it. Neither the arresting officer, her family nor her own lawyer could get her to confess a motive for the crime; she kept it to herself like an unspeakable secret. And since her family had failed to raise her bail, she had remained in custody.

At the moment, she was sitting at a plain wooden table in an interrogation room while a guard stood watch just inside the door. Staring blankly at the bare tabletop, Ruby was oblivious to the other presence in the room, lost instead in her own, private thoughts as she fiddled absently with a roll of Lifesavers. She had been unusually subdued ever since her daughter's visit three days ago—even the strip search to which she had been subjected a few minutes earlier had failed to elicit even the mildest protest. As she waited for John Creed to walk in, she looked nothing like an impulsive, cold-blooded murderess, and more like a lost, despairing spirit. It was a striking transformation, and one which her lawyer had noted with concern.

There was a knock at the door, and the guard turned around to look through the small, eye-level window. He nodded to the policeman on the other side, and let John Creed into the room. Ruby Mazzoni started to look up, but went on staring at the table instead, fiddling with the Lifesavers. John stared at the matronly, middle-aged figure with her head hung low, and marveled that this was the person who had tried to kill him.

He pulled out the chair opposite Ruby and sat down quietly. His eyes locked on to her face, waiting for her to meet his gaze. For almost a full minute, no one said a word. Ruby stared intently at the table; John stared intently at her. From what he had been told about Ruby's confession, he had expected her to be defiant and angry, livid at the sight of him. Instead, she seemed apprehensive, even ashamed. John was momentarily taken aback, but his anger ran too deep to be denied for long. When it finally became apparent that Ruby was unwilling or unable to say the first word, John broke the silence. "Hello, Ruby," he said in a stony voice.

A few seconds passed before Ruby looked up. A plain-looking woman under the best of circumstances, she would have been plainer still without her usual makeup were it not for the look of tragedy stamped on her face. At first, she didn't meet his gaze directly, focusing instead on a point somewhere behind his left ear. Her mouth twitched, but she said nothing. Behind her, the guard looked on impassively.

John tried again. "You know why I'm here," he said curtly. "I want some answers."

Ruby looked down again. After a moment, her eyes finally met John's. She had the stricken look of a woman who had been condemned, not by the state but by her own tortured conscience. John saw her lip quiver and thought that finally she was about to speak, but instead of replying, she chewed her lip and simply nodded.

"I really have only one thing to ask you," John continued. "I've thought and thought about it all these weeks, searching for something I might have said or done that could have set you off. But I keep coming up empty. I can't think of a single thing—when you think about it, Ruby, we barely know each other." He paused, anger flaring in his eyes, and demanded, "Why did you do it?"

Ruby flinched, then finally opened her mouth. "I want . . ." Her voice trailed off, and she glanced over her shoulder at the guard. "Would it be possible for us to be alone for a few minutes?" she asked meekly.

The guard shook his head. "You know I can't do that."

"Please," Ruby asked again. "I need to talk to Mr. Creed in private. I promise nothing will happen."

The guard was about to reiterate his refusal when John intervened. Desperate for an answer, he found it inconceivable that the pathetic woman sitting in front of him could still pose a threat to his physical well-being. "Please," he said, "just give us a few minutes. You can watch through the window to make sure nothing happens. I promise, for my part, that nothing will."

The guard didn't seem as certain as before, but still he shook his head no. "It's against procedure."

"Do me a favor," John responded. "At least check with Sergeant Marino. This is important."

The guard sighed, then opened the door and asked the other cop waiting outside to fetch the sergeant. Marino arrived a few minutes later, looking bothered. "What's the problem?" he asked.

"Mrs. Mazzoni and I would like a few minutes to talk in private," John explained. "This is awkward enough as it is, but it's impossible with a stranger in the room."

Marino scratched his chin. "I don't know—"

"Look, I assume you've already searched her for weapons," John interrupted. "And I've already gone through your metal detectors. You can search me again, if you want." He pointed to the door. "You can post a man outside to watch through the window—nothing could happen that he wouldn't have time to stop."

Marino thought it over, glancing from Ruby Mazzoni's pitiful countenance to John Creed's earnest expression. Creed seemed desperate to Marino, but not dangerous, and Ruby looked surprisingly broken since the last time he'd seen her, hardly a match for a man of Creed's size. "All right," Marino said sternly. "But just for ten minutes. And if my man sees anything even remotely threatening, the powwow's over. Got it?"

"Yes," Ruby said, nodding her head.

"Got it," John answered. "And thanks."

"We'll see if you thank me when your ten minutes are over," Marino replied. He walked out of the room, posting a man outside to watch through the glass.

As soon as the door closed behind them, John looked at the bus driver. "Okay, Ruby, let's talk. A few minutes ago you were about to say something—what was it?"

Ruby averted her gaze, staring with unfocused eyes on the roll of Lifesavers in her hand. She shifted uncomfortably in her seat and looked up. "Would you like one?" she asked weakly, holding out the candy.

"No, thank you," John replied impatiently.

Ruby drew back the roll and looked at it again. "Do you mind if I have one? They won't let me have cigarettes in here, and even after all this time I still get cravings."

"Go ahead," John replied evenly. His impatience was getting hard to contain, and the knowledge that this face-to-face meeting was obviously difficult for Ruby did nothing to lessen his anger. She had, after all, he reminded himself, attempted to kill him.

He watched her put a piece of candy in her mouth, and waited for her to talk. Then, as Ruby averted her eyes and sucked on the candy, John began drumming his fingers on top of the table. He glanced up at the clock; two minutes of their allotted time had already elapsed. Another minute passed, and John's face grew dark. Unconsciously, he folded his drumming fingers into an angry fist. "Dammit, Ruby!" he suddenly exploded, pounding the table. "Talk to me!"

Ruby jumped, swallowing the candy. As she stared at John with wide-eyed surprise, the guard outside reached for the doorknob. He was about to come in when John waved him off. "Sorry," he called out, raising his voice for the frowning guard. "Everything's all right." The guard seemed uncertain, but remained outside.

John looked back at Ruby. This time, she opened up. "This is not how I meant for things to turn out," she blurted.

"Yeah, I know," John shot back. The adrenaline in his system had weeks of anger and simmering resentment to back it up. "You meant for me to be dead by now."

Ruby blanched at his words and shook her head violently from side to side. "No, no! That's not what I meant! This whole thing has been a horrible mistake!"

"Come off it, Ruby," John replied heatedly; it took every ounce of his self-control to remain seated. "From what I was told, you said all along that you meant to kill me—the cop who questioned me in the hospital said you practically bragged about it!"

"No—" Ruby replied, bursting into tears. "I mean—yes, I did at the time . . . But that's because I didn't know I'd made a mistake!"

"A mistake!" John shouted, and immediately lowered his voice to an angry rumble. "You tried to ram me head-on with a bus! And you didn't look the least bit confused when you did it! I saw your face, Ruby—I remember it all now! You looked at me like you wished I was dead, then you hit the gas and headed straight for me! How can you call that a *mistake*?"

"Because I thought you were having an affair with my daughter!" Ruby confessed with a gut-wrenching sob. She buried her face in her hands and moaned, "God forgive me—I thought it was you. . . ."

John sat back in his chair, stunned. After a moment, he said in a near-whisper, "You thought I was having an affair with Beth?"

"Yes," Ruby wailed. She put down her hands and stared with wild, anguished eyes. She continued crying for several more moments, then valiantly tried to compose herself. "I knew that someone was . . . fooling around . . . with her. I thought it was you."

"But why?" John replied in a bewildered voice. "How could you think it was me?"

Ruby reached for the roll of Lifesavers again, and clutched it in her hands. She took a deep, hitching breath as she told him why. The tears kept flowing but slowed to a trickle and her chest heaved with emotion. "A few months ago, Beth started acting strange. . . ." She began in a halting voice. "When I asked her what was wrong, she said I shouldn't worry, that everything was okay. . . . But nothing changed—a mother knows when something's wrong with her daughter, Mr. Creed. Especially when it's . . . when it's a sexual thing," Ruby said, thoroughly miserable.

John nodded, listening; for the moment, he almost forgot his own anguish.

"When I couldn't stand it anymore, I snuck upstairs while she was at school one day and read her diary. It was pretty shocking. . . ." Ruby confessed with a look of shame. "It was obvious she was writing about an older man. She never mentioned his last name, but his first name was John."

She looked at John sorrowfully. "Beth always talked about you and about how much she enjoyed your class. And she always seemed to perk up when she was going to school, like she was looking forward to something. . . . You're the only teacher I know named John—I assumed it was you. . . ." Ruby closed her eyes. "That's why I tried to kill you that day."

"But it wasn't me," John said softly. "I would never do anything like that."

Ruby opened her eyes. They were red-rimmed and tearful, and laden with remorse. "I know that now. . . . I only found out who John was three days ago, when Beth came to visit me."

John waited for the rest, and then finally prompted her. "Who was it, Ruby? Another teacher?"

Ruby shook her head sadly. The effort seemed to cost her a lifetime. "My husband's name is John," she said simply, her confession complete.

John looked off to a corner of the room, attempting to give Ruby some semblance to privacy in which to grieve. He was emotionally drained, and more than a little confused. He had requested this meeting to demand the answers for the hell he'd been through; more than that, he realized, he had wanted to do everything possible to punish Ruby, short of killing her himself. And now his anger was slipping away in the face of a tragedy much larger than his own. He had survived this ironic comedy of errors; the Mazzoni family, he suspected, more than likely would not. "And that's why you wouldn't tell the police why you tried to kill me," he said softly.

Ruby's nod was almost imperceptible. "I didn't want everybody to know. . . ."

A long silence followed. Ruby unclasped her hands and stared once more at the roll of Lifesavers; she was craving a cigarette like she'd never craved one before. With a sigh that mourned far more than simply the loss of her habit, she carefully unwound the foil and removed a piece of candy. She started to place it in her mouth, and offered it to John instead. "Would you like a Lifesaver?" she asked in a worn-out voice.

John hesitated, then smiled weakly and accepted the gesture; under the circumstances, it seemed the right thing to do. "Thanks," he said softly, holding out his hand. Ruby reached across the table to give him the Lifesaver, and suddenly grabbed his hand instead. Her fingers wrapped around his in a desperate squeeze, and she stared balefully into his eyes, saying nothing. At first John was alarmed, but the intensity of the misery he saw in her eyes dampened his fear, and gave birth to a burgeoning sense of compassion he was powerless to stop. Before long, his lingering anger for what she had done began to sputter and die, and his heart went out to her with a matching intensity.

AND AS IT DID, a strange thing happened . . . Like highlights from a tape of Ruby's home movies, images and scenes from the bus driver's life began running through his mind. They were brief but powerful and laden with emotion, painful, private memories that he realized immediately couldn't be his own—

He saw the pages of a diary, and felt shock and disbelief, then a sinking sadness. He felt the anguish of having failed to protect a sweet child, the self-recrimination that eventually gave birth to an overpowering rage. . . .

From a bus driver's seat, he saw himself approaching in his bright red convertible, and felt the cold, blind rage find focus and sharpen as a decision was made in the blink of an eye. . . .

And finally, he saw Beth, Ruby's teenage daughter, sob uncontrollably as she revealed the truth in this very same room. He felt overwhelming heartache, disgust and horror, then the dawning of a devastating, searing remorse. . . .

When the images abruptly ended, John's eyes flew open, and he stared at Ruby with consternation, wondering against all reason if she had somehow bewitched him. But Ruby appeared lost in her own thoughts, and was staring at the tabletop; the expression on her face was completely without guile. John studied her awhile longer. His head throbbed from a headache that had come on suddenly, and then just as suddenly began to fade. It seemed to take with it the sting of the images that had just played in his head, while leaving behind a faint memory of pain, like the acrid smell of a blazing fire that had just sputtered and died. When Ruby finally looked up, there was no hint in her eyes that she knew what had just happened between them. Nor did John know, and that troubled him greatly.

The longer he thought about it, the more stunned he became. *It was as if he had somehow looked into Ruby's mind. . . .* And not only had he seen the events leading up to the crash, but he had shared her *thoughts . . .* and *experienced* her emotions—the acute pain and sorrow and thirst for justice, and her rage and remorse in the aftermath of discovering the shocking truth. *How is that possible?* he kept asking himself. Nothing remotely like this had ever happened to him before. He had no telepathic ability or psychic powers. He wasn't even sure he believed in such things.

Suddenly needing to leave, John removed his hand from Ruby's grasp and pushed back his chair. He got to his feet, trying to steady himself and hide his turmoil, then glanced uncertainly at Ruby once again. She returned his stare with a quizzical look, and a ghost of a smile flitted across her face; the burden in her eyes seemed to visibly lighten, as if she had just caught a glimpse of an elusive peace. Despite his consternation, John couldn't help but wonder what she was feeling. As if in answer, a faint glimmer of hope—hope for forgiveness and the release it would bring—abruptly washed over him.

Suddenly, Ruby reached across the table and clutched the hand that John had just freed. "I'm so sorry, Mr. Creed! What I did was wrong—my God, I almost killed you. . . ." Her eyes probed his, and she pleaded, "I know I don't have the right to ask, but can you ever forgive me?"

Even though he didn't understand what had happened in this room, John understood perfectly what he was supposed to do next. The burden he had lived with for the last several weeks—the pain of not knowing why Ruby had tried to kill him—was now a thing of the past, and it seemed only fitting that he free her from that part of her burden also. Still reeling from the experience of sharing her pain, but with a newfound peace taking root in his heart, he glanced down at Ruby and squeezed her hand. "I already have," he replied with a smile, then bade her good-bye.

The last thing he did before leaving the station was arrange for Ruby's bail to be paid.

EIGHT

Another Death, Another Tunnel

THREE WEEKS EARLIER, on the same afternoon when John Creed had temporarily died, eleven-year-old Matt Dandridge had passed away, too, after riding his bike into the path of a car. He had been taken to St. Joseph's Hospital and pronounced dead on arrival, but a few minutes later—as the ER doctor was working up the nerve to inform the boy's parents that his head injuries had been fatal—Matt miraculously stirred, mumbled a few words and lapsed into a coma.

Since that day, the members of Matt's family had made daily pilgrimages to sit by his bed in alternating shifts. They hoped and waited, gave up hope and waited some more, praying and willing his eyes to open—and hoping that if they did, they wouldn't be vacant. It had been a roller-coaster ride of the grandest proportions, and a grueling test of emotional endurance.

For his sister, Lori, it meant dealing with death—or at least its possibility—for the very first time, and a not-so-subtle revelation that youth wasn't insurance against the Reaper's call. Her days at school were like sleepwalking through a nightmare, her visits to the hospital like living the same dream. Even in her sleep, it was all she could think about.

For Kate Dandridge the wait was like teetering at the edge of a yawning pit, with a mother's worst fear lurking deep in the hole. After the first two weeks, she had reluctantly and dazedly returned to work, if only for something to distract her mind. That hadn't happened, but it helped pass the long hours when all she could do was wait and pray.

For Elliot Dandridge, the whole situation was sheer hell on earth. Not once since Matt had been old enough to understand had Elliot told him "I love you." Like his father before him, if given the choice between eating ground glass or admitting his feelings with three little words, Elliot might very well have reached for the glass. Now, he knew, he might never get the chance to say those words. Seeing his son in a comatose condition day after day was a constant reminder not only of that particular failing, but also of another costly mistake, namely, quitting his job instead of allowing himself to be fired.

Coming as it did on the very same day he had made that mistake, the timing of Matt's accident couldn't have been worse—not only did their health insurance have a high deductible, but now Elliot no longer had an employer to pay for the coverage. As a result, they faced the dilemma of paying the fifteen-hundred-dollar deductible *and* assuming the monthly cost of the insurance as well, all at a time when their income had decreased by seventy-five percent. It was only a matter of time before the family was faced with genuine financial disaster. Each morning when Elliot came to the hospital to man the day shift while Kate worked, he was acutely aware that he also needed to be out looking for employment to help avert that disaster, but he just couldn't face the intimidating process of applying for jobs. As a result, the crisis grew worse by the minute, and Elliot's sense of inadequacy and ongoing failure grew along with it.

On this particular day—the day after John Creed had affected his peculiar reconciliation with Ruby Mazzoni—all three of Matt's family members happened to be at the hospital. It was three o'clock, and Kate had just arrived to take over for Elliot; Lori, who had quit the track team two weeks ago, was with her. Elliot was in no hurry to leave, and after giving them a perfunctory greeting remained seated by the window of Matt's third-floor room, staring out at the parking lot below. There was a frown on his face, a look that Kate had seen often enough over the years but which seemed to have taken up permanent residence in the last few weeks; she was starting to resent it not only because it tended to drag her down too, but because she also suspected it contained more than an element of self-preoccupation and self-pity. At moments like this she wanted to shake her husband from his self-imposed lethargy and tell him to get up off his butt and go look for a job, or at least go do anything that might give him some relief from his deepening depression. But she didn't want to risk an argument, not here, not now, not in front of Matt. The last time they'd done that had help put their son where he was today.

Leaving Elliot to himself, Kate and Lori pulled up two chairs and assumed their usual places, Kate at Matt's side and Lori at the foot of the bed. The monitors behind and above the bed beeped and pulsed in the same steady rhythms they had kept without fail for the last three weeks. Kate and Lori had learned to ignore them; their eyes, when focused, were trained on Matt, who lay on his back, silent and unmoving, his breathing slow but reassuringly regular. His mop of blond hair was freshly washed and framed a freckled face that looked ironically peaceful, the eyes lightly closed, the mouth slightly open. The bruises were gone, and there were no casts or bandages since, surprisingly enough, he hadn't broken any bones when he was thrown from the bike; were it not for the aura of *wrongness* about him, it would have appeared that he was merely sleeping.

Sometimes it was easier to pretend that he was merely sleeping, and on those occasions Kate managed to do some of the work she had brought from school. But most of the time, she simply sat by her son's side, holding his hand or stroking his head and looking for signs. Once Elliot was gone she talked to Matt—her husband disapproved, calling it fruitless and maudlin—or sometimes she hummed or sang to him quietly. The conversations were one-sided, and sometimes Kate couldn't help but lapse into the "Momma's here" voice she had used with Matt when he was a baby. At other times, she relayed bits and pieces of what had happened at work, or told him who had called or stopped by the house, and what had been happening to his friends or neighbors. And in the moments when the enormity of what had happened threatened to overwhelm her anew, she would squeeze his hand, lean close to his ear and whisper that she loved him and wanted him back.

But that was when there was no one around, and at the moment her husband and daughter were there. Brushing back a lock of hair from Matt's forehead, Kate kissed her son lightly and settled into her seat at the side of his bed. She squeezed his hand softly and stared at Matt with a sad, sweet smile. "Hello, Matt. Momma's here." It was her usual greeting.

For the first week or two of the ordeal, Kate had secretly harbored the expectation that when Matt finally emerged from the coma, it would happen when she kissed his forehead and told him she was there. When that had not happened, she had not lost hope that he would ever regain consciousness, but she had stopped expecting it to coincide with her arrival. On that particular score, however, she had given up too soon. This time, no sooner had she spoken the magical words than the fingers of Matt's hand twitched in her own—tentatively at first, as if his fingers were reacting reflexively to her touch, and then with a stronger flexing and stretching, followed by a clearly deliberate act: they squeezed her hand. As Kate's heart began pounding, Matt's eyes began moving beneath his shuttered lids, then the eyelids fluttered and miraculously opened.

Kate held her breath as Matt turned his head slowly in her direction. His green eyes fastened on her own, and at first they appeared blank. Kate fought back the sudden fear that one unbearable nightmare had been exchanged for another that was worse, then Matt's eyes seemed to focus and a ghost of his long-lost smile spread across his face. "Wow," he gasped weakly, glancing wide-eyed around the room. "I'm back!"

In a heartbeat, he was surrounded by his family, who kissed him, hugged him, wept and screamed. If he hadn't finally yelled that he needed some air, they might never have let go. The commotion brought Anne Giovaniello—the nurse who had tended Matt since his arrival—running into the room. There was a disapproving scowl on her face, but it evaporated like frost before a blaze of sunshine when she saw what was happening. She ran outside to summon the doctor, and then hurried back to the room, where she waited for a turn to administer a hug to the little boy she had wanted to hug for so long.

When things had settled down a little, Matt glanced around the room and said, "I'm still in St. Joseph's, aren't I?"

"Yes, you are, sweetie," Kate Dandridge replied, brushing a tear of joy from her cheek.

"I thought so," Matt said hoarsely, but in a matter-of-fact tone. "It feels the same."

Kate started to nod, then gave Matt a quizzical look. Except for the moment when he had miraculously recovered from being clinically dead, only to lapse into a coma, Matt had been unconscious the entire time he had been in St. Joseph's. "Honey, the only other time you were in this hospital was the day you were born," Kate responded. "How could it feel the same?"

Matt shrugged, then winced and flexed his stiff shoulders. "It just does. It feels like it did when they brought me in." He paused and added, "You know . . . when I died."

Stunned that he knew what had happened that day, no one said a word. When Dr. Cohen walked in a moment later, the group around

Matt's bed still looked shocked. Having caught the tail end of the conversation as she entered the room, the doctor raised one eyebrow accusingly at Elliot Dandridge, then put the matter of who had needlessly informed the boy of his clinical death aside for the moment. A young woman with longish curly black hair and eyes that sparkled with warmth and spirit, Dr. Cohen flashed a reassuring (if somewhat astounded) smile at her miracle patient, and sat down on the edge of the bed. Reflexively, she reached for Matt's wrist to check his pulse. "Welcome back," she said, beaming with genuine relief. "How are you feeling?"

"Fine," Matt replied.

Dr. Cohen nodded, but her eyes made it clear that she was reserving judgment. "You ready to do chin-ups, then? Or maybe race me to the elevators?"

Matt grinned, then gave the doctor a sheepish look. "Well, I am kinda tired, I guess. Maybe later."

The doctor nodded again. "I thought so. Anything hurt?"

Matt shook his head. "No."

"Any headaches?"

"Nope."

Dr. Cohen made a notation on his chart. "Very good," she replied, smiling. "Now I'm going to ask you a question or two that might be a little harder. But try not to let them upset you, okay? The important thing is that you've already gone through the hard part. Try to remember that." The doctor waited for him to nod assent, then asked in a solicitous voice, "Do you know why you're here?"

Matt gave his parents a guilty look and said in a barely audible voice, "I rode my bike in front of a car and got hit . . . then I died."

Ignoring the others' discomfited expressions, the doctor searched Matt's face for a clue as to how to proceed; she had some experience telling patients they had died and been resuscitated, but she only divulged that information when it was absolutely necessary, and then always very carefully. Looking at Matt now, it was difficult to gauge how much he knew. All she saw was a guilty expression; beyond that he seemed to be extraordinarily calm. "And how do you know that you . . . died, Matt?"

Without hesitation, the boy answered, "Because I saw the whole thing. I saw Mom and Dad crying when they put me in the ambulance. And I saw you pull the sheet up over my head in the emergency room and tell the nurse that you were going to have to go tell my parents that I didn't make it. I remember you said, 'Damn' "—Matt shot his mother an apologetic look—" 'I hate doing this. I never know what to say.' "

Once again, Kate Dandridge was stunned, then worried; Elliot was dumbfounded, then worried too, but soon began to wonder if his son was having a bit of fun at everyone's expense. Lori and Nurse Giovaniello were staring, wide-eyed, obviously intrigued. But despite Dr. Cohen's hearing Matt render an exact quote of what she had said that day in the emergency room, her eyes widened only a little.

Choosing her words carefully, Cohen went on. "You were unconscious when the paramedics got to you, Matt. And you were still unconscious when they brought you in. As you already know, there was a brief time when I couldn't even get any vital signs . . . until you surprised us all by coming back." She paused and asked in a calm, nonjudgmental tone, "How could you have seen anything? Are you sure you're not just filling in the blanks?"

Matt thought about it for a second, and shook his head. With a shock, he began to realize that the people around him might not believe what he had to say, even if it was the truth. But he said it anyway. "No, ma'am," he replied earnestly. "I'm not making this up—and I know I didn't dream it. It really happened. I don't remember getting hit by the car, but I remember waking up in the street and feeling funny all over. . . . Then all of a sudden I was looking down at myself." Matt stopped, remembering. "I didn't look so good . . . and then Mom and Dad were kneeling over me while some lady stood by her car, screaming."

Kate Dandridge gasped and, reliving the pain, began weeping

quietly. Elliot was shaken, too, but his mind was racing, trying to make sense of it all.

"What do you mean, you were looking down at yourself, Spike?" Lori asked in an awed voice. Spike was the nickname she used for her brother.

Matt looked at his sister. "It was weird, like I was in two places at the same time, only one of me was floating."

"Cool," Lori responded. "Like what my psych teacher calls an out-of-body experience."

Matt shrugged, never having heard the term before. Dr. Cohen, however, nodded, and after jotting a quick note on the chart, stared at Matt thoughtfully. She had heard of the phenomenon, obviously, but had never encountered someone who claimed to have had one, and she was trying very hard to be objective and open-minded. At the moment, she was more concerned with hearing the rest of the boy's story before someone shamed him into silence than she was with making up her mind about the veracity of his claims. "And then what happened?" she prodded. "How did your . . . other self . . . get to the hospital?"

"I don't know, exactly," Matt answered. "I just sort of followed the ambulance."

"And you say you were in the emergency room?"

"Yeah, at first," Matt replied. "Then I . . . left for a while, right after you said what you said to the nurse." He paused, suddenly aware that if everybody was having trouble believing the first part of his story, they would really have problems with what came next. He reminded himself that what he was saying was God's honest truth, and that his mother had always told him he had nothing to be afraid of if he told the truth, so he swallowed hard, took a deep breath and prepared to go on.

"You left?" Cohen prodded.

"Yes, ma'am," Matt replied nervously.

"And where did you go?"

"Into the tunnel," Matt replied, his voice suddenly calm as wondrous images and soothing sensations flooded back into his mind.

Without waiting for anyone to encourage him, he described how he had suddenly found himself being drawn up into the sky, and then into a strange blackness that ended at the mouth of a long, dark tunnel. Speaking quickly, so as not to give anyone a chance to question his truthfulness, Matt recounted his dreamlike walk toward the beckoning light at the tunnel's end, reliving the excitement, the awe and the overwhelming joy even as he spoke. When he stopped speaking, his face was positively beatific.

Astounded, Dr. Cohen nonetheless clung to her clinical demeanor while the others around her were either slack-jawed with amazement or shaking their heads sadly from side to side. Assuming Matt had finished the story, she tried to wrap up the loose ends for him. "So I guess you left the tunnel and . . . reentered your body right before you . . . recovered?"

Matt didn't reply right away, still savoring the memory and thinking about what he hadn't yet told. When he finally spoke, his tone was matter-of-fact again. "Yes. I guess so."

Having always wondered why Matt had come back to life when her own medical efforts had failed, Dr. Cohen couldn't resist asking, "Why did you come back?"

Matt stared at the doctor and at each of his family members for a moment, buying time. Then, ashamed of himself for hesitating to tell the truth, he said simply, "They sent me back. My guardian angel told me it wasn't time for me to come to heaven yet."

Having already grown embarrassed by his son's story, Elliot Dandridge could no longer hold his tongue. "*Guardian angel? An angel* sent you back from *heaven*?" His voice was biting, part incredulity, part anger. The others were incredulous too—even Lori, who had been fairly accepting to this point—but no one else said a word.

Matt flinched at his father's tone and seemed to shrink into the covers beneath the patronizing glances of the people around him. His first reply was defensive, mumbled more into the pillow than in his father's direction, but after regaining his courage, his second was delivered in a strong, clear voice that was filled with conviction and a little defiance. "I'm telling the truth! My guardian angel was there at the end of the tunnel—where the bright light was coming from—and he told me it wasn't time and they were sending me back."

Somewhere deep in the recesses of his soul, Elliot Dandridge felt a twinge of guilt for his skeptical reaction, and he backed down a little—but only a little. He took a deep breath to try to steady his anger, and continued in a voice that was a little less harsh but still tinged with irritation. "Maybe this is just something you heard in Sunday school and then dreamed about—like that time when you watched *Invaders from Mars* and dreamed that Martians were blasting a hole through your bedroom floor. Remember? Maybe that's what it was." He shot a quick, disapproving glance at his wife, who took the kids to Sunday school almost every week, then turned back to Matt and forced a small smile. "Only this time it was angels instead of Martians."

Matt shook his head regretfully, hurt but not completely surprised at his father's reaction; Elliot had never much cared about church or anything connected with it. "It wasn't a dream, Dad. It really happened. Besides," he added, glancing at his mother, "Miss Thompson never taught us anything like this in Sunday school."

"That's for sure," Lori muttered. Kate Dandridge turned to her daughter and started to shush her, then did nothing. The same thought had been running through her mind, too; no one—not Pastor Buschkemper nor any of her former pastors—had ever taught anything like what Matt had described. For a variety of reasons—not the least of which was the burning desire to have her son back again, whole and sane—she wanted to believe Matt. But it was difficult. "It's not that we think you're lying, dear," she began in a tentative voice. "But you've been through a lot, and it does sound kind of . . . fantastic, if you know what I mean. Maybe it *was* just a dream—a very nice one, but still just a dream."

For Matt's sake, Dr. Cohen tried to steer the conversation back into safer waters. She still wanted to hear more, if there was any more to tell, but she had decided that could wait until she was alone with the patient. "If we can go on," she said, glancing at Mr. and Mrs. Dandridge, "I need to ask you another question, Matt." The boy nodded; he looked upset and hurt, but also relieved at the prospect of changing the subject. "You already know what happened in the emergency room," Dr. Cohen went on, "but do you know what's happened since then?"

"I've been unconscious," Matt replied matter-of-factly.

"Something like that," Dr. Cohen answered. "Do you know what a coma is?"

Matt puzzled over the word for a moment. "Not really."

"Well, we don't know a whole lot about it either, to be honest," the doctor went on, groping for an answer that might make sense to an eleven-year-old boy. "It's something like a real deep sleep, but more like being unconscious—like you said—only instead of coming to after a few minutes, you stay that way for a longer time."

Matt nodded slightly.

Dr. Cohen gave him a minute, then asked her next question. She tried to frame it delicately, because the duration of a coma—especially a lengthy one—was often a shock when revealed to a patient. "Do you know how long you've been with us, Matt?" she asked. "Here in St. Joseph's?"

The boy thought about it for a minute, and answered in a voice that was surprisingly unperturbed, "I'm not sure. Awhile, I guess—maybe a week or two?"

Dr. Cohen tilted her head slightly and pursed her lips. She smiled reassuringly. "Closer to a month, actually. But we took good care of you."

"And we were here with you the whole time, sweetie," his mother chimed in.

Matt favored his mother with a loving look, then addressed Dr. Cohen again. "I figured it was a long time," he said. "My guardian angel told me it would take a while for my body to heal after they sent me back. But he said it wouldn't seem like a long time because I'd be sleeping, sort of."

Kate Dandridge said it before Dr. Cohen could: "Your guardian angel told you that, too?"

Matt hesitated before answering. At first, he had been surprised at the reaction he'd gotten at the mention of his guardian angel: that half-amused, half-appalled look that adults give children when they think they're being asked to swallow a story that only a child—or an idiot—would think plausible. Now it hurt to see the look on his mother's face again. "Yes," he replied as the corners of his mouth turned down with resentment. "And he said he'd look out for me if I ever got into trouble. That's what they do. He said all of us have guardian angels while we're living down here."

Elliot Dandridge snorted and muttered, "Well, mine must have been taking a vacation lately."

"Oh, shut up, Elliot!" Kate snapped at her husband. Despite the incredulous look she'd first given Matt, she wasn't as willing as her husband to dismiss their son's story without at least mulling it over. And she had always liked the idea of guardian angels; hearing her husband deride it made her suddenly realize what Matt must be feeling. "Just because you don't believe in something doesn't make everyone else stupid for believing it," she said curtly. "Did it ever occur to you that a little bit of faith might do you some good?" She turned to Matt and said, "I'm sorry, sweetheart, if we gave you the impression that we think you're lying. *I* know you're not. We're thrilled to have you back, safe and sound . . . but we just never expected . . . this. Please try to understand. We want to believe what happened, but it may take a little time." She smiled sweetly and reached past the doctor to stroke Matt's hair. "Can you give us some time?"

"Sure, Mom," Matt replied, returning her smile. "I understand. I guess I might not believe it either, if it hadn't happened to me. But I'm glad it did."

"Well, on that note, I think it's time for me to leave," Dr. Cohen interjected. She looked at Matt's parents. "Mr. and Mrs. Dandridge, could you join me out in the hall for a minute?" She smiled at Matt. "Keep up the good work. I'll be back later to check on you."

After giving Matt another round of kisses and hugs, the Dandridges followed Dr. Cohen to the nurses' station. They were reluctant to leave their son so soon, even if only for a few minutes, but they were also anxious to talk to the doctor in a place where Matt couldn't overhear them. Elliot was still privately fuming over the way his wife had embarrassed him in front of the others, but he had decided to put it aside and save the discussion for later. Kate had already forgotten the exchange, but the words of Matt's account still rang in her head with an almost dizzying power, and she needed to hear Dr. Cohen say that Matt was okay.

"What do you think?" Elliot asked as soon as they were out of the room.

"Naturally, now that he's conscious, we'll need to run some tests," Dr. Cohen replied, "just to make sure nothing shows up that we didn't see before. And even if the tests come out negative, I'd still like to keep him under observation for a few more days. I know you're probably anxious to take him home, but I'd rather be safe than sorry." She reached out and patted Kate's hand, adding, "Don't hold me to this, but my hunch is that he came through it all right. If everything goes okay, within the next few days you'll have your little boy back."

Kate squeezed the doctor's hand and gave her a grateful smile, but a fresh wave of emotion kept her from actually saying what she felt. Elliot nodded vigorously and said their thank-you's for them, but he was still unsettled on one major point. "What's your opinion on this angel business?" he asked.

"Do you mean your son's account of what happened while he was clinically dead?"

"Yes. What was that all about?"

Dr. Cohen hesitated and said in a bemused voice, "This is the first time I've encountered something like this, but a colleague of mine has some experience with it. It sounds like Matt had an NDE."

"A near-death experience?" Elliot responded. He had expected a more pragmatic explanation from a medical doctor.

"That's what it sounds like," Dr. Cohen replied.

Elliot rolled his eyes, and his posture shifted into a more aggressive stance. "I thought the only doctors who believed in that kind of crap were the ones who got their degrees from one of those so-called medical schools down in the Caribbean."

"I didn't say I believe in them," Dr. Cohen replied, sounding a bit more defensive than she intended. Then she qualified her answer. "At least, I'm not sure I believe that people die and actually go to heaven for a few minutes, and then come back to their bodies. I *do* believe that there are such things as near-death experiences—there are too many documented cases to say they don't happen. I'm just not sure what they actually are. If you're asking me if I think you should be worried that Matt is suffering from some kind of psychotic episode or delusion, the answer is no. To be honest, he appears to be in a lot better shape than most people are when they come out of a coma."

"Then what do you suggest we do about it?" Elliot persisted.

"It's been my experience that kids that age—particularly ones who've been through such a serious illness—don't just make up stories like this," Dr. Cohen answered. "As I said before, even though this may be premature, I don't expect to find that your son suffered any brain damage. So, as far as I can tell, you've basically got two options: you can either write it off as a particularly vivid dream, or you can choose to believe that he's telling the truth."

Realizing they had gotten about as clear an answer as they were going to get for the time being—and anxious to excuse themselves before Elliot said anything else to antagonize Dr. Cohen—Kate stepped between the two of them and took the doctor's hand. "We appreciate everything you've been doing for Matt. Please forgive us if we sound impatient or ungrateful. We don't mean to be. It's just that—"

"There's no need to apologize," Dr. Cohen broke in. "You've been just fine. This has been tough on all of us. I'm just glad that it's almost over."

"You're very kind," Kate replied. She gave her husband a warning glance and added, "We really are very grateful."

"Yes, thank you," Elliot joined in, backing down.

"You're welcome," Dr. Cohen replied. She started to walk away, then turned back to the Dandridges. "One more thing—I almost forgot that the business office asked me to have you come down."

"Did they say what it's about?" Elliot asked guardedly.

"Something about your insurance," Cohen replied. "I didn't really ask. Doctors like to leave that kind of thing to the business office, you know."

Elliot frowned. "Okay . . . I'll try to stop by on my way home tonight."

"Actually, they said it was rather urgent. They asked me to send you down as soon as possible."

Elliot's frown deepened. He knew that the moment he'd been dreading—when the hospital would demand to know how he would pay his share of Matt's bill—had finally arrived. Unfortunately, he hadn't figured out how they were going to do it. "All right," he said tiredly, glancing at Kate. As he turned to go, his face was grim, and despite his relief at Matt's recovery, he couldn't fend off the thought that had plagued him more and more with each passing day, namely, that Matt couldn't possibly have picked a worse time to wind up in the hospital.

When he came back upstairs half an hour later, his face was even grimmer than it was before he left. And the look he gave his son when he entered the room made Matt begin to hope that his guardian angel hadn't forgotten his promise and was back on earth and paying attention.

NINE

John Goes Back to School, Holly Takes a Hike

AT THE END of his first day back at McQueen High, John felt as if he had been put through the wringer. Excited about going back to work that morning, all he wanted to do now was collapse in his favorite chair and rest for a while. But ten minutes after Margie drove him home, the telephone rang.

It was Will Gibson. "Hi, John. I'm running a little late. I should be there about five o'clock."

"What's going on at five?" John responded. He hadn't the faintest idea what Will was talking about.

There was a pause on the other end of the line. Will said, "Car shopping, remember? You and I are supposed to hit the lots this afternoon so you can get a replacement for your late, lamented convertible."

When John didn't respond right away, Gibson said, "First day back was kind of tough, I guess."

"Yeah," John replied, massaging his eyes, "It took more out of me than I expected."

"Maybe we should do it tomorrow," Will suggested.

John smiled, thinking how lucky he was to have so many good friends. "No, that's okay. Five o'clock sounds good. I ought to be catching my second wind about then."

FOUR HOURS LATER, John and Will were riding in a canyon-blue Jeep Cherokee that John had chosen from the lot at the first dealership they'd visited. The car was used, but it had very low mileage and had been so lovingly cared for by the previous owner that it looked and almost felt like new. After paying cash from the insurance settlement on his old car, they'd left Will's Sentra and gone to dinner.

"This is a great car," Will remarked for at least the third time since they'd driven off the lot. "I can't believe you made up your mind so quickly," he said. "It probably would have taken me days to decide."

John smiled. He liked the car, too—actually, he liked it a lot—but he wasn't half as enthralled as Will seemed to be. "Two months ago it would have taken me at least a month to make up my mind. I've always been inordinately attached to my cars, and if anyone had ever told me that a big yellow school bus was going to total my convertible, I probably would have lobbied my assemblyman to outlaw yellow school buses." He gave Will a wry smile as they pulled into the restaurant's parking lot. "That type of attachment seems kind of silly now."

Even so, John parked his new Jeep at the edge of the parking lot, as far away from the other cars as possible. After seeing Will's grin, he felt rather self-conscious, but rationalized his actions to himself, and then to Will, by saying he was only protecting the car against dings and scratches in an effort to preserve the resale value.

Once inside the restaurant, they were seated in a booth by the window and given their menus by a waitress who looked tired and bored. As she left to get their drinks, Will noticed that John's mood had suddenly shifted. He knew that periods of contemplative quiet—and more often depression—were a normal reaction to the type of trauma John had recently experienced. But John's moods seemed to be intensifying. Lately, there was always an air of preoccupation or sadness about him, even when he was smiling or laughing. Will decided it was time to ask him about it.

"Something got you down?" he asked, and immediately regretted the triteness of the question.

"Aside from having my whole life turned upside down by a school bus driver who made a mistake?" John replied.

"I'm sorry," Will apologized. "That didn't come out quite how I meant it. I wasn't trying to trivialize what you've been through—I know it takes time to deal with everything and get your life back in order." He gave John a concerned smile and said, "But it seems like something else is bothering you, too."

"I don't know," John replied, meeting Will's eyes only briefly before staring through the window at the parking lot outside. For a moment, he considered telling Will about the dreams he'd had, but decided against it. "I'm kind of tired these days. I haven't been sleeping very well. . . . Most of it's just stuff left over from the accident." He paused as the waitress brought their drinks and took the rest of their order. Then he continued. "I know all about post-traumatic stress, so I wasn't naive enough to expect that it wouldn't happen to me. But I guess I kind of hoped I'd only get a mild case. . . . I was trying not to let it show, but I must not be doing a very good job."

"There's no need to apologize," Will replied.

John nodded and went on. "Sometimes I feel stupid when I get this way. I went through a tough time, sure, but aside from the car, everything turned out okay: I'm alive, I'm getting my health back, I've still got my job and my friends"—he smiled warmly—"and I made a new one, besides. . . . It's just going to take some time to put it all behind me.

I've had nothing else to do but sit around and think for the last month or so, and that didn't help. Going back to work should give me a distraction. Unfortunately, this is a short week—we're off Friday. The last thing I wanted was more free time."

"If you're up to it, you could always help out down at the shelter," Will suggested.

John brightened. "You know, that's a great idea! I've been so wrapped up in my own problems that I completely forgot that I told you'd I'd like to do that. This is the perfect time—there's nothing like helping someone else to make you forget your own problems. Are you working there Friday?"

Will nodded. "From ten until two—the lunch shift. This week, I'm off on Friday instead of Saturday."

"Perfect," John responded, smiling enthusiastically. "I'll pick you up around nine-thirty. How does that sound?"

"It sounds great. But are you sure you wouldn't rather take my car? The neighborhood's not the best; you might not want to take that new Jeep down there. Nobody ever messes with the Nissan because it's too old to bother with."

John thought about it for a minute, and surprised Will and himself by saying, "What the heck—it's only a car. What kind of hypocrite would I be if I said I wanted to help the people in that neighborhood and then refused to drive my car down there because I was afraid one of them might steal it? If it does get stolen, we'll go out next week and find another one." He smiled with genuine satisfaction and said, "This is perfect, Will. Thanks for the invitation. I'm really looking forward to it."

∿

IT HAD BEEN another fruitless day of job hunting, and Holly Mandylor decided it was time for a trip to Red Rock Canyon, her refuge in the mountains just west of Las Vegas. After changing into a T-shirt, old jeans and hiking boots, she drove up to the canyon and parked her car at one of the scenic stops. She hiked up one of the narrow, rocky trails used by the tourists, then veered off the path and headed for a secluded spot she had staked out as her own several years ago.

With its boulders and outcroppings and shaded crannies, there were no end of places in the canyon to sit and think, and Holly's was not only high and secluded but had the added advantage of a spectacular view. To the east lay the city, its sprawling residential developments and towering casinos nestled in the valley against a dark and distant mountainous backdrop. Beneath her, red, rocky crags fell away precipitously to a scrubby brown floor that was dotted haphazardly with yuccas and creosote bushes, ironwood trees and sagebrush. And above and all around her was the endless blue sky, which never failed to soothe and exhilarate her spirit and make her feel connected to something greater and freer than she was at the moment. The city in the distance, the mountains and desert, the boundless blue sky, were all part of who she was, each of them important in a different way. And being in this particular spot where she could savor all three always focused her thoughts when nothing else could, and brought relief when she needed it, and sometimes inspiration.

As usual, it didn't take long to feel the magic of the place begin to weave its spell. Sitting cross-legged, she yielded to the solitude and breathed in the stillness. Soon, the weight of fear and uncertainty that had filled her heart seemed to shift and lighten, and when it was sufficiently lessened she turned to her problems with a calmer spirit and clearer head.

Having grown up in Las Vegas during a time that had been more boom than bust for the steadily expanding city, Holly had always taken it for granted that if a person wanted a job, there were jobs to be had. The casinos were the most obvious source of employment, and although not everyone she knew worked in one, most of them did. It used to be that there were always new positions being added—as dealers, waitresses, drivers, entertainers, bartenders, hotel staffers, or any one of a hundred miscellaneous jobs—and even during the most recent economic slump, there were still openings because people jumped around from job to job; the tourism business was very incestuous.

Holly had expected to land another position quickly, but it wasn't turning out that way. It was as if the bad luck that began when Turner fired her was still following her around. She had begun her search with hopes that were high, but not too high. She had stayed away from the big-name casinos because she didn't feel as if she had a realistic shot at any of them. Not that she had ever applied and been turned down; Holly just automatically assumed she wasn't cut out for the big-time. By her own estimation, she wasn't classy enough or pretty enough to carry rich men's drinks. And she also assumed she was too tall for their tastes; no matter how much a man claimed to prefer long-legged women, that only applied if the woman in question couldn't see his bald spot when she stood by his side. In reality, Holly got far more compliments than she did complaints about her height and looks, but she considered them potential handicaps, nonetheless.

She had confined her job search to what she thought of as the middle-class casinos, ones that were nicer than the roadside gyp joints or sleazy bars, and where an average cocktail waitress could serve an average clientele without feeling inferior or out of place. Surprisingly, she was told at each one that they were fully staffed and didn't expect an opening for some time to come. Of course, the fact that she couldn't provide a reference from her last job hadn't helped, but instead of suspecting that Gil Turner, the man who had fired her from the Golden Spur, had made a few phone calls and gotten her blackballed, Holly automatically assumed the reason she had failed was her own inability to simply measure up; it was an attitude that came easily after years of practice.

Now she wasn't sure what to do. Actually, she did know what to do—keep on trying—but she was beginning to wonder if anything would come of it. *Maybe this is the perfect time to go back to school,* she thought. She could attend full-time instead of working, maybe get a grant or loan and live on campus. She wouldn't have much money, but she'd be too busy to need much, anyway. And when she reentered the job market after getting her degree, maybe she could return to the casinos as a management trainee instead of a waitress. *Who knows where that might lead?* she thought, beginning to get excited—she might even wind up as Gil Turner's boss! Wouldn't that be a hoot?

Thinking that maybe she was on to something, Holly scanned the vista of desert and mountains, so inherently forbidding yet comforting to her, searching for a sign or at least some peace and reassurance. Farther down the rocky red slope, she spotted one of the burros that lived in the canyon; allegedly wild, they were nonetheless notorious for coming up to tourists and begging for food, even going so far as to stick their heads into open car windows. Holly stared at the animal and started to smile. At the same time, the burro glanced in her direction, returned her stare and let out a bray that sounded as if he had somehow read her dreams and found them funny.

"Shut up! What do you know about it!" Holly yelled down at the donkey, feeling angry, then silly. With a swish of his tail, the animal took off. But his noisy opinion lingered behind, and in spite of herself, Holly couldn't help but take it as a sign. "Who am I kidding?" she asked herself aloud. "This is *not* the time to think about college. I'm too old to live in a dorm with a bunch of teenagers! And the semester doesn't start for three more months—where would I live until then? I can't pay my rent if I don't have a job." She stared at the spot where the burro had stood, and shook her head. "I can always get a degree later. What I've got to do now is find a job." And since she barely managed to live from paycheck to paycheck, she had to find one soon, before her money ran out.

"I can do that," she said confidently to herself, falling back to her original, more familiar goal. She looked around for the donkey with a defiant smile, and waved her hand dismissively when she didn't see him. "Laugh if you want to," she said, raising her voice. "But I *will* find a job, and a good one, too! And I *will* get my degree—somewhere down the line. At least I won't spend my life walking around looking stupid and begging for food!"

Finally smiling for the first time in hours, Holly got up from the rock, ready to leave. Red Rock Canyon had worked its magic; she had sorted things out and was ready to try again. She laughed as the burro ambled back into view, then brushed herself off and shooed him away, laughing even harder when he cantered off. As he fled down the mountain, Holly started down, too, heading back to her car, confident she had faced her bad luck and scared it away.

Her optimism kept growing all the way back, right up until the moment she reached the parking lot and saw the very same burro standing in the spot where her old Chevy should have been. By the time she'd hitchhiked down the mountain and reported her car stolen, it was all she could do not to sit down and cry while she waited for the police to come pick her up.

TEN

Unfolding Memories, Puzzling Dreams

AFTER JOHN'S first day back at school, the rest of the week was an uneasy pairing of daytime normalcy and restless nights. Tuesday night was good, and brought his first restful sleep since returning from the hospital. The next night, however, turned out to be a restless one, and John slept fitfully, treading on the edge of portentous dreams. On Thursday, the dreams came back with newfound clarity and irresistible power, and John had barely gone to sleep before he found himself involved in the strangest one yet.

It began in the sterile white light of a hospital operating room. He was floating near the ceiling, watching as a team of green-clad doctors and nurses worked frantically on someone he soon realized was himself. More curious than afraid, he watched as their efforts failed and the "him" that was on the table—the body that was battered and covered in blood—eventually died. Then, as he pondered the fact that his body had died but he had survived, he was drawn up into a swirling, roaring vortex, and after an amazing trip through a lightless void, found himself standing at the mouth of a tunnel whose interior was glowing and pillowy like clouds.

There was a pinpoint of light off in the distance, and feeling a powerful attraction to it, he began to move forward. As he did, the distant twinkle gradually grew into a brilliant beacon, and soon he saw figures standing up ahead. He couldn't see their faces from so far away, but he instinctively knew they were waiting for him. With an escalating sense of awe and excitement, he quickened his pace and went deeper into the tunnel.

Before he had gone very far, the closest figure began moving toward him, and a feeling of joy and love washed over him as he recognized the face of his long-dead grandmother. In reality, he recognized her more as a matter of spirit than of sight; Grandma Creed's face was much younger, and the body he remembered as wrinkled and stooped no longer showed infirmity of any kind, and shone with an aura of wondrous light, much like the light that streamed from behind her. "Grandma . . ." he whispered, too moved to do anything but stand where he was. A moment later, he was lost in her embrace, with the voice he hadn't heard for the last twenty years now calling his name and welcoming him home. What surprised him at first was that even though her voice sounded clear and strong, her lips never moved except to smile. Instead of hearing her, he was somehow receiving her words and feelings through some form of telepathy, an honest and intimate and powerful exchange that far exceeded the limitations of speech or hearing. Before long, it seemed the most natural communication he had ever experienced.

After a while, they stepped back and looked at each other. "I've missed you, Grandma," John said, holding her hands.

"I know you have, Johnny," she replied with a comforting smile and a squeeze of his hands. "I'm so happy to see you I can hardly let go.

But there are others waiting for you, too." She motioned behind her, and after another long look at his face, she took his arm and led him down the tunnel, which grew wider and brighter the farther they went.

It was a reunion like none he'd ever imagined. Twenty people or more, all of whom he had loved dearly and missed after their deaths, were waiting along the way to greet him. His younger sister, Susie, who had died of leukemia at the age of twelve. His friend Mike Parker, who had succumbed to AIDS several months earlier. His Grandpa Thomas, favorite aunts and cousins. Practically everyone he cared deeply about who had gone on before was waiting and smiling, as happy to see him as he was them. One by one, with a smile on his face that never wavered, he embraced them all for a few precious moments, sometimes in silence, more often with tears or exclamations of joy. Eventually, his grandmother gently tugged at his arm and drew him aside.

"It's time to go," she said. Seeing his disappointment, she reassured him, "Don't worry, Johnny. You'll see them again."

He was reluctant to leave, especially after holding his kid sister for the first time in years, but something in Grandma Creed's manner suggested that the subject of moving on wasn't open to debate. "Where are we going?" he asked.

"Just a moment, dear," his grandmother answered, holding out her hand. There was something in it, a hard plastic name tag that was broken in half. "I believe this belongs to you," she said cryptically, pressing it into his open palm.

John looked at her in puzzlement, then turned the tag over and stared at the name. White letters beveled into a solid red background spelled out **HOLLY**. The rest of the name—if it was a name—was missing. "I don't understand," he said, shaking his head.

"You will, dear," she replied. "All in good time. Be patient." Grandma Creed gave him a smile and said, "Now it's time for you to move on. There's someone else who wants to see you, Johnny, and I don't think you'd want to keep him waiting." She gave him a knowing look and kissed him sweetly on the cheek, then gestured toward a figure standing deeper in the tunnel.

John started to protest, but even as he did his grandmother vanished. With a startled expression, he stared at the spot where she had stood only seconds before, and slowly lifted his gaze to the one who was waiting, wondering as he did whom it could possibly be. His speculation lasted only a second, and his eyes went wide as his spirit suddenly thrilled to the question's answer. After a moment's hesitation—and a lifetime of wondering—he started toward the radiant, familiar figure who waited in the center of the blazing light with outstretched arms and the most loving smile he had ever beheld. . . .

Almost immediately, the tunnel and the figure waiting in the light grew hazy and disappeared. With a profound sense of loss and a cry of protest, John found himself standing in a strange house instead— strange in the sense that it wasn't familiar, yet also because of a hint of something sour or rotten, as if a strong but invisible decay had set in. Morning sun shone weakly through the windows; except for a row of framed photographs hanging neatly on the wall, the room he was in was empty of people, furniture and any other evidence that the house was lived in.

The last photo caught John's eye, and he walked over to it with a feeling that he knew the child in the picture. It was of a boy, about ten or eleven years old, with a cute freckled face, green eyes and blond hair. It bothered him that he couldn't quite place the boy, especially since there seemed to be some urgency attached to knowing who he was, and as he stood there trying to figure it out, he heard a muttered oath come from one of the rooms behind him.

Surprised, he went in search of the voice. There was no one in the dining room, but when he entered the kitchen, he found a man sitting at a table, drinking. Since the boy in the picture had seemed vaguely familiar, John expected to find someone he knew in the kitchen, but the balding, middle-aged man was a total stranger. John started to introduce himself, but before he could speak, the man muttered another oath and slammed his drink down on the table. Then, he got up and walked right past John without so much as a word or a flick of his eyes. Bewildered, John waited in the doorway for a few moments, expecting him to return. When he heard a heavy tread ascending the stairs in the hallway instead, he decided to go after him.

Something in the house was definitely wrong—the empty rooms, the man and the negative energy were disquieting at first, and then for no apparent reason, faintly alarming. John hurried from the kitchen and made it to the stairs in time to see the man open a door at the right of the second-floor landing; on it was a life-size poster of former Cardinals slugger Mark McGwire, taking one of his legendary mighty swings. A boy's voice called out, "Dad?" from inside the room, and John could see the man's jaw clench as he hesitated outside the door. With another oath—only louder this time—he entered the room.

As the door swung shut with an ominous click, John inexplicably felt as if a fist had been slammed into his gut. He bounded up the stairs, taking them two at a time, and stood in front of McGwire a few seconds later. Without waiting to hear what might be going on inside, he turned the knob, threw open the door—

And stepped into an alley that was shrouded in night.

Completely disconcerted, he looked around frantically, trying to make sense of what had just happened. He was no longer in the house, that much was obvious. And the door through which he'd come was no longer there either. Instead, he was standing at the mouth of a dark, dirty alley that opened onto a street that wasn't the least bit familiar.

He considered backtracking into the alley, and actually took a few steps deeper into the shadows before accepting the futility of finding his way back. As surely as he had known that the boy was in trouble, he was equally sure now that there was nothing he could do to go back and help, just as he had been unable to return to the tunnel after it disappeared. With a mounting sense of frustration—and a nagging conviction that he would see the boy again—he exited the alley and walked down the street.

He hadn't gone far before he heard a commotion coming from the end of the block. Instinctively, he ducked into a shallow alcove at the entrance of a bakery that had seen better days, and peered around the corner in the direction of the noise. Three young men who appeared to be teenagers were standing under the street lamp. They were obviously quite drunk, gesturing with beer bottles and calling out epithets as the patrons of a small bar came and went across the street. One of the boys had a baseball bat in his hand, and each time he saw a customer, he'd point the bat and yell out something that made John's blood run cold; sometimes, especially if the customer made eye contact, the boy would grin and take an imaginary swing, right about the height where the person's head would be.

With his heart starting to pound, John realized that someone had to call the police, but that he'd make himself a target if he left the alcove. So he turned around to look for a pay phone inside the bakery—

And found himself standing in front of two large wooden doors that definitely hadn't been there a moment before. There were gold crosses on them, and they were gleaming softly in the morning sun, which had suddenly reappeared. Affixed to the wall at the right of the doorway was a black and gold plaque with ST. TIMOTHY'S CATHOLIC CHURCH written across the top in bold gold letters, and the hours for Mass listed underneath. The bakery had completely disappeared. John wheeled around and stared at the street, and saw that the rest of the neighborhood was gone, too, as well as the bar and the drunken teens.

It had happened again.

Suddenly angry, he lashed out at one of the doors with his foot. To his surprise, it slid open, and after a moment's hesitation, John slipped inside. He glanced around the church, looking for someone who might be able to tell him what had just happened, but saw only empty pews and burning candles, madonnas and saints. He stood still for a minute, until his anger began to fade in the reverent silence, and then slowly made his way down the center aisle. When he reached the front pew, he sat down wearily and shook his head, wondering where he was and why he was there.

He gradually became aware of muffled voices coming from the row of confessionals to his right. He had been about to leave, but decided to wait for the confession to end. Even though he suspected he'd be wasting his time, he had some questions he wanted to ask the priest—serious questions about the shifting realities of life and death, about boys and their fathers, and teenagers with beer bottles and baseball bats.

A few minutes later, one of the narrow, wooden confessional doors opened and a middle-aged man stepped out. His clothes, which looked as if they had once been fashionable, were shabby and unwashed, and his face was deeply lined and several days unshaven. As he started to walk away, and then went back to knock on the door of the priest's adjoining cubicle, there was a deference in his manner, an almost apologetic way that he carried himself that suggested someone who was down on his luck, and had been for longer than he cared to remember.

A young priest with a shock of red hair and a pleasant face opened the door and stepped out. "Yes?" he said, smiling at the man. "Is there something else?"

The man glanced down at his shoes for a few seconds before looking up at the priest. "There is one more thing, Father," he said meekly. "If I can ask you something . . ."

"Certainly."

"I haven't eaten since yesterday. . . . Could you spare a couple of bucks from the poor box so I can get myself some food?"

"I'm sorry," the priest replied in a firm but not uncaring voice, "but I'm not allowed to do that."

The man frowned bitterly and John thought he detected an air of cresting desperation about him, as if the man were already carrying the next-to-last straw on his aching back and had one eye on the last one as it prepared to fall. Still, considering his bloodshot eyes and the network of gin blossoms on the tip of his nose, it seemed likely that his disappointment had more to do with the need for a drink than the need for food. "But isn't that what the poor box is for?" the man shot back.

"That's exactly what it's for," the red-haired cleric answered tolerantly. "But we use it to help support our shelter. If you're hungry, we'll be more than happy to give you a meal there."

With a look of resignation on his face, the ragged man glanced at his wrist. John was surprised to see that he was wearing an expensive-looking gold watch; the priest seemed surprised also. "What time do they start serving lunch?" the man asked.

The priest glanced at his own watch and said, "We start at eleven. It's right next door. But you better hurry if you don't want to wait in a long line—there's a very great need in the parish, I'm afraid, and we usually have a big turnout." He smiled and added, "And if you need a place to sleep, you can come back tonight, although I wouldn't wait too late—the beds fill up fast, too."

The man nodded, gave the cleric a hurried "thanks" and started down a side aisle, heading toward the front door. John got up from the pew and walked toward the priest, intending to ask his own questions. But before he could do so, the priest called out to the other man, "My son! Did you forget to say your penance?"

The man turned around and faced the cleric with a sheepish expression that looked only partly genuine. If he saw John standing nearby, he gave no indication. "I'm sorry, Father. I guess I did." He dutifully came back up the aisle.

"Do you have a rosary?" the priest asked, noting that the man's hands were empty.

The man hung his head slightly. "No, Father. Someone stole it a long time ago, and I haven't had the money to buy a new one. . . ."

"Wait here a minute," the priest responded. He walked down the hall and disappeared through a doorway. When he returned, he was holding a rosary, which he pressed into the man's hand. He gestured toward the rail in front of the altar, looking right through John as if he were invisible. "Now you've got the equipment to say a proper Hail Mary," he said, smiling.

Wondering why both men were ignoring him, John waited until the man walked away from the priest, then cleared his throat and said, "Excuse me, Father."

The priest didn't respond, didn't even look in his direction. The man with the rosary paid no attention either, and walked right toward John as if he were not even there, never making eye contact, not even slowing down or veering to the side. As John stood there, amazed and beginning to get more than a little bit angry, the man just kept walking, and then walked straight into him—

And John felt the man actually pass through his body. He gasped at the sensation of merging atoms, and gasped even louder as they were torn asunder. For several long moments, his whole being was awash with tingling and pain, and his mind was roiling with images and thoughts and urges and fears, many of them alien, frightening or sad. He opened his mouth to scream, but found that he couldn't, and reached out for support from the priest or a pew. Instead he pitched forward into a hazy darkness as the dream abruptly ended, and he awoke in his bedroom with a pounding heart, the nightmare still intact and burned into his memory like an itching, painful, mysterious brand.

ELEVEN

John Creed Steps into a Dream

WHEN JOHN PICKED Will up the following morning, Will's first words were, "You look terrible! Are you sure you're up to this?"

John frowned, but nodded yes. He had no intention of reneging on his promise to work at the shelter; after last night, he needed a distraction even more than ever. "I just didn't sleep very well, that's all," he said.

Will shook his head. "If this is what you look like when you don't sleep very well, I'd hate to see you when you don't sleep at all. Maybe you ought to stay home and get some rest. We'll manage without you."

"I'll be fine," John replied a little more sharply than he'd intended. He offered Will a placating smile. "I appreciate your concern. But I'll be okay. Really."

"The old war wounds keeping you awake?" Will asked, referring to John's recent injuries.

John didn't reply right away, and stared straight ahead at the road instead. Thinking of what happened last night, he wondered if Will might be closer to the truth than he knew, for the onset of the dreams certainly seemed tied to the accident with Ruby. Ordinarily, he didn't remember his dreams or pay much attention to them. But the ones last night—like those he'd had the first night home from the hospital—were different, more urgent and powerful; he couldn't forget them even if he tried. The one about dying and meeting his grandmother in the unearthly tunnel, as bizarre as it was, had given him a disturbing sensation of déjà vu, as had the earlier dream about the accident—and that had turned out to be more fact than fiction. Since last night's dream seemed to pick up where that one left off, the implications were perplexing and a little overwhelming. He was beginning to wonder if something had happened when he died, after all, something he just hadn't remembered yet.

The parts of the dream that came after the tunnel—the drunken man in the empty house, the teenagers with the bat and the incident in the church—also seemed to have significance. They didn't feel quite the same as his trip to the tunnel, but they were too vivid and unsettling to dismiss out of hand. It occurred to him that maybe he'd suffered brain damage in the accident, after all. Dismissing the thought, he turned to Will and finally answered the question of whether his "war wounds" were to blame. "Something like that," he said cryptically, with an uneasy smile.

AS THEY PULLED up in front of the church, John immediately felt a stab of uneasiness. "St. Timothy's?" he said in a surprised voice, staring at the big wooden double doors and the black and gold plaque mounted on the wall. The doors had crosses on them, big gold crosses that gleamed in the morning sun, and the plaque gave the daily Mass times. It was the church in his dream.

"Yep," Will replied. "This is where I go to church. The shelter's next door."

"I didn't know it was called St. Timothy's—did I?"

"I don't know," Will responded. "I thought I mentioned it, but I might have called it St. Tim's. I usually do." He grinned and added, "I tried to get them to call it St. Will's, but Father Ryan said it just didn't have the same ring."

John finally remembered, and nodded. "That's right! You called it St. Tim's." He'd obviously gotten the name for the dream church from one of their conversations. And the entrance was much like any number of other church entrances all around the city. John smiled with relief as the mystery vanished. "I can't believe I didn't make the connection between Timothy and Tim," he said, smiling at last. "I must be losing it. You know what they say: once you turn thirty, it's all downhill."

Will laughed and climbed out of the car. "That certainly gives me something to look forward to."

John got out and joined Will in front of the church. "Don't rub it in," he replied. "Someday you'll reach the big three-oh, and you'll know what I mean."

"In that case, we better get a move on while one of us still can." Will pointed to a brick building next to the church, where a long line had formed. "The shelter's over there."

Timothy House was an old three-story brick structure that had once been a flophouse. The top two floors were still set up for overnight housing, but the ground floor had been converted into a large dining room and kitchen. The dining room was in front; its walls were painted in a cheery color and bore paintings of Jesus, the Blessed Virgin, Saint Peter, the pope and a variety of saints with whom John was unfamiliar. There were five long, Formica-topped tables with benches that ran the length of the room and a stainless steel serving counter next to one wall. Some of the volunteers, including several nuns and a priest, were carrying platters with cold cuts or steaming covered dishes from the kitchen and setting them on the counter.

"Looks like they decided to start early," Will commented, glancing at his watch. "From the looks of the line out front, today's going to be busy. Let's get you an apron," he said, steering John toward the kitchen. "And then I'll ask Sister Tracy what she wants us to do."

Seeing so many people come through the doors in search of a meal was a sobering experience. In John's world, food was a given and only required thought when a choice was involved; to the people filing past him, choice was a luxury and a regular meal more a matter of survival. As he stood next to Will, dishing out green beans from a huge, steaming pot, his view of the world and its capricious dependability was altered forever.

The experience changed John's opinion of Will Gibson, too. It was obvious that Will didn't work at the shelter to be politically correct, but because he cared. When someone reached his station, Will served him potato salad, and joked or talked for as long as he could without slowing up the line; and he did it sincerely, without the slightest condescension or hint of pity. After some initial uncertainty about what to do or say, John took his cue from Will and relaxed. Before long, he managed to forget about his dreams and began enjoying the work—

Until the man from the confessional in last night's dream walked up to his station and held out a plate.

John was so surprised he almost dropped the ladle into the pot of beans. Everything about the man was the same as in the dream—the clothes he was wearing, his demeanor and face; and when he opened his mouth and said, "I'd like some of those," his voice was the same, too. John was so taken aback that the man had to ask twice before he finally responded. With a puzzled expression, John spooned out a helping, then met his eyes and said, "I know you. Don't I?"

The man paused to consider it. "I don't think so," he said. "But I appreciate the green beans." He started to move on, then leaned over the counter instead. Thinking the man had changed his mind, John moved closer, his face tense but expectant.

"You want to buy a rosary cheap?" the man asked in a conspiratorial whisper. He reached into his pocket and partially withdrew a string of beads like the one John had seen the priest give him in the dream. "It's been blessed by the Holy Father himself, but I'll let you have it for only ten dollars."

John stared hard at the rosary, then even harder at the man, wondering if they really had met before, despite his denial. But he saw nothing in his eyes but desperation and petty greed. "Sorry," he replied in an equivocal voice, "I'm not Catholic." Before he could say anything else, the man stuffed the rosary back into his pocket with a look of disappointment, mumbled an apology and moved on down the line, leaving John to wonder if what had just happened was another piece of the puzzle falling into place or merely a strange coincidence. After a few minutes, he decided it was best to forget it, and he tried concentrating instead on the job at hand. But as the man sat down to eat his lunch, John's attention kept drifting to the table where he sat. He just couldn't shake the dizzying conviction that the man he had served was the man in his dream.

After a while, Will noticed John's preoccupied look and mistook it for a recurrence of his secret ailment—which it actually was—and walked over to ask if he needed a break. When John failed to respond or even seem aware of the social worker's presence, Will gently tugged at his arm and tried again. "John," he repeated with growing concern, "are you okay? You look like you're going to pass out or something."

"Huh?" John replied, tearing his gaze away from the man at the table. "I'm sorry, Will. What did you say?"

"I said you look like you're about to faint. Maybe you should take a break."

"No, I'll be okay," John responded, wiping sweat from his brow and glancing over at the man. He looked back at Will and said, "I just got a little overheated. I guess the steam and the heat lamps got to me." He smiled lamely and said, "I'll be all right. Thanks for asking."

Will narrowed his eyes and stared hard at his friend. This time he didn't buy the excuses. He grabbed John's arm and discreetly pulled him away from the counter. "Listen," he whispered sternly, "I can't just let you keel over right here and cause a commotion. We've still got a lot of hungry people to serve, and besides that, I've heard enough of your crap about how you just didn't get enough sleep last night! I don't know what's wrong—and I know you don't want to talk about it—but you're on my turf now, and I'm not going to let your problems intrude on these people. They've got enough of their own." He shook his head sadly and concluded, "Now, either you tell me what's wrong and let me take you to the doctor *now,* or you go sit down at one of the tables until you feel better. Those are your only two choices. Which is it?"

John stared back at Will with surprise and embarrassment, then, unable to resist, looked once again in the direction of the stranger. "Sorry," he mumbled. "Maybe I should sit down."

As Will watched him with a worried expression, John walked slowly but unwaveringly to the second table over and sat down directly across from the man who had tried to sell him the rosary. "Hi, I'm John Creed," he began, extending a hand across the table and trying to smile.

The man put down the ham sandwich he'd been eating, brushed his fingers on his pants and shook John's hand. "Hector Denton." He gave John a questioning look and said, "You're the green bean guy, aren't you?"

"That's me."

"Sorry about the rosary thing," Denton said. "But I'm a few bucks light, so I needed the money."

"Don't worry about it," John replied vaguely. "It looked like a nice one. Where'd you get it?"

Denton hesitated. "Father Ryan gave it to me." When John only nodded, he started to reach into his pocket for the rosary again, and

John saw a flash of gold at the edge of his sleeve. "You sure you don't want it?" Denton asked. "Like I said, it was blessed by the pope. It'd make a nice present if you've got any Catholic friends."

"No, thanks," John replied absently. The flash of gold had set his mind racing, and his hunch about Denton was gathering steam. Now all he needed was to see a watch—a gleaming gold watch that looked far too expensive for a man of Denton's means. Trying to keep the tension from his voice, he asked, "Do you know what time it is?"

Denton extended his arm and glanced at his wrist. Sure enough, his watch looked expensive. And it was also gold. "Five after twelve," he replied. Noting the paleness of John's face, he said guardedly, "You don't look too good. Are you okay?"

"I'm all right," John replied. It was difficult to talk, but he forced himself to act as naturally as he could. "I just got out of the hospital, and the friend I came with was afraid I was overdoing it and thought I should take a break."

"From the looks of you, it's a good thing he did," Denton replied, shoveling a forkful of potato salad into his mouth. He chewed and swallowed while John watched, then reached for his coffee and said, "Hospital, huh? What were you in for?"

"Car accident—someone hit me," John replied. He added in a meaningful voice, "I nearly died." He watched Denton's face for a reaction that might help him divine what connection there was between his dreams and reality—if there was a connection—but saw nothing.

"Must of been pretty bad," Denton commiserated. Then he added in a strange voice, "What happened to the other guy?"

"It was a woman, actually—someone I knew," John said thoughtfully. "It's a long story. . . . They put her in jail, but she's out now, awaiting trial."

Denton winced as memories of another accident rose up in his mind. "Oh, I see," he replied uncomfortably and looked away.

John wondered at the reaction and studied him closely. Denton picked up his sandwich and took another bite, trying unsuccessfully not to think about automobile accidents, particularly a hit-and-run incident two years ago. Even on the best of days it was never far from his mind, and now the images and emotions rushed back to center stage and refused to budge. Denton stopped chewing and put down his sandwich. Most people thought him lucky because a legal technicality had spared him a jail sentence, but he hardly felt lucky. There had been many times over the last two years when he wished he had gone to jail, because it would have been easier than what had happened instead.

Having lost his appetite, Denton pushed away his plate and glanced up. There was an anxious, almost desperate look on John's face, and it struck him that he wasn't the only one whose demons had followed him to the shelter that day. "Here," he said sympathetically, pushing the plate in John's direction. "Why don't you take the rest of my sandwich. I only took a couple of bites. You look like you could use it." He smiled wistfully and added, "I'd offer you something stronger, but I'm a little tapped out right now."

Roused from his own trance, John eyed the partially eaten sandwich and shook his head. "Thanks," he said, smiling uncomfortably. "But I'm not really hungry." Still obsessed with the watch, he asked, "What time did you say it was again?"

Automatically, Denton glanced at his wrist. "Six past twelve," he said, and held out his arm for John to see.

John leaned forward and drew the man's wrist nearer. He mumbled something, pretending to admire the watch, but focusing intently on Denton instead. Before long, everything in the room seemed to recede into oblivion; all that existed for the present moment was the two of them facing each other across the table, and the mystery of why Denton had appeared in his dreams and then in his life. The more intensely he focused, the closer he seemed to getting an answer, but suddenly he connected with something else instead. As if he had just opened a spillway, bitterness and negativity seeped into his mind, then came in a torrent, flooding his brain with images and feelings of despair and remorse, and words that might have come from Denton's confession—

"Bless me, Father, for I have sinned. I stole money from Willy while he slept last night, and used it to buy a bottle of cheap red wine—"

A bottle of cognac, a bottle of brandy and a party that lasted until three in the morning . . .

A hazy drive home, a left, a right, wondering if Mary would be awake when he got there, and knowing if she was there'd be hell to pay—

Suddenly, headlights up ahead, approaching fast—were they on his side of the road or was he on theirs . . .

A last instant of happiness, of blind, numbing bliss, then awareness and panic—and the awful screams . . .

Smashing metal, screeching tires, a car careening sideways over a dark, steep embankment and plunging like a meteor into the California ocean . . .

Suddenly—silence, sobriety and a fearful awareness, a decision made in haste, and a long drive home . . .

"Bless me, Father, for I have sinned. I stole money from Willy while he slept last night, and used it to buy a bottle of cheap red wine—"

Living with the guilt until the police showed up, and then living with the shame of undeserved freedom . . .

A pretty woman—his wife—with a deep purplish bruise disfiguring one eye, a woman who would be beautiful were it not for the bruise and the lines of unhappiness scored deep in her face . . .

Saying good-bye to no one, no children on the stairs, disappearing from people who had already left and let him go . . . and yielding to the cancer that would never let go.

"Bless me, Father, for I have sinned. I stole money from Willy while he slept last night, and used it to buy a bottle of cheap red wine. . . ."

And then John released Denton's wrist, and the vision was over.

Within the pounding of a headache that filled John's brain, he felt and also saw the *other* pain—Denton's pain—recede and fade until it lost its power. In its wake came feelings of deep empathy and love that welled up inside him. In his mind's eye, they sparkled like a cloud of energized fairy dust or twinkling stars, and surged across the mysterious connection with Denton, leaving John fatigued but inexplicably high. Once the headache was gone, John opened his eyes—not having been aware he had closed them to start with—and gazed at the face of the man across the table. Denton's eyes, once so troubled and lost, looked surprised and confused, and in the space of a few moments, tentatively peaceful. It was a subtle transformation, but remarkable, nonetheless, and John's thoughts went immediately to Ruby Mazzoni and how she had looked after the similarly inexplicable occurrence in the jail.

For a while, neither man said a word as each strove to comprehend what had transpired. Finally, Hector Denton smiled, a struggling smile buoyed by long-forgotten feelings of hope and relief, and he reached across the table and grasped John's hand for reasons he would never completely understand. Stunned by a repeat of what had happened with Ruby, John started to say something and found that he couldn't. A few seconds later, he passed out on the table.

TWELVE

Holly Gets an Interview, Elliot Gets a Drink

TRYING TO FORGET about Red Rock Canyon, Holly was still sleeping when the phone rang at 9 A.M. It was Tina Delaney, a girlfriend who worked at Caesar's Palace.

"Holly, guess what! I've got great news!"

"*Tina!* I'm trying to sleep!" Holly groaned into the phone. "Can't it wait?"

"Oh, come on," her best friend replied. "It's time to get up!" Then she repeated in an excited voice, "Guess what happened!"

"Tony Orlando asked you to be his new Dawn," Holly replied sarcastically.

"Yeah," Tina replied, giggling, "but I turned him down because Diana Ross came by earlier and needed a Supreme."

"Congratulations," Holly mumbled. "Now, if you don't mind, I'm going back to sleep."

"Boy, you really are out of it."

"Yeah, well, yesterday wasn't exactly the best day I've had in a while," Holly replied. "I thought I'd just stay in bed and try to forget about it."

"You didn't see Jimmy again, did you?" Tina asked with disapproval in her voice.

"Are you kidding!" Holly shot back, frowning at the phone. "I haven't seen that slimeball in months, thank God. You ought to know that!"

"Sorry," Tina replied. "It's just that every time you had problems with Jimmy, you always used to sleep in. . . ."

"He's ancient history," Holly replied flatly. "I've got other things to worry about now—like how to get the money to buy another car. Mine got stolen yesterday up at Red Rock Canyon."

"Somebody stole that piece of junk?"

Holly made a face at the phone, resisting the urge to hang up. Tina had a good job and a brand-new car, and she never understood how Holly had to struggle just to keep it together. "It may be a piece of junk, but it was the only piece of junk I had," she retorted.

"So what's the problem?" Tina asked brightly. "You can use the insurance to buy a better car!"

"No, I can't," Holly replied bitterly. "I only had liability. Full coverage would have cost more than the car was worth. So I'm out of luck."

"Well, don't worry about it—"

"Don't worry about it!" Holly practically screamed into the phone. "I've got to worry about it! How am I going to get around? How am I going to look for a job? By bus? Take a taxi? Come on, Tina. Things were bad enough as it was without somebody stealing my car, too!"

"Well, cheer up, girl," Tina responded excitedly. "They're about to get better!"

Holly shook her head wearily, then closed her eyes and covered them with her hand. "Tina, I know you're just trying to help. But do me a favor and spare me the cheerleader crap. That's the last thing I feel like hearing right now. This whole week's been a nightmare—the mother of all nightmares, if you really must know."

"I'm telling you, by tonight you'll forget all about it! Wait till you hear my news!"

On the other end of the line, Tina went into one of what Holly had come to know as her dramatic pauses, and in spite of her bad mood, Holly felt herself tensing in expectation. After a few more seconds of silence dragged past, Holly practically shrieked into the phone, "So, are you going to tell me your news or are you just going to let me have a heart attack and die?"

Tina giggled. "It's the greatest thing," she gushed, "just perfect! A girl I used to work with got a job over at the Mirage a few months ago, and last night when we went out, I told her I had a friend who was trying to get on at one of the casinos. And guess what! She said they had an opening—somebody just quit! Isn't that perfect? It's like karma or something," Tina exclaimed. "Anyway, I gave her your name and told her you've got experience. This morning, she called me and said you should come in!"

Thinking of all the other dead-end leads she'd had, Holly was wary of letting her hopes get too high, especially since it was one of the casinos that was out of her league. "The Mirage isn't going to hire me," she said skeptically. "Probably what will happen is that I'll get all dressed up to go down there, and they'll tell me they've already filled the job."

"No, they won't! My friend's got it all set up. Her new boss is sweet on her, and when she told him about you, he said to send you in."

"But that doesn't mean I've got the job," Holly pointed out, feeling more hopeful than she sounded, in spite of herself.

"I'm telling you, sweetie, it's already a done deal! Now get moving—you're supposed to be there at one. I'll pick you up around noon. Okay?"

"Okay," replied Holly, half in a daze.

"Good. I'll see you then!"

Holly hung up the phone with a trembling hand, then jumped out of bed and raced to the closet to see if she had anything suitable to wear. By the time Tina arrived three hours later, not only did Holly look stunning, she was also mentally prepared for the interview, having stilled the self-doubts and naysaying voices that lived in her head. As she left her apartment, she was practically bursting with a confidence that was as surprisingly comfortable as it was shiny and new. *The Mirage!* she kept thinking as she hurried to Tina's car. *The tips alone will make me rich!*

She latched on to that thought as her lucky mantra, and kept repeating it to herself on the way to the interview. They arrived at the casino with time to spare, and on an impulse Holly decided she wanted to go in by one of the streetside entrances and *really* experience the Mirage as it was meant to be experienced. They lingered out front by the famous volcano as if they hadn't seen it a hundred times, *ooh*-ing and *aah*-ing as explosions of flame burst high into the air, and once that was over, they went inside with smiles on their faces, strolling along with people wearing furs and diamonds that glittered almost as brightly as the casino itself. With each step that carried her closer to a job—an exciting, glamorous, well-paying job—Holly felt a sense of growing exhilaration and a surprising sense of being where she really belonged.

They eventually made their way past the shops and restaurants to one of the cavernous gaming rooms. Following the instructions her friend had given her, Tina led Holly across the noisy floor, past busy slot machines and crowded blackjack tables to a door marked EM-PLOYEES ONLY. She opened the door and ushered Holly inside, and led her down the hall to another door marked PRIVATE. Holly's heart was racing, and even though the din of the casino faded as they walked down the hall, Holly's gorgeous smile and her faith in the outcome of the impending interview never wavered an iota. Even allowing for the possibility that this wasn't a sure thing, Holly had already decided—indeed, she felt it in her bones—that when she looked back on this day in the distant future, she would point to it and say, "*That* was the day that changed my whole life, the day I interviewed for a job at the Mirage!" And she was right.

When they reached the office at the end of the hall, Tina turned to her and whispered excitedly, "Not that you'll need it, but good luck!" Holly smiled and hugged her fiercely. They gave each other the once-over, making sure nothing had gotten mussed or crooked or smeared in the time since they'd left the car, and Holly knocked twice on the door and went inside. Tina followed.

A tall, middle-aged balding man with a sunlamp tan and a smile that Holly knew was every bit as dangerous as an invisible shark stood up behind a desk and spread his hands in a familiar greeting. It was Gil Turner, the man who had fired her only a few weeks earlier. "Well, what do you know! Holly Mandylor! You're the last person I ever expected to ask me for a job!" His smile changed subtly as he walked in front of the desk, and now he looked more than anything like a sadistic little boy who had just trapped a fly and was trying to decide how best to pull off its wings. Holly, for her part, felt about as big as that fly, and the smile that had taken her hours to build crumbled in an instant like a house of cards. Tina, who hadn't known that Turner was her friend's new boss, was as flabbergasted as Holly.

"I guess what they say is true," Turner went on with exaggerated irony. "Never burn your bridges—especially in a town as small as this—because you never can tell where the person you left behind will wind up next." As Holly watched, too stunned to reply, he held out a piece of paper. "I guess you'd like to fill out an application—here, let me get you something to write with." He smirked, then reached behind him and brought back a pen. "I think you'll find the application's not too difficult to understand—and unlike the work you've probably been doing for the past few weeks, you can actually keep your clothes on while applying for this job."

Holly stared at her ex-boss with an abject despair that slid quickly into murderous rage. It occurred to her that Turner had known all along who would be applying for the job—after all, Tina's friend had told him all about her—and the realization that the man who had screwed up her life had orchestrated this farce just to get one more chance to twist the knife in her bleeding back was more than Holly was willing to endure. Recalling the satisfaction she had felt when she stabbed her high heel through the cowboy hat of Turner's treacherous friend at the Golden Spur, it suddenly occurred to her that it would feel ten times better to do the exact same thing to Gil Turner's crotch. As Turner leaned against his desk and started to laugh at the host of emotions that played on her face, Holly visualized quite clearly the surprise and pain that would be on his face—a mirror image of her own expression when she had walked in the door—and found that, even though the fantasy was extraordinarily tempting and a fitting revenge, she just couldn't do it. Actually, she *could* have done it, and *wanted* to do it, but she wouldn't allow herself to return pain for pain, no matter how justified it seemed. Instead, she summoned what little dignity she had left, and met Turner's eyes with a cold, clear gaze. "I'd rather go hungry and live on the street than work for you," she said with such heartfelt scorn that he actually flinched. With Tina at her side, she turned on her heel and walked out the door, slamming it behind her.

Instead of storming down the hall, she decided she had earned at least one small indulgence, and taking out a tube of bright red lipstick, she scrawled a warning to all future applicants in bold red letters across Turner's door. Feeling rather childish but a whole lot better, she smiled at the insult, then left the Mirage and never went back.

EIGHTEEN HUNDRED MILES AWAY, in a suburb of St. Louis, Matt Dandridge was just getting home from school. It was a Friday afternoon, the end of his first full week since getting out of the hospital. The last five days had been busy ones for Matt, and uncertain ones, too. After missing so much school near the end of the semester, he was in danger of having to repeat the fifth grade, and was trying like crazy to make up what he'd missed during the month he'd been out. Under ordinary circumstances, having so much to make up would have completely demoralized him, especially since he didn't like homework to begin with. But Matt wasn't the same boy he had been prior to the accident, and even if he wasn't entirely thrilled with the prospect of tackling a mountain of homework, he understood its importance. More than that, it kept him too busy to think much about what was going on with his family.

When he went into the house, he discovered that he was the first one home again. It had been that way every day that week—something else that had changed since coming home from the hospital. It used to be that when Matt got home, his mother had already been there for an hour or so; his sister, Lori, would show up between four-thirty and five, unless she had a track meet; and his dad usually got home at five o'clock sharp. But these days, his mother was working a lot of overtime (partly to pay his medical bills, Matt realized guiltily, and partly, he suspected, to avoid his father). And although Lori had quit the track team, she rarely came home before six o'clock, only staying long enough to eat dinner or help Matt with his homework before leaving again; Matt suspected that she, too, was avoiding their father.

His dad, on the other hand, seemed to be avoiding something else. From the snatches of conversations he'd overheard between his parents, what Elliot seemed to be avoiding was finding another job. Matt knew he had applied at one place, at least, because he had heard him on the phone, asking if his résumé had been received. And he was usually already up and dressed when Matt left for school, which seemed to mean that Elliot was going out looking for a job. The only problem was, when his dad came home after being gone all day, he smelled so strongly of liquor that sometimes it was noticeable from ten feet away, and his mood was even worse than it had been that morning.

Matt was used to the moods and tried to accept them, but the drinking was something that made him nervous. His father had never been much of a drinker until the terrorists had flown those planes into the Twin Towers in New York. From that time on, his dad had never been the same. None of them had, Matt realized—he still dreamed about that terrible day and everything that had happened since. Sometimes, it felt like a shadow hanging over him, or a shadow waiting in the road up ahead.

His dad had obviously felt the shadow's presence, too. And now that he was out of work, he was drinking almost every day. Matt didn't dare ask his father about it—although he knew his mother did when she thought that he and Lori were out of earshot. Nonetheless, Matt knew that his dad was spending his afternoons (and sometimes his mornings) in a little corner bar a few blocks away, drinking by himself or telling his troubles to the bartender or anybody else who would listen. He knew because it was one of the things his guardian angel had shown him in heaven.

He had been shown other things, too. Mostly glimpses of what would happen when he went back to his family. It had been like watching home movies, or more like the time his mother had taken him to a play and they had watched the actors from balcony seats—only this time his family were the actors, performing short bits from some larger story that Matt couldn't see. The short bits were so frightening that he had been reluctant to leave heaven and go back to his family. A warm, bright light had filled the tunnel where he and his guardian angel stood, a light that made Matt feel as if every day in heaven would be a Saturday afternoon, warm and sunny, with exciting things to do, and bright colors and music and good feelings all around him. Even though he loved his family very, very much, that just wasn't something he wanted to leave.

In the end he had left because his guardian angel convinced him it was the right thing to do. "God wants you to go back. He still has important work for you to do," he had told him. "Think of it as a mission—and try not to get discouraged, because if things get too tough, I'll be there to help." Then he had smiled reassuringly and said, "When your mission is over, I'll be waiting for you right here. I promise." And that had been that. The next thing Matt knew, he was waking up in the hospital.

After the reaction he had gotten when he told his family about his guardian angel, Matt had decided he wouldn't tell anyone else, not his friends or classmates, not even Miss Thompson, his Sunday school teacher. He hadn't discussed it with any of his family again, either, and none of them had brought it up since he'd come home from the hospital. They looked at him funny once in a while—especially his father—but if anyone still thought he was crazy, no one was saying so, at least not to him. Matt had decided it was best to keep it that way, so he'd made up his mind never to tell anyone, not even his mother, about having a mission, or to ever breathe a word about the things he'd been shown, things that were now starting to happen.

It was a hard secret to keep. There were times—like today—when it bothered him so much that it was all he could do to keep from running to his mother and blurting it out. Usually when he felt like that, he'd go over to Tommy's to play video games; or if Tommy was gone, he'd stay home and hide beneath the porch, pretending to have found his way back into the tunnel, where it was safe to tell secrets and talk about a mission. But since Tommy and his family were leaving for the weekend, and Matt was home alone, with no one to tell, he decided he'd start on his homework instead.

A few minutes later, he changed his mind. No sooner had he gotten up to his room than he saw his father lurching up the sidewalk, looking drunk and angry. Matt immediately raced downstairs and fled out the back as fast as he could. Pausing at the side of the house to peek around the corner, he watched in dismay as his dad stumbled up the walk. Once he heard the front door slam, he crept around front, keeping well below the windows so he couldn't be seen, and scurried under the porch.

He hadn't really exerted himself much, but Matt was panting as he crawled into the darkness of his secret place. He was shaking, too, not out of fear of some unseen creature lurking under the porch, but from the knowledge of the rest of the afternoon's events. He had known this was the start of it—that his father would come lurching down the sidewalk in a drunken rage—because he had been shown that, too, and he didn't want to be around when his mom came home and found out that his dad had smashed his car into a tree down the street. Seeing that once was more than enough.

THIRTEEN

A Complicated Confession

WHEN JOHN CREED regained consciousness, he found himself in the passenger seat of his car, with Will Gibson driving. He ran a hand over his face, blinking his eyes to clear away the fog. "What's going on?"

Will glanced across the seat, relieved. "You passed out at the shelter, and I'm taking you to the emergency room."

"I really don't need to go to the hospital, Will. Aside from feeling stupid, I'm okay."

"Sorry," Will replied firmly. "You're going anyway."

"But—"

Will cut him off, slapping the steering wheel in exasperation. "You were unconscious for several minutes, John! That's serious!" Convinced his friend was hiding or ignoring a serious condition, he went on, "It's time to stop pretending nothing's wrong when it's so obvious that something is. If you don't want to tell me, that's fine, but I'm taking you to the hospital, anyway!"

John closed his eyes and blew out a weary breath. "Listen, Will, you're right—you've been right all along," he began in a placating voice. "There is something wrong, and it is related to the accident— at least I think so—but the problem isn't physical. I know it looks that way because I fainted, but it isn't. So going to the hospital isn't going to help." Will glanced at him uncertainly, and John went on, "I'm sorry I wasn't honest with you. I didn't mean to make you worry—"

"Of course you made me worry!" Will responded, but not as angrily as before. "What else am I supposed to do when a friend keeps telling me he's all right and then almost goes face-first into a plate of potato salad?"

John stared back, shamefaced. "I know you deserved an explanation, and I wanted to tell you, but I just wasn't ready to talk about it. . . . I wasn't sure how you'd react."

"I realize we haven't known each other that long," Will responded, "but I pride myself on being a pretty good judge of character, and I'm very picky about choosing my friends. There isn't anything you can tell me that would make me think less of you."

John smiled wanly, accepting the compliment. "It wasn't that I didn't feel like I could trust you. I just wasn't sure what was going on—and I'm still not, really. But if you're still willing to listen, I think I'd like to talk about it," he said in a thoughtful voice, hoping that perhaps the mere process of telling would make it clearer to himself.

"I've been ready for a while now," Will said.

"Okay," John answered. "Let's go someplace where we can talk. Why don't we go to my house? It's as good a place as any."

～

ENSCONCED IN HIS FAVORITE CHAIR with Alex sleeping by his feet, John looked at Will and admitted, "I don't really know where to begin. I guess that's a cliché, but it seems to be particularly appropriate, because I'm really *not* sure where to begin."

"Well, from what you said earlier, it has something to do with the accident," Will coaxed. "So I assume it started while you were in the hospital."

John frowned, thinking. "Sort of. But it really seemed to start gaining momentum after I came home." He hesitated and said rather self-consciously, "This is going to sound bizarre, Will. . . ."

"You'd have to come up with something pretty outrageous to top some of the things I've heard," Will reassured him, trying to hide his concern. "And even if you do—like I said, we're friends. I don't dump friends just because they have problems."

John smiled tentatively and forced himself to go on. "I keep having these dreams. . . . They started in the hospital, but, at first, they were just jumbled bits and pieces that didn't make sense. After I came home, they began to form a pattern."

"What kind of a pattern? Is it a recurring dream?"

John furrowed his brow. "Yes and no. It's not like any recurring dream I ever heard of. Instead of being the same every time, it seems to pick up where the last one left off, like some surreal TV show, doling out plotlines with each new episode."

Will leaned forward in his chair. "And you think it's connected to the accident?"

John nodded. "The accident was the first thing I dreamed about. That's why I had to see Ruby Mazzoni last week."

"She's in it?"

John nodded again. "She was the first time. I dreamed about her the night I came home from the hospital. . . ." In a voice that was bemused but steady with conviction, he went on to describe that night's dream. He told about the boy who had jumped on the bike and pedaled away, and about how he had tried to catch him and wound up behind the wheel of his sports car instead, shortly before Ruby rammed him with the bus. "I hadn't been able to remember anything about the accident until I had that dream. Then I saw everything. . . . The more I thought about it, the more I realized it had to be a repressed memory finally breaking through. That's why I had to talk to Ruby and find out why she did it, because it was finally real to me."

Will blew out a soft breath and sank back into the chair. At first he said nothing, staring at John with sympathetic eyes. "It must have been like going through it for the very first time," he said finally.

"It was," John admitted, seeing the bus grille filling his vision again. He looked at Will with reservation and said, "If it had ended there, I could have dealt with it. But it didn't. Last night I dreamed about dying in the emergency room. . . ."

Will arched an eyebrow and ran a hand over his scalp, frowning. "No wonder you've been upset. . . ."

"The dreams are so vivid that I've been having trouble shaking them."

"When I was in school, my psych professor used to say that dreaming your own death wasn't all that uncommon," Will responded. "He said it had more to do with your mind acknowledging an important change in your life than it did with actual death. As if your subconscious were laying your old self to rest so that you could move on in a new direction. Maybe that's what it means—that you're ready to move in a new direction."

"If it were just a dream, that might be true," John replied, having already considered the possibility. "As I said, the 'dream' about the accident wasn't symbolic at all; it turned out to be painfully real. And the one I had last night felt exactly the same way. . . ." He hesitated, acutely aware that Will might not be nearly as accepting from this point on. "The astonishing thing," he continued, "is that not only did I actually witness my own death, I saw what happened *after* I died."

Will hesitated, then asked, "What do you mean?"

"I 'dreamed' what happened to me after I died," John repeated. The awe and incredulity in his voice were a near match for the expression dawning on Will's face, and he held his breath, wondering if his friend could make such a large leap of faith without benefit of actually having lived the experience.

After a moment of stunned silence, Will finally responded. His voice was as neutral as he could manage: "How is that possible?"

For the next fifteen minutes, as Will listened wide-eyed but respectfully, John told him what he'd dreamed, recounting in great detail what had happened in the emergency room and ending with being greeted by his grandmother in the tunnel. When he paused to let Will absorb what he'd said, his friend averted his eyes and was silent for a while. Then he looked up and said, "Did anyone at the hospital ever tell you what went on in the ER that night?"

John shook his head. "No. The only thing Dr. Tolar said was that they 'lost' me for a while." He leaned forward and stared intently at Will. "Even if someone had told me, that still wouldn't explain the rest of the experience."

Will thought about it for a second. "No, I guess it wouldn't," he agreed, visibly struggling. "And you're absolutely convinced that it wasn't just a dream?"

"I'm not *absolutely* convinced, no," John replied. "But it sure felt real."

Will ran his hand over his head again and whistled softly. Alex's ears went up at the sound, and she glanced at Will with anticipation; John's face bore a look of expectation also. "I've heard of this before," Will replied slowly. "But I never really expected it to happen to someone I know. . . . It sounds to me like you had a near-death experience."

Relieved that Will had reached the same conclusion he had been considering, John nodded soberly. "I think you may be right," he said. "It sure sounds like an NDE. I've been dancing around it for the last few days, but there doesn't seem to be any other logical conclusion." He smiled uncertainly and added, "I guess it took hearing someone else say it before I could accept it myself."

Overwhelmed by the enormity of what they had just said, both men lapsed into a thoughtful silence. Will looked away, finding an invisible focus point in a corner of the room, and after a few moments, he suddenly turned back to John; his gaze was intense. "My God," he said. "Think of what this means!"

John nodded. Without realizing it, he frowned. "I've thought about it a lot. It's practically all I *can* think about."

Will met John's frown with one of his own. "I may be out of line for saying so, but you don't seem very happy about it. . . . I know it has to be an overwhelming experience, to say the least, but I would have thought this is the kind of thing a person would get excited about. Instead, you look like you just lost your last friend."

"If that's all there was to it, I *would* be excited—I'd be ecstatic," John responded, clearly torn. He paused and added, "But I keep having these other dreams. . . ."

Will looked confused. "You mean, besides the one about the NDE?"

"Yes," John replied. "Remember, I told you the dream about the accident started out with a boy on a bike? Well, I've dreamed about him again, as well as some other people."

"Do you know them?"

"No. They're all strangers."

"Did you see them in the tunnel?"

"Not that I remember."

Will shook his head. "Then I don't see the connection."

"I'm not sure I do, either. But they started at the same time as the other dreams. And in their own weird way, they seem just as real."

Will thought for a moment. "They probably just seem that way because you decided the other one was real."

John considered it briefly, then shook his head. "I'd be inclined to accept that if it weren't for something else. . . ." His voice trailed off, and he glanced down at the dog and absently stroked her head, trying to decide how much more to say. He had already unburdened himself more than he'd intended, and, up to this point, Will had been far more accepting than John might have been had their roles been reversed. He had no intention of bringing up the strange incident in the jail or the real reason he had passed out at the shelter, if only because he hadn't the faintest idea what to make of it himself, but he realized that even if he didn't reveal everything to Will, he still had to tell him more than he had. He glanced back up and tried to look and sound as reasonable as he could. "Besides the dream about Ruby, at least one of those other dreams turned out to be true."

Right away, John knew he had finally overstepped the limits of Will's credulity. He had expected as much, and couldn't fault his friend for the look on his face; he was having a difficult time believing the story himself. When Will finally spoke, the awe was gone from his voice, replaced by self-consciousness, and he looked like someone who had suddenly found himself in the middle of a room strewn with eggs and was weighing the prospects of finding a way out without breaking any eggshells. "What do you mean, it turned out to be true?" His tone was mild but faintly challenging. "Are you saying you met the boy you dreamed about?"

"Well, no," John answered. "Although I can't shake the feeling that I know him somehow."

"Well, there's nothing inherently strange about that," Will countered. "People and places in dreams often seem familiar, and they ought to—they come from your own subconscious."

John stared intently at his friend and shook his head. "The man I dreamed about last night didn't come from my subconscious. He came from St. Tim's."

Will's eyes narrowed. "What do you mean?"

"You know the man I was talking to when I passed out today? Hector Denton? Have you ever told me about him?"

"No," Will answered guardedly. "I've never seen him before."

"I'd never seen him before today, either," John said. "But I dreamed about him last night."

For John's sake, Will took a moment before replying. "I don't know," he said doubtfully. "It's certainly a strange coincidence, but that's all it can be—a coincidence."

John leaned forward in his chair. "What are the odds that I would manufacture a total stranger in my dreams, and then meet him the very next day?" he parried.

"Pretty slim," Will admitted. "But just because two things happen close to each other doesn't mean it can't still be a coincidence. Besides, a lot of people look alike."

John nodded. "That's what I told myself when he came through the line—I even asked him if I knew him, and I didn't. But his face was exactly the same as it was in the dream, right down to the gin blossoms on his nose! And his voice was the same!"

"That's remarkable, but it still doesn't mean it has to be the same man—"

"What about the watch?" John demanded.

"What watch?"

John scooted closer to the edge of his chair, becoming more animated. "How many people have you seen down at the shelter wearing expensive gold watches?"

"None. Most of them are too poor to own a watch, expensive or otherwise."

"Exactly," John said, his head bobbing up and down. "But this guy had a watch! I remember in the dream I thought it was odd that someone dressed as shabbily as he was should be wearing such an expensive-looking timepiece. When I sat down with him today, I asked him what time it was so I could see if he had the same watch, and he did! Up until then, I'd been telling myself that it *was* just a coincidence—a weird one, but a coincidence, nonetheless. Even when he had offered to sell me the rosary I saw in my dream, I was still willing to believe it wasn't the same man. But the watch was the clincher. There were just too many things to ignore."

Will wasn't convinced. "What was the man doing in your dream?" he asked. "Was he in danger, too, like the boy on the bike?"

"Not the same kind of danger," John answered. He shuddered, re-membering the overwhelming guilt and crippling despair he had felt from the man right before John fainted. "I got the sense that his was a more spiritual danger. He had just finished making his confession." He paused and added meaningfully, "In the dream, the church we were in was St. Timothy's. And the front of it looked exactly the same as it did when I saw it today."

In spite of himself, Will was initially intrigued. Then he reverted to the role of devil's advocate: "That makes sense. I'd already told you St. Timothy's runs the shelter."

"That's true," John conceded. "And even though I've never been to your church before this morning, I realized I've probably driven past it. So it is possible that I've seen it before. But that still doesn't explain the man. I know it sounds impossible, but I'm convinced the guy in the dream and the guy at the shelter are one and the same. What I don't know is why I dreamed about him at all—or about the boy, for that matter."

"I don't know, John. . . ." Will responded. "It's not that I think you're making it up, but it's kind of hard for me to believe your dreams can predict the future." He smiled apologetically. "There has to be an-other explanation."

John nodded somberly. "I'd like to believe that—part of the rea-son I told you was that I thought you might be able to come up with a more reasonable alternative." He paused, then continued when Will said nothing. "Look, Will, I'm not necessarily claiming my dreams are prescient, but I also can't ignore the fact that they appear to have coun-terparts in reality. I *do* believe I'm dreaming about real people. What I don't know is how or why. None of it makes any sense, and until I *can* make sense of it, I can't be sure that I really had a near-death experience either, because all of the dreams seem to be wrapped up together."

Will looked at his friend with concern, as troubled for John as John was by the whole affair. He also couldn't help feeling disappointed that the wonder and hope that the possible NDE had given them both had been tarnished and complicated by the rest of the dream. Sensing they had reached an impasse, Will said, "I wish I could help you. I just don't know what else to say. . . . Maybe you should sleep on it and see how you feel tomorrow. You've been through a lot, and today wasn't easy, either. A good night's sleep might give you a new perspective. . . . Or maybe you'll have the dream again, and this time you'll be able to make some sense of it." He got to his feet and laid a hand on John's shoulder. "I'm glad you confided in me, and I'd like to talk about it again," he said with a small smile. "I want you to know I believe you. I just don't know what to make of it. I hope you're not offended."

John wearily got to his feet. "You haven't offended me. You're a good friend, Will. I don't blame you for being skeptical. Most people would have laughed in my face and then carted me off to the nearest institution."

Will grinned slightly, trying to mask the worry he felt. "Naw, I wouldn't do that. But if you faint on me again, I *will* take you to the hospital."

"We'll see," John replied vaguely. He shook his head, then forced a smile. "Thanks for everything. And thanks for bringing me home— although I don't remember giving you permission to drive my new car," he added with a weak grin.

Will laughed, grateful for a lighthearted moment. "I guess I could have called an ambulance when you passed out, but I figured that might be my only chance to drive the Jeep."

Both men laughed again, and Will handed over the car keys so John could drive him home. John accepted them, and after a slight hesitation, held them out again. "Here," he said. "Why don't you drive? Don't worry, I haven't had any dreams about you putting a dent in it."

Will gave him a wry smile. He looked at the keys wistfully, and reluctantly declined. "No. It's a tempting offer, but I don't want to push my luck. I don't even want to risk scratching the paint."

"Last chance," John responded, jingling the keys.

Will grinned but didn't take them, and both men headed for the front door. John paused in the doorway and impulsively gave Will a hug. "You're a good friend, Will," he said once again. "This is the second time you've kept me from going insane. I owe you big-time."

Will smiled warmly, then opened the door and stepped outside. "Like I told you before, you better watch that talk about owing me— you never can tell when I might have to collect."

FOURTEEN

The Painful Proof

JOHN SPENT the rest of the day mulling over his conversation with Will, but as nighttime drew near, he was no more enlightened than before. Finding himself even more hopelessly lost in an emotional, spiritual and intellectual limbo, he toyed with the idea of calling his friend, and then finally gave in around ten o'clock and dialed the number. After three and a half rings, an answering machine picked up and John replaced the receiver without leaving a message. Feeling slightly stupid for forgetting that most single guys usually went out on Friday nights, he decided the best thing to do was to take Will's advice and sleep on the problem.

The last thing he prayed about before drifting off to sleep was that the dreams would return and furnish him with new clues. Or if that didn't happen, then at least tomorrow might bring him a new perspective. Privately, he hoped for the first scenario, and that he would awake in the morning with clear, irrefutable, unambiguous proof. He soon fell asleep, and not long after, his prayers were answered by a longer version of a previous dream.

IT WAS LATE. He was standing in an alcove, the streetside entrance to a run-down bakery. Across from him was a small bar, its lights barely visible through smoked-glass windows, its patrons merely shadows shifting inside; the neighboring businesses were closed for the night. Three teenage boys stood at the corner, grouped around the street lamp on John's side of the street. They were obviously drunk, and one of them carried a baseball bat.

Instinctively, John pulled back into the cover of the darkened alcove. The boys gave no sign of having noticed him; instead they were staring at the bar's entrance. Before long, two men emerged, talking and laughing. The teenagers shouted at them, gesturing with their beer bottles. "Fag alert!" the short, muscular one called out shrilly. The tall boy in a high school letterman's jacket parroted his words in a voice made deeper by cigarettes and beer, while the third one yelled, "Hey, fags! Check this out!" and swung his bat in a vicious arc; the message, while unspoken, was frighteningly clear. The patrons stopped laughing and hurried away.

Soon, another man approached the bar from the other direction. This time, the drunken teens abandoned their corner and headed straight for him. They surrounded the man and began yelling in his face and jabbing his chest. Even though no punches were thrown, John could see that the level of violence was escalating, and he looked around frantically for a pay phone to call the police. There was none in sight.

As John watched with a sinking heart, the short, stocky boy pulled back a fist and buried it hard in the stranger's stomach. When the man doubled over, gasping for air, the teens closed in and proceeded to beat him. There was no time for John to call the police, so he ran toward the street, screaming at the boys to leave the man alone.

He didn't get far before something unexpected happened—as soon as he reached the sidewalk's edge, his vision grew dark and began to fail. He drew up short, then started running again, but with each step that took him closer to the melee, his vision kept fading, as if he had unknowingly crossed an invisible boundary—on one side he could see, on the other he couldn't. Frustrated and frantic, he staggered back toward the sidewalk. As soon as he did, his vision was restored.

Before long, another patron came out of the bar, and John cupped his hands to his mouth and shouted, "Call the police! *Go back inside and call the police!*" But the man never looked his way, not even when the warning was repeated in a voice that should have been heard at least a block away. John tried again and got the same result, and it was at that point he finally understood that for some strange reason, he was completely powerless to stop what was happening. Not only was he being prevented from going beyond the sidewalk's edge, but evidently he couldn't make himself seen or heard either. For all practical purposes, he wasn't even there.

But John couldn't accept that—especially when he saw the man who had just left the bar immediately run to the victim's aid. Determined to at least try again to warn him, John started back into the street. This time his vision went almost completely black in only a second and he was suddenly overwhelmed by a nagging sensation of déjà vu—he somehow knew that time and space were about to shift and he would be removed from the scene by some invisible force whether he agreed to it or not. "*Wait!*" John screamed. The cry was as much a protest at being removed as it was a warning to the Good Samaritan. "*They've got a baseball bat!*" he yelled at the man. "*Go back inside and call the police!*"

No sooner had he cried out than two things happened. First, as if in answer to his protest, his vision cleared and the scene before him swam back into focus. And second, the Good Samaritan who had gone to the aid of the unfortunate stranger saw the baseball bat with his very own eyes—as it whiffed through the air and slammed into his stomach with a sickening *thud.*

John cried out again as the man doubled over and fell to the ground, but his passionate outbursts fell on deaf ears. As he started across the street—unseen by the others but with his own sight restored—the other two teens abandoned their first victim and converged in a frenzy on the second hapless man. By the time John slowed to a stop in the middle of the street, he was crazy with frustration and sick with horror, and the attack was proceeding with earnest abandon.

"Where do you get off buttin' into our business!" the tall boy screamed at the second victim, burying his hard-soled sneaker into the prone man's ribs.

"Yeah," the short one joined in. "You should've left well enough alone, you know?" He uttered a sharp, shrill laugh that gave John chills, and followed his friend's kick with one of his own.

The man on the ground gasped—not loudly, but loud enough for John to hear—and drew himself up into a fetal position; even struggling to shield himself, his fists were clenched in an aggressive position, as if he were just waiting for the breath to get up and fight. When he finally tried to get to his feet, the third boy—who had been watching from the sidelines with an unreadable expression—took a step forward and drew back his bat. But teen number two beat him to the punch, and slammed his beer bottle against the Good Samaritan's head.

The only thing worse than the sickening *thunk* of glass meeting skull was the resounding *crack* that reverberated in the air when the victim pitched sideways and landed headfirst on the concrete sidewalk.

"*Stop it!*" John screamed at the top of his lungs. "*For God's sake, stop it! Leave him alone!*" His voice sounded in his own ears like the blare of a trumpet, but none of the others even flinched or turned around.

Their victim lay on the ground—mouth open slightly, lips brushing the sidewalk—with his legs akimbo and a baseball cap partly covering his eyes. Then, a trickle of blood oozed past his ear, and he curled back into a fetal position and started to moan. The moans started softly, then quickly grew into a plaintive wail of anger and pain.

All three boys stared down at the man with disgust on their faces, and the one with the bat prodded him with it in the small of the back. "Come on, *faggot!*" he hissed, drawing back the bat as if ready to swing. "Get up! You've got till the count of three!"

John gasped in horror and looked around frantically, praying that someone had called the police. The teenagers broke into a fresh round of laughter, then the boy with the bat abruptly stopped laughing and counted, "*One!*"

The man stopped moaning and the fingers of his right hand balled into a trembling fist. He turned his head slightly and peered at the man they had first assaulted, who was also lying prone a few yards away. Then, he looked back at his attackers. "Why?" he croaked and fell silent again.

The teen with the bat snorted. "*Two!*"

The man on the ground tried to crawl away, grunting in pain, but the tall boy stepped in front of him and blocked the way. "I said *stand up!*" the boy with the bat repeated. "Step into the batter's box and take it like a man!"

His victim said nothing, but his hands closed again into tight, angry fists.

With a sly smile, the boy stepped across the man's body and kicked him in the stomach. He bent down, leaning closer to his bloody face. "You know, you fight like a girl." He spat in disgust and, using the fat end of the bat, jabbed the man in the shoulder and flipped him onto his back.

In spite of himself, John moved closer. The man's baseball cap had fallen away from his head, giving John his first good look at the victim's face—

It was Will Gibson. Looking up with angry, terrified eyes and bleeding from the head in at least two places . . .

John fell back in shock. He stared at Will with tormented eyes, his rage and frustration rising to an almost unbearable level as he realized that all he could do was stand by and watch. Never in his life had he felt so helpless. Never had he felt so utterly useless. . . .

Still standing over Will's body, the teenager stared down at him with inscrutable eyes. He abandoned his countdown and hoisted the bat high over his head. "Let's finish this one off."

The instant the bat tipped in his direction, Will bucked like a wild man, slamming his boots into his attacker's shins. The boy fell backward, cursing in surprise, and as he reached for Will's ankle with his one free hand, Will drew back his foot and buried it hard in the teenager's crotch.

The boy yelped in surprise and rolled on the ground with his hands between his legs, cursing and howling with pain. When Will lurched to his feet, the tall boy hung back, staring at all the blood, but the third boy went after him and tackled him hard. Having used all his strength in the initial escape, Will crashed to the sidewalk and was easily pinned.

Panting as if he had run a hundred-yard dash, the boy with the bat stumbled to his feet and stood still, moaning softly. His eyes were burning with a hatred that had been stoked into a roaring fire. After a few moments, he gripped the bat tightly with skinned-up hands and staggered toward Will. When he reached the spot where Will and the short boy lay tangled on the ground, he gestured for his companion to move aside. The teenager did so and Will rolled over onto his back to face his attacker, then lay there unmoving, too weak to get up.

A few yards away, John started to pray.

"Up on your knees!" the boy demanded hoarsely, flicking the bat.

"Hey, man, that's enough," the tall boy protested nervously. "Let's get going before someone calls the cops." When his suggestion was met with silent scorn, he took off down the street and soon disappeared. The short boy looked uncertain, but stayed behind.

Looking angrier, if possible, than he had before, Will's attacker repeated his earlier demand. "Up on your knees!"

Will stared up at the teenager and silently but clearly mouthed the word *no.*

The boy glared back for only a moment, then swung the bat straight at Will's lower rib cage. The crack of breaking bones could be heard across the street. "I said, *get on your knees!*"

Somehow Will managed to do as he was told. His body swaying slightly as he knelt on the concrete, he wiped blood from his mouth with the back of his hand and met the boy's eyes with pain-wracked defiance.

In return, the teenager grinned. As he did, the wail of sirens sounded in the distance. He glanced up briefly with a look of annoyance, then looked back at Will, who had turned to stare in the same direction. The boy shook his head slowly from side to side and muttered an obscenity. As John watched helplessly with widening eyes, he hoisted the bat with both hands on the handle, jerked it behind him, then whipped it forward and smashed Will Gibson in the back of the head.

JOHN AWOKE with a start in the darkness of his bedroom. His heart was pounding, his stomach was in knots and his brain was reeling with shock and fear—fear that his prayer for conclusive proof might just have been answered.

Be careful what you ask for, his mother had always said. *Because you never can tell when you might just get it.*

John stared at the ceiling and prayed to God this wasn't one of those times when his mother was right. . . .

Will.

He couldn't stop thinking about Will Gibson.

About his face when the teenager straddled his body.

And the sound of the baseball bat hitting his head . . .

Most of all, he couldn't shake the guilt and frustration of having stood on the sidelines while everything happened.

If it really *did* happen.

Maybe the proof he had been given was that it *was* just a dream and nothing more.

Then again, maybe it wasn't. And if Will was in danger, he couldn't just stand by and let it come to pass.

If it hadn't already . . .

In a near-panic, he sat up in bed, turned on the light and dialed Will's number. It rang once, then twice, and as it started on the third ring, John's heart beat faster and the knot in his stomach began to tighten even more. On the fourth ring, Will's answering machine picked up, as it had earlier that night. Crestfallen, John broke the connection and, on the off chance that Will might be working, dialed the number of Washoe Medical Center. He wasn't there either.

There were any number of places where Will might have been that had nothing to do with John's dream, and he tried to convince himself that was the case. But the argument rang hollow and dangerously false, because of Ruby and the tunnel and Hector Denton, and after only a minute of trying to be rational, John threw on some clothes and got into his car.

He headed straight for St. Timothy's. He couldn't be sure that the bar he had dreamed of was close to the church—if it existed at all—but the two had been linked in a previous dream. And even though he couldn't recall seeing such a place when he'd gone to the shelter, that didn't necessarily mean it wasn't close by. Ten minutes later, when he arrived at St. Timothy's, it looked like his hunch had been right, after all.

With a sinking feeling, he slowed to a stop a block past the church. Up ahead was the bar. A large crowd had gathered outside, and three police cars were sitting in the middle of the street, their radios squawking and red lights flashing. As John parked and jumped out, he heard the strident sound of approaching sirens, and a moment later, two ambulances arrived.

He ran toward the crowd, afraid of what he'd find but driven by the need to know about Will. Even as he drew closer and found that everything around him was a perfect match for what he had seen in his dream, he still kept hoping that it wouldn't be Will who was lying on the sidewalk.

In a rising panic, he shoved his way to the front of the crowd, unmindful of the curses and hostile looks from the people around him. He caught a glimpse of a man being loaded onto a stretcher by a team of paramedics, and he felt a burst of hope—it wasn't Will! But another stretcher went by a few seconds later . . . Despite the swelling and blood that marred the second victim's face, John saw with eyes suddenly hot with tears that it was Will, after all. . . . In that awful moment, he realized beyond a doubt that the near-death experience and prescient dreams were as palpably real as the body rolling past him. It was a life-changing revelation, a shove past the fork in the proverbial road, but an epiphany that came at a frightful cost.

As they loaded Will into an ambulance, John pushed his way closer. "Where are you taking him?" he shouted over the angry buzz of the crowd. When the paramedics didn't answer, he tried again in a louder voice. They still didn't respond, but a policeman turned around and stared at John with a thinly disguised look that was uncomfortably similar to one he had seen on the teenager's face in the dream. "They're taking your little buddy to Washoe Med," the policeman replied in a patronizing voice. "Now, why don't you run back inside and let these people do their jobs, okay?"

John returned the cop's stare just long enough to make a point, then turned around and headed back to his car. As he made his way along the edge of the crowd, he happened to walk past a police cruiser from which a familiar face peered through a side rear window at the busy scene. The sneer on the face was eerily unmistakable, if slightly more sullen—it was the boy with the bat he had seen in his dream.

John drew up short, stopped in his tracks by a powerful burst of conflicting emotions, and stared at the teenager, fighting off the urge to lunge at the window. For a few tense seconds, they glared at each other in a mutual exchange of revulsion and anger. The boy then offered up a chilling smile, shouted "Batter up!" through the thick glass window, and began laughing hysterically. John recoiled in shock, and as he turned away, fighting off a wave of sudden nausea, the boy's maniacal laughter followed him down the street and still echoed in his ears long after he was gone.

FIFTEEN

Gift and Giver

AFTER RUSHING to the hospital, John Creed spent the next ninety minutes pacing the floor of Washoe Med's emergency room waiting area, surrounded by people who were also pacing or watching TV or simply sitting and crying. Every fifteen minutes, he approached the front desk to inquire about Will and each time he was given the same reply: "Mr. Gibson is in surgery. I don't know his condition." It was a maddening litany, and even after asking a nurse who had taken care of him during his own hospitalization to intervene, he was no better off than before; it was simply too soon to tell how Will would fare.

When he wasn't pacing, he sat by himself in a corner of the room, worrying and praying and waiting for news. He spent much of that time fending off bouts of intense frustration over his ongoing role as hapless bystander; it particularly galled him that he couldn't even make phone calls to let people know what had happened to Will, because he didn't know Will's friends or family. When Father Ryan from St. Timothy's Church (and Thursday's dream) came in with a group of people around 1 A.M., John introduced himself and spent the next several hours waiting with them.

At 4 A.M., they finally got word that Will was out of surgery and was being moved to a bed in intensive care. In typical hospital fashion, the nurse refused to let anybody see him because none of them was a member of his immediate family, but once everyone except Father Ryan and John had gone home, the priest persuaded her to change her mind. Half an hour later, they were shown to Will's room.

When he walked in the doorway, John was profoundly shocked and immediately reminded of how his own body had looked when he watched himself die in this very same hospital. As banged up as he had been then, Will looked even worse, and were it not for the fact that the social worker was breathing on his own and in a very deep sleep instead of a coma, John would have given up all hope of ever talking to him again. Even so, the odds didn't look good—after being savagely beaten to within an inch of his life, Will's grip on that inch looked precariously weak.

Father Ryan had evidently reached the same conclusion. He turned to John with a remorseful look, as if apologizing for confirming their shared worst fear, and quietly administered the last rites to Will. Once he finished making the sign of the cross over the bruised and bandaged body lying on the bed, he stared intently at his parishioner for a very long time, his lips moving almost imperceptibly in silent prayer. Then, obviously laboring under the strain of the night's events, he smiled weakly at John and wearily bade him good night.

John remained behind, and with the permission of a nurse who was one of Will's friends, drew a chair up to the bedside and settled in for the night. For the next hour or so, he gazed sadly at Will's face or at the beeping monitors, or stared off into the distance, silently praying.

He eventually drifted into a dreamless sleep, and when he opened his eyes almost an hour later, Will was also awake.

"Hi," Will whispered in a thin voice.

"Hi," John replied, cautiously relieved. "How are you feeling?"

A ghost of a smile played across Will's face. "Like I was hit by a truck," he answered weakly. He started to glance around the room, but as soon as he moved his head, a small, soft moan escaped his lips. He lay still for a few seconds, and turned slowly back to John. "Washoe?" he asked in a strained voice.

John nodded and asked worriedly, "Do you want me to get a nurse?"

"I don't think so." Will closed his eyes and took a careful breath. He opened them again and stared at John, saying nothing.

John scrambled for something to fill the silence. He had always been good with emotional crises but never knew what to say to people who were in physical pain; under the present circumstances, it was even harder than usual. "Do you remember what happened?" he finally asked.

Will's answer came out slowly, in a hoarse near-whisper. "You know me . . . always sticking my nose where it doesn't belong." He gave John a small, wry smile and said in a more serious voice, "They got another guy, too. . . . How is he?"

"He's doing fine," John replied, wishing that Will were doing even half as well as the man he had saved. "He's here, too, in a room upstairs. He wants to thank you as soon as you're up to it." Will smiled at that, and John went on, "You know, what you did took a lot of guts—"

Will started to protest, but John cut him off. "No false modesty, okay?" he said gently. He leaned closer, and his voice grew impassioned as all the emotions of the last eight hours welled up inside him. "You know, most people would have just looked the other way or gone back inside to call the police. But no, not you . . . It looked to me like you ran to help him without even thinking twice about what might happen."

Will looked puzzled at first, then simply astonished. John nodded and gave him a meaningful look. "That's right," he said softly, "I know what happened—I saw the whole thing."

No sooner had John made his startling revelation than two nurses and a doctor came bustling in and converged on Will's bed, asking questions and checking all the monitors and medical paraphernalia attached to his body. Automatically, John stood up to move out of the way, but when he went no farther than the open doorway, one of the nurses politely but firmly suggested it might be a good time for him to go eat breakfast. John looked at Will, who was still staring at him intently with an unspoken question, and reluctantly agreed.

When he returned, Will was asleep and remained that way for several hours. John dozed also, but was awakened periodically by the arrival of visitors, including Father Ryan and several of Will's coworkers, who stopped in on their breaks. Most of them left after only a few minutes—some because they didn't have much time but usually because it was too upsetting to stay—but John never strayed farther than the open doorway. He had unfinished business to attend to with Will, and he owed him too much to leave him alone.

In midafternoon, not long after Father Ryan had left, Will finally woke up. His breathing was more labored than before, and it looked to John as if he were in a great deal of pain, but the first thing Will did was resume that morning's conversation, as if only seconds had intervened instead of hours. "You dreamed it, didn't you?" he asked weakly, referring to John's statement that he had seen the beating. It was clear from the set of his eyes and mouth that he already knew what the answer would be.

John nodded gravely. "It was just like the others. I woke up as soon as it was over. . . ." He stared at Will, not sure what to say next, and suddenly averted his eyes when he was caught unaware by a painful wave of resurgent guilt. After collecting himself, he said in a voice that cracked with emotion, "I went straight to St. Timothy's because I had a hunch the bar was somewhere close by. I wanted to warn you, but by the time I got there, it was already too late—" His eyes filled with tears and he whispered hoarsely, "I'm sorry I didn't get there in time. . . . I'm so sorry, Will! I would have given anything to keep it from happening!"

Will waited for him to look up again, then met his gaze with eyes that were filled with awe and compassion. When he finally spoke, he didn't challenge John's claim as he had the last time they had discussed the dreams. Instead, he nodded almost imperceptibly and said softly, "Then all of it was true. . . ."

John nodded slowly. "Yes. Everything—the NDE, the other dreams . . ." Again, he stopped short of adding the mysterious emotional connection he'd experienced between himself and Ruby, and then later, between himself and Denton. "After last night, there's no doubt in my mind. . . . I know you think I should be ecstatic or relieved or grateful or something, but after what happened to you, I only feel guilty."

"There was nothing you could have done, John," Will reassured him. His voice was so weak that John strained to hear him. Then, Will added pensively, "I think that's the way it was supposed to be."

"But *why?*" John asked miserably and with a touch of anger.

Will smiled weakly. "Who knows . . . There's a reason for everything. Even this," he added philosophically, indicating the bandages on his upper body and head. He blanched in pain and carefully laid his arm back down on the bed, saying softly, "It seems to me you've been given a rare gift, John. I think you should concentrate on finding out how God wants you to use it, instead of wasting your time feeling guilty. What happened to me wasn't your fault."

Ashamed for bringing up his own problems when Will's were so much worse, John stared thoughtfully at his friend, and changed to a safer, more appropriate subject. "Is there someone you'd like me to call?" he asked.

Will thought about it for a moment, and said, "Most of my friends work here. They probably know already."

John nodded. "Several of them looked in on you today while you were sleeping. . . . How about your family? Do you want me to call you parents and let them know you're in the hospital?"

The vehemence of Will's answer caught John by surprise. "No!" he said sharply, and his expression clouded with a different kind of pain. He looked away and said in a slightly tempered voice, "Not yet. Maybe later . . ."

While John was trying to decide how best to pursue the matter, which was obviously emotionally charged but too important to let go, Will moved on. "You might call Father Ryan for me," he said, breaking the awkward silence. "I'd kind of like to see him."

"He was here last night and again this morning—as a matter of fact he's the one who convinced the nurse to let me in to see you," John answered, carefully omitting any mention of last rites being administered. It occurred to him that he'd forgotten to tell Will that the priest had been in the dream with Hector Denton, but there didn't seem to be any point in telling him now. Instead, he went on, "He said to tell you he'd be back later."

"He's a good priest," Will answered. "And a very good friend."

John nodded. "He seems like it. . . ."

An awkward silence returned, and for several minutes, neither man said a word. Finally, Will looked at John and said in a low, apologetic voice, "I'm sorry I didn't tell you."

"Tell me what?" John asked.

"That I'm gay," Will answered. "I would rather have told you myself than have you find out the way you did."

"It doesn't matter. It's not a big deal, Will." John grinned and added, "At least now I'll be able to use the old 'some of my best friends are . . . ' line."

Will laughed self-consciously and smiled with relief. "I planned to tell you eventually. But we haven't known each other very long, and I was afraid you might think I was trying to pick you up."

"I wouldn't have thought that," John answered. "At least, not seriously. You've never said anything to make me think you were interested in being more than friends—luckily for you," John added, grinning. "I would've hated to disappoint you."

Will grunted and replied with a sardonic smile, "Well, I'd hate to disappoint *you*—to be honest, John, you're not really my type."

John hesitated before replying, trying to decide if he should be offended. Instead, he laughed, shaking his head and looking slightly embarrassed. In a more serious vein, he asked, "Does Father Ryan know?"

"Sure, he knows," Will answered. "He lets our support group meet in the church—which would get him in a lot of trouble if the bishop knew." He shifted in his bed as if trying to get comfortable, then inhaled sharply and closed his eyes. When he opened them again and resumed talking, his voice was a little weaker than before. "That's why I happened to be at the bar," he said, frowning. "I was meeting a few friends who had gone there to have a beer after the meeting. The irony of it is that I don't even like bars. That was the first time I'd been there in months . . ."

John nodded but remained silent, giving him the time to say what he needed to say. Will stared at the ceiling, then closed his eyes and was quiet for so long that John had almost decided he was sleeping—or worse—when the social worker suddenly opened them again and resumed the conversation. All the while, his gaze remained fixed on the white acoustical tile six feet above his head, and his voice grew weaker and more troubled as he talked. "You know, I understand the fear—people always fear what they don't know. But I can't understand the hatred . . ." His voice trailed off, and John stared at him, puzzled. A moment later, he realized that Will was talking about the boys who had attacked him.

Will turned his head slowly and met John's eyes. When he spoke, there was bitterness in his voice, and simmering anger, but more than anything else, there was a profound but bewildered sadness. "The funny thing is, while it was happening, I kept thinking about that old saying our parents taught us when we were kids—you know, 'Sticks and stones may break my bones, but names will never hurt me.'" He paused, and his eyes grew fierce, and his voice more vehement. "That was easy for them to say! No one ever screamed *fag* or *queer* in *their* faces!" He lowered his voice and shook his head sadly from side to side, despite the physical discomfort it caused. "The fact is, the names hurt worse, because all the people who don't have the nerve to pick up a baseball bat use them instead. And they do it with the same intent." He stared at John with a sad, meaningful look and added, "It especially hurts when those people are your parents . . ."

Taken aback, John stared at his friend and wished he could do something to ease his pain. Recalling the offer to call Will's parents, he said, "I'm sorry. I had no idea. . . ."

"It's okay. You didn't know. . . . It was a long time ago. I guess I should have gotten over it by now." He paused, then clenched his jaw and gingerly touched his fingers to the side of his head. "Damn, my head hurts . . ."

John was instantly alarmed. "Do you want me to get a nurse?"

"No," Will answered, waving him off. "It's only a headache. I just got myself worked up." He closed his eyes for a few moments, and when he opened them again, they were filled with pain. "On second thought," he said in a tight voice, "maybe you should ring for the nurse. . . ."

This time the nurse allowed John to stay, but only until she had finished tending to Will and he was fast asleep. "We've increased his pain medication," she explained. "He's going to be out for a while—probably until late tonight or tomorrow morning. Perhaps you should go home and get some rest."

"Is he going to be okay?" John asked.

"I couldn't tell you, Mr. Creed," she replied candidly but with concern in her voice. "I hope so. But he's got a long way to go." She added in a more officious tone, "Now why don't you go home and come back later? We've already let you stay a lot longer than we're supposed to."

John shook his head. "Thanks, but I'm going to stick close to the hospital. I'll be in the waiting room."

AROUND 2 A.M., John was sleeping fitfully on a couch in the intensive care waiting room when he was awakened by the same nurse who had been on duty the previous night. "Mr. Gibson is asking for you," she said with a serious expression. "You can come back for a while, but you have to promise not to tire him out. He's still very weak and in some pain." John solemnly promised to do as she said, and followed her back.

If possible, Will looked worse than before. The head of his bed was elevated slightly, and he was lying very still, with his eyes fixed on the doorway, waiting for John. The room was fairly dark, with only one small lamp burning, but the pain etched on his face was clearly visible. If the long rest and increased medication had done him any good, it was difficult to tell. John hesitated before walking into the room. "How are you feeling?" he asked in a conversational tone, trying to hide his concern.

"I've been better," Will replied feebly. "I'm surprised you're still here. . . . It's okay to go home, you know."

John shook his head. "Maybe later." He drew a chair up next to the bed, then sat down and looked at Will with an ironic smile. "You know, it seems as if most of the time we've known each other, one of us has been in the hospital. It's a hell of a way to start off a friendship."

"True," Will said, averting his eyes. He lapsed into a brief but pensive silence, then said, "I'm sorry I dumped all that crap on you earlier. Sometimes I start feeling sorry for myself and get carried away. You know—gay man's angst. There are so many other people in the world who are going through such worse things right now that I feel guilty for even bringing it up."

"Don't apologize," John replied. "You have a right to be upset. Besides, it isn't as if I haven't done the same thing to you."

Will smiled sadly. He moistened his lips and glanced at a paper cup on the table that was just out of reach. "Could you hand me those ice chips?" he asked.

"Sure," John said, giving him the cup. "Do you want some help?"

"No, thanks. I think I can manage." Will took the cup and gingerly raised it to his lips, tipping a few ice chips into his mouth. After letting them melt, he returned to the subject of their earlier conversation. It obviously cost him a great deal to do so, both physically and emotionally; the words came out slowly, at times almost inaudible. John would have steered the conversation back into less stressful waters, but realized it was futile, because the subject was clearly one Will felt compelled to discuss.

"I know it's normal to feel angry after what happened," he started out in a sad, paper-thin voice. "The problem is, that's not the only thing I'm angry about. It's only the most recent. . . . Do you know I haven't even talked to my parents in almost four years?" He paused and looked away again. When he turned back and began to explain, there was regret in his voice, and hurt. So much hurt that John couldn't help but be moved. "I'll never forget the looks on their faces when I told them I was gay," Will went on. "I knew they weren't going to be thrilled, but I never thought they'd react the way they did. . . . They stared at me like I was a stranger, like I had suddenly turned into some sort of freak. And then my father started in with the names . . . I guess it's hard for any father to hear that his son is gay, but I think black men have an even harder time with it. For some reason, a lot of African Americans think all gay men are white."

Will paused. He started to raise the cup of ice chips to his mouth, but his hand shook so badly that he let it drop back to the bed instead. "So I took off," he went on, frowning. "I left the very next day, and wound up out here. I haven't spoken to them since. . . . I guess I never really gave them a chance to come to terms with it. I was so caught up in my own hurt feelings that I never stopped to think of how it must have hurt them. I probably didn't make it any easier for my little sister to come out to them, either," he added regretfully. "Deidra's gay, too."

John raised his eyebrows, surprised to learn that Will had a sister. Then he nodded sympathetically. "Naturally you were hurt—your parents handled it badly. The truth is, they probably weren't prepared to have that conversation. It's a difficult thing, finding out your child is homosexual, and most people don't have any idea how to react or feel, so they say the first thing that comes into their heads. Most people need time to adjust." He half smiled, hoping he was right, and added softly, "Maybe you should let me call them, Will. Chances are, they feel differently by now. At the very least, you should let me call your sister."

Will held his gaze for several long moments, looking emotionally drained and physically exhausted. Finally, he mumbled, "Maybe you should," then closed his eyes and nodded off.

Once Will was asleep, John let out a heavy, pent-up sigh and regarded his friend with anxious eyes. It was difficult to see him in such multifaceted distress; harder still to think that the physical beating that had resurrected old wounds might also be the thing that robbed him of the chance to heal those wounds and find some peace. It was all so frustrating, so hard to do nothing when Will was in pain. *You owe him more than you've done so far,* he silently chided himself. *A lot more.*

As the minutes wore on in the darkened room, an idea took root and grew in John's mind. Remembering Ruby Mazzoni and Hector Denton, two other tortured souls who had crossed his path recently, John found himself wondering if he could do for Will what he had seemed to do for them. He still wasn't sure what had actually happened in both of those cases, or if his strange, new ability was real or imagined, but it seemed pretty clear that some type of emotional or energy transfer had somehow occurred, as if he had taken some of their pain and replaced it with hope. Whatever it was, he was absolutely convinced that it wasn't a coincidence; over the last twenty-four hours, he had ceased to believe there was such a thing, at least for him. For now, it was enough to know that whatever he had done—even if unintentionally—had left Ruby and Hector visibly relieved, even peaceful, it seemed, as if the burdens they carried had become suddenly lighter. Remembering the looks on their faces, John stared at Will and thought, *Maybe I can do something for him, after all.*

For the first time in a while, he regarded his friend with a hopeful heart. He had a very strong hunch he was on the right track, and the more he thought about it, the more convinced he became. More than anything, it felt as if he were being led to the idea and discouraged from engaging his rational doubts; why he should feel that way was still a complete mystery, but the feeling was strong and came from a place that felt unwise to ignore. Although he didn't know why his new ability worked (if it really worked at all) or why he could do it (if he was really the one doing it), he thought he understood how to initiate the connection. Even if it turned out that he was deluding himself, he owed it to Will to at least make the effort. Afterward, he would make the call to Will's sister and parents.

Feeling slightly self-conscious and more than a little bit anxious, he glanced outside to make sure no one was coming, then began clearing his mind. He put his hand on Will's and stared at his friend for a very long while, tuning out everything else around them, and focusing instead on all the love and hope and forgiveness he could summon. When he felt ready he shifted his focus to Will, and not long after, the connection took place. As soon as it did, John's mind was flooded with words and emotions and unfamiliar faces that were ten times more bitter than anything he expected—

A teenage friend's face looming before him, his features contorted with fear and disgust, from his lips a vow that he would never stay friends with a guy who was queer—

A friendly face with an easy smile that tells a joke that secretly hurts him, then laughs and expects him to laugh in return—

Discomfort, resentment, the shame of staying silent; and the hard, hot nugget of defensive anger he has long carried with him grows slightly larger and a little bit hotter than it was before . . .

A man and a woman—father and mother—staring uncomfortably; one begins to cry, the other begins to shout, and a volatile exchange of emotions ensues; hateful things are said and names are spoken that throw up barriers around wounded love; a line is blindly crossed and twenty years of memories become too charged to touch—

Like a developing pearl, his anger grows, adding layers of hurt, abandonment and shame; like a cancerous tumor, it eats at his happiness and self-esteem; he is alone and lonely, and secretly bitter . . .

A trio of teenagers, drunk and laughing; they beat him with beer bottles and sneaker-clad feet and a baseball bat of scarred, hard wood; they rape his dignity with the same hate-filled names his father had called him, then laugh as he fears they will rape his body; the assault is thorough, striking body, mind and wounded spirit—

The pain is excruciating; hatred and violence flood his soul, and the pearl grows so enormous it threatens to crush him; now he holds it in his hands, watching it turn black, as black as the heart of the boy who beat him; forgiveness is elusive and dancing out of reach; and the pearl burns his hands, but he can't let go . . .

He can't let go . . .

He can't . . .

let . . .

go . . .

. . . He finally lets it go.

When the pearl was released after a mighty struggle, the emotions faded and vanished from John's mind. Similar to what happened with the man in the shelter, John felt healing energy flow across the space between himself and Will, as if it were drawn into the vacuum left by the passage of pain and sorrow. This time John opened his eyes as he felt it happen, and he was surprised and excited actually to see the energy. It was a bright, white-gold light that pulsed with vitality, similar to the cloud of sparkling dust or twinkling stars he had imagined before. He also saw a field of energy around Will, highly charged particles that shimmered unevenly at the edges of his body like a semitransparent cloak of blues, greens and reds that were streaked with black. When John's light touched them, it shot through the aura like a bolt of electricity; the blues and greens intensified, overwhelming the reds, and the patches of black began to shrink and fade, giving way to a network of white-gold light. It was an astounding sight.

Once the transformation was complete, John's head was throbbing and his stomach ached, but his heart was hopeful because he knew it had worked. And as the anger he had taken from Will Gibson dwindled to little more than a hazy memory, so too did his doubts about this peculiar gift he'd somehow been given; he still didn't understand it, at least not completely, but he believed it was real. Now all that remained was to see the effect it had on Will.

Will opened his eyes and stared at John with a strange expression. He opened his mouth slightly and started to speak, but closed it again without saying a word, as if groping for a question he couldn't quite form. After a lengthy silence, he did it again, and John grew alarmed. "Are you all right?" he asked.

Will's mouth turned down in an uncertain frown. "I don't know. . . ." he said softly. "I feel kind of strange."

John started up from his chair. "I'll get the nurse—"

"No!" Will said. "Not that kind of strange. I just feel . . . I don't know . . . weird but in a good way, I think. If that makes any sense."

John hesitated and sat back down. The alarm he had felt became tentative relief, and as he began to believe that Will's feelings were the signs for which he'd been looking—proof that his gift had actually helped—he felt a solemn satisfaction that maybe, at last, he had paid back a small measure of the debt he owed him.

Will fell silent and stared hard at John with probing eyes. "What did you do?" he asked finally in a voice that was husky with unabashed awe.

"What do you mean?" John replied, keeping his voice neutral.

Will narrowed his eyes, and shook his head slightly. "I feel . . . peaceful," he said. "Like I've just come from confession—like I just came from the mother of all confessions . . ." He looked away and his expression became distant, as if he were turning inward to verify that the weight was actually gone. When he turned back to John, the serenity in his eyes was unmistakable. "I don't know how you did it," he said slowly and with wonder in his voice, "but I can't shake the feeling that whatever just happened to me happened because of you." He offered John a small but grateful smile, then reached out and weakly squeezed his hand. "Thank you," he said softly, but with great emotion. His eyes snapped shut and his hand began to tremble, gently at first, then with alarming violence as his arm followed suit.

John stared at his friend, too stunned to move until Will's eyes flew open with a searing look of unmistakable agony. John jumped up to get help, but Will wouldn't let go. Instead, he squeezed John's hand harder with a viselike grip and said in a series of short, ragged gasps, "Looks-like-it-was-just-in-time . . ."

John's eyes widened in dismay, and he turned toward the doorway and looked out at the nurses' station. "We need a doctor!" he bellowed. A nurse looked up, and he waved at her frantically with his free hand. "He needs help—*now!*" John glanced down at Will, who had started to moan, and shook his head angrily from side to side. "Dammit, Will, don't die!" he croaked. "Not now, of all times . . ."

Will started to smile reassuringly and grimaced instead. He reached up with his other hand and tried to massage his temple. "It'll-be-okay," he said choppily through gritted teeth. "*You*-should-know-that. . . ."

John shook his head slowly from side to side with desperate denial. A part of him was aware that Will was right, but that didn't make it easier to watch what was happening. And it didn't stop the tears that streamed from John's eyes, or soften the shock or ward off the emptiness he was already feeling as Will's grip grew weaker. Every fiber of John's being was screaming out, *"No!"* as the doctor and nurses rushed into the room and the space around him exploded with frantic activity. Rather than release Will's hand and move out of the way, he held on tighter, afraid to let go.

"Mr. Creed, you have to leave." The nurse's voice was firm, no-nonsense and urgent.

John just kept shaking his head, staring at Will.

"Mr. Creed!" she repeated, more sternly this time. "You're interfering! Go wait outside!" She reached for his hand to pry loose his fingers, but before she could manage, Will's tremors subsided and after taking a long, deep, hitching breath, he looked up at John with calming eyes and said in a whisper, "Please, John, let go."

The sound of his voice finally got through where the nurse's couldn't, and John snapped out of his daze and released Will's hand. He took a step back, but couldn't look away or make himself leave, because to do either one would be saying good-bye.

Will held his gaze and tried to smile. "Look for me when you go back," he said cryptically in a ragged whisper. His voice was tortured with physical pain, but his eyes were serene, half-focused elsewhere, as if reminding John of the special knowledge they secretly shared. "I'll be waiting . . . I promise . . . And please tell Deidra—and my parents—that I love them. . . ." Then his eyes went glassy and rolled back in his head as his entire body began shaking violently.

The seizure that followed was even worse, and John attempted to stay and see Will through it, but in the end, he couldn't bear to watch any more. Crying uncontrollably, he sobbed, "I'll miss you," and staggered from the room.

It was the last time he saw Will Gibson alive.

SIXTEEN

Wishing for an Angel

ELLIOT DANDRIDGE FELT lousy when he woke up on Monday morning. As if the hangover weren't enough, his conscience was waiting for him with something he'd been dreading: an objective assessment of what he was doing and where he was going. He spent the next half hour trying to go back to sleep so he could avoid the matter, but when he finally climbed out of bed it was with the unshakable realization that he needed to shape up and pull himself together, that he'd been screwing up royally—drinking every day instead of looking for a job, wrecking one of the cars, snapping at the kids and generally messing up his life and that of his family. It was a painful epiphany, a searing-hot moment of crystal clarity too strong to ignore.

The look Kate gave him a short while later as she left for work only reinforced his guilt. He didn't get a kiss and a "Have a good day." Instead of a smile, he got a look of disappointment, with hints of resentment or something worse. It occurred to him that he'd probably been getting that look for a while, but today it finally registered, and it cut him to the quick. Kate's smile was one of the things that kept him going and made him feel good when nothing else would. It was what had made him impulsively pop the question on only their third date. And now it was gone, and it was all his fault.

Elliot realized he had to do something to get the smile back, and for his own sake he needed to do it today. *You could go out and get a job, and lay off the booze,* his conscience suggested. He thought seriously about it for a while, but decided those were things that would take too long. What he needed was something he could point to today; he'd work on the others, starting tomorrow.

He began by cleaning the house, throwing himself into it with so much energy and noise that Matt and Lori came downstairs early, rubbing their eyes—from sleep, at first, then disbelief. Elliot greeted them both with a warm "Good morning," and an offer of breakfast, which they awkwardly declined; half an hour later, they left for school earlier than usual. Unperturbed, Elliot continued working. He dusted, swept, did the laundry and dishes. He went after cobwebs and even mopped the kitchen. It felt good to be productive, and when he finally stopped working in the early afternoon, he was tired but smiling. Still, he reflected as he relaxed on the sofa and watched TV, he needed to do more, something extra special that would say to his wife, "I'm sorry I screwed up, but I'm going to do better."

At first nothing occurred to him, but an afternoon talk show came to his rescue. The topic was longtime relationships, and more specifically, how to put the spark back into them after they'd started to fizzle. The panel of experts—a sexologist and a counselor who had written a book—had a long and imaginative list of ideas, several of which Elliot liked but reluctantly rejected; given recent events, he was afraid they might do more harm than good. When the sexologist suggested a gift of lingerie—"Something *she* likes, not just something that turns *you* on," he cautioned—Elliot was inspired. Kate likes teddies, he mused with a smile, and she still had the figure to fill one out nicely. He could buy one with the money he won last night on the baseball game. Yes, that's what he'd get her—an expensive new teddy, black or maybe blue. Something that reminded her of better days. Something that told her he thought she was sexy and desirable and pretty. Something that said he was sorry he'd forgotten just how much he loved her and needed her smile.

KATE DANDRIDGE WAS GETTING DESPERATE, and she was desperately trying not to let her children know. On the other hand, she had tried everything she could think of to make her husband realize just how bad things were getting. Elliot, as usual, refused to deal with it. Regardless, the bills kept coming. And as Kate opened the front door upon arriving home from work, she found more bills on the floor where they had dropped through the mail slot. With an expression of dread, she bent over and picked them up by the corners as if they were hazardous waste, and carried them into the kitchen, where she dropped them on the table.

Elliot better get a job pretty soon, she thought angrily. *Or we won't even have a house for the bills to be delivered to.*

And there were plenty of bills. Even before Matt's accident and Elliot's unemployment, they had already fallen behind. Elliot's slipshod budgeting had seen to that, and Kate hadn't realized just how bad their finances were until he stopped paying bills altogether and the job had fallen to her. Now they were so far behind that Kate didn't see how they could possibly catch up. Even working full-time, her salary didn't begin to cover the income they'd lost when Elliot got fired. Or quit. Or whatever he'd done to put them in this mess.

Kate stared at the bills and frowned. She hated feeling like this. She hated being desperate and perpetually angry. It wasn't in her nature.

Not even after all these years with Elliot, who always found a way to test her patience. But even though things had been bad before, they had never come close to how they were now, and Elliot had never seemed so cavalier about finding another job. The responsibilities they had shared (more or less, she mused) had all fallen to her, and were slowly but surely turning her into someone she really didn't like.

She meant to sit down and have a Pepsi and maybe check the latest news on CNN before opening the mail, but her fingers seemed to have a mind of their own. Before she knew what she was doing, she was thumbing through the bills and laying them out on the table. Visa. MasterCard. The mortgage. State Farm. The bill for the furniture they had bought on credit. Why did they all have to come at once? She shook her head glumly, and began opening the envelopes, one by one.

The mortgage was still current, thank God for that. The furniture store was a different matter and was making noises about repossession; Kate made a mental note to contact the store and see if she could work something out. She picked up the State Farm envelope with great trepidation. After Elliot's drunken encounter with a tree down the street, she wouldn't be surprised to find a cancellation notice on their car insurance. But the envelope contained a bill for their six-month premium, and Kate breathed a small sigh of relief, grateful for the temporary stay of execution.

The next bill wasn't too bad, either. They only owed MasterCard a comparatively small amount; Kate laid the bill aside, grateful for something she could safely put off paying. She started to open the Visa bill, then stopped. They shouldn't be getting a bill from Visa—it was their only credit card with a zero balance, the one they kept free for emergencies; she had been thinking of it particularly as their ace in the hole against losing their furniture, if it came to that. *Maybe it's just a notice that our limit has been increased,* she thought hopefully, trying to banish the suspicion that was forming in her mind. *Or one of those interest rate changes they're always sending out.* With nervous fingers, she tore open the envelope and looked inside. It was a bill, after all—and the zero balance had jumped to the sum owed of fifteen hundred dollars.

Kate sat down and stared at the statement with angry disbelief. There were twenty new charges in twenty days, all cash advances from an automated teller. The first thing she thought of was that their card had been stolen, but another possibility—the likeliest possibility—soon pushed that aside. It had to be Elliot, although God knew how he had managed to spend that much money. She had confronted him several times about the drinking and how much it cost, and on the occasions when he deigned to give her an answer, he indignantly claimed to be running a tab—a small one, he said—or that friends were paying for most of the rounds. Even if that was a lie, which it obviously was, that still wouldn't explain the amount on the statement. Not by a long shot.

How were they going to manage another monthly payment when they couldn't keep up with the ones they had? And what would they do for crisis money, now that Elliot had wasted half of it? Then another thought occurred to her: How much more had he withdrawn since the statement was run? After seeing that a week had already elapsed, she put down the bill and started to cry.

WHEN LORI WALKED in a few minutes later, Kate was still hunched over the kitchen table, hands covering her face as she cried. The teenager immediately dropped her schoolbooks on the table and went to her. "Mom, what's wrong?" she asked, tenderly pulling Kate's hands away from her face.

Mother and daughter faced each other, mirror images except for the differences wrought by age. In answer to Lori's question, Kate simply handed her the Visa bill.

Having become her mother's confidante over the last few months,

Lori immediately knew the implications of the credit card statement. After staring at it a few moments, she put it down and gave her mother an empathetic look. "Oh, Mom," she said. "He didn't!"

"He did," Kate answered.

Lori looked at the rest of the envelopes lying on the table. "How bad is it?"

Kate shook her head and tried to decide how much to tell her. She was grateful for the way Lori had risen to the challenges of the last couple months, and she wanted to tell her everything, to get it all off her chest, but it didn't seem right to give her the full, unadulterated version. "I don't know," she said in a tired voice. "It's bad, but I guess it could be worse." And then, before she realized what she was saying, she added, "But if something doesn't happen pretty soon, it's going to get worse real quick."

Lori glanced at the bills again, then looked at her mother. "I think it's time for me to get a job," she said.

Kate gave her a stricken, guilty look. The last thing she wanted was for Lori to start working because Elliot wouldn't. "I don't know, honey. I'd rather you concentrate on your schoolwork. . . ."

"School's almost over, Mom," Lori reminded her. "Finals are next week."

Kate looked surprised, having forgotten in the uproar of the last few months that the semester would end soon; luckily, her job with the district was year-round. "Well, let's wait until after finals, and then we'll talk about it," she replied, forcing a shaky smile. "Okay?"

"Okay. In the meantime, I'll ask around to see who's hiring." Lori smiled and bent down to hug her mother. "It'll be all right, Mom," she said reassuringly. "We've been through this before."

Kate hugged her back fiercely, and Lori started to leave but stopped in her tracks when they heard the front door open. Both women exchanged nervous looks, wondering if it was Elliot. When Matt walked in instead, Lori uttered an audible sigh of relief. "Hey, Spike," she said with forced heartiness. "How's it going?"

"Fine," Matt replied guardedly, glancing suspiciously from one woman to the other. By now he was so finely attuned to the tension in the house that he immediately knew when something was wrong. "What's up with you guys?"

"Not much," his sister answered evasively. "I just got home. Mom and I were just talking."

"About what?"

"Nothing, dear," Kate answered. Her eyes were still red-rimmed and her voice, while stronger, still trembled a bit. She silently chided herself for letting her son see her like this, for making it so obvious that something was wrong. Still, she wasn't about to confess what was happening, because Matt already felt responsible for the whole mess as it was. "Just, you know, girl talk," Kate went on, trying to sound lighthearted. "Nothing an eleven-year-old boy needs to hear."

"Oh," Matt replied, clearly unconvinced.

"How was school?" Kate asked, changing the subject.

"Okay," Matt replied with a slight frown. "But Miss Jahn gave us a lot of homework."

"Well, you better go upstairs and get started on it, then," his mother replied, wanting him out of earshot—and if possible, out of the house—when Elliot came home. "The sooner you get it done, the sooner you can go outside and play with your friends."

Matt went over and gave her a kiss and a knowing look, then grabbed a Pepsi from the refrigerator and went upstairs.

No sooner had he left than the back door opened and Elliot walked in. For once he looked to be in a rare good mood. "Hey," he said in an expansive voice, "it's my two gorgeous women!" He beamed at Kate, not noticing the tension on her face, then looked at his daughter and threw his arms open wide. "Come give your old man a big hug," he said to Lori, who glanced nervously at her mom, and did as she was told. "Mmmph, that feels good!" Elliot exclaimed, and winked at Kate. Lori gingerly disengaged herself from his bear hug, then held up her books, anxious to leave. "Well, I better get started on these," she said. After a quick, questioning glance at Kate, she left the kitchen as fast as she could.

Smiling hugely, Elliot turned to Kate. "God, you *are* gorgeous!" he said again. He bent down and gave her a big, sloppy kiss, never noticing in his excitement that she failed to reciprocate the sudden affection. Nor did he notice the not-so-subtle fury in her eyes or that her hands were balled into fists at her sides. Smiling, he stepped back and glanced around the kitchen. "Notice anything different?" he asked, referring to his cleaning job.

Kate frowned impatiently. "You're sober—for once," she said tartly.

Now Elliot frowned, but only for a second. "No—oh, never mind," he said, going back to the door and picking up the shopping bag he had left on the floor. Smiling with anticipation, he reached inside and pulled out a beautifully wrapped box. "Here," he said, thrusting it toward her. "This is for you."

"What is it?" Kate asked suspiciously.

"Open it and see!"

Not sure what to make of it all, Kate looked at the box uncertainly, then slowly unwrapped it and lifted the lid. Inside were two teddies, one black, one blue. Later she would regret that she hadn't handled things better, but right then all she could think about was whether their emergency Visa had paid for the garments. "Where did you get the money for these?" she asked without any of the delight her husband expected.

Elliot was instantly crestfallen, but tried to salvage the moment. "I won a hundred dollars on last night's game," he explained, forcing a smile. "Pujols hit a homer in the bottom of the twelfth."

"How nice for him," Kate replied in a sarcastic voice.

Elliot shook his head. "What's eating you?" he asked sourly. "I thought you'd like them."

"That's not the point. I want to know where you got the money," Kate demanded.

"I told you, I won it."

"No. I mean, where did you get the money to make the bet?"

"I've got a little," Elliot replied defensively, taking a step back.

"A little mad money?" Kate said testily.

"Something like that . . . "

"And I suppose it just falls out of the sky every day," Kate went on, gathering steam, but trying not to shout on account of the children, "or maybe the unemployment fairy creeps into our room every night and puts a little something under your pillow." She picked up the Visa statement and waved it in front of him. "Or maybe it comes out of a little machine down the block!"

Elliot stared at the bill with narrowed eyes, and looked at his wife with clear defiance. "What if it does? It's my card too."

Kate jumped to her feet and held out the statement. "This is supposed to be our emergency money!" she said in a trembling voice. "Remember, Elliot? And you're throwing it away on booze and bets!" She turned and tossed it on the table, then gestured at the other envelopes laid out around it. "How am I supposed to pay all of these?" she demanded in a desperate voice.

"A few more nights like last night—" Elliot began, forgetting he had vowed to swear off the bar.

"How much money did you lose before you won that lousy hundred dollars?" Kate cut in. "Two hundred? Five hundred? From the looks of that statement, you lost quite a bit! A few more nights like last night, and we'll be ruined for good!" She took a step forward and leaned into his face. All of the mounting frustration and fear and anger of the last few months welled up inside her and her voice grew louder as her emotions kept building. "It's bad enough that you've been drinking up our money," she went on. "But now you're gambling it away, too! What're you going to do when you hit the limit on the Visa?" she asked. Then she added with heavy sarcasm, "Surely you don't plan on getting a job!"

Elliot flinched as if she had just reached out and slapped him. His face grew dark and his voice grew hard, and his earlier resolve to turn over a new leaf flew right out the window. "I've got a plan," he said evenly. "Don't you worry about me."

Kate gave him a withering look. "It's not you I'm worried about!"

Elliot glared at her for a moment, and said, "Obviously not." He scooped up the gift box and started to walk away.

Kate felt a sinking sensation as he turned his back on her and headed for the door. "Where are you going?" she croaked, suddenly more afraid than angry. It had felt good to get her pound of flesh, but the last thing she wanted was for Elliot to go get drunk.

Elliot turned around. The expression on his face was one that Kate had never seen before, and one she hoped she'd never see again; it froze her in her tracks until after he was gone. "I'm going to the bar," Elliot replied coldly, dumping her gift in the trash with elaborate fanfare. "People appreciate me there. Don't bother waiting up."

IN HIS SECRET hiding place under the porch, Matt sat in the darkness after sneaking outside, listening to the argument and waiting for it to end. It was hard to sit there and listen instead of running off to Tommy's. It made him feel the way he felt when he hadn't prepared for a test at school, or when he watched scary movies by himself late at night—all he wanted to do was to jump up and run as fast as he could without ever looking back. Listening to his mom and dad fight made him feel exactly like that, only ten times worse. And lately, it seemed they were fighting all the time.

Once he heard the back door slam and saw his father head down the sidewalk, Matt waited awhile longer, and crawled out from under the porch. Frowning, he glanced down the block to make sure Elliot was gone, then went around front and plopped down on the steps. After glancing over his shoulder at the front door, he sat there for a moment, shaking his head. Things were getting worse, and he couldn't understand why, because he was doing everything he could think of to make them better. He said his prayers every night, and never forgot to include his family. He tried harder in school. He even made his bed and picked up his room without waiting to be told. But obviously that wasn't enough—if he had been sent back from heaven to help his family, then he was failing miserably.

I wish my guardian angel was here, he mused, and kicked at the step. *Or I wish he would call me. Maybe he could tell me how to accomplish my mission.* But his guardian angel had been strangely silent, and Matt didn't know if that meant he was supposed to figure this out for himself or if his angel was still in the tunnel. Either way, he was starting to wish he'd get a little help.

There was one thing he could do, it suddenly occurred to him: he could call Mr. Qualls and see if he'd hired someone for the paper route yet. The day before the accident, his principal had asked him if he was interested in the job, but Matt had forgotten about it. *That would help out,* he thought with a glimmer of hope. *It wouldn't be a lot, but it's better than nothing—if the job's still open.* Of course, he'd still need a bike—his had been pretty well totaled in the accident, and he hadn't had the nerve to ask for a new one—but Tommy had an old one he'd probably let him borrow or maybe even buy. The thought of getting back on a bike was a little bit scary, but not half as scary as what was happening to his family. And since his hospital bills were part of the problem, it was the least he could do. Suddenly excited, Matt jumped up from the steps, raced inside and headed straight for the phone. Fifteen minutes later, he had his very first job and a replacement for his bike.

~

DESPITE HER HUSBAND'S snide suggestion, Kate Dandridge did wait up for Elliot to get home. Her intentions weren't to rehash the argument in the hope of getting a better result—she knew better than to do that when Elliot was drunk—but to settle the problem in a different way. So when Elliot stumbled in at a quarter to two and promptly fell asleep on the living room couch, Kate waited ten minutes and came downstairs. After carefully removing the wallet from the back pocket of his pants, she tiptoed to the moonlight streaming through the window, took out the Visa and replaced the wallet. Then, she made her way quietly to their upstairs bedroom, found a pair of scissors and quickly cut the card into a dozen tiny pieces.

JUST DOWN THE HALL, behind another bedroom door at the top of the stairs, a worried but determined boy had just fallen asleep after hours of lying awake and staring out the window. His mind, as usual, had been dwelling on his family and his guardian angel, and the sacred promise that bound them together. So, naturally, in his sleep he dreamed that night of the very same things—

Of his mother and father, the fights, the drinking, and dark shadows lurking in the corners of their house . . .

And of a red brick building with bars on the windows, and a man and a woman standing by a Jeep parked out front. The woman seemed familiar, but he just couldn't place her. The man, however, he recognized right away—it was his guardian angel, the man in the tunnel whose name was John—and he was calling Matt's name and telling him to come meet him.

SEVENTEEN

The End of the Tunnel, the End of Dreams

FOR THE FIRST WEEK after Will's death, John felt as if he were trapped in a long, bad dream. The first few days were the worst: driving home from the hospital after being told Will was dead, the crying jag triggered by Bobbi Smith's visit and, throughout it all, the overwhelming sense of shock and loss. He had also made the call to Mr. and Mrs. Gibson, and it had been every bit as difficult as he had expected. After Will's services—a somber funeral Mass conducted by Father Ryan and attended by several hundred people, including Will's parents and sister (whom John immediately liked)—John had gone back to work on Wednesday morning, grateful for something else to occupy his mind.

But work helped him get through only part of the day. The hardest times came when he was alone in the evenings, and especially at night. Watching the news only made him feel worse, and when he went to bed he rarely slept for more than a few hours. The next morning he always woke up feeling fatigued, depressed and uncharacteristically irritable. When the school semester ended the following week, it didn't take him long to add restless to the list.

That he seemed to have stopped dreaming was part of the problem. The events of Will's death had decisively answered most of the questions that had plagued him for months, but he still had no answer to the question of *why*.

Why was he sent back after dying in the hospital?

Why was he given the mysterious power to ease someone's spirit by sharing the thoughts that caused emotional pain?

And why, above all else, was he given these dreams of people in trouble if he wasn't meant to help them avoid the danger? That burden had gotten too heavy to bear.

After what happened to Will, he needed those answers even more than before, so it was particularly frustrating that now, of all times, he had ceased to dream. Of course, he knew the dreams would return, if for no other reason than there were so many loose ends. But his grief and the waiting were driving him crazy. He also had a hunch—and it was a very strong hunch that was almost as daunting as being left in the dark—that the lull in his dreams was the calm before the storm.

RATHER THAN SIT back and wait for the dreams to resume, John tried to find answers by other means. He started by checking the psychology books in his own personal library, but soon realized that he was looking in the wrong place. His college textbooks didn't have a single listing for near-death experiences, and although several of his more recent books did, the information he found was sketchy, at best; most of the authors treated NDEs more as a curiosity better left to theologians than as a viable subject for psychological concern.

The next day he went to the public library to look for anything remotely connected to near-death experiences. He knew there had been some well-publicized research done over the last ten or fifteen years—although he hadn't paid it much attention—and he started there. But the articles in the psychological journals had the same biased attitude he'd found before, coupled with an almost fanatical determination to prove that NDEs could be entirely explained by physiological events. Although he didn't have the kind of proof that would have convinced the authors, John knew they were wrong, so he went back to the card catalog to look for titles that sounded more open-minded.

He was pleasantly surprised to find there were quite a few books on the subject, including several best sellers he had previously ignored because they had seemed too sensational or questionable to take seriously. Now, of course, they didn't sound so sensational at all, and with a twinge of guilt for having dismissed them so easily, he searched the shelves anxiously. An hour later, he had chosen several that looked highly promising, as well as a few titles on death and dreams.

That evening, he threw himself into his reading with the single-mindedness of a religious convert, and the more he read, the more his need for additional knowledge grew. He read firsthand accounts of ordinary people who had NDEs, case studies by doctors and medical researchers who had started out skeptical but wound up believing, and literature from some of the world's great religions that described the same experience without giving it the label. Almost everything he read struck a chord deep within him, as if some inner voice were telling him, *This is truth! Pay attention!* By Saturday, when he had read most of the books—and some of them twice—he no longer felt isolated and depressed and confused. He also knew he had taken a small but important step toward understanding not only the last few months of his life, but his past and present and future as well.

It was reassuring to know that he wasn't alone, and interesting to compare his own experience to others. Many people reported going farther in the tunnel and experiencing things John hadn't encountered—or at least remembered, as yet—but there were also many similarities: the out-of-body experience, the indescribable feelings of peace and love, the trip through the void, being greeted by loved ones. And even though he seemed to be unique in two crucial matters—the prophetic dreams and his strange psychic ability—having everything else validated helped him feel better about his own experience. It also seemed to confirm his long-held suspicion that there was more to remember—much, much more—and after climbing into bed shortly before midnight, he fell asleep praying that his dream would continue that very same night.

And it did . . .

LEFT ALONE in the tunnel after his grandmother disappeared, John turned and saw the person she had said was waiting for him. Up ahead was a figure standing in the blazing, white-gold light that had illumined the entire way from the mouth of the tunnel. John stared in wonder and realized that the figure wasn't merely standing in the light, but was somehow the *source* of it—a being who had the shape and face of a man, but who was clearly not a being of flesh but of light, a light that suffused his entire form and radiated beyond him like a dazzling aura of purity and power. It was a man whose identity he instinctively knew, and whose countenance was easily the most beautiful sight he had ever beheld, full of love and compassion and joy and strength, and his presence was overwhelming and completely daunting, yet radiated reassurance and unconditional love. There was no doubt in John's mind that this Being of Light at the end of the tunnel was Jesus, and with no further hesitation, he began the last leg of his trip down the tunnel.

Jesus smiled and held out his hands as he drew near, but John fell to his knees and met his gaze timidly with a heart that was bursting with conflicting emotions. The doubts and fears he had felt after dying—and the lifetime of doubt that preceded that moment—came back to him now and filled him with shame. "I'm sorry," he said simply, and lowered his head.

A hand reached down and drew him gently to his feet. At the touch, a host of emotions flooded John's mind: astonishment and awe, relief, excitement, sublime serenity and, most of all, love, a love like none he had ever experienced. "Your fear in the void was perfectly understandable," a rich, soothing voice reassured him; as had happened with his grandmother, he received the words directly in his mind, without the need for speech or hearing. "And your moments of belief far outweigh your moments of doubt. No one holds them against you."

John gazed up into his Lord's eyes and knew it was true. He felt transformed, transcendent, exalted, whole; one with himself, the Light, the whole of creation. And as the Light reached out and embraced his body—his *spiritual* body, he suddenly knew—John's entire being was suffused with pure, overwhelming love. It was every hug and kiss, every hope and dream, every moment of laughter and happiness and freedom rolled into one. It was unconditional love, and it banished all doubts and painful emotions, all secret insecurities and feelings of isolation and guilt and shame. A perfect love that filled him with joy and comfort and purpose, and which gave him the strength to face what came next.

Much like a high-speed, three-dimensional movie or a hologram that was more real than reality itself, episodes of John's life began flashing before him. Mean or hurtful or selfish things he had done in his life played out before his eyes, as well as acts that were good or thoughtful or loving. One after another, the choices he had made sprang back to life—good and bad, those that helped him grow or held him back, and several he hadn't even realized were choices at the time.

Not only did he see the events of his life, he *relived* them also, re-experiencing the full force of his thoughts and emotions without benefit of self-deception or rationalization; the light that surrounded him illuminated everything with the power of truth. He also saw the impact his choices had had in shaping his life. He saw how the times when his existence had seemed pointless or headed for disaster had always been preceded by doubt and fear, and he saw the energies he had drawn on—both positive and negative—to move himself forward or hold himself back.

What made the review even more extraordinary was that not only did he reexperience his life from his own point of view, he also experienced the emotional impact on the others involved. He felt their hurt and disappointment or anger and pain when he'd wronged them; he shared their comfort and gratitude or joy and love when he'd shown he cared. More important, he saw how each of his acts—both good and bad—had a far-reaching, ripple effect on the people around him: like a pebble dropped casually into the middle of a pond, a kind or caring gesture was often passed on by the person he'd touched, and so on down the line of almost infinite contacts; likewise, a cruel or thoughtless act had the same effect.

The experience illuminated the path of his life, and he realized that path was a spiritual journey. His existence as a spirit from eternities prior to his physical life was also revealed, as well as his choice of when his earthly life would begin and how it would unfold. He was shown how his life had been a learning experience, a priceless opportunity for spiritual growth. Indeed, the whole reason for living was to experience the challenges life had to offer, its moments of hardship and pain and loss, as well as its moments of joy and discovery and, ultimately, love.

He also learned that that there had been far fewer coincidences than he might have supposed, that virtually everything in his life had happened for a reason that was part of a plan. And he saw that when he'd felt overwhelmed or helpless in the face of his problems, he hadn't been alone. Like a man dying of thirst in the middle of a desert, who for reasons of pride or lack of faith believes the water in the distance is only a mirage, he had simply neglected to look beyond himself and accept the help that was there all along. Angels and loved ones—both living and dead—had always been around him, and God was never farther than a prayer away.

Yet, despite the mistakes and shameful failures, the review of his life was a transcendent experience, and John realized that this was the inevitable judgment he'd always been taught was every man's fate— the only difference being that it was light-years away from what he'd expected. There had been no fiercely scowling white-haired God reciting John's sins and pronouncing judgment; rather, the Being of Light had stood by his side, radiating love and unconditional acceptance. Sensing no condemnation from his heavenly "judge," only satisfaction and joy as John grasped the lessons of what he was seeing, it finally came to him that the purpose of the review wasn't to judge and condemn but to instruct and uplift, to help him learn from his mistakes as well as his successes. It was a profound revelation, and once the life review had ended, his heart was overflowing with gratitude and love.

As the last of the images faded from view, a lifetime of questions flooded his mind. Emboldened by the knowledge he had just received, he couldn't resist asking for yet more answers:

Is this heaven?

In a manner of speaking. There is a veil that separates heaven from earth, rendering it invisible to earthly eyes. At this moment, you are parting the veil.

And is there a hell?

Not close by. Those who are afraid to approach the Light create their own hell for as long as they wish. You may have sensed some of them as you traveled through the void.

Do you meet everyone who comes through the tunnel?

Eventually. But a spirit who chose to be Jewish in his earthly life might be greeted by Moses or an angel of mercy, and a Muslim by Mohammed. And a Buddhist might be welcomed by Buddha himself.

I was always taught you were the only Way . . .

There are many ways. I am the Light, and the Light is Truth, and the way to Truth is love, because God is love. Earthly religions all claim to teach the Truth, but they disguise it with rules and man-made doctrines. What matters most is love, and anyone who lives by love already believes in the Truth and comes to the Light. You are all God's children, regardless of the religion you chose in your life.

Why does there have to be so much suffering in the world?

There doesn't. The truth is that you are responsible for more of your own pain and hardship than you know. You are children of the Creator, made in His image. That means your thoughts, your words, your actions, all have creative power. And what you create is up to you. Negative or fearful thoughts and words and actions literally call into being the negative conditions that cause hardship and suffering. In the same fashion, thoughts and words and actions that are positive or loving bring about happiness, prosperity and health. It is a gradual process, done piece by piece, like the construction of a building. Often, you do not even realize it is happening. Therefore you must constantly be aware of what you think, say and do.

This holds true, as well, for humanity as a whole. What each of you can do individually, you can also do collectively. That is why you have wars, why your environment no longer functions the way it was intended and why natural disasters are occurring more often. It is not God's doing, but yours.

But why does God permit us to make such a mess of our personal lives? And why is there so much evil and tragedy in the world right now? Why does He allow us to do the things we do to each other and to the planet?

Because free will is inherent in the power to create. You cannot create if you cannot choose. Every moment of every day, you are deciding between positive and negative alternatives—between love and fear— and the decision you make creates your reality by the energy it attracts. When you or someone around you chooses negative energy, suffering ensues.

Even so, something positive can come from negative choices. Suffering often precedes growth, just as death precedes life. The first is a transition that makes the second possible. Remember, crucifixion is always followed by resurrection. So, in suffering lie the seeds of blessing. All creation serves a purpose, including the struggles your world is experiencing now.

What purpose can possibly be served by diseases like cancer? Or the worldwide AIDS epidemic?

AIDS is not a punishment, as some would have you believe. It is a disease, nothing more. To say so is an affront to the Heavenly Father. Before beginning your earthly journey, each of you chooses the life experiences that will help you achieve spiritual growth. Often, that includes suffering. And sometimes, it is chosen not only for your own sake.

To suffer for the sake of others is the noblest calling a spirit can accept in his earthly life. Many of those suffering with cancer and AIDS and other afflictions are doing so not just for their own growth but for the growth of others. They suffer to teach you about life and death, about fear and love, about courage and compassion. And you treat them the way you have always treated prophets: you listen from afar, afraid to get too close; you apprehend that their words are true, but refuse to embrace them because the growth that would require calls for more courage than you think you have; then, you shun them and send them away, until the day finally comes when you can bear to listen again. Such spirits should not be despised or pitied, but honored.

This really isn't a dream, is it?

No. But when you go back, you will not remember it until it comes to you in a dream.

Go back? I thought I died.

You did, but it was not your time. You still have important work to do. . . . It won't be easy, but you won't be alone. And I will give you a gift to remind you of me and to help you complete your earthly mission.

I don't understand. . . .

You will. All in due time, as your grandmother said. When you need

*to know, you will. But not before. For now, there is something I want
you to see. . . .*

John glanced down and saw a bright red piece of plastic being
held out to him. He took it and saw that it was the second half of
the broken name tag his grandmother had given him before sending
him on to the end of the tunnel. This piece spelled out MANDYLOR in
the same white beveled font used on the other. With a puzzled expression, he joined the halves. Complete, the name tag read HOLLY
MANDYLOR. He turned it over and looked at the back. Beneath the silver
pin it said GOLDEN SPUR CASINO, LAS VEGAS, NEVADA. When John glanced up
with a question on his lips, he was directed to turn around and look
behind him.

The tunnel was gone and in its place was the living room of what
appeared to be a small apartment. The furniture reminded him of
his own in the sense that all of the pieces didn't quite mesh into a single decorating scheme, as if the owner had started out with hand-me-
downs and had only been able to replace them one at a time. The
main difference was that this room showed evidence of a female touch,
and even though the furnishings were in various stages of newness or
wear, most of them were pretty and had been arranged in a way that
showed great thought and care. It was a work in progress, but a warm
and inviting one.

As he watched, a young woman came into the room carrying a
drink in one hand and a sheet of paper in the other. Tall and dressed
in an ankle-length robe of emerald silk, she had auburn hair and
large, innocent-looking eyes the same shade of green as the robe she
wore. Her face was angular and would have been pretty had it not
looked so troubled and filled with despair, and there was an open and
vulnerable air about her; even if it was nothing more than the overall
effect of her wide eyes and frown, it made her obvious distress that
much more painful to see. John's heart immediately went out to her,
and he realized there was something about her that seemed familiar,
even though he'd never seen her before. And then he knew, without

actually being told, that the woman was the one to whom the name tag belonged—Holly Mandylor.

As if in confirmation, the woman walked over to the coffee table, set down her drink and picked up an identical red name tag that had been lying in an unused ashtray. She held it in her open hand, staring at it forlornly. After a few moments, her fingers closed on the tag and she shifted her attention to the sheet of paper she held in her other hand. She read it once with an inscrutable expression, and laid it carefully in the middle of the glass-top coffee table. Then she opened her fist, glared at the piece of shiny red plastic that bore her name, grabbed it with both hands and snapped it in half. A small sob escaped her lips, and she stared at the pieces, one in each hand, then tossed them disdainfully next to the sheet of paper she had laid on the coffee table. Picking up her drink, she closed her eyes and drained the glass, then walked to the bathroom with unsteady steps. . . .

SHE FELT LIKE A ZOMBIE. Hollowed out and empty. Drained of all emotion. Dead but still moving. And the least little thing, whether it was answering the phone or getting out of bed, was more than she could manage. Everything seemed to require more effort than she felt like giving. *Everything except this,* she thought as she trudged into the bathroom.

This wasn't the first time she'd been through a rough patch, when things fell apart and conspired against her putting them back together. And it wasn't even the worst time. But the snowballing effect of a long line of setbacks and bitter disappointments, of fresh starts gone bad and of bleak, lingering moods was more than she could take. The despair had gotten too familiar, and seemed to have insinuated itself into every corner of her mind. Now it was always with her, and the lullaby of darkness it whispered in her ear made perfect sense—these days, it was the only thing that made sense. Going on certainly didn't—how could she go on with no job or money, with no place to live and no one to love? It wasn't fair. . . . And she just . . . couldn't . . . deal with it anymore. . . .

At least someone will find the note and tell Gil Turner what he did to my life, she mused with macabre satisfaction.

She supposed it was a bit melodramatic to name her ex-boss in the note, but she felt like she had to. One way or another, he'd had a hand in everything that had led to this point. He'd stabbed her in the back by firing and blackballing her, and then added insult to injury with that so-called interview at the Mirage; since that humiliating disaster, everything had just gotten worse. Thanks to Turner, she was cut off from the casinos she loved so much, had no money to speak of and was losing her apartment at the end of the month. *You just can't mess with people's lives like they don't mean anything,* she thought bitterly. *It's wrong—no, it's worse than wrong: it's just plain evil.* And if there was any justice in the world, her note would cause him some trouble, too.

Frowning furiously, Holly bent over the bathtub and put the stopper in the drain. She hesitated for a moment and pulled out the knob, turning it to the left so the water would be nice and hot; she'd heard that made it go faster. Then she straightened up and watched as the tub began filling with steaming water.

She slipped off her robe and let it fall to the floor, and leaned over to test the water. It was hotter than she normally liked, but it wasn't her intention to take a bath anyway. She shook her head with great sadness, still finding it difficult to believe it had come to this, then stepped into the tub. She eased into the water. After the initial shock, the enveloping heat almost felt good and she could feel her muscles begin to relax. With the cloud of steam rising up all around her and the sound of water splashing and bubbling, she could almost imagine she had slipped into a hot tub to soak away the troubles of a trying day.

But she couldn't and she hadn't.

The bitter irony of it all welled up inside her and she turned to stare at the single-edged razor that waited in the soap dish a few inches from her hand. *There* was the only real permanent solution to all of her problems. She'd already considered all of her options, and one by one, they had turned to smoke. She no longer had the energy, or even the inclination, to continue trying and she couldn't see the point of living without hope. Why keep getting back up and dusting yourself off if you knew you were just going to get knocked down again? It seemed like all of her life had been like that—just when things started working out, something would happen to screw it all up. She stared at the rising water and thought grimly, *Only a fool would think that's ever going to change. Jinxed is jinxed, till death do us part.*

For as long as she could remember, bad luck had followed her like Mary's little lamb. The sad thing was that as often as bad luck had screwed things up, there were just as many times when she had done it all by herself. And there was certainly no reason to think that would ever change, either—she was who she was: a person who craved happiness more than anything in the world but always found a way to scare it off fast when it got too close.

She had the intelligence and self-awareness to recognize the pattern of her own self-sabotage, but most of the time she didn't realize what she was doing until it was already too late. The process was simple but so deeply ingrained that it was difficult to stop: as soon as she realized things were going well—in her job, a relationship, or her life in general—it seemed like some perverse part of her mind always insisted that she pinch herself to see if she was dreaming, and if the answer was no, it whispered in her ear that she probably didn't deserve her current good fortune and would end up losing it. Since that was one of her greatest fears—that she'd wake up one morning and find it gone, that the cosmic forces in charge of such things would realize their mistake and take it away because she wasn't judged worthy—she usually took the initiative and beat them to the punch. Oh yes, she knew the pattern, and she knew it was wrong, but being aware of the problem and being able to fix it were two different things.

Of course, this wasn't one of those times when she was responsible for screwing things up. For once she was innocent, a victim of forces beyond her control. Even so, there was no comfort in it. Trouble was trouble, regardless of who caused it. If she didn't cause it, then fate or chance or just bad luck would always step in and pick up the gauntlet. That was a pattern she also knew.

After turning off the water, she picked up the razor and stared fixedly at its edge for a very long while. It was a brand-new blade, with no nicks or dull spots. If she was lucky—for a change—the job would go quickly, and it would all be over in a matter of minutes.

For once in her life she was grateful she had no parents, or a husband and children she had to consider. With so many tragic deaths in the world over the last few years, who would notice one more? Tina would be upset, as would a few other friends, but they would get over it. With any luck, Turner would feel guilty, but she didn't think it likely. All in all, she was pretty much free to do as she wanted. . . .

Still holding the razor, she turned off the water, then stared into space and brushed back a strand of damp, limp hair that had fallen in her eyes. *Are you sure you want to do this?* she asked herself again.

Yes . . . the answer came back after a long hesitation. *What else is there?*

Dancing topless for a crowd of leering old men? Waiting tables in a Denny's for the rest of her life? Those things would kill her just as surely as the razor; the only difference was that they would take longer to do it. Holly shook her head and started to cry. No, this was the way it had to be. A few cuts, some blood and the whole thing would be over. Once and for all, without dragging it out. She reached up with her free hand and wiped away the tears, then slowly lowered her arm down to the hot, steaming water. After one last glance at the damp, sharp razor, she inhaled deeply and touched its blade to the soft, wet skin of her trembling wrist. "If there is a God, I hope He understands," she whispered hoarsely. With a gasp of pain, she pushed in the blade until it broke the skin, made a quick, long slice as deep as she could, then switched the blade hurriedly to her other trembling hand and sliced her right wrist in exactly the same way.

EIGHTEEN

Men with a Mission

WHEN JOHN WOKE UP at 4 A.M., his heart was pounding and his mind was racing. *My God!* he kept thinking, over and over, in awe then shock, excitement then horror. Within a few short minutes, he had been taken to the pinnacle of human existence and then stared into the abyss of human despair. *My God!* seemed the only appropriate response.

He couldn't stop thinking about what had occurred at the end of the tunnel. It *was* something for which he should be grateful, as Will had said. It was a miracle in every meaningful sense of the word, and his mind still reeled from the memory of the moment the Light had touched him. The feelings of completeness and harmony and love were with him still, and would be, he knew, for the rest of his life. From this point on, he would never be the same, and he would never again think of his NDE as anything other than the ultimate gift a man can receive while still on this side of the celestial veil.

He also couldn't stop thinking about one of the responsibilities that evidently came with the gift: Holly Mandylor. The implications of what he'd been shown were disturbingly clear: here was someone else who was about to die before her time—and at her own hand—someone who had hit rock bottom and given up on life, who didn't understand that she wasn't alone. And for whatever reason, it had been entrusted to him to keep her from ending her life prematurely. It was a sobering challenge, but after Will's tragic death and the encounter he'd just had with the Being of Light, it was one he never even considered declining.

It was also a situation that recent experience had taught him was probably urgent. Like most of the other tragedies he had seen in his dreams, he couldn't tell if Holly's was past, in the present or slated for the future. It was theoretically possible she was lying in a bathtub bleeding to death at that very moment—the windows of her apartment had been dark in the vision, so the events he had seen would happen at night—but the following evening seemed a likelier possibility. Regardless, he wouldn't merely wait until he knew for certain.

The first thing he did after turning on the light was reach for the phone. Because Holly Mandylor was such an unusual name, it only took a minute to get her number from Las Vegas directory assistance. After thanking the operator, he hung up and stared at the number scribbled on the notepad. What would he say if she answered the phone? *I know what you're planning, and please don't do it?* He thought about it for a while, and realized there really wasn't anything else he could say. Holly was a stranger, and if he told her the whole truth, she'd think he was nuts and cut the connection before he was halfway done. But if he kept it anonymous and deliberately mysterious, she might be shaken up enough to rethink her plans.

Still, he knew he hadn't been drawn into the affair merely to make a phone call; at best, that would only be a stopgap measure.

He would make the call, but only to buy time, and then he'd leave for Las Vegas as soon as he could—and hope he'd have a plan to explain his appearance by the time he arrived. Holly's failure to answer the phone a few minutes later, and then when he called twice more over the next half hour, only confirmed his conviction that he had to leave.

By the time the sun came up, he was almost packed. Initially, he had thrown only a few things into the oversized gym bag, but after recalling the despair on Holly's face, he realized it was likely he'd be gone for more than one night. He couldn't just walk into someone's life, tell her to cheer up and go on his way. So he emptied out the bag and hurriedly packed a suitcase instead, taking more clothes and some of the books he was reading.

When he walked into the living room, Alex took one look at the suitcase and ran behind the couch, whimpering. John set down the luggage, then went over and squatted next to the dog. "It's okay, Al," he cooed, stroking her head and giving her what he hoped was a reassuring smile. "I won't be gone long. A few days, tops." Privately, he wondered if that would be the case, and when Alex looked unconvinced, he kissed her on the head and gave her a hug. She obviously missed him a great deal when he was away, and the feeling was mutual, to say the least—when Dr. Bucheit had spayed her a few months back, John had missed her terribly, even though she had stayed at the clinic for only one night. Now he was tempted to take her along, but after mulling it over, he realized that wasn't feasible. Instead, he'd call Bobbi on his way to Las Vegas and ask her to dog-sit, as she usually did.

He'd have to ask Bobbi to call Margie Mullins, too, and let her know he'd be gone for a few days. He still wasn't sure what excuse he'd use for leaving so abruptly, but he couldn't just say he was on a mission from God. He knew he'd have to explain everything once he got back—he'd kept the full story of his experience to himself too long, and it wasn't the type of thing that was meant to be kept secret—but there wasn't time now. He went to the phone and dialed Holly's number one last time. When no one answered, he picked up the suitcase, waved good-bye to Alex and headed for the door.

WHEN ALL OF THE OTHER KIDS filed out of the Sunday school room, Matt Dandridge stayed behind to talk to his teacher. He liked Miss Thompson a lot, partly because she laughed at his jokes and partly because he felt he could trust her, and he often hung around after class was over. Today, however, his motives weren't just social; he had an important question he needed to ask, and he knew that if anyone could answer it honestly and without making him feel stupid, Miss Thompson was the one.

After some hemming and hawing, he finally worked up the nerve. "Miss Thompson," he began sheepishly, "can you answer a question for me?"

As if sensing this wasn't going to be merely one of those how-did-Jonah-live-in-the-whale? questions, Miss Thompson stopped tidying up the classroom and gave Matt her undivided attention. "If I know the answer I will," she replied, smiling.

Matt nodded absently, and glanced away for a moment. When he looked back at Miss Thompson, his expression was serious, especially for Matt. "Are we here for a reason?" he asked.

Miss Thompson's eyes widened slightly, as if the question surprised her. "What do you mean, Matt?" she asked cautiously.

"Does God put us here for a reason?" Matt responded. "You know, like, does everybody have a mission to accomplish?"

"I guess you could put it that way, yes."

Matt knit his brows in concentration. "Do you know what your mission is?" he asked in an earnest voice.

Miss Thompson considered the question, then answered, "I think so." She smiled. "Part of it is to teach Sunday school."

"Did God tell you that?"

"Not in so many words, I guess," Miss Thompson replied. "But I feel like it's what He wants me to do."

Matt thought about it for a minute. "So God doesn't really tell people what their mission is?"

"In one way or another He does. But sometimes He wants us to figure it out for ourselves, I think." Miss Thompson smiled again. "That's what makes life interesting."

Matt nodded and his gaze drifted away as he considered the answer.

"It sounds like maybe you've been thinking about what your mission is," Miss Thompson prodded.

Matt looked up. His expression was sober. "Yeah, I have. I've been thinking about it a lot."

Miss Thompson nodded approvingly. "That's good, Matt. I'm glad to hear it." She patted his arm and added, "I'll be sure to include you in my prayers and ask God to help you figure out what it is."

"You will?" Matt replied hopefully.

"You bet I will," Miss Thompson said with a warm smile. "That's what friends are for." Then, she added in a less lighthearted tone, "But don't give up if you don't get an answer right away. Sometimes it takes a while to figure out what God wants us to do. Important things often take time."

Matt nodded again, thanked his teacher and got up to leave. He had already had an idea of what his mission might be, and talking to Miss Thompson made it a little clearer, although he still wasn't sure. He just hoped she was wrong about needing more time. The way things were going, there wasn't much left.

WHEN MATT GOT HOME a few hours later, he felt better than he had in several weeks. After talking to Miss Thompson he had reached a decision: this was the day things would start turning around, the day he would begin to accomplish his mission. The key, he had decided, was to get his parents into a better mood. Walking home from church, he had thought of a way—two ways, actually. He realized they wouldn't fix things completely, but for the first time in weeks he was actually hopeful.

He only stuck around the house long enough to see what kind of mood everybody was in, hoping that for once it wouldn't be a bad one. The house was kind of quiet but no crisis was brewing that he could tell. Not only that, but his dad had stayed home instead of going to the bar. It looked like today was a good day for his plan.

The first thing he did was go down to Main Street. He liked the mall better than the riverfront shops on Main Street, which was a restored historical area with riverboats and cobblestone streets. But it was his mother's favorite place to go on Sunday afternoons, and the last time Matt had gone with her she had seen a small silk flower arrangement in a shop called the Flower Petaler. She had wanted to buy the arrangement but talked herself out of it because of the family's money problems. Matt knew she still wanted it because every once in a while she'd mention the flowers and give a little sigh, like she always did when she saw something pretty that was more than she could afford. So today he was going to use some of the money he had just earned from his new paper route to buy the arrangement.

He also had a surprise in mind for his dad. When Matt had bought the bike from Tommy the previous week, Tommy's father had mentioned that he had two box seat tickets to next Saturday's Cards-Cubs game that he needed to sell; he was willing to part with them for only ten dollars. Matt had immediately thought of his dad but hadn't had the money. Now he did.

By four o'clock, he had baseball tickets in the pocket of his jeans and a beautiful silk flower arrangement he'd bought from the Flower Petaler. Since his reason for taking the paper route was to help pay the bills, he was a little bit worried his mom might get mad that he'd spent some of his money. But he'd only spent a little, and if the gifts made his parents feel better, as he suspected they would, then it was worth the risk. As he snuck into the garage to hide the flowers until after dinner, he couldn't help hoping that after today things would get better, and then keep getting better until everything was okay and his parents were the people they used to be.

"I DON'T KNOW, Matt," Kate Dandridge said uncertainly. "I appreciate the sentiment, I really do, but I'm not sure you're ready to cook an entire meal by yourself."

"Aw, come on, Mom," Matt replied with an earnest smile. He was trying to implement phase two of his plan: preparing Sunday dinner for the rest of his family, something he'd never attempted or even considered before. He had approached his mom with the idea a few moments earlier as she read a magazine at the dining room table. Lori was standing behind her, looking over her shoulder. "You deserve a day off," Matt continued. "Wouldn't you rather watch TV or read or something? I can do this. I know I can."

"Go on, Kate, let the boy try it," Elliot weighed in from his spot on the sofa. He had stayed home this particular Sunday afternoon— partly to watch the baseball game but mainly because he was too hungover to even think about walking the five blocks to the bar—and the last thing he wanted was to hear his son whine. "If he wants to help out, let him help out."

Matt glanced at his dad, surprised but grateful for the unexpected support, and took it as a sign his plan would go well. He looked back at his mother and gave her a smile she found hard to resist. "Come on, Mom. I'll do a good job, I promise. Really."

Kate looked at her son's imploring green eyes and felt her reservations begin slipping away. "I don't know . . ."

"It sounds like a great idea to me," Lori chimed in, sensing what her brother was trying to do. "If it'll make you feel any better, I'll give Spike a hand."

Kate finally gave in. "All right," she said, smiling, "I guess it's okay. Just try not to make a mess—and use the cookbook!"

"No problem," Matt replied, grinning at his sister. "Don't worry about a thing, Mom. It's under control."

The meal wasn't fancy, but it turned out fine. Lori had tried to minimize the chances of a culinary disaster by steering her brother toward spaghetti and meatballs, something simple that everybody liked. Lori had actually made the meatballs but Matt had done the rest of the cooking under her watchful eye, and he had done a good job without making a mess. Lori was impressed, and she told him so.

Matt finished eating before everyone else, and as he accepted the compliments (including one from his father) it was all he could do to contain his smile and growing excitement. The meal had gone even better than he'd hoped, and as it neared its end, everyone was more relaxed than they had been in weeks—Elliot actually smiled a few times and even joined in the conversation, if only halfheartedly. It was a welcome pause to everyone around the table, a bittersweet reminder of how things used to be. To Matt is was proof he was on the right track and that it was time to move on to phase three of his plan.

Since there would be no dessert—that had been one of the first things to go when money got tight, along with steaks on Sunday and Friday-night shrimp—Matt excused himself from the table as everyone was finishing, and hurried out to the garage to get the surprises for his parents. He returned a few minutes later carrying a large brown bag and smiling hugely.

"Mom. Dad," he said, looking at each of them. "Close your eyes."

Kate and Elliot exchanged puzzled glances. "Why?" Kate asked.

"Yeah," Elliot echoed, "what are you up to?"

"Don't worry, I'm not going to play a trick on you," Matt replied, smiling slyly. He glanced at Lori and winked, and Lori looked back, trying to suppress a smile; Matt had told her of the surprise while they were fixing dinner and she had solemnly promised not to give it away. "Just close your eyes, *please*."

Elliot looked at Kate. "Guess we better do as he says," he proposed with mock seriousness. "We don't want to get grounded or anything." Kate laughed and quickly agreed. She was intrigued as much as Elliot, and even more than that, she didn't want to do anything to jeopardize the near-normalcy they were experiencing; it had been far too long since the last time she'd seen it.

After they closed their eyes, Matt placed the silk flowers on the table in front of his mom and set the baseball tickets in front of his dad. After milking the drama as long as he could, he looked at his parents and said, "You can open your eyes now."

Kate was thrilled when she saw the surprise, and the look on her face was exactly the one Matt had hoped to evoke. "Oh, Matt, they're beautiful!" she said, giving him a hug and a big, enthusiastic kiss. "I've wanted these ever since I saw them at the Flower Petaler!"

"I know," Matt said proudly and kissed her again. "That's where I got them." Grinning from ear to ear, he turned to his father, primed for a similar reaction.

It was immediately obvious that he wasn't going to get it. Elliot held the tickets in his hands, but instead of smiling, he stared at his son with a look of suspicion and dawning anger. Little by little, Matt's grin disappeared.

"Where'd you get the money to buy baseball tickets?" Elliot asked. His voice was low but volatile, like approaching thunderheads.

Matt swallowed guiltily and briefly considered lying; he felt like he had just wandered into a pit of quicksand. Kate and Lori were as stunned as he was, and dismayed by the shift in Elliot's mood; each held her breath, both of them half hoping Matt would think to lie, too.

Because Kate feared her husband would be touchy on the subject, all three had conspired to keep Elliot from knowing about Matt and Lori's jobs until his drinking abated or he found employment, whichever came first—if either came at all. He had been gone so much, and so drunk when he came home, that it had been easy to maintain the deception; no one mentioned Matt's paper route or Lori's new job at the dress shop in the mall, and Matt always hid his new bike at the back of the garage behind Elliot's car—since the car wasn't drivable and wouldn't be fixed until the insurance check arrived, it seemed like the safest place to hide it from his father. And it had been; Elliot never went near the car and had no intention of doing so anytime soon. Unbeknownst to Kate, he had already received the insurance check—and then a policy cancellation notice a few days later; and since he no longer had insurance to drive the car, there didn't seem to be a point to getting it fixed. Instead, he had cashed the check and squirreled away the money to replace the Visa that Kate had repossessed. So both sides had their secrets, but only Matt's—and Kate's and Lori's—were in immediate danger of being exposed.

"Are you listening to me, Matt?" Elliot demanded. "Where'd you get the money to buy these tickets?" He suspected he already knew the answer, and he didn't like it. It made him angrier than he'd been in weeks.

"I—I thought you'd like them," Matt offered lamely, staring down at his sneakers.

"That's not the point," Elliot responded. His eyes were flashing as he held up the tickets. "Where'd you get the money?" he repeated hotly.

Ironically, about halfway through dinner, Matt had decided he would tell his dad he had gotten a job. He had figured that since Elliot was in a decent mood and the dinner was going well, the baseball tickets would please him so much he wouldn't be angry. He had even thought his dad might be proud—not to mention grateful—that he had used his own money to buy the tickets. But it was painfully clear he was wrong, and that instead of helping, his little surprise had actually backfired. "I got a paper route," Matt mumbled, flushed with shame; he had no idea why he should feel so badly, but he did, nonetheless. "I wanted to help out. . . ."

"*You wanted to help out!*" Elliot hissed. "*Help out with what?*"

Matt glanced at his mother, and looked back at his shoes. He was keenly aware of his father's gaze but couldn't bear the thought of meeting his eyes. More than anything else, he wanted to disappear, to fade like a ghost in the morning sunlight or be swallowed by a hole in the floor beneath him. Kate and Lori wanted very much to help him, but were temporarily paralyzed by their own complicity in the secret that now had them all in trouble. "You know," Matt answered meekly, "I wanted to help out with the bills and stuff. . . ."

Elliot glared at his son, his temper aroused like a waking lion. "You wanted to help out!" he said with a sneer. "*You* wanted to help out?" He turned to Lori with the same withering gaze. "And I suppose you're helping out, too!"

Lori said nothing, and merely looked at the floor.

"I might have known," Elliot said bitterly. He glared at his wife. "I'll bet this was your idea. You really get a kick out of rubbing my face in it, don't you? Everyone contributes—everybody can find a job except poor, pathetic Elliot!"

Kate's eyes flashed with anger, partly at Elliot's self-pity but mostly for the way he had ruined Matt's surprise. "You can't find a job unless you look for one, Elliot," she reminded him tartly. "This was the kids' idea. They wanted to help."

Elliot stood up. His face was red and his voice a growl. "I don't need your damn help," he spat.

Matt and Lori flinched. Matt felt like crying but was afraid to make things worse.

"They're not doing this to help *you*," Kate shot back, getting to her feet. "They're doing it for the family! Somebody's got to do something—we're sinking in a sea of unpaid bills and all you do is sit in that bar and throw away our future!"

Elliot glared ominously at each of them in turn. His hands were clenched in tight, angry fists. "Well, I guess that's my job," he replied in a biting, sarcastic voice, "making a mess so the rest of you can pitch in and clean it all up!" He suddenly lashed out and swept half the dishes from the dining room table; they crashed against the wall and several of them shattered in a shower of glass and broken china.

Terrified, Matt and Lori ran to their mother. Elliot stared at the debris with a twisted smile, and turned to his family. "There, that ought to make you happy," he snarled, breathing heavily. "Another opportunity to clean up one of Elliot's big messes! Now, if you don't mind," he went on in a mocking tone, "I think I'll make everybody *real* happy and go get a beer and watch the game with people who don't try to help out behind my back!" With a bitter smile, he started to leave, then turned back and held up the tickets. He glanced briefly at Kate, then focused on Matt. "Oh, and thanks for these. They'll come in real handy: they ought to fetch enough money to keep me in beer for the rest of the night." With a hollow laugh at the stricken expression that came to Matt's face, he turned on his heel and stormed out of the house.

LATER THAT NIGHT, after six hours of nonstop drinking and brooding over what had happened earlier, Elliot came home around 1 A.M. He stumbled through the front doorway, flipped on the light with a scowl on his face and staggered up the stairs to the second-floor bedrooms. He stopped at the door at the top of the landing. After opening it, he stepped inside and closed the door behind him as quietly as he could. Across the room, Matt was lying on his bed, bathed in the moonlight that streamed through the window; his face bore a frown, and he was tossing and turning.

Elliot made his way to the bed and grabbed his son by the shoulders, shaking him awake. Almost immediately, Matt's eyes flew open and he sat up with an alarmed expression that didn't go away when he saw that his father was the one standing over him. Elliot let go of his shoulders, then drew back a hand and slapped Matt hard. "That's for showing me up this afternoon," he snarled in a hateful whisper. "If you know what's good for you, you won't do it again." He turned and left without uttering another word.

Matt watched him leave with tear-filled eyes, then sat in the darkness, crying softly. This wasn't the first time his father had hit him, but it was the first time he'd ever hit him like that, and it scared him so much that he couldn't stop shaking. After a while—once he was sure Elliot wasn't coming back—he got up and knelt by the bedside. "Please, God," he prayed in a hitching voice. "Please send my guardian angel real soon. I think I'm going to need him—things are getting pretty bad around here, and I don't know what to do." Then, he climbed back in bed, whispered the "Amen" he had forgotten to say and cried himself to sleep, wondering what was keeping the man in the tunnel, and wishing he had asked him where he'd be if he needed him.

Eventually he dreamed, and interspersed between the images of all that had gone wrong over the last few months, he dreamed once again of his guardian angel. The scene was the same as it was before: the man named John standing with a woman in front of a building with bars on the windows. Only this time he saw the words on a sign above the door:

KANSAS CITY POLICE DEPARTMENT
17TH PRECINCT

NINETEEN

Needle in a Haystack

EARLIER THAT MORNING, in the wake of his audience with the Being of Light, John Creed had been buoyed by a sense of serenity and near-invincibility that made the prospect of finding Holly Mandylor seem an easy matter. But by nine o'clock that evening, John was starting to panic. He knew he shouldn't—*Have a little faith*, he kept telling himself—but that was getting harder to do as darkness began to fall with no sign of Holly.

After arriving in Las Vegas that afternoon, he had found the Golden Spur—the casino named on the broken red badge he'd been shown in the tunnel—only to find that Holly no longer worked there. Undaunted, he had used a combination of persistence and outright lies—the truth was too complicated, and time too valuable—to wheedle her address from a former coworker. There had been no one home at Holly's apartment, and because the idea of waiting felt too much like doing nothing at all, he had gone back to the Strip. But after hours of searching the endless blocks of crowded casinos, sidewalks and streets, he had come up empty and it had finally occurred to him that he might have been too smug about his prospects, naively convinced that failure wasn't possible in a mission that came from heaven itself. *That isn't necessarily the way things work,* he reminded himself, glancing nervously at his watch for the umpteenth time in the last two hours. Even if God was all-powerful, that still didn't mean He was pulling all the strings like a master puppeteer. The overall design had allowed for some latitude—maybe a great deal of latitude, for all he knew. *Which means it's up to me to find this woman,* he reminded himself soberly.

Now he found himself racing against nightfall and the maddening traffic to get back to the apartment before Holly came home and did something both of them would regret forever. To make matters worse, the Jeep was running out of gas. For the last twenty minutes, he had checked the fuel gauge almost as many times as he'd checked his watch. Now he glanced at it with an imploring look, as if he could somehow coax the needle to move off the *E.* "Just a few more miles," he pleaded with the car, and parenthetically, with the powers that had sent him four hundred miles to intervene with a stranger. "You can do that, can't you? Just this once?" He reached out and gave the dashboard an encouraging pat. As he did, a memory caught him unawares, that of Will Gibson lovingly patting the same dash not very long ago as he *ooh*-ed and *aah*-ed over the Jeep. And then hard on its heels came another recent memory of the last time he'd been racing toward the scene of a nightmare, unsure of what he'd find when he finally got there. John shook it off quickly, rejecting the bad omen, but he couldn't help musing that his new car was already laden with too many bittersweet memories.

Five minutes later, having reached the scruffy outskirts where Holly's apartment complex coexisted with second-rate casinos and tourist traps, the car finally decided that fumes weren't enough. As it passed one of the roadside casinos, the Jeep shook once, then lapsed and lurched, and John realized with dismay that waiting to refuel was no longer an option. Crossing his fingers, he turned off the road and eased the faltering car into a blacktop parking lot, irritated with himself for not making it to Holly's apartment, but grateful that he'd gone as far as he had.

Appropriately named the Roadside Casino, his unscheduled stop was a sprawling Western-style complex with a combination casino and lounge, a large souvenir shop and an old-time cafe with gas pumps out front. The car coasted to the pumps and John jumped out and began filling the tank, frowning impatiently. He glanced up at the sky as the last reddish glow of sunlight disappeared, then grimaced and looked at his watch once again. His eyes flicked to the pump, and he stared at the numbers on the slowly turning dials, willing them to go faster, as fast as his heart had begun to beat. When that didn't happen, he turned and stared at the brightly lit restaurant, absently scanning the faces of the people who were seated behind the large plate-glass windows. A few anxious seconds later, his look of desperation changed to one of bewilderment, then spread into an excited, ironic smile. He laughed and shook his head with amazed relief, glanced at the restaurant and laughed again. Sitting in a booth only fifty feet away was a lone young woman with reddish brown hair and a familiar face—the woman he had seen last night in his dream. . . .

FRESH FROM HAVING CHECKED herself out of Clark County Hospital, Holly Mandylor was sitting in a gaudy red booth in the Roadside Casino's Old-Time Cafe. Next to her on the seat lay a green soft-sided overnight bag, filled with only the barest of necessities. She had left her apartment ten minutes earlier, and although she hadn't been particularly hungry, as soon as she'd seen the cafe it had suddenly seemed like a very good idea to get something to eat before heading out of town.

Staring out at the parking lot and the highway beyond, her mind barely registered the busy surroundings. The memory of the suicide attempt and the shame of being held for psychiatric observation still smarted keenly, and the anger and despair that had landed her there had abated only slightly. She supposed she should be grateful that Tina had come by the apartment last night and let herself in when Holly didn't answer—and she *was* glad to be alive, or rather she was glad she wasn't dead—but she still felt adrift, with no real direction. *So here I am starting all over again,* she mused guiltily. *Always giving up and running somewhere else.*

In her heart that felt wrong, but in her head it felt right. Now that she had run out of options in Las Vegas, the only thing she could think of beside suicide—which, after last night, she had solemnly vowed she'd never try again—was to make a fresh start in a brand-new place. She had always lived her life by one simple rule: never get so attached to something or someone that you can't walk away. Now that rule seemed more practical than ever. The mountains, the desert, the glamour of the casinos, most of her belongings, her history and friends—she would leave them all behind and try not to look back, hoping for a future that was kinder than the past.

Now all she had to do was figure out where she wanted to go, which wasn't going to be easy, considering she could barely function, much less make a complicated decision. She stared at the place mat, a colorful U.S. map that highlighted all the routes leading into (and out of) Las Vegas, and considered the possibilities. She thought about California first, but discarded the notion; everybody thought about California, and half of them moved there. Besides, the cost of living was too high, and to someone without a job, that was reason enough to look elsewhere. She briefly considered Reno and then rejected that, too; it was different from Las Vegas, but not different enough. As she idly moved on to thoughts of Arizona, her waitress approached the table and set down a Pepsi.

"Your food'll be up in a minute," the woman said. There was a smile on her face, but her voice was indifferent, bordering on petulant. Fiftyish and trim, she had dark curly hair and a pretty but sharp-featured face that looked as if it might go from laughter to anger without missing a beat. She was wearing a colorful apron over a short, desert brown dress with fringe on the hem, and seemed as uncomfortable and self-conscious in the pseudo-Western attire as a cowboy dressed up in a suit and tie. Holly couldn't help but think of a fish out of water, and felt an instant kinship.

"Thanks," Holly answered. She smiled weakly, and, on impulse, stuck out her hand and introduced herself. "Hi, I'm Holly. Holly Mandylor."

The waitress's expression softened and she offered a more genuine, if surprised, smile. "Glory Roseman," she replied after a brief hesitation, shaking Holly's hand. "It's nice to meet you."

Having initiated the conversation without really knowing why, Holly now found herself in the unusual position of not knowing what to say next. She glanced down at the map on the place mat, idly fingering the corners, and looked back up at the waitress. "You know anything about Arizona?" she finally asked.

"Arizona?" Glory repeated. She frowned and rattled off an answer in a sharp, sardonic voice: "It's a desert. It's hot. It's got Indians, Mexicans and most of the New Yorkers who didn't move to Florida when they finally retired."

"Sounds like Las Vegas," Holly observed.

The waitress rolled her eyes. "Don't I know it! Like this is the kind of place where I wanted to wind up! I see the same kind of people I saw when I lived in New York, only now I'm doing this," she said, gesturing at her uniform with her order pad and pen, "while they're all living it up, playing golf and tennis."

"You're a New Yorker?" Holly replied. She'd noticed the woman's accent right off, but hadn't thought much about it; with so many tourists in Las Vegas, different accents were common.

"An ex-New Yorker," Glory answered with more than a touch of rancor. "Now I'm not anything. Just a glorified slave in some cheap cafe."

Holly nodded. "Yeah, waitressing is tough," she commiserated, finding herself drawn into the conversation, despite her mood. "That's what I used to do. It's murder on your back."

"Tell me about it!" Glory agreed, grabbing her lower back in the-atrical fashion. "And I thought sitting at a desk all day was torture—this is ten times worse!" She glanced around the busy room, as if checking to see if her boss was watching, then pulled a pack of ciga-rettes out of her apron pocket and slid into the booth opposite Holly. "And the air out here," she said, lighting the cigarette, "what it does to my sinuses—don't even ask! I'm lucky I'm still breathing, the air's so dry."

"Really," Holly replied, thinking that the cigarette probably didn't do her any good either.

The waitress gave her an appraising look. "Let me guess," she said, pointing the cigarette at Holly's head. "You're a native, right?"

Holly nodded.

"Then I guess you're used to it," Glory replied. She glanced around the room again, and this time caught the eye of the cafe manager, who was glaring at her from the kitchen door. Ignoring the packed dining room, Glory looked at him defiantly and yelled, "I get a break, don't I!" She held his gaze, as if daring him to come over, and signaled the other waitress to cover for her awhile. "I'm telling you, I wish I'd never moved to Las Vegas," she went on. "No offense," she added quickly, "but this isn't Manhattan."

"You actually lived in Manhattan?" Holly asked wistfully. She had always wanted to go there, but had never gotten closer than Amarillo, Texas—which wasn't even close, in any respect.

Glory took a drag from her cigarette and exhaled slowly. "On West Fifty-Seventh. I was a network liaison to the Oprah show and a few other syndicateds—until those cutthroats at the network let me go!"

Holly nodded sympathetically. "You, too, huh? I used to be a cocktail waitress at the Golden Spur. Some baldheaded jerk fired me because I wouldn't put out."

"Men are pigs."

"This one was," Holly agreed, glancing down at her wrists. Two lines of white gauze had crept into view, and she discreetly tugged at the cuffs of her long-sleeve blouse, hiding the reminders of where that firing had led. "He just about ruined my life, and he enjoyed every minute of it!" For the first time since yesterday, the deadness in her eyes and voice gave way to a brief but enervating burst of passion. "I loved that job! I liked the people, the casino—I even liked my boss until he started treating me like dirt. I gave that place three good years of my life, and it didn't mean a thing!"

Glory nodded fiercely. "You think that's bad," she said, leaning closer and jabbing the air with the smoking cigarette, "try giving twenty-five years to some heartless corporation and then have them toss you out like a piece of garbage!"

"You're kidding!" Holly replied, appalled. "Twenty-five years?"

"You bet. I had a high-paying position, an office with a view, an apartment in Manhattan, you name it. Don't get me wrong, it wasn't all roses: it was a stressful job—half the people in TV are maniacs and the rest are morons, so they can drive you up the wall without even trying—but I liked what I was doing, and people respected me. Now look at me. My back's a disaster, my feet are killing me, my sinuses are a wreck and I might as well be making minimum wage!" Glory shook her head angrily. "All those years, and then just like that—" she said, snapping her fingers and staring fiercely at Holly, "—they suddenly decide they don't need you anymore! You know how hard it is to find a good job when you're my age? Don't ask—it's impossible! I tried for forever. When my savings finally ran out, I had to give up my apartment and move out here to live with my mother. Imagine being fifty-two years old and living with your mother! At least I don't have to worry about some crazy religious fanatic crashing a plane into my building anymore."

Holly nodded sympathetically, and then thought about her own mom, who had died when Holly was ten. Right now having a mother to move in with didn't sound all that bad. Still, she could understand what it felt like to lose everything. It made you feel empty and about three inches tall. She fumbled for a response that would make Glory feel better, but all she came up with was, "Yeah, life is unfair."

"Unfair isn't the word for it," the waitress replied, her voice suddenly pensive. "Sometimes it makes me so mad I don't know whether to scream or just cry."

Holly shook her head in silent agreement and reached across the table, taking Glory's hand in both of hers. She gave it a squeeze but hastily let go when she realized she'd exposed the bandages again. "Yeah, I know the feeling," she said self-consciously, putting her arms in her lap and staring down at the table. When she finally met Glory's eyes again, it was immediately apparent that the woman had seen the telltale gauze. Holly's face flushed with shame and she averted her gaze, first to her bag, then out at the highway. As much to herself as to the wide-eyed waitress, she added, "Sometimes life will get you if you don't watch out."

When Holly finally worked up the nerve to look at her again, Glory smiled awkwardly, then stubbed out her cigarette and got to her feet. "Listen to me," she said, slightly flustered, "going on and on like a silly old woman when your food's probably up and getting cold already."

"It's okay," Holly responded, not quite successfully forcing a smile.

"It most certainly is not. Let me go get your order. I'll be right back."

As Glory hurried away, a man walked into the restaurant and stood by the checkout counter. He was tall and handsome, a few years older than Holly, with thick blond hair and striking blue eyes that seemed to flash with recognition when he met her gaze. The man smiled. His smile was sweet but seemed tentative, even slightly nervous, and under less preoccupied circumstances, Holly would have found it endearing and reciprocated in kind. Instead, she glanced back down at the table after acknowledging the gesture with barely a nod.

As she stared at the map, considering Arizona again, Glory returned with her food. "Here you go," she said cheerfully, setting down the steaming plate. Holly couldn't help but notice that Glory carefully avoided looking at her wrists, which were once again resting on the table's edge. "Everything look okay?" the waitress asked. "Do you need anything else?"

Holly shook her head, embarrassed anew. "No. Everything looks fine. Thanks."

"Okay. Enjoy. This place might be a dump, but the food's pretty good, believe it or not." She smiled self-consciously and cleared her throat, then added, "Sorry I unloaded like that on you earlier. You sure took it like a sport. Most people would have complained to the manager, or at least walked out."

Holly smiled wanly. "Don't worry about it. Everybody needs somebody to listen sometimes."

Glory nodded sagely. "All the same, I appreciate it." She stole a quick glance at Holly's wrists, then lowered her voice and said, "If you need someone, I get off in a few hours. I'd be happy to return the favor. I mean it."

"I appreciate the offer," Holly replied, genuinely moved. "But I'm okay."

"Are you sure?"

Holly smiled, and tried to make it convincing. "Yes, I'm sure. Thanks."

Glory held her gaze for a moment longer, then reached out and tenderly patted her hand. "It'll be all right, trust me. You just keep looking for whatever it is you're looking for, and don't give up. You'll find it. Things'll work out—for both of us. Just you wait and see." She smiled warmly and glanced at the man who was waiting to be seated. When she saw that he was staring with undisguised interest—not at her, but at Holly—the wheels started turning in Glory's brain. After giving him a quick once-over and deciding he might be just what her new friend needed, she glanced around the dining room to make sure the tables were still all taken, then turned back to Holly with a knowing wink. "Looks like you've got a secret admirer," she said, inclining her head in the man's direction. She grinned and said in a mischievous tone, "I better go seat him before he takes his business elsewhere."

TWENTY

Dinner at the
Roadside Casino

As the waitress hurried away, Holly turned her attention to the food on the table. Recalling Glory's assurance that things would work out, she shook her head doubtfully and picked up a fork. It was hard to believe her life would get better—she didn't really think it could get any worse, but she couldn't imagine a sudden change in luck either. The only thing Holly could visualize with any clarity at all was a future that got her out of Las Vegas as soon as possible.

John Creed, on the other hand, couldn't believe his good fortune: he had found Holly Mandylor—or rather, he had been led to her. Now all he had to do was figure out how to introduce himself without scaring her away. As it turned out, he needn't have worried, for the waitress coming toward him was already working on that very same problem.

"One?" Glory asked, smiling sweetly and picking up a menu from a stack by the register.

John nodded absently, still staring at Holly. "Yes. I'm by myself."

"We're a little busy," Glory explained, waving the menu at the crowded dining room, "so it might be a while before a spot opens up. If you don't mind sharing a table, I could seat you with someone else," she said slyly. "That way you wouldn't have to wait so long. I know that's not how they do it out here, but we do it all the time back East."

John started to decline the offer, picturing himself getting stuck in an endless conversation with a garrulous stranger while Holly finished her meal and slipped away, but before he could object, Glory pointed at the booth where Holly was sitting. "I don't think that young lady would mind sharing her table. Would that be okay?" Without waiting for a reply, she turned and led John to Holly's booth.

Holly glanced up at Glory, expecting her to ask if the food was okay. Instead, Glory put her on the spot. "You wouldn't mind some company, would you?" she asked, stepping to one side and gesturing for John to sit down. "The place is full and I didn't have the heart to make this gentleman wait." Remembering how impressed Holly had seemed earlier with all things New York, Glory added, "We do this all the time in Manhattan. I can't remember the last time when I had lunch there by myself." She winked and added provocatively, "Some of those lunches turned out pretty well."

Both John and Holly winced with embarrassment. John would have preferred to meet another way, but he had to admit Glory's well-intentioned scheming did solve his problem. Before Holly could think of a polite way to say she'd rather be alone, Glory all but pushed John into the booth. The waitress handed him a menu. "I'll be back in a minute to take your order," she said, then hurried away, a self-satisfied smile lighting up her face.

John gave Holly an apologetic look. "That waitress is something else," he said, trying to break the ice. Now that he was actually with the person who had vaulted into his consciousness less than twenty-four hours earlier—a woman who didn't know she wasn't a total stranger to him—he felt uncharacteristically self-conscious and at a loss for words, finding it difficult to be natural in so unnatural a situation, especially when there was so much at stake.

"She's nice, though," Holly replied, trying to mask her discomfort. It embarrassed her to realize that Glory had assumed some tragic love affair was the root of her problems.

"Oh," John said, hoping he hadn't misspoken. "Is she a friend of yours?"

"Not really, I guess. We just met a few minutes ago."

John nodded but couldn't come up with anything to say. He glanced at the menu, wondering how to proceed, and Holly returned her attention to her food, wondering if it was rude to start eating without him. After one bite of her hamburger, she decided it was, and put the sandwich back on the plate. Preferring conversation to another awkward silence—especially since there was nothing else to do if she wasn't going to eat—Holly smiled weakly when John looked up. "Are you from Las Vegas?" she asked.

"No," John replied, straining for a normal conversational tone. "I'm from Reno."

"You didn't stray too far from home then," Holly observed.

"About four hundred miles. It wasn't a bad drive, though."

Holly nodded, and frowned slightly when a small rumbling noise drifted up from her stomach. Hoping John hadn't heard it, she glanced down at her plate and wondered if maybe it would be okay to have a french fry or two, just to stall an encore. Deciding that was better than putting them both in the position of pretending not to hear her stomach's complaints, she finally gave in. "So, how's your luck been running?" she asked, nibbling on a fry.

John started to say his luck had turned around the moment he walked into the restaurant, but drew up short when he noticed the bandages on Holly's wrist. Quickly his eyes flicked to her other wrist and saw the same thing there. "Actually," he said slowly, trying to cover his shock, "I didn't come here to gamble. . . ."

Holly swallowed and looked up. "Oh," she said. "I guess not. You could do that at home."

All John could do was nod in agreement as he tried not to stare at her bandaged wrists. He was stunned to see that the suicide attempt had already happened—simultaneously, no doubt, with the previous night's dream—and it was so distressingly similar to what occurred with Will that old feelings of sorrow and guilty failure came surging back. It was only the realization that this time things had turned out differently—no one had died or was in danger of dying—that gave him enough composure to hide behind a shaky but passable facade.

Unaware of what he had seen, Holly replied, "You must be here on business, then." She discreetly scanned the room, looking for Glory, and was relieved to find her hurrying toward their booth.

"I'm sort of on vacation," John replied as the waitress walked up with pad in hand.

"Vegas is a good place to take a vacation," Glory said, jumping into the conversation. "Lots of interesting people here. You never know who you'll meet." She glanced down at Holly and winked, then took John's order.

After Glory left, Holly asked, "So if you didn't come here to gamble . . . why Vegas?"

"I guess you could say I'm on a spur-of-the-moment driving trip."

"Really," Holly said, knowing the appeal of the open road, of movement, of freedom, of leaving things behind. She glanced down at her bag and then out at the highway. As soon as this unusual meal was done, she'd be embarking on her own impromptu excursion— that is, assuming someone stopped to pick her up when she stuck out her thumb; driving trips were awkward when you didn't have a car. "I think that's probably the best way to take a vacation," she said, her voice suddenly wistful. "So where are you headed?"

John furrowed his brow, wondering the same thing. He had

assumed Las Vegas was the end of the line, but since it was obvious that someone had already prevented Holly from ending her own life—and because her travel bag seemed a pretty good indicator that she was going elsewhere—he realized his assumption might have been wrong. With a flash of insight that was more hunch than epiphany, he began to understand the timing of their meeting: as he had originally suspected, his involvement with Holly—whatever form it would take—would be longer and more complex than merely stopping a suicide. And until he had a clearer understanding of what that would be, he had to make sure he didn't lose sight of her, a task that was potentially fraught with problems. "Where am I headed?" he finally said. "Wherever the road leads me, I guess. I didn't really make any plans beyond tonight." He nodded in the direction of her bag and added, "How about you? Are you coming or going?"

"Going," Holly replied in a distant voice. "I've had enough of this town."

John tried not to show his consternation. "Where are you headed?"

"I've been thinking about Arizona, for starters. But I'm not sure that's far enough away. I'll probably wind up going wherever the road takes me, too. Someone stole my car, and hitchhikers can't afford to be choosy."

Realizing he had the perfect opportunity to solve both their problems, John started to offer her a ride—at least on the first leg of her journey—but decided to wait. The last thing he wanted was to scare Holly off by appearing too eager. Instead of pursuing their mutual lack of direction, he offered his sympathies on the car and changed the subject. They spent the next fifteen minutes talking about a variety of mundane things, until Glory returned with a large serving tray bearing two orders of food.

The first thing she did was clear Holly's barely touched dinner from the table and replace it with a fresh but identical order. "I thought you might like some food that's actually still hot."

"You didn't have to do that!" Holly protested.

Glory served John's food and waved her off. "You came in here to get a hot meal, and a hot meal is what you're going to get. Now," she said, favoring them both with an encouraging smile, "enjoy your food. If you need anything else, just flag me down."

Holly was shaking her head, but grinning, as Glory went back to the kitchen. In spite of herself, she felt her earlier resentment at the waitress's meddling slipping away. What had started out as a routine stop on her way out of town was turning out to be a bizarre but interesting send-off, and had given her a break from her gloom and confusion. The waitress and the unexpected dinner companion had made her feel almost normal, at least for the moment. It wasn't a big thing, but after the last few days, it wasn't a small thing either.

With the food's surprisingly appetizing aromas filling the air between them, John and Holly soon fell to eating. As John stared absently at his plate or off into the distance, thinking about what his next step should be, Holly reflected on their meeting. She was surprised to realize that she found this stranger attractive—not because he wasn't handsome; he was—but because her mind was so weighed down with more important matters that it seemed frivolous that she should even notice. She also couldn't help sensing that, aside from appearing a little preoccupied, he seemed genuinely nice and naturally friendly. Unlike most men who had ever shown her any kindness or attention, he didn't appear to harbor any secret agenda. It occurred to Holly that she was probably being naive, that just because a man spent half an hour in her company without making veiled or suggestive remarks wasn't absolute proof that he had an honorable nature. But she doubted it. And even if her positive feelings about the man weren't something she was inclined to pursue at such an unsettled time, it was nice to know that all of her emotions hadn't died in that bathtub the previous night.

Eventually it occurred to her that they hadn't introduced themselves. There didn't seem to be a point to doing it now that the meal was almost over, but Holly didn't feel right about it. "You know," she said, getting John's attention, "here I am sharing a meal with you, and I'm embarrassed to say I don't even know your name."

Having already known Holly's since the previous night, it had slipped John's mind that he had never told her his. Smiling guiltily, he smacked his head lightly with the heel of his hand and said, "You're right!" Putting down his fork, he stuck his hand across the table and said, "I'm sorry. I'm John Creed—previously known as the Man With No Name."

Holly laughed, and reached out and shook his hand. "I'm Holly—" she began, and abruptly broke off before saying her last name. She had exposed the bandage on her wrist again, and to her shame and horror, John had noticed and was trying to look away. It had been painful enough when it had happened with Glory, but now that she had done it again the shame came flooding back, even stronger than before, sweeping away her tenuous sense of contentment. She silently chided herself that she might as well have climbed on top of the table and displayed it openly for the rest of the customers, so that everyone could have known that she was weak and stupid. Instead, she pulled back her arm and pushed down her sleeve with as much dignity as she could muster. The next thing she knew, there were tears in her eyes; they spilled down her cheeks slowly at first, then came in earnest. Disgusted with herself all over again, Holly crumpled the paper napkin that lay in her lap and tossed it on the table with a trembling hand. She turned away from John and fumbled for the travel bag. "I think it's time for me to go," she whispered in a broken voice. "I'm sorry . . ."

Caught off guard, John could only stare with surprise and mounting concern as the woman he had searched for now prepared to flee. Acting instinctively, he reached out and grasped her hand, holding it firmly but tenderly, and said in a voice that was filled with concern, "Holly, wait! We all make mistakes. . . ."

Still sobbing, Holly turned back to him but couldn't meet his eyes. "Some of us make bigger ones than others."

"But they're still just mistakes," John responded in a soft but earnest voice. "It's one of the things that makes us human—and I don't think we can do a damn thing about it except maybe grow a little stronger so it doesn't hurt so much the next time we screw up."

Holly stared down at her plate with a bitter smile. Her tears abated but her chest was still heaving as she tried to stave off a fresh wave of sobs. Finally gaining a little composure, she picked up the napkin and swiped at her nose, then drew the travel bag closer. "I really ought to be going," she reiterated, still averting her gaze. She started to withdraw her hand from John's grasp, but instead of letting go, he only squeezed tighter. Surprised and a little frightened by the intensity of his grip, Holly glanced up sharply, finally meeting his gaze. Not knowing what to expect, she was almost as disconcerted by the understanding and unadulterated concern she saw in his eyes as if she had found unadulterated lust there instead. For a few long seconds, they simply stared at each other without uttering a word, and John's demeanor remained so completely without guile and unflinchingly earnest that, amid the painful emotions roiling in Holly's breast, she felt a consoling warmth reach through and touch her. It was a subtle experience, but it calmed her just enough that her urgency to leave subsided a little.

Afraid that the moment would slip away and that Holly would leave—even worse, that she might try again to kill herself—John decided to take a chance. Loosening his grip on her hand, he gave her a tentative smile. "I know we just met and you don't even know me," he began slowly, hiding the tension he actually felt, "but I'd like to propose something: come with me on my trip, at least for tonight. . . . It only makes sense—you need a ride and I could use some company, and neither one of us is in a hurry to get anywhere in particular. I promise I have no ulterior motives. What do you say?" He grinned slightly and added, "I've been told that most of the time I'm pretty good company."

Remembering the old axiom that if something appeared too

good to be true, it probably was, Holly was initially wary, especially since that something involved hitching a ride with a man she hardly knew. Then she reminded herself that she'd be taking a chance if she accepted a ride from anyone she didn't know, too. Either way, it was a risky proposition, but one she had already decided was her only practical means of getting out of town. That redefined the question: Was John Creed the stranger she wanted to trust? When she thought about it, her gut feeling was that she could trust him. But there was another issue to consider. "You're not just offering me a ride out of pity, are you?" she finally responded in a defensive voice. "Because even though I could use the lift, I don't need anyone to feel sorry for me."

"If I felt sorry for you, I'd just buy you a bus ticket and move on down the road," John replied matter-of-factly. He smiled sadly and said, "I don't pity you, Holly. But I do know what it's like to have your whole world turned upside down. It's not necessarily the best time to be alone, and, like I said, I could use some company. After the first few hundred miles, it gets kind of lonesome with no one to talk to."

Holly nodded slightly and narrowed her eyes. "Swear to me you aren't some kind of pervert or creep." She realized even as the words left her mouth that it was an essentially meaningless demand, not to mention silly. No one who was a creep would admit to it so easily, and anyone who wasn't would resent the question. It occurred to her too late that it would serve her right if he withdrew his offer. Still, it was a valid concern.

Instead of showing offense, John said solemnly, "I swear it will be okay. If I turn out to be a creep or a pervert, you can leave me in the desert with the foxes and snakes—as well you should." He gently released her hand and ventured a speculative smile. "And who knows, it might even turn out to be fun—in a purely safe and respectable way," he added hastily.

Holly thought it over a little more, wondering once again if he was as nice as he seemed or if he was just a good actor. Again, her gut or her heart or some small inner voice—whatever it was that seemed to respond to this man—told her he was okay. A moment later, she made the decision, but still felt it prudent to give herself an out. "I can't promise I'll be very good company," she said half apologetically. "And I don't really know how long I'll stick around."

"That's okay," John responded, trying not to sound as relieved as he felt. "I can't make any guarantees, either. When you decide you've gone as far as you need to go, or when I decide it's time for me to head home, then that's it. Fair enough?"

For the first time since bursting into tears, Holly allowed herself a small, shy smile. "More than fair. Thanks. I guess we've got a deal." With a flash of self-deprecating humor that surprised her almost as much as it surprised him, she added, "I hope you understand if I don't offer to shake hands on it."

TWENTY-ONE

Peering into Shadows

"WHERE DOES MADAME wish to go?" John asked with exaggerated civility once they were in the car.

In spite of her nervousness, Holly laughed. "Home, James," she answered, playing along. "Wherever that turns out to be."

"Does Madame have a direction in mind?"

Without hesitation, Holly answered, "East."

"Any particular point east?"

"I don't know. Do you have a destination in mind?"

"I hadn't decided yet. I was kind of waiting for something to come to me," John answered honestly.

Holly thought about it a moment. "Have you ever seen Hoover Dam?"

"Only in pictures."

"Why don't we go there? It won't be the same as seeing it in day-time, but it's still an experience even at night."

Realizing he was committed to winging it until he got a better idea of how to proceed, John readily agreed. "Sounds good to me. I take it you know the way."

"It's easy to get to," Holly replied, pointing at the road in front of the casino. "Just go south on the highway and follow the signs. It's about twenty minutes away."

HOLLY STARED OUT THE WINDOW in silence as they headed out of town. In one way or another, she had started her life over more times in her twenty-seven years than she cared to remember. Some-times it had been hard and sometimes it had been easy. But this was the hardest—running away from the place she had always called home. When they neared the last of the neon-lit casinos, it occurred to her that this might be the last time she'd ever lay eyes on Las Vegas, and a pang of regret shot through her heart. As sharp as it was, she also felt a sense of bittersweet relief.

Like a tableau on the fringes of a slowly strobing light, Holly's face was alternately etched with sorrow or bathed in shadow as they passed beneath the street lamps lining their way. John studied her dis-creetly, and everything he saw—the set of her mouth, the weariness in her eyes, the way she held her body—was a subtle reminder that the woman he had befriended had ventured into a tunnel very different from his own and was still in the process of gradually emerging. Re-specting her emotions, he joined in her silence and used the opportu-nity to consider contingency plans should Holly change her mind about leaving Las Vegas. After a while, she turned to him and asked, "So what do you do when you're not driving around the country?"

"I teach psychology and sociology. Mostly to high school seniors."

Holly recalled the psychological "help" she had just gotten in the hospital. "Oh, I see," she replied, suddenly uncomfortable.

"Don't sound so disappointed," John responded, mildly amused at getting the usual reaction. "It's not like I'm a hit man or something."

"Sorry. I didn't mean for it to sound that way. It's just that shrinks are always poking around inside people's heads and analyzing what they're thinking."

John smiled. "Well, you can relax. First of all, I'm not a shrink. And second, I can't read minds. Even if I had one, a crystal ball's not something I'd take on vacation."

In spite of herself, Holly grinned, but the expression faded as the irony of her concern quickly sank in—it was silly to worry about protecting her secrets when John already knew the one that shamed her the most. "I'm sorry," she responded. "I didn't mean to offend you."

"No offense taken. I get that sort of reaction all the time."

"You'd think I'd be more sensitive," Holly went on. "You don't exactly get a good reaction when you tell people you're a cocktail waitress, either."

"Really?" John responded. "I always thought that was kind of a glamorous job in Las Vegas."

"That depends on where you work. The Golden Spur wasn't all that glamorous. It was okay—definitely better than the place we just left—but it wasn't like Caesar's or the MGM Grand. Still, I have to admit I kind of liked it. I met a lot of people, made some pretty good friends. And I'd still be there," Holly added, suddenly animated, "if it weren't for that damned cowboy hat."

When John glanced at her quizzically, Holly recounted the events leading up to her firing. Once she had finished, she accepted the outrage John expressed on her behalf, then lapsed into silence and stared out at the darkness, herding the emotions the incident had resurrected back into a place where they weren't so painful. Eventually, she turned back to John and asked, "So what's your story? What made you suddenly decide to take off all by yourself on a trip to nowhere?" Then, fishing a little, she asked, "Didn't your wife want to come along?"

Having expected Holly to simply accept his story about an

impulsive road trip, John hadn't anticipated she might ask why he had gone. "I'm not married," he replied, buying some time by answering her last question first, "so I'm pretty much free to take off when I want to. . . . I was involved in a pretty bad car accident a few months back that put me in the hospital for a while," he explained soberly, pointedly omitting his near-death experience. "I've been kind of restless ever since, especially since school let out. When I woke up this morning," he said, hedging just a bit, "I decided that getting away for a while might be the best thing."

Holly nodded sympathetically. "It sounds like the last few months haven't exactly been a picnic for you, either."

"Not really. But it hasn't been all bad. And it certainly hasn't been dull."

"Yeah, bad luck seldom is . . . So why'd you come here? Vegas is the last place you ought to go if your luck's running bad. God knows that's why I'm getting out."

"Like I said, I didn't come here to gamble."

"That's true. I forgot," Holly replied. After a moment, she smiled and said, "Well, I'm glad you came to Vegas. Otherwise, right now I'd probably be standing in front of the restaurant with my thumb in the air."

"I'm kind of glad I did, too," John responded, amazed once again by the series of events that had led him here. He fell silent, staring out at the dark and winding road, and suddenly pointed out the windshield as they came around a bend. "Whoa, I guess we must be here," he said. Up ahead, flanked by dark, looming mountains and glowing streetlights, was Hoover Dam.

They parked in an adjacent lot and headed toward the walkway atop the dam. It was darker than John had imagined it would be; the seven hundred feet of concrete stretching down to the river at the canyon's bottom was breathtakingly lit by a series of floodlights, but the sidewalk and highway that ran along its crest had only street lamps to light them, and the mountains jutting up on either side of the dam were forbiddingly dark above the reach of the lights. The night air was also surprisingly still; there was no deafening roar from millions of gallons of rushing water, only an audible trickle from the spillways on either side and the faraway sound of the river below. Since it was a Sunday night, they were practically alone; the only other people were a man and a woman standing far away, near the end of the railing, and a security guard at either end of the dam. All in all, the atmosphere was rather eerie for such a famous place, with some of the site's grandeur lost or obscured by nighttime shadows, and its awesome power only sensed by the knowledge they were standing atop a massive, man-made structure that held back the force of the Colorado River.

"Pretty impressive, huh?" Holly said as she strolled along the walkway.

"Not in the way that I thought it would be," John replied, glancing at the mountains on either side. "But, yeah, it still looks impressive, even if does feel like we're out in the middle of nowhere."

"It is kind of dark," Holly agreed. She stopped to let him catch up with her, and they walked on casually, saying nothing, until they reached the center of the dam. By unspoken mutual consent, they stopped again to get a different view. From that vantage point, the brilliance and enormity of the wall beneath them was even more staggering, a strikingly unnatural contrast to the black, moving surface of the water far below and the canyon and mountains stretching off into the darkness.

In such a rarefied atmosphere, it wasn't long before Holly and John slipped into a contemplative mood. Minutes passed as they remained that way, each comfortable in his own, personal silence. The other couple left and returned to their car, completely unnoticed. The sound of running water in the sunken spillways droned on, unheard. Even the lights and sounds of an occasional passing car failed to impinge on their respective reveries. Her arms folded and elbows resting on the rail, Holly stared off into the distance, pondering the events of the last twenty-four hours. Next to her, John leaned on the metal barrier with both hands, staring almost fixedly at a spotlight below him. Like Holly, his thoughts had been recaptured by what had happened the previous night, as if his mind had only been waiting for the first quiet moment to relive his encounter with the Being of Light and the vision that had led him inevitably to this place. Amid the challenge and uncertainty of what had ensued, he could still feel that light surrounding him with love, supporting his spirit with patience and strength.

As his thoughts drifted back to Holly, he turned his head and stared at her for a moment. Finally, he said softly, "What are you thinking about?"

"Just saying my good-byes," Holly answered wistfully.

"Having second thoughts?" John asked gently, trying not to sound leading. He couldn't help thinking the situation would be a lot less complicated if they went back to Las Vegas.

"No. Not at all," Holly answered, shaking her head. "It was time to move on." Having said it for the first time without the usual feelings of shame and despair, it dawned on Holly that maybe she had turned a corner of some kind, that it might actually be possible she was running *toward* something instead of running away. It was a faint feeling at best, but novel enough to hold on to.

John nodded. After a moment, he motioned up ahead. "Want to check out the rest of it?"

"Sure. The experience wouldn't be complete unless we made it all the way to the other end."

With Holly in the lead, they made their way leisurely toward the far end of the walkway, each with a hand skimming along the rail. Every few yards, they stopped to peer briefly over the side, exchanging exclamations of awe before moving on. After they had covered barely a hundred feet, something in the air suddenly seemed different, and John frowned and slowed his pace, then abruptly stopped; a second or two later, Holly did the same. For no apparent reason, and independently of each other, both of them had begun to feel uneasy as they neared the place where the observation walk ended and the dark mountain wall of the canyon rose up. John looked for the security guards, but they were nowhere in sight.

Saying nothing, John looked past Holly to the craggy wall of rock beyond. Extending above the walkway, the mountain that formed that side of the canyon was a formidable mass of shadows, and darkness within shadows, visually impenetrable and completely silent.

John edged a little closer. After his eyes had adjusted to the subtle gradients of black and gray, he peered intently at the rocks without the slightest clue as to what he was seeking. Twice he thought he saw something out of the corner of his eye, but when he turned to look, whatever it was had gone or blended in an instant with the craggy terrain. Intrigued, he crossed the few steps to Holly's side and saw that she was staring in the same direction. Her face looked troubled, bordering on panicked. "Do you see something?" John asked in a hushed tone.

Holly jumped slightly at the sound of his voice. "Huh?" she replied distractedly, tearing her gaze away from the mountain. One look at John's face told her she had not been imagining whatever was going on. "Do you feel it, too?"

John nodded and gripped the rail tightly, warily edging his way forward for a closer look.

Holly reached out and grabbed his arm. "Wait, John," she said in a shaking voice. As if playing to the thing lurking in the shadows, she added with a forced casualness, "Let's go back. We've already seen all there is to see."

"Hold on," John whispered. He raised his hand, cueing her to be silent, and cocked an ear in the direction of the mountain. He could have sworn he'd heard something, but now—nothing. Holly tugged at his arm, turning to glance longingly in the direction of the parking lot.

A figure was standing in the middle of the walk, an aura of light glowing softly around him as he looked in their direction. Holly was startled by his sudden and unusual appearance, and let out a small shriek. John wheeled around, ready to tell her in more emphatic terms to be quiet, but the words died in his throat as his eyes looked beyond her and saw Will Gibson. His dead friend looked whole again, without the bandages and bruises that had marred his face the last time John had seen him, and his voice sounded clear and urgent in John's head, even though John didn't see his lips move: *Get out of here, John! You don't know what you're dealing with. Take Holly and go back to the car as fast as you can.* When John only stood there, staring in disbelief, Will urged him more forcefully, *Go on! Do it now!* As soon as John moved, Will vanished into thin air.

If possible, John was even more shocked than Holly, who had seen the apparition but not heard the warning. Too stunned to move, he only stood where he was, shaking his head slowly from side to side, as if clearing his head from a vivid dream. There was no doubt about it, it had really been Will. "Who—what was that?" Holly croaked. The sound of her voice finally snapped him out of it, and with the look of disbelief fading from his face, John answered in a thoughtful, awestruck voice, "Someone who came to warn us to get out of this place." After one last glance at the mountain behind him, he grabbed Holly's hand and they headed for the car as quickly as they could.

AS THEY DROVE south into Arizona, the feeling that had overwhelmed them on the dam gradually faded, leaving them numb in its wake. John answered Holly's questions about their ghostly visitation as best he could, but aside from knowing who it was and what he had said, he was as mystified as she was by Will's appearance. And when it came to the matter of what lurked on the mountain, he could only speculate, having seen no more than Holly had.

As unnerving as the episode had been, John's thoughts quickly came to focus exclusively on Will. His grandmother had once told him that his grandfather had visited her a week after his death, and a friend who had recently passed on from AIDS had also claimed to have had a similar visitation from his long-dead mother, but while

John had been careful to appear accepting, or at least open to the possibility that such things could happen, privately he had remained skeptical—until now. What he had written off as magical thinking on his grandmother's part and an innocent delusion on the part of his friend wasn't so easy to dismiss after his own experience. His first thought had been to label it a hallucination, but that didn't explain why Holly saw it too. And all the other rational explanations that came to mind—it had been a trick of the light, or a man that simply looked like Will—didn't hold up, either. Illusions didn't speak, and strangers—even ones who looked familiar—didn't just vanish into thin air.

It eventually occurred to him that if it was possible to die and still come back—as he had indisputably done after the run-in with Ruby—then maybe it wasn't so far-fetched that Will could return from the other side, too, even if he was in a different form. The more he considered it, the truer it rang. He already had ample proof of life after death, and of equally strange things—prophetic visions, spiritual revelations, the ability he'd been given to read someone's mind—so accepting that a deceased friend had suddenly appeared to warn them of danger didn't seem so unreasonable. Once he got past the surprise of the experience, it was comforting to think that Will was watching over him.

That did not settle the matter of what had actually prompted Will's warning, though, and after replaying what he had felt (but had not seen), John still could not fathom what had threatened them at the dam. Needing some explanation, even a temporary one, he finally decided it might have been a wild animal, a coyote, perhaps, or whatever else roamed that strange terrain. The possibility didn't exactly explain what they had felt, but with no evidence to the contrary, he reluctantly decided it would have to do, especially since nothing had actually harmed them.

Having made some tentative sense of the incident, John tried to relax and figure out where to go from there. He glanced over at Holly and decided she seemed to be handling everything okay. As a matter of fact, she had accepted the idea of having seen a ghost much quicker than John, even though she still found it mildly unsettling. She also hadn't decided yet whether to blame John for the visitation, since the ghost was someone he knew. The intense sensation of despair and danger she had felt just prior to Will's appearance had scared her more, but now that they had put some miles between themselves and the dam, her initial terror had subsided, giving way to a milder anxiety and a subtle sensation of mystery and awe.

Even without the incident at the dam, it had been an eventful day for both of them, and by the time they entered the town of Kingman, Arizona, an hour later, the adrenaline rush was a fading memory and fatigue had set in. Noticing Holly was having trouble staying awake, John said, "Both of us have been yawning for the last ten miles. What do you say we find a place to stop for the night?"

"That's a good idea," Holly agreed, stifling another yawn. She usually stayed up long past midnight, but the last few days had taken a toll and the thought of sleep was incredibly appealing, especially now that they were safely out of Nevada.

There were several motels grouped along the highway, and when they finally found one whose sign said VACANCY in bright red neon, John pulled into the lot and parked in front of the office. "How does this look?" he asked Holly.

"If you like it, it's fine," she replied. "I think I'm going to sleep in the car—if that's okay with you." Not only did she want to avoid the possibility of having to say she didn't want to share a room, Holly also was loathe to spend the money. Having borrowed three hundred dollars from Tina, she needed to make it stretch until she found a town that felt right to settle down in. Until that happened, she planned to stay in motels only when she couldn't find a cheaper alternative, like a women's shelter, the YWCA or even a safe place outdoors.

John was taken aback by her answer. "In the car?" he repeated, glancing out at the darkened parking lot. "That wouldn't be very safe." When it dawned on him that he hadn't known Holly long enough to gain her trust, he shook his head and turned to her with an expression he hoped was reassuring. "Don't worry, I'm sure they've got two rooms. And if they don't, there's bound to be at least one of these places with more than one vacancy. I just don't think sleeping in the car is a good idea."

Feeling as if she were being backed into a corner, Holly lowered her eyes and admitted the truth: "To be honest, I'm on kind of a limited budget. It's nice of you to be concerned, but I'm sure I'll be fine."

John was insistent: "Holly, it's too dangerous—especially for a woman. Like you said back at the restaurant, you never know when you'll run into a creep—or worse."

Holly glanced up, suddenly concerned. "You don't think your friend from the dam will show up again, do you?" she asked anxiously, referring to Will. Dealing with a ghost twice in the same night was more than she thought she could handle at the moment.

John shook his head, deciding Will's visitation was a once-in-a-lifetime occurrence. "No, I don't think so," he replied thoughtfully, then hastily proposed a compromise on the matter of the room. "Look, let me pay for your room. You can even consider it a loan, if you like. But I've got some insurance money left over from the settlement and I intend to spend it—if I'd brought someone else with me, I would have done the same thing." He paused and gave her an uncompromising look, adding, "If you sleep in the car, then I will, too—and tomorrow we'll both feel too crappy to enjoy the trip. It's not like I'm offering to put you up at the Ritz or anything," he finished with a small smile. "We're talking about the Rest-E-Z Motel, after all."

Holly thought it over, trying to decide if the offer was charity or generosity, and after deciding it was the latter—and that it was rude to refuse if no harm would result—she reluctantly gave in. "Okay," she said, frowning slightly. "But I'm not really comfortable with it." John smiled but said nothing, and hurried inside to check on the rooms.

When he returned a few minutes later, he handed Holly a key.

"We're in luck," he announced. "They had two rooms left—you're in ten and I'm in eleven." He cleared his throat and added delicately, "The manager said there's a connecting door, but it locks from either side. I assumed that would be okay with you."

"That's fine," Holly answered self-consciously. She regretted having made him think she didn't trust him but didn't see how it could have been avoided. Trying to make it up to him, she smiled and said, "Thanks for everything. I appreciate what you've done." And remembering one of her grandmother's old sayings, she added lightly but with genuine sentiment, "May it come back to you tenfold—or however many times good deeds are supposed to come back."

John laughed appreciatively and said, "You're welcome—and thanks."

After agreeing to sleep late the following morning and get together for breakfast around ten o'clock, they parted for the night. Once inside her room, Holly unpacked the things she would need for the next day, discreetly bolted the lock on the connecting door, then slipped out of her clothes and climbed into bed. Soon after, she was fast asleep.

WHEN THE CLOCK on the nightstand marked 2 A.M., John was still awake, his mind in overdrive, refusing to shut down. The day had been the equivalent of an emotional roller coaster. Driving to Las Vegas to hunt for Holly, finally finding her at the restaurant when he'd almost lost hope, persuading her to go with him, the danger at the dam, Will's shocking visit, the understandable tension between two perfect strangers—all seemed to require more processing and thought before they'd let him rest. Beyond all that, there still remained the issue of where to go from here, but that turned out to be easier to deal with than some of the others: he simply told himself that whatever he needed to know would come to him when it was time. That was the way things had worked so far—as difficult as it had been to accept at times—and it was finally sinking in that that was the way they would continue to go. *Looks like you're finally getting it,* he told himself wryly. Of course, the true test would be if tomorrow rolled around and nothing had come to him.

Having gained that small but crucial insight, he let go of the rest of his concerns, and yielded to the weariness that suffused his body. As on so many other recent nights, he drifted into sleep expecting his dreams to be eventful and revealing. At the very least, he expected to be shown his next move, and maybe, he hoped, he would continue his dialogue with the Being of Light. Now that he'd hooked up with Holly it seemed likely, especially since each time he remembered a piece of his NDE he always had the feeling that, as astounding as it was, there was still more to come .

If that were true, then his budding patience was put to the test as the night progressed, for the mysterious tunnel and the magnificent Light who waited at its end failed to recall him. In their stead, however, were delivered two revelations, one reassuring and the other portentous. The first was in the form of a vivid vision of John and Holly visiting the Grand Canyon, smiling and talking as the sun went down. The other was of someone from his earlier dreams: the balding middle-aged man whom John now knew—for whatever reason— was the father of the boy from several other dreams. The last time he had appeared in one of John's dreams, he had seemed a harbinger of trouble, although the threat he posed hadn't been very clear. This time, however, he was buying a gun. . . .

TWENTY-TWO

Approaching the Abyss

KATE DANDRIDGE WAS THE FIRST one up on Monday morning, and a restless night's sleep had done nothing to dispel her disappointment and fury over Elliot's reaction to Matt's baseball tickets. Grimly rushing through her morning routine, she pointedly avoided the living room, where her husband was sleeping, afraid to risk another chancy encounter, mostly because Elliot had become so unpredictable, but partly because she didn't trust her own frazzled temper. Lori was already gone, having spent the night at a friend's house, so Matt—who had borne the brunt of the previous day's disaster—would be alone with his father when Kate left. That made her uncomfortable, but it didn't feel right to encourage her son to hide from his father. She went to work hoping that Matt would leave on his own.

After Matt had been awakened by his dad in the middle of the night—not for an apology but for a slap in the face—his sleep had been restless, too, and plagued with dreams, most of them nightmares involving his father. Over and over, his mind kept returning to one scene in particular: Elliot standing in the moonlight next to his bed in that terrifying moment right before he hit him. The expression on his dad's face had stung much worse than the hand that followed, and the fear it caused him refused to go away even in the light of a brand-new day.

He stayed in bed much longer than usual, hoping his dad would go somewhere. When Elliot finally left around 10 A.M., Matt scrambled out of bed and ran to the window to watch him leave. Once the coast was clear, he threw on his clothes and grabbed his sneakers, and ran downstairs for a quick breakfast.

He was putting on his shoes when the doorbell rang. Thinking his father had come back home without his key, Matt froze. With his foot drawn up on the kitchen chair and his fingers tangled in the laces of one sneaker, he turned his head slowly in the direction of the living room, then turned and stared at the door behind him, wondering if he should sneak out the back. When the doorbell chimed again, he finished tying his sneaker with growing trepidation, and crept into the dining room to see who was at the door.

Drawing back the drapes just enough to peek outside, he was relieved to see that it wasn't his father, after all. The man on the porch was much taller and younger than Elliot Dandridge, with a red bandanna tied around a mop of thick brown hair. A large truck with BAKER BROTHERS painted on the side was parked at the curb, and opening its rear door was a younger and slightly shorter man with long blond hair tied back in a ponytail. Glimpsing furniture inside the open trailer, Matt naturally assumed they were making a delivery and went to let them in.

"Hi," Matt said after opening the door.

"Hi," the older of the two men said without smiling. "I'm Marv

Baker. That's my brother Jeff," he added, gesturing over his shoulder with a clipboard. "We're here for the living room set."

"And the TV," Jeff reminded him.

Matt gave them both a puzzled look. "Did you say you're *here* for the living room set or you're here to *deliver* the living room set?"

"We're here to pick one up," Marv replied flatly.

"Yeah, we're the *repo* men," Jeff explained. Strangely, he smiled.

"Are your parents home?" the older Baker went on, looking past Matt's shoulder into the house.

With a sinking feeling, Matt finally understood. "I better call my mom." He raced back to the kitchen and called his mother without thinking to close the door. When he returned, Marv and Jeff were already loading the sofa onto the back of the truck. Matt stared in shock at the big empty spot on the carpet and ran outside as the Baker brothers started up the walk to get the next piece.

"Wait a minute, you guys!" he exclaimed, frantically waving and backpedaling toward the porch when the men didn't stop. "My mom said to hold off. She's going to make a call and straighten this all out."

"It's too late for that, kid," the younger Baker said, almost apologetically.

"But there's been some kind of mistake!" Matt wailed, stopping at the porch steps and unconsciously blocking their way. "It's *our* furniture!"

"Not anymore, it isn't." The man with the bandanna pointed at the clipboard. "Look, kid," he said in a voice that conveyed how often he'd heard this before, "this is a work order from the furniture store to pick up a living room set at this address. If your mom works something out with them later, fine. But right now we've got a job to do." He brushed past Matt and went back inside.

Matt followed him in and tried calling his mother again, but Kate's line was busy and stayed that way for the next few minutes. Finally, he gave up and wandered back into the living room, where he watched with dismay as the men methodically but quickly cleaned out the room.

When they unplugged the TV and carried it to the door, Matt trailed behind them, open-mouthed and miserable, feeling as if he were losing a favorite friend.

"This turned out to be a piece of cake," Jeff Baker said to his brother as they moved carefully down the walk with the heavy TV.

Marv smiled for the first time. "Yeah, it's always a lot easier when the parents aren't home."

"I feel kind of sorry for the kid, though," Jeff said, nodding. "I wouldn't want to lose my TV."

"I'm just glad he didn't jump on my back the way the last one did," Marv responded. "I wish they were all this cooperative."

Jeff started to agree but frowned instead. Before he could say anything, Marv felt a forceful tap at the back of his right shoulder.

It was Elliot Dandridge, who had just returned after walking several blocks to Denny's with a raging hangover, only to discover he'd spent all of his money the night before. "What the hell do you think you're doing?" he demanded.

Angry at being jabbed in the back, Marv replied testily, "What the hell does it look like we're doing? We're repossessing the furniture you didn't pay for. Now if you'll kindly move out of the way, this TV is getting heavy."

"I don't care if it weighs a ton," Elliot exploded. "Now put it back in the house—and unload the rest of my furniture, too," he added, seeing the sofa and chairs in the open trailer. "I want everything back exactly where it came from."

"That's what we're doing: taking it back where it came from," Jeff retorted. His tone was almost flippant, but his eyes made it clear he was ready to get serious if Elliot provoked him.

Even though both of the Bakers were younger and stronger, Elliot was too mad and embarrassed that this was happening in full view of the neighbors to be intimidated. But the Bakers were too experienced to be intimidated by him. When they tried to detour around him, Elliot cursed in frustration and snatched at the television, trying to wrest it away. A brief struggle ensued, and as Matt watched from the doorway with a sinking feeling, the TV went crashing to the concrete walk. There was a sickening sound of splintering wood and shattering glass, and then a pregnant silence as all three men stared in surprise at the ruined TV.

Jeff Baker spoke first. "Well, that's one less thing for us to carry."

"And one more thing he still has to pay for," his brother added through clenched teeth.

"Like hell I will!" Elliot snapped, flailing his arms. "You two . . . *thieves* . . . are going to buy me a new one!"

Marv cocked an eyebrow at him. "I don't think so," he replied in a low voice. "You're the one who broke it."

"*You're* the ones who broke it!" Elliot sputtered, shoving him hard in the chest. His face was reddening and the vein in his forehead was visibly throbbing.

Ready to defend his brother, Jeff raised his fists and stepped in between them, but Marv grabbed his arm and held him back. They closed ranks and faced off with Elliot over the TV's remains, grim-faced and waiting for him to make another move. His own hands bunched tightly into fists, Elliot was too full of white-hot fury to speak. He glared at the brothers and then down at the ground, tempted to grab a leg from the broken TV and beat them until they promised to give back his furniture, but after a few delicious moments of savoring the image, he wordlessly turned around and stormed up the walk to the open front door.

When he got there, he smacked Matt hard on the side of the head.

"Hey!" the Baker brothers yelled in unison, starting toward the house.

Elliot faced them with a look that stopped them in their tracks. "If you know what's good for you," he hissed, "you'll mind your own business." Then he slammed the front door with a resounding *crack*.

While Marv and Jeff stood by the truck, debating what to do, Elliot slapped Matt again. "You let them in, didn't you?" he said savagely. Matt yelped and shied away, but before he could say anything, Elliot grabbed him by the collar and dragged his face to within inches of his own. *"Didn't you?"* he screamed. "I bet you even helped them, didn't you—you're such a *helpful* boy. . . ."

Too terrified to speak, Matt could only stare and try to keep from crying.

"What's the matter, did the coma make you stupid?" Elliot jeered. He slapped Matt a third time on the side of the face.

"Don't, Dad! Please," Matt croaked, his eyes open wide in full-blown terror. "I'm sorry . . ." He began to sob. "I didn't know who they were."

Until that moment, Elliot's attention had been focused entirely on his son's infuriating presence. Now he made an incoherent, guttural sound and the anger in his eyes seemed to harden and compress as his gaze drifted past Matt and fell for the first time on the room behind him. The sofa, both chairs—including his favorite—the end tables, the coffee table and the TV were gone. All that remained were the photos on the wall and two lamps they had purchased from a different store. If he had been furious before, seeing the barrenness of the room set him off even worse. "Son . . . of . . . a . . . *bitch!*" he roared, shoving Matt away as he spat the last word. With his arms flailing, the boy stumbled backward and landed in a heap against the opposite wall. As the breath was knocked from his body with a painful *whoosh*, the room rumbled with the sound of the truck pulling away from the curb outside.

Ignoring his son, Elliot surveyed the emptiness with a terrifying expression, his dwindling self-awareness pushed further aside by a powerful, blinding, free-floating rage. He shook his head slowly from side to side, and as his face grew redder the knuckles of his fists grew whiter and whiter. When his anger had been stoked to the point where he felt as if his whole body would explode, he glanced around the room for something to smash or hit or throw, something that would help him vent his rage. It wasn't long before he settled on Matt, who whimpered softly at the look on his father's face and scrambled to his knees, ready to run.

After a slight hesitation, Elliot raised a fist and started toward him.

He was halfway across the room when the small, faint voice of his struggling reason brought him up short with a single word: *Don't.* His anger only stalled, he stared intently at his son for a few seconds longer, then abruptly turned and snatched up a lamp that was sitting on the floor. As Matt let out a cry and leapt to his feet, Elliot hurled it across the room in the other direction, where it smashed into the wall with a resounding crash and shattered into a hundred porcelain fragments. Elliot smiled perversely, staring at the hole in the plaster wall, then stormed up the stairs. After raiding the secret lockbox in the back of his closet, he left the house without so much as a glance at Matt, and headed for the bar with a wallet full of money and a burning thirst.

"HOW FAR IS the Grand Canyon from here?" John asked. Having wound up sleeping until almost noon, he and Holly were having a late breakfast at a Denny's restaurant down the street from the motel; Holly had just asked if he had decided on a destination.

"About a hundred miles, I guess," Holly replied, trying to hide her disappointment. Having hoped to see other parts of Arizona where she might want to move, like Flagstaff or Phoenix, the idea of spending the day sightseeing made her toy with the idea of finding another ride. But after considering how lucky she had been the first time out, and reminding herself that she was basically ambivalent about Arizona, she decided to be patient and abandoned the idea.

If she had known John's real motivation for going to the Grand Canyon, she might have felt differently. After the previous night's dreams, John's sense of being on a mission was even stronger than before, and the vision of the Grand Canyon had firmly convinced him that Holly was part of it. Although the other vision—that of the man buying a gun—was a little less explicit in its implications, his fear that the boy who kept appearing in his dreams was in growing danger was also reinforced, as well as his suspicion that somewhere down the road—and possibly soon—he would have to get involved. It occurred to him that both visions might be connected, but it was difficult to see how. The one thing he was sure of was that he and Holly should go to the Grand Canyon and stay for the sunset. "Does that sound okay to you?" he asked, wondering what he would do if Holly said no.

Holly debated with herself one last time, and agreed. "Sure," she replied in a neutral voice, hoping that on the way back she could convince him to stop at Flagstaff for the night. "I haven't been there since I was a little girl."

WHILE JOHN AND HOLLY were getting to know each other better on their way to the Grand Canyon, Kate Dandridge was arriving home from work. Having failed to persuade the furniture store to call off the repossession, she had thought she was prepared for what she would find when she walked into the house, but it was still a shock to lay eyes on the harsh reality—which, in addition to one hundred and fifty square feet of bare floor, involved a shattered lamp and a hole in the wall three feet above it. It was this that made the desecration near-perfect in her mind, the final touch that would be a daily reminder of all that had gone wrong, and it let loose the tears she had been trying to resist, because she knew without asking that the movers hadn't thrown the lamp at the wall; it was just the kind of thing that Elliot would do.

When the tears finally slowed, she got a broom and dustpan to clean up the mess. She considered covering the hole with a painting, but decided to leave it, like evidence at a crime scene, until Elliot came home. Once she finished, she wandered back into the kitchen and disposed of the lamp, then sat down and stared forlornly through the window at the sidewalk outside, wondering why Fate—with a big hand from Elliot—had decided it was time to rough up their lives. No answer came, and seeking comfort in its place, or at least an audience for her darkening mood, she reached for the phone to call her mother, but hung up the receiver before finishing the number. Her mother, she remembered, would rightly put the blame on Elliot's shoulders and launch into a stern but well-intentioned lecture on why it was time to consider divorce, or at the very least counseling—both of which Elliot would never consider. Since Kate couldn't stand the thought of a lecture and was too embarrassed to share this particular problem with her friends, she wound up turning back to the window and shadowboxing instead.

She had repeatedly rehearsed and revised a confrontation with Elliot by the time Matt rode past the window and into the backyard. Despite his earlier trauma, he had dutifully run his paper route after dragging the remains of the shattered TV into the garage, and the sight of him coming home reminded Kate that he had been the one who called her to say the furniture was being repossessed. No one had answered when she called back later, and she had been so upset ever since that it had completely slipped her mind that Matt was involved. Now it struck her that it must have been traumatic for him, and she was overcome by regret and a keen sense of failure. With an expression that did little to hide her emotions, she went to the back door and waited for her son, hoping he wasn't taking it too badly, and praying he had left before his father had come home and made the mess.

Noticing his black eye as he trudged up the stairs, her heart sank and her fingers tensed around the doorknob. "Honey, what happened to you?" she exclaimed as he walked through the door. Gingerly touching the black and purple bruise, she pulled off his baseball cap and tilted his face upward to get a better look. "Are you okay?" she asked with motherly alarm.

"I'm okay," Matt mumbled.

Kate waited, then prompted him again. "Matt, how did this happen?" she repeated softly, hoping against hope that he had run into a door or gotten into a fight, either of which was preferable to what she suspected.

Matt scuffed the floor nervously with the toe of his sneaker. He considered lying, but instead replied, "It doesn't hurt too much."

Kate again gently took his face in her hands, lifting it to hers. "That's not what I asked you," she said, forcing a stern note into her voice. Softening again, but with a look that made it clear she wouldn't back off, she reiterated, "Matt, honey, who did this to your eye?"

Matt swallowed hard. "Dad," he finally admitted and looked away.

Her worst fears confirmed, Kate stiffened momentarily, then got to her feet. "Oh, honey," she cried, gathering Matt into her arms and hugging him fiercely. "I'm so sorry. I'm sorry you had to be here when all of this happened." Vowing to herself that Elliot would never lay a hand on her son again, Kate took Matt by the shoulders, looked him in the eyes and said in a trembling but determined voice, "Your dad will never do this to you again. I promise." After one last hug, she sent him upstairs and sat down at the table to wait for her husband.

ELLIOT HAD DOWNED so many beers that he shouldn't have been feeling the slightest bit of pain. Yet his head was pounding with a dull, throbbing ache across the width of his forehead, and over the last few hours his thoughts had become painful and increasingly volatile, ranging far and wide from remorseful flashes of momentary insight to the obsessive grip of irrational rage.

Now that five o'clock had rolled around, the bar was starting to get busy, but Elliot barely noticed the increasing noise as he sat at a table in the darkest corner of the ill-lit room. He was even less aware of the people who had drifted in over the last half hour and taken the tables on either side of his own. He was too busy thinking.

After storming out of the house, it had taken every bit of three hours to calm himself down, and for the last few minutes, aided by the effects of an alcohol low, he had gradually slipped from being angry to maudlin, drifting unawares into a reflective mood. *I sure made a mess of dinner,* he thought, casting back to yesterday's ill-fated meal, which had ended with a tantrum that now seemed shameful. *Lately, it seems like I'm making a mess out of everything.* And what he had done to Matt this morning—it had felt good at the time, even irresistible, but now he wasn't so sure it wasn't out of proportion to the boy's mistake. He had swatted his kids before, even spanked them a few times, but he had never actually hit them, not with such force and uncontrolled anger.

Elliot peered into the smooth, amber surface of his Budweiser and saw the ghosts of the past few months of his life. The late arrivals. The contentious meals. The discussions with Kate that had inevitably escalated into confrontations. Matt's terrified expression when Elliot had grabbed him that morning. And throughout it all, the countless hours spent in this bar . . . His frown deepened. "I've got to stop drinking," he said thickly to himself and took another swig.

Of course, the drinking was more a symptom than the problem. If he could only straighten out what had gone wrong in his life, he wouldn't need the beer—or at least not so often—but at the moment, figuring out how to do that seemed impossible. It was like being surrounded by a family of angry bears and having only one bullet in a shaking gun; there were just too many targets and too little firepower. Everything was so complicated and unrelenting; just when he thought he could deal with a problem, along came another one. Like yesterday, which had started out fine and then gone straight to hell. It had been a perfect Sunday afternoon, just like old times, and he actually had been enjoying the company of his family, something he hadn't done for what seemed like forever. He had almost felt like his old self again, like he had gotten a reprieve and was on the verge of a smoother run that would help him turn things around.

And then Matt had brought out the baseball tickets and it all fell apart.

The boy was just trying to make you happy, a small voice said in his head.

Before the guilt could set in, another, more persuasive voice spoke up and said it wasn't so: *The boy was rubbing your face in your troubles, that's what he was doing. He wanted to remind you that since you can't get a job, you can't afford a ball game—or flowers for your wife—without someone's charity. And the other two were in on it. You know that they were.*

Elliot shook his head uncertainly, then took another drink and considered both scenarios. There was a time when he never would have thought of the second one, but after the events of the past two days, it seemed that Matt *was* turning against him, or at least didn't like him. He couldn't remember the last time they'd actually sat on the porch and talked or watched a ball game together, something they used to do religiously every Saturday afternoon. Matt always seemed to find an excuse to disappear as soon as Elliot showed up, and even when the boy did stick around, he completely ignored him as if Elliot weren't even there or wasn't worth talking to.

Lori was treating him differently, too. The change was more subtle than in Matt's case, but it was there. Mostly it showed in little things. Her face didn't light up when he walked into the room, like it used to do. She seldom kissed him good night or gave him a hug. And at times she acted as if she was downright afraid of him. Someone else might not have noticed, but how could he miss it? He knew his own daughter. *Or at least, I used to know her,* he thought sadly.

As if it weren't enough that his kids had become strangers, his wife had changed, too. Kate was so damned moody these days and too wrapped up in herself to give him any support, not to mention affection; she'd cut him off weeks ago, with no sign of a thaw in the foreseeable future. Unlike Matt, she didn't try to avoid him. Instead, she always seemed to be waiting when he walked through the door, ready to criticize the way he was treating the kids—particularly Matt—or barrage him with questions about what he'd been doing, and then whine and complain when he didn't spout the answers she wanted to hear. Every time he'd had difficulties before, she'd been there for him with sympathy and encouragement, and stuck by his side until he found a new job. What made this time so different? He didn't have a clue. Well, he *did* have a clue, he thought, glancing at his beer, but just because he wasn't handling unemployment as well as before wasn't grounds to abandon him. If anything, Kate should have worked that much harder to help him get through it. But she hadn't and she wouldn't. She had turned against him when he needed her most. And after losing their furniture—which wouldn't have happened if Matt hadn't let those men in—she'd be on him even worse.

The more he thought about it, the deeper it cut him to realize his family were trying to abandon him. All he'd ever tried to do was provide for everyone. It wasn't his fault he'd lost his job. He wasn't any happier about being broke than the rest of them—if anything, he felt ten times worse. Couldn't they see that?

Of course, their finances wouldn't have been so screwed up if Matt hadn't done something stupid like getting hit by a car. He must have told the boy at least a hundred times to watch out for cars when he rode his bike, but he hadn't. So, on top of everything else, they had all those medical bills. *That* was the difference between this time and all the others when he'd been out of work. The accident changed everything and blew the loss of his income all out of proportion. Matt's timing was lousy, to say the least.

Now everything was in danger of falling apart, and just because he couldn't wave a magic wand to make it all better, he was suddenly the bad guy. It was still hard to believe. He was used to betrayal from other people—actually, he'd come to expect it—but he'd always thought he could count on his family no matter how bad things got.

Looks like you were wrong, the second voice opined. *And not only do they hold you responsible for not fixing the problem, they blame you for causing it. As far as they're concerned, everything's your fault.*

No wonder he couldn't muster the courage to look for another job. *Who in his right mind would bust his butt for people who don't even like him?* he mused. *A fool, perhaps. But I'm no fool.*

Then again, maybe he was—hadn't he spent the last eighteen years working at jobs he disliked, just so his family could have a good life? And look what it got him. It would serve them right if they *did* lose everything. He wagged his head angrily from side to side, then drained his beer and slammed it on the table. The situation at home was becoming intolerable. The looks, the arguments, the veiled accusations all had to stop. The disrespect, the lack of support, his very own children undermining his marriage—he had tolerated it too long, and now he was through. *As soon as I get home,* he thought, getting up from the table, *I'm going to put an end to this nonsense, once and for all.*

TWENTY-THREE

The View from the Edge
of the Visible World

"THIS IS REALLY SOMETHING, isn't it?" Holly said in an awed voice. She and John were standing with a few dozen other tourists at one of the Grand Canyon's popular lookout points. The view was breathtaking, and Holly suddenly found herself glad they'd come.

John's eyes were riveted on the colorful panorama. "It's incredible," he agreed. "I should have done this a long time ago."

Holly understood his feelings. As someone who often felt a stronger, more direct connection with nature than she did with people, Holly felt the intrinsic and immediate pull of this place. The day was warm, without a cloud in the sky, and the wide-open blue above the enormous landscape made the sky and the canyon appear endless, stretching into infinity from the point where she stood. The colorfully striated zigzag fissures were almost too long and too wide and too deep to take in, and despite the presence of the others around her, the inherent solitude and peaceful energy of the ancient place was near-overwhelming, too profound to grasp. It managed to thrill and at the same time humble her, and it wasn't long before she found herself under the spell of a sublime epiphany, an instinctive and spiritual—if only rudimentary—understanding of her place on the planet. At that moment, she began to see her problems from a new perspective, one in which her attempted suicide and lingering despair seemed not only self-indulgent but grossly inappropriate. While the insight wasn't a miraculous cure for her deep-seated depression, it did ease her spirit and open her mind to new possibilities.

In the wake of his meeting with the Being of Light, John was also operating from a new perspective. As it was for Holly, the canyon's grandeur was a reminder of his place in the universal plan and gave him a seldom-experienced sense of oneness. Like him, the canyon was part and parcel of the divine Creator, an earthly reflection of eternal reality, and it called forth the feelings he had experienced so intensely on the other side—the awe, the joy, the clarity of being. As soon as he had fastened his gaze on the sight, he had immediately felt stronger, more settled and less daunted by the uncertainty surrounding his unfolding mission.

After their initial exchange, John and Holly fell reverentially silent, still not having moved from the spot where they had first glimpsed the canyon. They made a striking pair: two tall, handsome figures standing in the sunlight. Unlike most of the other couples standing at the rim of what could easily pass for the edge of the world, they stood apart and not touching as they scanned the horizon, but the distance between them was short and friendly.

After the three-hour drive from Kingman to the canyon, the uneasy relationship between the two former strangers was beginning to change. Little by little, Holly was letting down her guard, and the easier it became to talk to John, the easier it was for John to respond in kind. Sharing a similar spiritual experience was taking them a step further (although neither was consciously aware it was happening) and they were edging beyond merely tolerating each other's company to a place where they were actually beginning to enjoy it.

After a while, John inclined his head toward the beaten path that led off to their left through the scattered trees along the rim. "Want to see what it looks like from a different angle? I assume that leads to another vantage point."

"Several, actually," Holly replied. "If I remember correctly."

"Then let's check them out."

Holly grinned. "I'd never forgive you if we didn't."

They spent the next half hour exploring the path, stopping along the way at each open juncture for a different view. Finally they came to a clearing where the vista opened up even wider and more spectacular than it had anywhere else. A broad, flat boulder sat at the edge of the lookout point, and a teenage couple were sitting cross-legged on it, holding hands, with their heads almost touching as they took in the sights. John and Holly agreed it was the best seat in the house, and as soon as the other couple vacated the rock, they hastily claimed it.

They were still perched there an hour later, willingly yielding to the canyon's spell. Holly hadn't felt so good in a long, long time, and as she dangled her legs over the wide-open space that stretched out below her, she closed her eyes and had the sudden conviction that if she rose to her feet and stepped off the rock, she would fly as high as the loftiest eagle and soar effortlessly over the canyon if she actually desired. It was a liberating thought and she savored it happily, wishing it were true.

When she finally opened her eyes, she smiled dreamily and leaned forward to peer over the edge of the boulder. The precipitous drop to the chasm below immediately brought her back to reality, and she reminded herself with a sigh of regret that if she stepped into the air she would plummet to her death, not soar to freedom. For the first time it struck her how surprising it was that there was no fence or barrier along the rim to keep people from falling over the edge. Having so recently been given a reprieve from death, Holly reflexively scooted back a few inches and redirected her thoughts to happier things, like wondering what a sunset over the canyon would look like. When the idea refused to go away, she turned to John and asked, "Do you like sunsets?"

John glanced up with a look of surprise. The dream that had prompted him to bring Holly there had involved the two of them watching the sunset, and while the ex–cocktail waitress had been daydreaming about flying, he had been trying to work out a scenario that would keep them there for the next few hours. Now he realized that if Holly was leading up to what he thought she was, the mechanics of the situation already had been worked out for him. He smiled to himself, then more deeply at Holly. "That's one of the main reasons I go to the ocean every chance I get," he replied with sincerity. "The sunsets are spectacular."

Holly was delighted. "I can't believe it!" she responded, grabbing John's arm. "I knew there was a reason why I took you up on your offer to give me a ride—I must have sensed you were a kindred spirit!" She flashed an unself-conscious, almost goofy grin, an endearing gesture that hadn't gotten much use over the last few months. Then her voice grew reflective. "Sunsets are just about my favorite thing in the whole world. I can get totally lost watching the sun go down over the mountains back home."

John understood completely. He felt the same way, even if he didn't vocalize his feelings as freely as Holly. He started to suggest that they wait until sundown before leaving the canyon but Holly beat him to it. "Why don't we stay for the sunset?" she said with an infectious enthusiasm, squeezing his arm. "It would be a shame to miss it in a place like this!"

"You must be a mind reader," John laughed, shaking his head. "I was just thinking the same thing."

"Great! Then it's settled."

John's stomach growled, and he looked at his watch. "We've still got a few hours. Want to get something to eat and come back?"

Holly glanced down at their rocky perch. "And lose this place?" she said, appalled at the thought. "If we give it up now, we might never get it back."

"Hmm . . . true," John replied, smiling apologetically. "But, to be honest, I'm really getting hungry." He wanted to see the sunset from that spot almost as much as Holly, but his stomach was insistent.

Holly tried to hide her disappointment, then abruptly beamed. "I've got an idea!" she said excitedly. "May I borrow your car for a little bit?"

Ever since the first time John had seen her in his vision, Holly had always appeared depressed, at best; now she seemed happy, even excited, and John was so taken aback that at first he didn't understand what she was asking. When he realized she was asking for the car, his knee-jerk reaction was that he would rather risk starvation than turn over his keys to someone he had just met the day before. An image of Holly driving off in the Jeep, never to return, sprang to mind. Just as suddenly, he felt ashamed for entertaining the idea; he had not known Holly very long, but he instinctively knew she wasn't a thief. Being careful to hide his initial suspicion, he asked as nonchalantly as he could, "Why?"

"It's a surprise," Holly replied brightly. "I just need to go into town for a bit. You can stay here and read or something, and save our spot." She let go of his arm, crossed her heart and added with mock seriousness, "Don't worry, I swear I won't take off on you. I'll be back before you know it, and I'll bring back something so you won't pass out while we're waiting for the sunset."

John could not help but be intrigued. Since the request came so close on the heels of her not-so-coincidental suggestion to stay for the sunset, he didn't want to risk derailing the scenario that seemed to be unfolding. And it made him feel so good to see Holly emerging from her depression that he didn't have the heart to tell her no. "All right," he said, nearly matching Holly's lighthearted tone. "But be careful with my Jeep. I haven't had it that long."

"I'll be careful. I promise," Holly replied as John fished the keys from his pocket and handed them over. "Do you want anything from the car before I take off?"

"Maybe I will grab something to read while you're gone," John answered, swinging his legs over the boulder's side and getting to his feet. He held out his hand and Holly gave him back the keys. "Be right back," he said and headed up the path to where the car was parked.

He returned five minutes later carrying a beach towel and one of the books he'd brought with him. "Got everything I need," he said, climbing back up on the boulder and handing Holly the keys.

"You're sure you don't mind waiting here all by yourself?" Holly asked, jumping down to the ground.

"Don't worry about me. I'll be fine." John smiled and waved as she turned to walk away. When she had gone, he spread the beach towel over the rock, glanced one more time at the now empty path, then opened the book and began to read.

AS HOLLY MANEUVERED John's car through the winding roads leading away from the canyon, it struck her again how remarkable it was that she could feel so good only forty-eight hours after deciding she could never feel good again. *Thank God for Tina,* she mused, thinking of the friend who had dragged her from the tub and rushed her to the hospital. *As soon as I get settled, I've got to do something to let her know how grateful I am for giving me another chance. . . .*

There had been moments when she wasn't sure she could ever make good on a second chance—even though she was determined to try—and now she wondered if she had been too pessimistic. The more she thought about how quickly her mood had rebounded, the more amazed she felt . . . as well as a little guilty. *What kind of person goes from opening up her wrists to being higher than a kite in only a few days?* she wondered. *Am I that shallow?* She considered it briefly, and decided not to pursue that particular train of thought. Putting her rejuvenated mood under too close scrutiny might cause it to melt like a delicate snowflake. Supposedly Lot's wife had been turned into a pillar of salt for looking back; maybe the wise thing to do was to heed the example.

Besides, this was the first time she had ever driven a car as big as the Jeep Cherokee, and she needed to pay more attention to what she was doing than what she was feeling, or risk having an accident. *That would go over big,* she thought, conjuring up an image of handing John back the keys to a banged-up car. How would she explain that— "Thanks for all you've done. I guess I was so busy being grateful that I didn't see that ditch until I was already in it"? Considering John was one of the reasons she was feeling better, wrecking his car was the last thing she wanted to do. If it weren't for him, she wouldn't have wound up at the Grand Canyon or maybe even have gotten out of Vegas when she did, both of which had done wonders for her.

But John had done much more than merely give her a ride. Despite her self-preoccupation, Holly recognized that not only was he being kind but he was doing it without treating her like an emotional cripple, which was more than most people could have managed after seeing her bandaged wrists. She suspected the reason for his sensitivity went beyond mere kindness—at times she couldn't help noticing that beneath his ready smile he seemed to be hiding his own uneasy secrets—but regardless of what motivated him, she was grateful for the way he had treated her so far.

Most men would have expected something in return by now, she mused. Of course, before it was all over John might, too, but somehow she doubted it—not that the thought of something eventually developing with him was distasteful, because it certainly wasn't. . . .

Holly shook her head and looked in the rearview mirror. "Better watch where you're going," she admonished her mirror self, and not in regard to the road she was driving. "You've known this guy less than twenty-four hours and already you're jumping to conclusions. Even if it does come to that, this is hardly the time to get involved with somebody." No, even if she happened to feel good at the moment, thinking like that was definitely dangerous when her emotions were still in such a state of flux.

Turning her attention back to the road, she mentally backpedaled to safer territory. *That doesn't mean you can't enjoy his company,* she told herself, trying to prevent the pendulum that had swung so far one way from swinging all the way back to the opposite side. Nor did it mean she should rethink the plan that had popped into her head back at the canyon. Holly was a staunch believer in showing appreciation when someone did something for her, and the idea of surprising her traveling companion with an impromptu picnic as the sun went down still seemed the perfect way to let John know she wasn't taking him for granted. It was hardly as grand a gesture as taking her on his trip and paying for her hotel room the previous night—and unfortunately she had to burn up more of his gas to go get the food—but it was the best she could do on a limited budget. *At any rate,* she mused, *it should be a lot of fun.* After the last few months, that was almost as important as everything else.

～

BACK AT THE CANYON, John had long since forgotten his reservations about loaning Holly the car. He was too engrossed in a book written by a man who had had a remarkably detailed near-death experience, one which was far more elaborate than anything John had remembered so far. Reading it was a landmark experience, not only because it answered so many of his questions about life, but also because it helped him understand his own NDE.

After half an hour in which everything around him might as well have disappeared, he put down the book and gazed thoughtfully around the canyon with a new sense of discovery and burgeoning excitement. He returned to the book and read several passages again, more slowly this time and with intense concentration. After finishing them a second time, he closed the book and stared off into the distance, not seeing the canyon but something beyond.

He realized that it was no coincidence that he should read this particular book in this particular time and place. And it was ironic, he thought, that he had seen the author on television several times prior to his own NDE, but had been afraid to take him seriously, even though he was fascinating and seemed genuine. Now, after all of his research and speculations and prayers, after weeks of being plagued by a burning question posed by his own experience, he felt as if an important door had been opened, and he finally understood his newfound gift, the one he had been promised during his NDE.

More important, he had a pretty good idea of how he was supposed to use it, and when and with whom.

TWENTY-FOUR

The Last Straw

WITH HIS CREEPING madness having won another battle with his fading rationality, Elliot Dandridge came home from the bar loaded for bear. Kate Dandridge was loaded for bear, too. She was more or less resigned to having lost their furniture, but Matt's black eye still had her so enraged she hadn't stopped pacing the kitchen floor for the last half hour. Matt was in the bathroom having an ice pack applied by Lori, who had returned from her friend's, and both of them froze, along with their mother, when the front door opened and Elliot came in.

Slamming the door behind him, Elliot planted himself in the middle of the living room, weaving slightly and scowling like a drunken monarch returning to the heart of an ungrateful kingdom. If possible, the barren room made him even angrier than before. He glanced in the direction of the kitchen and shouted, "Kate, get in here! We need to talk!"

Kate muttered under her breath, "You bet we do," and headed for the living room with a look that was the equal of Elliot's expression. She wanted to walk right up to him and slap his face or punch him in the nose, but the sight of her husband with his wild, puffy, bloodshot eyes and the drunken stance that gave him the appearance of being loose and dangerous made her opt for caution. She stopped at the edge of the dining room, a few yards away from where Elliot stood.

Without preamble, he announced, "I came home to tell you that things are going to change around here—starting right *now!*" His voice was stern, meant to be authoritarian, but the words were slurred.

It was obvious from his belligerence that he wasn't referring to his own behavior, and Kate summoned her courage and took up the gauntlet. "They sure are!" she shot back, moving closer. Her voice was low and wavering, barely under control. "You've really outdone yourself this time, Elliot! As if losing our furniture wasn't enough!" Elliot started to reply and she cut him off. "What kind of monster gives his own son a black eye?" she demanded heatedly, her voice rising as she moved a step closer. "Do you think it's okay to punch out an eleven-year-old boy?"

Having by this time more or less dismissed the incident with Matt, Elliot was caught off guard; he had expected Kate to be upset about the furniture instead. When he replied, his self-righteous tone had turned defensive. "He just let them walk right in and take everything!"

"So you used him as a punching bag!"

"He's old enough to know better than to let repo men in," Elliot countered, regaining his momentum. "If he hadn't been so stupid, none of this would have happened. He's the one you ought to be yelling at! Besides," he added with heavy sarcasm, "I didn't hit him that hard. . . . If I'd known he was so *tender,* I would've pulled my punches."

Kate gaped at him with shock, and Elliot smiled perversely, glad that his shot had hit the mark. In the bathroom down the hall, Lori and Matt stared at each other, stunned and scared.

Kate shook her head in disgust. "You've really convinced yourself that it's his fault, haven't you?" she said incredulously, her voice a near-whisper. She took a step closer and jabbed the air in front of Elliot's face with a trembling finger. "*You're* the one who brought that misfortune on us, not Matt!"

"What!" Elliot exploded, truly surprised. "By the time I got here, they'd already cleaned us out! How the hell can you say it's my fault?"

"Because it's the truth!" Kate responded acidly, discarding all caution. "And maybe if you weren't so damned drunk, you'd realize it!" Exasperated, she waved an arm in the air and let it drop at her side. "If you'd gone out and gotten a job we could've made the payments. Matt may have let them in because he didn't know any better, but you're the reason they came in the first place."

Elliot narrowed his eyes and glared at Kate. He wasn't entirely surprised that she was pinning it on him, but he had allowed himself to think that maybe she wouldn't. Now he felt victimized and betrayed, once again abandoned when he needed support. It was further proof that the conclusion he had reached about his family's loyalty was right on target. "Nice try," he replied, managing to sound both hurt and mocking. For several long months, despite accusations and insults, he had kept his opinion on the cause of their troubles completely to himself, nurturing it with self-pity and beer after beer until it grew into a conviction, an unspeakable truth that no one in the family had the courage to voice. Now he decided that if the nonsense was going to end, if people were ever going to stop treating him like the nasty hind end of a mangy dog, that painful truth had to come out in the open—the blame finally had to be placed where it rightfully belonged. With the telltale vein throbbing in his forehead, he moved a step closer to Kate and stuck a finger in her face. "Didn't it ever occur to you," he hissed with scathing condescension, "that if your *precious* little boy hadn't pulled that stunt that landed him in the hospital, we might have been able to pay those bills? That I might have had a chance to get over losing my job before having to deal with another setback? *That's* where it all started! If Matt had to play dodge-'em with a car, why couldn't he have picked a better time to do it?"

"A better time?" Kate gasped, horrified. She reached back and grabbed one of the dining room chairs to steady herself. In the bathroom, Lori turned to Matt with a sorrowful expression, and pulled him into her arms, covering his ears. "*A better time!*" Kate repeated. "Our son almost died—he *did* die—and you have the audacity to say you wished he'd picked a better *time?* You make it sound like he did it deliberately, just to make things tougher for you."

"I didn't say that," Elliot responded heatedly. "Stop twisting my words! I know it was an accident—but what about the paper route? And the tickets? And the flowers? You can't tell me he wasn't trying to make me look bad with those! 'Poor old Dad just can't stand the pressure,'" he mimicked in a singsong falsetto, derisively giving voice to his son's imaginary thoughts, "'so I guess it's up to me to be the man of the house.'"

Kate blew out a long, tense breath, trying to fathom what was happening to Elliot. In some ways he had always been difficult, but she had managed to deal with it because there was so much else about him that was easy to love. He was a good man—a loving husband and father, even if he did not always know how to show it—and she knew that at his core, somewhere beneath all the anger and confusion that were changing his personality, that good man was still there. But at the moment she could not see him. Everything seemed surreal to her—Elliot standing there with his wild-eyed look, and his hateful words ringing in her ears. It made Kate sick to her stomach and incredibly sad. When she finally spoke, it was in a calmer voice tinged with that sadness. "Elliot, I think it's time we got some help," she said, choosing her words carefully and trying to sound nonconfrontational. "It seems like everything's falling apart around here, and I don't think we can fix it without some professional help."

"You mean a shrink." Elliot's voice was deceptively neutral.

Kate gave a tentative nod. "A psychologist or a counselor of some kind." Knowing how he felt about counseling, she added hastily, "There's no shame in it, Elliot. It's like anything else: if you've got a problem you can't fix, you find someone who can help you fix it."

Elliot's eyes narrowed, his frown deepened. "We're both adults here," he replied, his voice heating up once again, "and neither one of us is stupid—despite what you think—so why don't you stop acting so coy and just say what you mean? When you say, 'I think it's time *we* got some help,' what you really mean is that you think it's time *I* got some help."

After a slight hesitation, Kate said softly, "Yes. I do."

At the bar, Elliot had stopped just short of convincing himself that his wife had completely turned against him. Now his last few doubts crumbled like dust. Staring silently at Kate, a sinking feeling spread through his chest as he realized bitterly that she completely misunderstood the point he was trying to make. It seemed painfully obvious to him that she no longer understood or even cared what he was feeling. "Do you think I've enjoyed the last few months?" he asked quietly, his voice laced with hurt. "Do you think I enjoy living like this?"

"I don't know," Kate answered, matching his tone. "I would hope not. . . . That's why I think you should get some help."

Angry again, Elliot shot back, "I hate it when you trot out that patronizing tone! Why am I the one who's always at fault? Why am I the one who suddenly needs help?"

"You really don't know?"

"It's a mystery to me," Elliot replied sarcastically. "Why don't you enlighten me?"

Completely exasperated, Kate ticked off a list of pent-up grievances. "First, you haven't really looked for a job. Then you wrecked the car. You ran up the Visa that was supposed to be our ace in the hole. You miss meals, or when you are here, you pull some stunt like you did yesterday. You're always at that *stupid* bar, and I never know when you'll come home—or if you'll even make it home—"

"Here we go with that again," Elliot interrupted, dismissing her words with a wave of his hand.

"Yes, here we go with that again," Kate shot back. "You should have been out getting another job, Elliot, so we wouldn't have to worry about losing our furniture—or our house, for that matter! But instead you spend all of your time drowning your sorrows in a bottle of beer, which only makes everything worse! What happened to you?"

"Well, it wasn't the beer," Elliot responded, defensive once more.

"It *was* the beer! Don't you understand? You've turned into a drunk! A self-pitying, pathetic—and violent—drunk!"

Elliot moved a step closer and raised his fist. "Watch yourself, Kate!"

"Is that your new way of dealing with problems?" Kate said sarcastically, pointing at his fist. "You never used to act like this, Elliot. Now look at you—yesterday you practically wrecked the dining room, today you put a huge hole in the wall and beat up your son and now you're ready to do the same thing to me!"

Elliot's expression grew thunderously dark. "Are you about finished?" he demanded in a low, ominous voice.

"No, I'm not finished!" Kate retorted. Months of resentment and silent frustration came rushing out in a scathing torrent, too powerful to check. "If you're determined to drink your way to the bottom, I can't stop you. But I'll be *damned* if I'll let you take us down with you! You're right, Elliot—things *are* going to change around here, one way or the other!"

Elliot's eyes narrowed. "What's that supposed to mean?"

"It means we can't go on like this," Kate said plaintively, looking away. She took a deep breath, turned back to her husband and threw down her trump card. "If you won't face what you're doing to yourself and your family . . . well, one of us will have to make different living arrangements."

Elliot was stunned. Of all the buttons Kate could have pressed to make him crazy, that was the one. "What are you saying, that you'd take the kids and leave me?" he asked in a voice that was strained with disbelief.

"No, I was thinking more along the lines of kicking you out!"

Down the hall, the Dandridge children stared at each other with growing dismay and held their breath. Elliot answered his wife with a contemptuous snort. "Fat chance," he replied.

Kate stared hard at her husband and made a decision. "Fine," she responded wearily, turning to go. "If you won't leave, then the rest of us will."

"Like hell you will!" As Kate started past him, Elliot grabbed her arm and yanked her back. "No one's going anywhere," he growled, squeezing her wrist.

Kate's eyes went wide, first in fear, then anger. "*Let go of me,*" she hissed. "I don't want you ever touching me again! And don't touch your daughter and don't touch your son!" She glared at him defiantly, egged on by adrenaline and the prospect of leaving all the misery behind. "Now get out of my way. I've got bags to pack." With a violent jerk, she freed her arm.

Elliot started to reply, but lashed out instead with the back of his hand. He slapped her so hard that Kate went reeling toward the dining room table with a split lower lip and terrified eyes, falling against the high-back wooden chair behind her. It bit into her back with a painful gouge and tumbled over with a resounding *crack* on the hardwood floor, sending Matt and Lori running from the bathroom to see what had happened. When they got there, they saw their mother struggling to her feet, her hair in disarray and her lip growing puffy and smeared with blood. Both of them cried out for their father to stop, but Elliot ignored them and closed in on Kate, shoving her violently.

She stumbled backward with flailing arms and fell against the glass-fronted china cabinet. There was a terrific crash of shattering glass as her arm smashed through it, then she let out a scream and collapsed on the floor, dazed and bleeding.

Lori echoed the scream and ran to her mother while Matt stared in shock, too stunned to move. For a second that seemed like an eternity to him, his mind and legs were frozen in time, then fear and outrage blitzed their way through and he ran to his father and jumped on his back, kicking and punching and screaming that Elliot was killing his mother.

Kneeling at Kate's side, Lori took one look at her mother's arm and tried not to faint. A gash above the elbow was long and deep, and bleeding profusely. Trying not to sound as panicked as she felt, Lori turned to Matt and instructed him urgently, "Call nine-one-one!" When Matt didn't hear her over his own cries of rage, she stopped worrying about scaring him and screamed instead: *"Cut it out, Matt! Call nine-one-one and tell them to send an ambulance before Mom bleeds to death!"*

Matt's upraised fist froze in midair and he stared uncomprehendingly at Lori for a second, then raced to the phone and called for an ambulance. Meanwhile, Elliot, who had barely even noticed his son's furious attack, remained standing where he was, breathing fast and ragged while he stared in disbelief at the growing pool of blood beneath his wife's arm. A few minutes later, while Lori applied a towel as a makeshift tourniquet, he turned wordlessly on his heel and walked out of the house.

WHEN LORI AND MATT brought their mother home from the emergency room a few hours later, they were all relieved to find Elliot gone. The question, of course, was: Would he dare to come back? All of them hoped not, but none more fervently than Kate. After getting her arm stitched, bandaged and placed in a sling to keep it immobile, and then lying to the doctor about how it had happened—because after twenty years of marriage she wasn't quite ready to make it a legal matter—the last thing she could have handled was seeing Elliot again, even if it were to hear him beg for forgiveness. Only in passing did she wonder where he would spend the night, and then only to vow that it wouldn't be at home.

Thanks to painkillers, her arm and back were manageable for the time being, but she was physically drained and emotionally exhausted, and the only thing she could think about was climbing into bed and banishing the day's nightmare from her conscious mind. Now that Elliot had so dramatically called her bluff, tomorrow she would have to get up early and pack some bags. She would also have to call her mother and tell her they were coming, something she dreaded more than almost anything else. But for now she barely had enough strength left to climb the stairs while Matt and Lori locked up the house. As an afterthought, she crept into Matt's room and carried his baseball bat back to her bedroom. For added insurance, she called down to the children and told them to be sure that after they locked their doors they should also jam a chair under both of the doorknobs.

AFTER LEAVING THE HOUSE, Elliot had sought refuge in his usual place and in his usual way, but after buying his first beer it had suddenly occurred to him that maybe he should have gone someplace where he couldn't be found so easily. If Kate had called the police or told the doctors how she had gotten injured, he might be in trouble.

His first inclination had been to get as far away from St. Charles as possible, but that had been impossible without a car and more money than he had in his wallet. After considering a few other options that were equally unworkable, he finally realized the prudent thing to do was to simply find a place where he could lay low until he knew for sure if he was in trouble or not. He wound up at the Hampton Inn a few miles away, registered under an alias.

After being holed up in his room long enough to down half of the six-pack that had been his only luggage, he was still jumpy. *Were doctors required to notify the police in cases of suspected domestic abuse,* he wondered, *even if Kate hadn't fingered him at the hospital?* He wasn't sure, but he seemed to recall hearing about some law being passed. Which meant that if he had stayed at the bar some self-righteous cop (who probably put his own wife in her place more than once, he bet) could've swaggered into the bar and dragged him away like a common criminal.

Even though it hadn't happened, the possibility made him angry all over again. The more he thought about it, the likelier it seemed that if Kate got the chance to get him into trouble, she'd probably take it, just to get even. Never mind that he hadn't done anything worthy of jail. He had hurt her, true, and felt a remorse of sorts, but as shocking as it had been to see his wife bleeding on the floor, a part of him still felt that she'd had it coming. You just couldn't provoke a man like that and expect to walk away, not when his world—and the whole world, for that matter—was falling apart. Couldn't she see he had already been scared and struggling even before he lost his job?

By the time the six-pack was down to only one, he had mellowed a little and couldn't help wondering if Kate was okay—and equally important, if she had mellowed, too. But he realized it was too soon to expect a change of heart from a woman he'd sent to the emergency room only a few hours earlier, and he fell back to wondering about the seriousness of her condition. That had a bearing, after all, on whether taking him back was even an option.

Calling the hospital was out of the question. For all he knew, St. Joseph's had tracers on all of their phones. It was safer to call the house, assuming anyone was there. He glanced at his watch. It was almost ten. Unless the hospital was keeping Kate overnight, she'd probably be home by now. He walked over to the bed and sat down next to the phone, then dialed the number. *What am I going to say if somebody answers?* he suddenly wondered. Before he could think of something, someone did pick up, and Kate's tired, groggy voice drifted across the line. "Hello?" she answered. When Elliot said nothing, she repeated, "Hello?"

His chest suddenly tight with mixed emotions, Elliot quietly hung up. He had his answer: Kate was okay. Now all he had to worry about was how to talk her out of leaving—without promising to see a shrink, which he would never do. Forgetting his last beer, he picked up the remote control and turned off the TV, then lay back on the bed and thought about his family. Despite today's fight and months of being ignored or treated like a pariah, he just couldn't imagine living without them. The very idea was unacceptable, too painful and threatening, the ultimate abandonment at the very time of his ultimate need. *But what if you can't talk her out of it?* he wondered. After having thought about it all evening, he thought about it some more, and over and over, he kept coming back to the same grim conclusion: one way or another, he would never let it happen.

OBEYING HIS MOTHER'S instructions, Matt went to his room early, as did his sister. But he didn't go to bed. He was too tired and miserable, and his eye still smarted where his father had punched him. More than anything else, he was just plain scared. Scared for his mother, his sister and himself. Scared for the future. Even scared for his dad. Sitting at his desk in his darkened room, he stared through the open window at the night outside, halfway keeping watch for an approaching figure that might look familiar, but mostly just thinking about how bad things were getting and trying very hard not to hate his father.

Ever since his dad got fired, it seemed like it had been one thing after another, with each new problem worse than the last. Matt felt like he was riding a roller coaster that had crested a hill and suddenly plunged downward—only on this particular ride, just when you thought you'd reached the end of a really nasty drop, the bottom fell out and you started falling again, farther and faster, with a fearful darkness rushing up from below.

Earlier that evening, he had been convinced that darkness had finally gotten them. When he first saw his mother bleeding so badly, he was sure she would die. Even when the doctor reassured him that his mom would be okay, he still couldn't stop shaking and expecting the worst.

What would happen when his dad came back?

Would his mom try to leave again?

And if she did, would he hurt her again, maybe worse than before?

His dad was the one who played catch with him in the backyard, who had taught him to ride a bike, the man he sometimes feared but never like *that*. . . . But his dad was a totally different person these days. It was as if some pod creature had secretly taken his place, only the pod creature was mean and drank and hit when he got mad. Even though the old Dad usually blamed someone else when something went wrong—like the new Dad did—he had never gone this far.

Because his father blamed him for their current problems, and because he'd already felt partly responsible anyway, Matt couldn't help but feel guilty for what had happened to his mother, and it was tearing him up. Even his mom's repeated reassurances that he wasn't to blame, that it was his father's fault and his alone, did little to ease his conscience. After all, he was the one who'd made his dad mad in the first place. And now his mom was paying the price.

Frowning, Matt got up from the window, then walked across the room and quietly opened his door. For the third time in the last half hour, he glanced miserably across the hall toward his mother's room, fighting the urge to go and see if she was okay. He still couldn't shake the nagging fear that maybe she'd stop breathing or start bleeding again and no one would know until it was too late, but he also didn't want to wake her if she was only sleeping. Finally, the uncertainty was too much. Treading softly across the floor so as not to make it squeak, he went to her door and opened it slowly. A small lamp was on in the corner of the room but Kate was asleep. As far as Matt could tell, she was breathing normally. The bandaged arm rested on the sheet she was sleeping under, and it also looked okay, with no sign of blood.

Matt breathed a quiet sigh of relief but remained in the doorway, watching her sleep. Every time he looked at her it was hard not to see his father knocking her into the china cabinet, and hard not to hear the sound of shattering glass. Hard not to remember the terrible expression on his father's face as he watched her lie there, covered in blood.

Once again, he wondered what would happen tomorrow or the day after that. It was only a matter of time before his father came back, and when he did, Matt knew they were going to need help. Otherwise . . .

Without realizing he was doing it, Matt began to cry and edged closer to the bed. A few steps later he stopped, and shortly thereafter the tears stopped, too. *Enough with the crying,* he silently chided himself. *That isn't going to make Mom any better. And it won't stop Dad from doing this again.* He swiped at his eyes, then took a deep breath and crept back toward the hall. By the time he reached the doorway he had come to a decision: it was time to stop crying and do something instead—something to protect his mom from his dad, and if possible, to protect his dad from himself.

As they had so often of late, his thoughts turned naturally to his guardian angel, who had promised to help if Matt's mission got too tough or he got into trouble. If this wasn't enough trouble for a guardian angel, what was? He'd already tried every way he could think of to fix things on his own, and when that hadn't worked he'd prayed real hard for John to show up, but so far nothing had happened. Now he was getting desperate. As his father sometimes said, desperate times call for desperate measures. Matt needed John *now.* So, if his guardian angel wouldn't—or couldn't—come on his own, *he* would have to go to his guardian angel.

Of course, it occurred to him, *it would help if I had an address or something.* He knew John was a teacher, but he didn't know where. The only other things he had learned about him in the tunnel were that he had died too soon—like himself—and was being sent back—also like himself—and that he had seemed like a man who would keep his promises. *He saw the same things I saw in the tunnel—he has to know what's going on,* Matt mused. *So what's keeping him?* He thought about it, and finally decided it really didn't matter. John had promised to help and Matt believed that he would, if for no other reason than guardian angels just didn't lie. For all he knew, John was waiting for word that Matt wanted help, and he probably didn't realize he hadn't told Matt how to reach him.

If his dreams had been telling him where to find John—and after his near-death experience, anything seemed possible—it was a pretty good bet that he lived in Kansas City, although it was kind of strange that each time he'd seen him it was in front of a jail. Regardless, Kansas City, was where he had to go. Smiling faintly to himself, and glad to have settled on a course of action, Matt glanced once more at his sleeping mother and was suddenly beset by second thoughts. *You sure you want to do this?* he asked himself silently. His mom hadn't really believed him when he told her he'd met his guardian angel; if he went to Kansas City because of a dream, and then failed to find John, she'd probably put him in the nuthouse or at least ground him for life.

And if his dad found out . . .

But he *would* find John. He was sure of it. The way things were going, he at least had to try.

Firm in his resolve, Matt stared tenderly at his mother and was overcome by the urge to kiss her before leaving. He was halfway to the bed before he realized what he was doing and that waking her up would jeopardize his plans. Aiming a hopeful smile in her direction instead, he whispered in a voice that was virtually inaudible, "I love you, Mom." Then he closed the door behind him, and hurried to his room as quietly as he could.

An hour later, he had packed his knapsack and was ready to leave. After sliding a note under his mother's door, he crept downstairs and out to the backyard. Without looking back, he hopped on his bike, and with grim exhilaration set out through the quiet, nighttime streets in a desperate quest to find his guardian angel.

TWENTY-FIVE

A Picnic and a Sunset

KNOWING.

Sitting on the boulder with a book in his lap, waiting for Holly to come back, John turned the word over in his mind for the umpteenth time since it had come to him. *Knowing.* Such a simple word for such a powerful gift! Because of his experiences with Ruby and Hector and Will, he had a rudimentary understanding of the nature of his gift, and Saturday night's dream of meeting the Light had answered the question of where it had originated. Now, as he thought about how he had felt while reading this book and others like it, how some instinctual spiritual connection had allowed him to experience—to *know*—them as true, he realized that in a similar way his new ability allowed him to make a deep, empathic spiritual connection and *know* certain people. Now that he had a name for his new gift, much of the mystery surrounding it fell away, triggering an epiphany-in-progress that allowed the last missing pieces to fall into place.

Lacking a physical body during his time in the tunnel, he had experienced everything with his spiritual senses. Communication had been instantaneous and direct, clear and unambiguous in tone and meaning. His ability to "see" had been similarly enhanced, unhindered by the limitations of physical sight. It was as if blinders had been removed from his eyes, and he had seen colors and energies and spiritual beings that were always there but out of the range of normal human perception. He had experienced the Light for who He really was, and he had seen the true essence of people he had known in his earthly life, had seen beyond the memory of their physical existence to the spiritual beings they had been all along. In short, he had truly "known" them.

During the "knowing" experiences he'd had since returning, he was actually using those same spiritual senses. He was being allowed to "know" some of the people around him, to have an intimate understanding of their fears and pain and deep-seated sorrow, and share with them the love and compassion they needed. He understood now that emotions have energy, and that love is the ultimate healing energy. He had seen it very clearly with Will Gibson, had seen how it banished the darkness in his aura and replaced it with light. In the same way that unconditional love had made him feel forgiven during his life review, so too did his sharing of the same love give the people he "knew" a taste of forgiveness and peace and hope. It eased the burdens they had carried for years, and freed them to move closer to self-forgiveness and forgiving the people who had brought them pain. Ultimately, it freed them to move on with their lives with a new-found strength and sense of hope.

John gazed absently at the yawning canyon and smiled. Finally he could accept what Will had suggested, that the NDE and the dreams and the knowing were precious gifts to be used and treasured. Because the power to help others in such a profound fashion—even if he wasn't always sure where it was leading—was something he had striven for all of his life. It was a humbling but exciting and fulfilling responsibility. Enlightened by this deeper knowledge, he began to understand how recent events had led him to Holly, and why.

Ever since discovering that he hadn't been meant to prevent her suicide, he had wondered why he had been sent to her. He had begun to suspect it had something to do with his knowing ability but hadn't been sure, and there had been too many unresolved questions about his gift to use it again without a stronger sign. Now he was convinced that sign had been given, and despite the gravity of the process and the painful empathy that gripped him at the moment of transfer, he found himself eager and increasingly excited at the prospect of using it later that evening.

HOLLY RETURNED less than an hour before sunset. John waved and broke into a grin as she appeared on the path carrying a large wicker picnic basket in one hand and a cooler in the other. Holly grinned, too, and hurried over to the boulder. "See, I told you I'd come back," she teased, plopping the carriers on the beach towel–covered rock. John hopped down beside her, and she opened the basket with a look of anticipation.

John peeked inside and saw that it was packed to the top. There were potato chips, bread, fried chicken and fruit—and that was only the top layer. "Wow!" he said, laughing. "When you said you'd bring back some food, you weren't kidding, were you?"

"Nope," Holly replied, still grinning. Then she added anxiously, "Does it look okay?"

John reached into the basket and inspected the bottom layer of food, then did the same with the cooler. In addition to everything else, Holly had bought sodas, potato salad, some cold cuts and cheese, and a bottle of wine nestled in ice. "I don't know," he said with mock seriousness. "I think you forgot something."

"I did?" Holly croaked in a drooping voice. "What?"

"I see the apple . . . but where's the roast pig?" John replied and burst out laughing.

"Very funny," Holly said, slapping him playfully on the arm. "For a minute, I thought you were actually serious."

"Are you kidding? It looks like you emptied out a delicatessen! When I said I wanted some food, I didn't expect you to bring back a ten-course meal! A burger would have been fine." He glanced at the open carriers again and gave Holly a grateful look. "I have to admit, though, this looks a heck of a lot better than a warmed-over burger."

"Good," Holly replied, pleased that her surprise had worked. "I thought it might be fun to have a little picnic while we watch the sunset. Bringing back a burger just didn't seem appropriate."

John agreed and they set about emptying the basket and cooler.

It wasn't long before they had laid out a casual but ample meal on their private rock. There was barely enough room for them to sit, but it was a pleasant setting for an impromptu picnic. Along the rim, other tourists also settled in, and a few billowy clouds languidly sailed into view, their undersides glowing softly with an orangish hue as the sun dipped close to the horizon.

Sitting cross-legged next to Holly, John smiled at the sight, and it suddenly occurred to him that if he could somehow stand off to the side and look at himself and his picnic partner perched on the rock, he would no doubt be seeing the very same tableau as in the previous night's dream. Even after everything that had happened recently, it was an eerie feeling—living out a future he had already seen—but this time he was filled with hopeful expectation instead of foreboding. A moment or two later, the surreal feeling was gone, but his heart remained buoyant as he filled his plate and started to eat.

It had been a long time since either of them had felt so good, so at ease with themselves and their recent history. As a result, they ate unhurriedly but with relish, carrying on a lighthearted conversation. They occasionally stopped to acknowledge envious stares from passing tourists or to point out features in the landscape they hadn't noticed before, but throughout it all, they kept a watchful eye on the blazing sun. Eventually their conversation turned to teaching, and as John waxed enthusiastic about his chosen career, Holly stopped munching on a chicken leg long enough to observe, "I don't think I could ever be a teacher. You must really like kids."

John responded with a thoughtful smile. "There are some days when I'd probably give you a different answer, but, yeah, I guess I do."

"Ever think about having your own?"

"Sure. But everybody tells me that once I get over turning thirty it'll go away," he replied with a laugh. Then he added more seriously, "How about you?"

A fleeting pensiveness touched the corners of Holly's smile, and she nodded solemnly. Since high school, she had fantasized about having a daughter or a son someday, partly because she wanted to do better as a parent than the aunt who raised her, but mostly because she loved the idea of having a little Holly or Rachel around, or a little Marc or Paul, or maybe all four. Unlike some of her friends who talked about having children as if it were the end of all happiness, Holly had always seen it as just the opposite. Ironically, the fear that she would never realize her goal of having a family was one of the factors that had led her down the path to near-fatal despair. Like so many of her dreams, it had shone brightly but ultimately seemed more than she could hope for or deserved, and it still bothered her greatly that she had come so close to cutting off all possibility of ever finding out. At the moment, that dream didn't seem quite as impossible as it had before. "Yes," she finally answered, "I would like to have kids." Then she added in a voice that she hoped didn't betray her tentative affection for John, "That is, when I meet the right person and the time is right—and when the world isn't such a dangerous place. My biological clock still has a few good years left on it, which is one of the reasons I left Las Vegas."

"I would have thought Vegas was a great place to meet people," John responded.

"It is. And a lot of the people are nice, but the city seems to attract more than its share of creeps, too."

"Not the romance Mecca it's cut out to be, huh?"

"Not by a long shot," Holly answered emphatically. She laughed and added, "Unless you mean the kind of romance you can charge to your MasterCard."

John chuckled and nodded. "I've about decided that finding the right person is a tricky proposition, wherever you live." No sooner had he said that than he recalled how he and Holly had met; there hadn't been a trick to their meeting at all—if a person believed in divine assistance. It turned out to be a double-edged thought: reassuring to know that something so important wasn't dependent on chance, but vaguely unsettling to realize that he had thought of their meeting—if only in passing—in a romantic vein.

"As far as I'm concerned," Holly agreed, "dating is about as much fun as Russian roulette—and most of the time the odds aren't as good!" She laughed, and before she knew what she was doing, admitted, "You know, you're the first decent man I've met in ages."

There was an awkward moment of silence between them and John matched her self-conscious smile. "Thanks," he said, "I think you're pretty . . . decent, too."

Like the sudden derailment of a smooth-running train, their conversation lurched to a halt. Both of them realized they had wandered prematurely onto sensitive ground, and they found themselves searching for a diversion of some sort, anything to allow them to pretend the exchange had not happened.

Luckily, the sun came to the rescue. As its perimeter touched the rocky, far-off horizon, the clouds lit up with a sympathetic fire, and a little girl in a group a few yards away delightedly exclaimed, "Wow, Mom! Look at that! The clouds are turning *gold!*" Having lost track of what was happening in the sky above them, Holly and John were startled from their silence and automatically looked up.

Realizing that the much-awaited event had finally arrived, Holly suddenly remembered the wine. "I almost forgot something!" she said, pulling the bottle from the cooler. She set it on the towel, fished two plastic wineglasses from the picnic basket and handed them to John. "I bought this especially for the sunset," she explained as she found the corkscrew and applied it to the bottle. "I always make a toast when I watch the sun go down—even if I don't have anything to toast with!"

"Sort of like wishing on a star, I suppose," John observed, smiling.

Holly returned the smile, surprised that he had understood. "Exactly like that—only I figure my chances are better if I wish on a big one!"

She held out the bottle and began pouring the wine. "I suppose I should let this breathe," she apologized, "but if we wait any longer, it'll all be over."

"My poor man's palate won't notice the difference anyway."

"Good," Holly replied, already staring into the distance. The setting sun was wondrously large and wondrously brilliant, and the surrounding sky a pastel blue, awash in a dreamy, heavenly light. The colorful canyon formed a magnificent stage on which the last bursts of light would soon spend themselves, and within a matter of moments, the horizon and its accompaniment of drifting clouds were magically transformed into a glorious display of gold and crimson and violet and rust. The sight was breathtaking, every bit as moving as Holly had hoped, and with an ecstatic smile, she raised her glass to the departing sun. "Here's to the perfect end of a perfect day!"

His eyes riveted on the sky, John echoed her toast. Thinking of how he intended to help Holly that night, he added his own: "And to new beginnings!" Finding that to her liking, Holly repeated it, extending her glass in John's direction. They tapped them against each other, laughing at the weak-sounding *plink* of the plastic, then turned to the sunset and drank the wine.

As the sun sank lower and the colors slowly shifted and started to deepen, they stared at the sky with rapt attention, silent and unmoving. For a few brief moments, they were virtually transformed into primordial creatures, unable to do anything but stare and ponder, their hearts and minds free of all emotions and thoughts save those that were part of an instinctual response to the light and immensity and mystery of the sun. John found himself thinking that this must have been how the ancient sun worshippers had felt, overwhelmed by the beauty and power of it all, and a little anxious, perhaps, at the thought of its loss. It struck him as telling that even the advances of science had done little to diminish those instinctual feelings, or to negate the sun's status as a potent archetype, a symbol of the ultimate universal Power who nurtured the world with His own brilliant light.

Holly was similarly awestruck, but her feelings were more personal and less philosophical than John's. Bolstered by the recollection of other glorious sunsets, she reexperienced the wonder and serenity and hope of earlier times. For her, this wasn't an isolated event but a continuing process or work-in-progress, with each new experience built on the foundation of previous sunsets, like an ascending stairway reaching hopefully toward the heavens and the source of it all. It was a time for reflection and maybe even renewal.

The sun disappeared all too soon, and Holly and John sat very still in a reverent silence as the rest of the tourists began drifting away. Before long, the canopy of stars slid slowly into place. Holly and John were alone on the rim, but neither of them noticed; they were still thinking of the sunset, and then of each other, the person with whom they had shared the experience.

It had been one of the most spectacular sunsets John had ever seen, and he felt totally relaxed, suffused with a deep inner peace he had rarely known this side of the tunnel. When he finally spoke, his words were delivered in a faraway voice but came straight from the heart: "Thanks for the picnic. I wouldn't have missed it for the world."

"You're welcome," Holly answered in a similar tone. "It *was* fantastic, wasn't it?" After a short silence, she added, "I'm glad I had someone to share it with. Thanks for staying—and for trusting me enough to loan me the car."

John smiled shyly. "No problem. It was certainly worth it. Be-sides," he added, telling a little white lie, "I wasn't really worried."

"Yeah, sure," Holly retorted. Her tone was teasing, but her voice was subdued in the quiet night air. "I know how you men are about your cars—afraid someone's going to scratch it, or a bird's going to poop on it. You must've been a basket case watching a perfect stranger drive it away."

"Well, maybe a little," John confessed with a small laugh. "But af-ter what we've been through—that business at the dam last night and then this incredible sunset—I'd hardly call you a stranger. Maybe a perfect traveling companion, but never a perfect stranger."

Even with a glowing moon and a sky full of stars, there was barely enough light to see each other's face, and Holly was glad that John could not see her blush. "Thanks," she said softly, and found herself impulsively leaning over to give him a kiss. John was surprised but couldn't help but respond. The kiss was brief, but to both of them it felt powerful and long overdue. When it was over, Holly averted her eyes to the darkened canyon.

John followed her gaze, and a pensive silence returned. After a few minutes, John tried to lighten the mood. "Well, here we are again," he said wryly, gesturing toward the graduated darkness below them, "taking in another famous view when it's so dark you can barely see your hand in front of your face."

Holly laughed and the uncomfortableness passed. "We do seem to have a habit of doing that," she agreed, then reached into the cooler and pulled out the wine bottle. "I think that calls for a toast, don't you?"

"Why not?" John responded, glancing up at the sky. "We already toasted the sun, so it seems only fair that we toast the moon—although I better make this my last one, since I have to drive."

Holly nodded. After the toast, she said, "You know, I'd be happy to take a turn behind the wheel any time you get tired. I'm not usually much on cars, but this afternoon, it was kind of fun driving something nice for a change. I've had so many old clunkers that I'd forgotten what a nice car feels like. I kinda like it."

John smiled and remembered how much Will had liked the car, too. A wave of sadness washed over him, and he took a sip of wine to give it time to pass. "Yeah, I'm kind of fond of the Jeep, too. Although at times I still miss my convertible." He shook his head, recalling the insurance photos he had seen after the accident. "It's too bad it got trashed. I loved that car."

"That was the accident you told me about?" Holly asked, recalling one of their first conversations. All John had told her at the time was that an accident had put him in the hospital, and since he had seemed reluctant to discuss it and she had been preoccupied with her own problems, the subject had died.

"That's the one," John answered. Unsure whether the setting and the wine were loosening his tongue or if he was getting his courage from a different source, he decided to tell her about his near-death experience. "It happened back in the spring," he began in a quiet voice. "I was driving home from work, and a school bus—of all things— rammed me off the road."

"My God!" Holly gasped. "You're lucky you weren't killed!" Her mouth dropped open when John hesitated then responded, "Actually, I was . . ."

Holly stared at him with an incredulity that was easy to see even in the darkness, so before she could accuse him of pulling her leg—or even worse, of being crazy—John launched into the story of that fateful day. He knew he was taking a calculated risk, but sensed somehow that he was supposed to tell her before attempting the knowing, and that not only would she believe him, but that her belief was necessary to pave the way.

For the next half hour they sat on the boulder at the canyon's rim, two solitary figures surrounded by the remnants of the earlier picnic. Each held a half-filled glass of wine while John told his story, slowly and quietly but with great conviction. Steering clear of any mention of the other dreams, he stuck to the NDE itself, telling everything he'd been able to remember so far and omitting only the name tag and the gift he was given. Holly listened intently, never saying a word, her only reaction an occasional subtle facial expression that was hard to interpret by the light of the moon.

After finishing, John sat quietly and waited for her to break the silence. At several points in the tale Holly had almost spoken, feeling too much skepticism or amazement or emotion to keep inside. But she had held her tongue and waited to hear everything before passing judgment, because, as astonishing as John's story was, something deep inside her had told her to listen. She had heard accounts similar to John's on TV talk shows, but she had always reserved a measure of doubt in the matter. Now she was forced to consider it more seriously. Still, years of working in Las Vegas casinos had taught her not to automatically believe everything she heard without asking a few questions—no matter how appealing it sounded.

"I'm not sure what to say," she began in a pensive voice. "The whole thing is so . . . incredible." She paused and glanced up into the sky before meeting John's eyes. "Are you sure it wasn't a hallucination?" she asked delicately. "Maybe it was caused by the drugs they gave you."

"I'm absolutely positive," John answered in a soft but unequivocal voice. "It came to me in a dream, not a hallucination."

"Then maybe that's all it was—a dream," Holly offered, half hoping it wasn't.

John shook his head and smiled wanly. "Actually, there've been two so far. I call them dreams, but they're more like visions or memories. . . . Believe me, I've never had dreams this vivid or real, especially about things that turn out to have actually happened—like the emergency room. There are only two ways I could have known what went on in there while I was clinically dead: either I really did have an out-of-body experience or someone told me later. And no one told me."

Holly decided to believe him, but there were still aspects of the story she had difficulty accepting. "I've never been what you'd call a very religious person," she said in a tentative voice, "but I do believe in God. . . . Still—not that I'm accusing you of lying or anything—the thought that you actually met this . . . Being of Light . . . is kind of hard to swallow. It's just, I don't know . . ." she said with a shrug, and glanced down at her wineglass, fingering the stem.

"I know," John answered, automatically smiling. The mere mention of the encounter still raised goose bumps on his arms and filled him with a sense of indescribable joy as if some otherworldly current had just shot through his body. "But it really did happen. . . . It sounds crazy, but when you think about it, it really isn't, not if you believe in some kind of heaven. It only stands to reason that we'd see God there. We're just so accustomed to thinking that no one ever has proof until he's dead and gone that it's kind of hard to accept when someone who's alive says he already knows."

Holly grudgingly admitted, "I guess you're right." Her acceptance was tentative, but it was as much as John had hoped to get at that stage of the discussion. He resisted the urge to explore it some more, and waited instead for another question.

Holly took her time before speaking again, because in some ways she had an even greater stake in the answer to the next question than in all of the others. John's account of being reunited with his grandmother and sister in the tunnel had moved her profoundly, and flooded her heart with bittersweet emotions and a powerful yearning for his claims to be true. Now that need pushed aside her fear, and after taking a sip of wine to steady herself, she broached the subject. "My mother's been dead almost twenty years. . . ." she began with an almost palpable ache in her voice. She looked away, blinking back tears. "Do you think it's possible . . ." she tried again, but found herself unable to finish the question.

Knowing how it felt to long to see a loved one who had already passed over, John gently placed his hand on Holly's and smiled sympathetically. "You'll see her again. I'm sure of it," he said tenderly. "She'll probably be there to greet you, like my grandmother was."

Holly nodded gratefully but was unable to speak. Soon she was giving vent to the tears, both happy and sad, that she'd held back throughout much of John's narrative. For several minutes she stared out into the darkness, contemplating the reunion she had dreamed of for years. When the tears finally stopped, her need to believe everything was stronger than ever.

Gently withdrawing her hand from John's, she wiped the dampness from her cheeks and composed herself, then turned to him and brought up another matter that had troubled her earlier. "There's one thing I don't understand," she began in a still-shaky voice. "How can God let someone die too soon? It seems like He could just snap His fingers and prevent it from happening."

"I asked myself the very same question," John admitted. "I guess He could—if He wanted to. But I don't picture God sitting around up in heaven or somewhere off in the cosmos making sure everything follows some master plan that's carved in stone. I believe He cares about what we're doing and does intervene when we want Him to, but for the most part I think we're allowed to make our own decisions and live with the consequences. Otherwise, how would we ever learn anything? What would be the point?"

Holly had never thought of it that way before. As a matter of fact, she had seldom thought about it at all, except at the moments of her bleakest despair, when she had felt the most vulnerable and alone, tempted to blame God for letting her suffer. "So you think everything happens for a reason—even your accident?"

"Yes—although I wouldn't want to go through it again," John replied with a wry smile. It occurred to him that in answering Holly's questions he was drawing the parts of his experience into a cohesive whole, and, for the first time, putting into words the beliefs and attitudes he had formulated since the experience but never consciously expressed. It was in that moment that he realized just how fundamentally his NDE had altered his view not only of death, but of life as well. When he continued, it was with as much a sense of self-discovery as wanting to share what he had learned with Holly. "Remember when I told you about seeing my life played back for me?"

Automatically, Holly's eyes flicked to the wounds on her wrists, which she'd covered with colorful wrist bands in place of the previous day's obvious white bandages. "I remember," she answered softly. The life review had made an indelible impression and filled her with dread, despite John's description of it as a liberating experience.

"I learned two things from that," John went on, leaning a little closer so he could see her better. "First, we should be careful how we treat other people, because someday we're going to know exactly how it feels. And second, when we do make mistakes or fail, God doesn't hold it against us. But He does expect us to learn from the experience."

"That almost sounds too good to be true," Holly replied.

John gave her a half smile. If for no other reason than her attempted suicide, he had already suspected she was one of those people who wouldn't forgive herself for past mistakes and so found it difficult to believe that anyone else would either. With the sense that the time for the knowing was drawing near, he hoped the surprise he had planned would help her leave the past behind. "That's because most of us were taught to think of mistakes as something we're supposed to be punished for," he replied, "instead of something we should learn from."

Uncomfortable with the subject, Holly nodded politely and said, "But that still doesn't explain how God could let you die when it wasn't your time."

"As it turned out, He didn't," John responded with a small smile. "But He could have, I guess. Like I said, I think there's a general plan for each of us, but it's not inflexible. It allows for choice and can be changed by our own free will or by someone else's." He paused, choosing words carefully for a truth he'd just recently begun to understand. Then he looked at Holly with a thoughtful expression. "Maybe what we think of as mistakes are actually part of a larger plan for our lives. God is the only one who knows for sure, because He's the only one who can see the big picture. What that bus driver did was wrong, but I know for a fact it wound up helping her teenage daughter, who was in a bad situation. And, as strange as it sounds, it changed my life in a profound and positive way—a lot of good things came from it." He smiled and added, "Like meeting you, for instance . . ."

Holly smiled but said nothing. John continued: "Tragedies are traumatic because we don't understand what is really happening. But nothing can truly harm who we really are, because who we really are is indestructible and much, much more than our physical existence. Life goes on, always. Nothing can change that. I believe everything that happens to us is an opportunity for growth, and that just because it doesn't make sense at the time doesn't mean it can't turn out to be beneficial in the long run. That might sound like pie in the sky, but I know it's true. And it may not explain everything, but it explains a lot."

Keenly aware that a great deal was riding on how convincing he'd been, John tried not to worry when Holly averted her face without saying a word. The minutes dragged out, but John forced himself to wait while the silence all around them seemed to deepen with the darkness. What he didn't know was that Holly had decided to believe him—although the decision had been made on a level much deeper than conscious thought—and, as a result, she was struggling with the emotions that acceptance had aroused. Paradoxically, his words had had the effect of both filling her with hope and overwhelming her with regret, the latter of which had rapidly gained strength as John had shared his philosophy of life. Holly tried her best to hide her turmoil, but finally she broke the silence with a soft and barely audible sob. Another followed in its wake, and she spoke in a hitching voice that was filled with self-reproach. "If life is all about learning from our mistakes, then I'm a miserable failure. . . ."

John frowned. "You're being too hard on yourself," he said gently.

"No, I'm not!" Holly replied, still averting her face. "I'm one of those people who never learns from her mistakes, John. I just keep screwing things up, over and over—and if I don't screw them up, then someone else does it for me! I've failed at everything I ever tried—career, school, money, relationships." She added with a bitter, self-deprecating laugh, "Even suicide!"

Pained to see her in such distress, John gently laid his hand on Holly's shoulder. "It's all right, Holly," he said in a soothing voice.

She turned to him with a thoroughly miserable look. "It's *not* all right!" she shot back angrily, jerking her shoulder from beneath his hand and spilling some of the wine from her glass. "Look, I've pretty much lost everything I had—my job, my car, my dignity—and what I did manage to hold on to, I just walked away from when I left Las Vegas. Now here I am sitting out in the middle of nowhere, with nowhere to go and no one to care where I wind up. Maybe everything's all right with your life, but it's not with mine!" Shutting her eyes as the tears began flowing, she shook her head sadly and said in a breaking voice, "No, it is definitely *not* all right. . . ."

Angry with himself, John was momentarily at a loss for words. Ordinarily, he would never have trivialized or denied her feelings by saying something as facile as "Everything's all right" when it obviously wasn't. But he had been caught off guard, having expected a positive reaction, or at worst, skepticism—anything but a self-deprecating tirade and tears. Now he had to figure out how to undue the damage he had inadvertently caused. His instinct and training told him to apologize and acknowledge Holly's feelings, offering himself as a sympathetic listener, but it was so soon after the near-fatal episode with the razor that he was concerned that would amount to little more than a psychological Band-Aid. And it was painfully clear to him that Holly's reopened wounds were too deep for mere Band-Aids. Upon further reflection, he realized it was time to do what he had been planning earlier that evening—the time for the knowing had finally arrived.

A great calm came over him as he realized what he had to do.

Holly sat next to him in the darkness, clutching her wineglass with her head still down, her face turned away as she continued to cry. John stared at her with great compassion and love, and said in a slow but steady voice, "I never intended to make light of your problems, Holly. I'm sorry. You're right—everything isn't okay." He added softly, "But if you'll let me, I'd like to help."

He reached for her wine, and as his fingers closed tentatively on the stem of the glass, Holly's eyes flew open. She regarded him quizically and with a hint of mistrust, but said nothing as he gently took the glass and set it on the rock. Nor did she offer any resistance when he placed his hand on top of hers. "Don't worry," he said quietly. "I'd never do anything to hurt you. Let's just sit here for a while and look at the stars."

Holly had no idea what John was planning, but her instincts told her it was still safe to trust him. The warmth of his hand was so comforting on hers, and the care in his voice so genuine and soothing that she finally did as he asked and glanced up at the sky. John stared at her sadly and sent off a short, silent prayer for success. Then he followed her eyes and gazed at the stars, clearing his mind of everything except Holly and the pain she was feeling. Not long after, the knowing began.

TWENTY-SIX

Visions of Demons

ONE MOMENT HE WAS PEERING up into a vast, star-filled sky, and the next he was suddenly falling through space. Down and down he hurtled through darkness, and at first he thought he had slipped off the boulder and was plunging to his death in the canyon below. When the sensation abruptly ended, he was standing on the steps of a pink-and-white mobile home on a bright, sunny day.

Disoriented, but with the feeling he had done this a thousand times, he opened the door and stepped inside. His eyes skimmed a room that was furnished with old, mismatched pieces, and settled out of habit on the full-length mirror next to the couch. He walked over to it, and in place of his own reflection, he saw a tall, skinny, red-haired girl of nine or ten staring back. When the girl pushed back her bangs and broke into an endearing but slightly goofy grin that John had seen only earlier that day, his disorientation faded and the situation became clear: he was experiencing the same vicarious knowing he had experienced with Ruby and Will and Denton, only this time it was stronger, more real and detailed than ever before. The falling sensation of a moment ago had been Holly's, not his, an empathic sharing of her emotional state. The girl in the mirror was Holly also, and he was seeing through her eyes as she had seen almost twenty years ago.

"Hi, Mom! I'm home," Holly called out in a light, chirpy voice, dropping her notebook on the TV. Getting no reply, she crossed the narrow living room and peeked into the kitchen. But the room was empty. "Mom?" she repeated.

That's weird, she thought. Her mom was always in the kitchen fixing her a snack when she came home from school.

Shrugging, she grabbed an apple from the counter and headed for the hall. "I'm home, Mom," she said once more. She took a bite out of the apple, and John's connection with her was so strong that he could actually taste the sweet juiciness of the fruit.

Holly started down the hallway and drew up short. There was a large, discolored, wet-looking spot on the beige carpet in front of the bathroom. The door was closed, and she thought she could hear a faint trickle of water coming from inside. Thinking her mother had started to draw a bath and gotten distracted by something else, Holly hurried toward the bathroom to shut off the water.

When she stepped in front of the door, her sneakers squished on the carpet and she felt wetness soaking through the sides of her shoes. With an exclamation of disgust, she stepped back and glanced down at her feet. A wet, pinkish stain ringed the soles of her white canvas sneakers. *What in the world . . .* she wondered. An instant later, something went *click* in her brain and her disgust gave way to sudden alarm. Stepping back onto the stain only because she had to, she grabbed the knob and threw open the door.

What she found inside made her want to scream and run and tear out her eyes. But her lungs and legs might as well have been stone, and blindness was no answer because the horror she had seen could never be erased by a lifetime of darkness. She had no choice but to take it all in—the murky pink water that seeped over the side of the overflowing tub, her mother's vacant eyes staring up at the ceiling, and the limp, bloodied wrist that hung in space beyond the edge of the tub. When she finally looked away and saw the note taped to the mirror—*I'm sorry, I just didn't know what else to do*—she ripped it from the wall and threw it in the trash, thinking that if she removed the confession, the sin might not be true. And when she ran to the tub, sobbing hysterically, and reached into the water—the warm, pink water—and grabbed her mother's arms and shook her and shook her, trying to make her wake up or move or speak, only a small part of her realized it was too late. Even when her aunt arrived and gasped at the sight of Holly's bloodstained clothes, she still couldn't bring herself to admit what had happened, because she still didn't believe it.

Fast-forward.

Three days later, after seeing her mother's casket lowered into the ground, Holly's denial began to crumble. The dam finally burst and reality overwhelmed her, sweeping her away with a wall of emotion that bore her on its crest and threatened to drown her. John felt it all now—the grief, the anger, the acute vulnerability, the fear and confusion, the pain of being abandoned with no one to love her. He felt it so sharply the emotions might have been his own. He also felt the beginning of young Holly's retreat toward the emotional caution she thought would protect her from being hurt again.

Fast-forward.

Holly was a few years older now and living with her mother's older sister, an aunt she doesn't like very much. Standing just inside the door of a well-appointed living room where her aunt and uncle are seated on the sofa, listening to a local television evangelist, Holly is trying not to fidget as she asks for permission to go on her first date.

The reply was swift and to the point. "No, you may not," her aunt Liz replied sharply. Uncle Wendel didn't look as if he would have given the same answer, but he didn't interfere. He never interfered in anything that happened between his wife and Holly. Aunt Liz shook her head in annoyance and sighed. "Thirteen's too young to be going out with boys. You know that, Thelma." Holly made a face, angered as much at being called by her given name, Thelma, as she was by the answer. "We've had this discussion before," her aunt went on in a tired, irritated voice. "So don't ask me again. *I'll* let you know when it's time to start dating."

Holly knew from experience that the best thing to do was just let it drop, no matter how disappointed she was. "Yes, ma'am," she said, not quite masking her anger. Head down, she turned to go, but her aunt called her back. "Aren't you forgetting something?"

Holly gritted her teeth and shut her eyes, counting to ten as her mother had taught her to do when she was tempted to say something that would get her into trouble. She turned back around. "May I be excused, Aunt Liz?" she said in a strained, singsong voice.

"Yes, you may, Thelma."

Holly grimaced and turned to leave, counting softly again as she headed for the door. Her aunt knew it drove her crazy to be called Thelma; *that* was a discussion they'd had even more times than the one about dating. *Five . . . six . . . seven*—"Stubborn old bat," she muttered before going on to eight. "My name's Holly, not Thelma."

Like a pistol shot, her aunt's voice rang out behind her. "*What* did you say, young lady?"

Holly wheeled to face her, the count washed away by a wave of petulant, pent-up anger. "I *said* my name is *Holly*, not Thelma!"

Liz snorted derisively. "I'll call you whatever I want, little miss! Just because your mama went along with this name-change nonsense doesn't mean I will. In this house people keep the name they're born with," she said, glancing at Wendel as if he were the one who had laid down that law. "Thelma Smith may be a bit plain for your tastes, but a plain, honest name is nothing to be ashamed of—and heaven knows it suits you a lot better than *Holly*. Next thing, I suppose you'll want to change your last name, too!" Liz snorted again and dismissed her impatiently.

Seething and mortified, Holly left the room. When she was halfway down the hall she decided that changing her last name *was* a pretty good idea, and that she should march back into the living room and tell Aunt Liz that she had decided to do it—and that she wasn't going to wait until she got married, either. Before she had re-traced all of her steps, she stopped, hearing her aunt speaking to Un-cle Wendel in a low, hushed voice, as if she were talking about things Holly shouldn't hear. Hugging the wall, Holly tiptoed closer until she was able to make out what her aunt was saying.

"—hadn't been so foolish, she wouldn't have had that child and her life wouldn't have turned out the way it did! I tried to tell her that man was trouble, but she wouldn't listen. Naturally, she got pregnant and he took off. . . . She spent the next ten years paying for that mis-take. And now we're paying for it."

Uncle Wendel's voice cut in, calm in contrast to his wife's agitated tone. "I wouldn't put it like that, Liz. Thelma doesn't mean to be any trouble. And compared to a lot of others, she's a pretty good girl."

"She's just like her mother, is what she is!" Liz's voice shot back. "And she'll probably come to the same bad end. I can already see the signs."

Stung by her aunt's words, Holly bit her lower lip to keep from cry-ing and backed down the hall on trembling legs. As soon as she thought she was safely out of earshot, she fled to her room, where she closed the door and burst into tears. She had always known her aunt wasn't ex-actly fond of her, but she had assumed it was because she wasn't used to children. She had never suspected Aunt Liz felt like that—about her or her mother. And she had always felt guilty for her mother's death, that she was somehow to blame and could have prevented it if she had only been better. Now that her fears were confirmed, Holly was devastated. She couldn't get the accusation—and her aunt's smug prediction—out of her head. John felt her gag on the poison and swallow it down. . . .

Fast-forward.

Rapid-fire, in a fashion similar to his own life review, came other critical junctures in Holly's life. The poison stayed with her throughout them all, and several times John stood vicariously at a crossroads where Holly was faced with an opportunity to purge it from her system, to deal with her past and get back on a truer, happier path. On each occasion, she made the wrong choice. Sometimes she was too distracted to recognize the moment for what it truly was. At other times she pulled back—often at the last minute—fearing the unknown and choosing instead what she already knew, even though it filled her with pain and misery. Each time when she acted out of fear, letting her tumultuous past dictate what she did with her education, her career and how she handled relationships, the poison grew stronger. And Holly grew increasingly unhappy, restless and confused. Her self-esteem dwindled, and she became increasingly fearful of committing to anything—and to anyone who might hurt her by walking away. The result was a spirit entombed in the center of a multilayered casing of disappointment and self-doubt, loneliness and shame, a spirit that was still capable of enthusiasm and joy but chronically incapable of sustaining either one for more than a few days.

Fast-forward.

John stood with her at another crossroads, one he had witnessed as an invisible spectator only two nights ago. At the time, watching the experience had been disturbing enough, but now that he was actually living it, feeling the emotions that Holly had felt, the pain was unimaginable and threatened to crush him as it had almost crushed Holly.

He felt smothering despair as Holly turned on the tap, felt the hopelessness and helplessness to do anything but die.

As she slipped from her robe, he shared the sensation of being emotionally empty, a mere husk of a person whose bright, shining spirit had been eaten by a cancer until almost nothing was left.

He saw the beckoning darkness when she stepped into the tub

and closed her eyes briefly, saw it opening its arms in preparation to receive her, and heard the voice of oblivion whispering a promise of a tangible end to the pain and lovelessness and the never-ending need to make sense of it all.

He felt the trembling of her body as she eased into the water, and her confusion as she weighed two terrifying alternatives: whether to fight back the darkness and try one more time, or give it all up, once and for all. The debate was brief but seemed to take forever, until the scale with surrender sank slowly down.

He experienced keenly the cold, sharp touch of the razor's edge as it rested lightly on unbroken skin, the last hesitation, then perverse relief and dark exhilaration as the razor sliced downward, parting the flesh and letting all the pain and blood flow free.

Finally, he shared her descent into the nether regions of fear and felt her yield to the embrace of the seductive darkness. When the fear closed in, once and for all, he snatched it away and took it as his own, sending Holly love and hope in its place. . . .

∽

JOHN SLOWLY OPENED his eyes to a darkness that was at first indistinguishable from the darkness he had just left. Only seconds had elapsed since completing the exchange, but it felt like days—long, trying, exhausting days. . . . Of the four knowings he had experienced so far, this one had been the most draining and intense, and he was left feeling numb and his body heavy, as if he had literally taken on the weight of Holly's sorrow.

After a few disoriented moments, the sensation faded. Holly's moonlit face swam into view, surrounded by an aura much like the one John had seen encompassing Will after their experience. Holly appeared stunned, but her eyes hinted at the stirring of a fledgling serenity. "What just happened?" she asked softly.

John gave her a pensive smile. "I gave you a taste of what I experienced in the Light."

Holly's eyes flashed with surprise, and she stared intently at John while a stream of thoughts cascaded through her mind. Earlier, she had believed his account of a near-death experience, but now, as his words illuminated the change in her emotional state, she finally began to grasp at least a fraction of the wonder and truth of what he had told her. She smiled fleetingly. "But how? I don't understand. . . ."

"I don't completely understand it myself," John admitted in a hushed voice, wondering how much to tell her. He knew it was possible that Holly might feel violated by the revelation that he had known her thoughts, so he decided to tread lightly. "It's the gift I was promised by the Being of Light. . . . When I reviewed my life, there were a lot of things I was pretty ashamed of. But He kept me so close that it just wasn't possible to hold on to negative feelings about my past when I was completely surrounded by such unconditional love. I think this ability I came back with operates on the same principle. It makes it possible for me to share positive energy—love—with other people, and that helps them feel better about themselves, just like I was helped. More than anything else, I guess, it shows them the power of forgiveness."

Holly thought about it for a while, glancing out at the darkened canyon, the stars, the moon. Every time she watched a particularly spectacular sunset, she couldn't help but feel the bright light of the sun bathing her with energy, a universal energy that cleansed, rejuvenated and inspired her spirit. Red Rock Canyon had a similar effect on her. She felt it very clearly in those moments of solitude when the rocks and the desert and the endless sky gave her refuge from the demons of everyday life. Remembering those things, the leap of faith that was required to believe John's words turned out to be a short one.

There was still one burning question left to be answered. "Do you do this all the time?" Holly asked.

John shook his head. "Only a few times, so far . . . Only when I'm supposed to."

"Then why me?" Holly asked in an awed voice. "It's not like I'm ungrateful . . . but what did I do to deserve it?"

Before John could answer, a third voice spoke in the stillness of the space around them. "It's time to move on."

Startled, John and Holly turned and saw Will Gibson. He was standing just beyond the edge of their boulder, hovering in the air above the yawning canyon, his body glowing softly with a wondrous light. John reached out to him. "Will!"

"The menace that stalked you last night at the dam is coming for you again," Will announced in an urgent voice. The expression on his face was troubled. "You've got to leave while you can."

"What are you talking about?" John replied. Like Holly, he was confused and suddenly scared.

"There's no time for questions," Will said in an unequivocal voice. Already his image was beginning to fade. "Get going!" he reiterated. "Before it's too late." And then he was gone.

John and Holly stared at the spot where Will had been, and Holly turned to the man who had brought her along on this metaphysical roller coaster. "Who *are* you?" she whispered.

John frowned and motioned for silence, peering intently into the moonlit shadows all around them. He saw nothing out of the ordinary but knew that someone or some *thing* was close by; he could already feel the free-floating dread spreading through his gut, the same instinctual warning he had experienced at Hoover Dam. Soon, Holly felt it, too.

She reached for John's hand and glanced around anxiously. "Do you see anything?" The silence of the night had suddenly deepened; the insects, the birds, the very trees themselves seemed afraid to be heard.

"No," John replied in a tight voice. Sitting out in the open at the canyon's edge, they felt exposed and alone, vulnerable to attack from any point in the darkness—behind, in front, above and below. He glanced up the path in the direction they had come. They were too far from the car to reach it quickly, because the path—which ran perilously close to the canyon's rim at several places—was all but obscured by the night. Yet with each passing second, the air grew more charged with the unmistakable electricity of approaching danger. Realizing they were squandering whatever time they had left, John shot off a fervent silent prayer, then climbed down from the boulder and reached for Holly's hand. Holly took it eagerly, slid her legs over the side of the rock and jumped down.

Because of the darkness, both of them had to resist the urge simply to flee blindly up the path. Instead, they took a few tentative steps, glanced nervously over their shoulders, then hurried away from the clearing as fast as the night and uneven ground allowed. They did not look back.

They had put about one hundred feet between themselves and the boulder when the worn, meandering path narrowed and grew darker, crowded by an overgrowth of tall brush on both sides. John and Holly hesitated momentarily, then plunged into the deeper darkness only because they had no other choice. As they made their way through it, the thick, ragged undergrowth clutched at their ankles and whiplike branches lashed their upper bodies and faces with sharp, pointed leaves. Still, they redoubled their pace, driven by an ever-increasing sense of foreboding—for all they knew, whatever was chasing them was getting closer and closer.

They had not gone very far into the difficult stretch of the trail when a rustling suddenly came from the growth on their right. Holly let out a cry of surprise, slipped in the loose dirt and rock and fell to her knees. Barely missing a stride, John shot out his hand and quickly hauled her to her feet as a small rodent of some kind ran out from the bush and scurried across the path. They felt a rush of gratitude for the momentary reprieve, then John set his gaze tensely but resolutely on the path, and wordlessly got Holly moving forward again.

Once they had cleared the overgrown stretch of trail, the way was still difficult to make out, but at least now they could see five or six feet in front of them. They could also feel their pursuer gaining ground. Energized by another boost of adrenaline, they broke into a run, plunging through the darkness with their hearts pounding in their ears. The knot that had formed in Holly's stomach grew bigger and tighter with each passing second, and her legs were going rubbery and trembled so badly she wasn't sure how much longer she could run. Over and over again, she told herself that this couldn't possibly be happening, that it had to be a dream. But each time she willed herself to *wake up! wake up!* she kept returning to the sounds of their ragged breathing, the pounding of their feet and the unnerving stillness of the night all around them. John accepted from the start that it wasn't a dream. All he could think about was getting Holly to safety.

Before long, they spied the muted glow of the lights of the parking lot off in the distance to their left. John immediately veered blindly off the path in that direction, motioning for Holly to follow. Three anxious strides later he lost his footing and lurched sideways, skidding on the near-invisible edge of the canyon. For a second that seemed to stretch out for an eternity, he teetered on the edge, arms pinwheeling in the air above the yawning blackness while he wondered if it all had come down to this. It wasn't that he was afraid of dying again—the first time had shown him that it was nothing to fear—but after all that had happened between himself and Holly in the last twenty-four hours, it seemed too ironic and unfair for it to end now, like this, not to mention that his death would leave Holly in danger. He looked at her once with disbelief in his eyes, then his balance tipped in favor of the yawning canyon.

TWENTY-SEVEN

Visions of Angels

WITH NO THOUGHT of what would happen if John pulled her over with him, Holly lunged for his arm and yanked him back before the canyon could claim him. As they fell into each other's arms, gasping for breath and shaking with relief, John peered tensely into the shadows, fully expecting to find that they had escaped one form of death only to face another. Surprisingly, whatever had been chasing them was nowhere in sight. Not only that, John suddenly knew, but he—it?—had given up, perhaps assuming that John had plunged to his death. Whatever the reason, they were safe—for the moment.

As John opened his mouth to tell Holly the good news, they were suddenly engulfed by a glowing white light that emanated from behind them. John smiled knowingly and turned Holly around to see its source—a very tall and muscular being who glowed with a radiant light. Clothed only in a coarse white robe that hung to his knees, he had a shaggy mane of long, black hair and a countenance that intimated an equal capacity for incredible love and incredible power.

"Are you an angel?" Holly blurted out, staring up in astonishment at the face that was not quite human.

The being favored her with a radiant smile. He replied telepathically in a rich, deep voice that made Holly feel warm and awed at the same time, "Yes. I am."

Holly started to say something else, but her voice trailed off, as it finally sank in that she was talking to an honest-to-God angel.

Having already encountered the Being of Light, John was relatively nonplussed about meeting one of his messengers. Suddenly, he couldn't help feeling angry. "Where were you when we needed you?" he demanded between ragged breaths. "Whatever was after us almost made me run right off the cliff!"

"You almost made yourself run right off the cliff," the angel replied, nearly matching his tone. "I assumed you would remain on the path to safety. Obviously, I was mistaken." He paused, then smiled slightly. "Even so, I must admit that both of you were very brave. And I was with you every step of the way. If you had needed my assistance, I would have given it at once."

John felt his anger drain away, but he was still bothered by the question of why they had been placed in peril in the first place. "Why in the world is someone stalking us—all the way from Hoover Dam, if what Will said was correct?" he demanded. "After all we've been through, why would God even let this happen—what purpose could it possibly serve?"

"As is usually the case, there is more going on here than meets the eye," the angel replied patiently. "Your pursuer was sent to stop you from completing your mission." Then he added cryptically, "It was sent by someone other than God."

A shiver went through John, then he demanded, "But why did *Holly* have to be put in danger?"

"As I said, you have a mission—*both* of you," the angel answered, delivering news that was a revelation to John, and to Holly as well. "There are forces that do not want you to complete it."

As John pondered the implications of what he'd just heard, Holly stared at the angel, dumbfounded. "Mission?" she repeated weakly, shaking her head. "What are you talking about?"

"Yes," John chimed in. "What exactly is this mission? I haven't the faintest idea what to do next." Thinking of the still-unexplained dreams of the blond-haired boy, he added, "I assume it has something to do with the child in my dreams, but I need more information if you expect me to do something. That is, if you expect *us* to do something," he corrected himself, still getting used to the idea that it was now Holly's mission, too.

The angel nodded gravely. "I know. And the time has come for you to be given more of what you need to know." He pointed toward the canyon, and a pocket of air began shimmering in front of them. It coalesced into a colorful, three-dimensional screen like the one John had watched during his life review. As he and Holly stared wide-eyed with awe, the rest of John's near-death experience played out. . . .

JOHN WAS STANDING in a blaze of light at the end of the tunnel. As the vision of Holly's attempted suicide faded from view, he turned to ask the Being of Light what it meant. But Jesus was gone, and in His place stood John's grandmother. John stared at her, puzzled, and asked, "Where did He go?"

"Don't fret yourself," she answered with an understanding smile. "You'll see Him again, when it's time."

John frowned, but nodded; he could still feel the warmth of the Light all around him. Referring to the vision he'd just been shown, he asked, "Who was that woman? And why did I have to see that?"

"So many questions!" Grandma Creed exclaimed, grinning mildly. "You're just as curious now, Johnny, as you were when you were a little boy." Her expression turned serious. "Don't worry. After you go back, you'll know what it means, but not until you need to know. That's the way it works, Johnny: everything in its time, and only when you are ready to receive it. Have faith. And a little patience." She smiled again and said, "Right now, there's someone else I want you to meet."

She turned and peered down the tunnel. John followed her gaze and saw an angel holding the hand of a wide-eyed, blond-haired boy of ten or eleven. "Here's another one who's only here for a visit," Grandma Creed told him. "You're supposed to meet him before he's sent back." John once again gave her a puzzled look, but his grandmother ignored him and went to greet the boy as the angel disappeared.

She brought him over, beaming. "John, this is Matt Dandridge," she said, gently nudging the boy forward. "Matt, this is John, your guardian angel."

Caught off guard, John gaped in surprise. The only thing he could think to say was "Hi. It's nice to meet you."

Looking a little tentative himself, Matt looked up at Grandma Creed and said with a child's frankness, "He doesn't look like an angel."

Grandma Creed laughed. "Well, there are angels, and then there are angels," she said. "Sometimes people can be guardian angels, too, if our Heavenly Father wants them to be." She smiled warmly and added, "He makes sure every little boy has at least one to watch over him— and often, more than one. You may not see them, but they're there, all the same. Isn't that right, John?" she said, turning to her grandson.

"Yes, that's true," John agreed, realizing as he spoke that it indeed was true; he wasn't sure how he knew, but the knowledge felt more like a memory than a discovery. As the surprise of learning that he was to be the boy's guardian angel began to wear off, he found himself warming to the notion, although he had no idea what the job would entail.

"John had an accident today, just like you," Grandma Creed went on explaining to Matt. "But it wasn't his time to come Home just yet, and God is sending him back so he can finish the work he was meant to do." She smiled gently and added, "Like watching over you."

Matt's eyes went wide and he frowned. "I don't have to go back, too, do I?"

"I'm afraid so."

After a moment, Matt folded his arms across his chest and shook his head vigorously from side to side. The expression on his face was obstinate, filled with a child's unflinching determination. It also showed his fear and bitter disappointment. "I'm not going back. No way."

John regarded him with a wry smile. Having felt the same way when he'd been asked to return, he understood Matt's reluctance to give up the heaven he'd only just reclaimed. But he also understood the need to go back. He glanced at Grandma Creed, and she nodded in response. "You have a family, don't you?" John asked the boy.

"Yes." The answer was given almost grudgingly.

"What about them?" John asked softly. "I'm sure they'd miss you terribly."

"They can get along without me," Matt replied stubbornly, but with less conviction than before. He gazed down at his feet and almost whimpered, "Please . . . don't make me go back. They'll be okay."

Grandma Creed placed her hands lovingly on the boy's shoulders. "But what if they won't?" she asked. "What if they need you?" Smiling sweetly, she cupped a hand under his chin and lifted Matt's face until his eyes met hers. With a nod of her head, she directed him to look at the holographic images that had sprung to life in the space before them.

The three of them watched silently as Matt and his family acted out scenes that grew increasingly disturbing, visions of a future that was close at hand. With each successive scene, Matt's face became grimmer and his resolve less firm, until finally he reached out and squeezed John's hand, as if suddenly feeling the need for a guardian angel. John was greatly troubled, too, and as he watched, the budding protective feelings he felt for the boy grew stronger and stronger.

When it was over, Matt turned to Grandma Creed and said in a small voice, "Maybe those things won't happen if I don't go back."

Grandma Creed shook her head with great sadness. "And maybe they'll be worse, dear."

"But I'm just a kid! What can I do?" Matt croaked.

"Tell them about the love you felt here," Grandma Creed responded. "It doesn't matter whether you're a little boy or a grand-mother like me—if you share God's love you can always make a difference. Have faith in yourself, Matt. God does. That's why He's sending you back." When Matt still looked doubtful, she continued, "Everything might not work out like you want, but you have to try. That's all God asks. He has a plan for your life, Matt—He expects great things from you when you grow up—but you have to go back to make it happen."

Without knowing exactly why, John began to sense that Matt's return was important not only to his family, but for other reasons as well. He also understood that part of the mission he'd been given by the Light was to help Matt through the bad times looming on the horizon. It was a sobering responsibility, but one from which John would never walk away. Still holding the boy's hand, he squatted down in front of him and smiled reassuringly. "Think of it as a mission," he said. "A mission from God. And if things get too tough, all you have to do is let me know and I'll be there to help. Okay?"

Matt looked into John's eyes and said, "You promise?" It was obvious that he was still greatly torn between staying in heaven and returning to earth.

John smiled, his heart suddenly filled with love for the boy. "I promise," he said solemnly.

Matt glanced off into the distance. After a few moments, he said in a small voice, "Okay . . . I'm ready to go back."

John pulled him into his arms and gave him a long, fierce hug.

After telling him what to expect when he returned to his body, which had been seriously injured in the bicycle accident, he let go of Matt's hand, gave him one final hug and waved farewell. Matt gave him a brave smile, cast one last glance at Grandma Creed and disappeared.

John stared thoughtfully into the tunnel for a while, and turned to his grandmother. "He's a special little boy, isn't he?"

"He certainly is," Grandma Creed replied. "And brave, too. It's not going to be easy for him when he gets back to the world."

John nodded, frowning. He couldn't help but wonder what his own life would be like after returning. "I hope he's okay."

"He will be. God will help you see to that."

John thought about it for a moment, and his frown deepened. "But why did he have to see all that?" he asked, referring to the future both of them had seen. "No wonder he was afraid to go back. I would have been, too. It seems like more than a child should have to bear."

"I know," Grandma Creed replied. "But we have to trust God's plan. Showing him those things was necessary to convince him to return. You needed to see them, too, Johnny. Don't worry, God knows Matt's limits, and most of what he saw will be removed from his memory." She paused, and added with fresh concern in her eyes, "But as bad as that was, he was spared the worst." She pointed to the spot where the vision of Matt's family had just played out, and the "worst" she referred to began to unfold.

John stared intently as the vision came into focus. A lone figure sat cross-legged on the floor in a darkened room. The man was silent, but the air was filled with the ominous sound of approaching thunder. Lightning flashed. Harsh white light exploded through the room, and John saw that the man was Matt's father. Staring at a row of family photographs on the wall, his cheeks were wet with recent tears, and his eyes were red and puffy and grim. Lightning flashed again, and John saw his hands curled in his lap. One of them was trembling and clutched at the handle of a gleaming pistol. When lightning flashed a third time, the face of Matt's father hardened into a terrifying mask of desperate resolve, and he struggled to his feet and headed for a stairway. The last thing John saw before the vision ended was the man climbing the stairs and entering a bedroom, the gun at the end of his outstretched arm. . . .

John turned to his grandmother with a horrified expression. "When will this happen?"

"As you reckon time, soon enough," she replied enigmatically, and with great sadness.

John closed his eyes and shook his head slowly from side to side, finding it increasingly difficult to accept riddles in lieu of answers. "Can't you be more specific?" he asked, unable to mask his frustration. "I'm supposed to be this boy's guardian angel, but I don't know when he's going to need my help—and I don't even know where he lives, for that matter!"

"I'm sorry, Johnny," Grandma Creed replied. "All I can tell you is that you'll know when it's time, and that you'll find him by going to Kansas City. Other than that, I can't be more specific." She smiled slightly and gave his hand a reassuring squeeze. "Trust me, it's better this way."

"It is, John," a voice—*the* voice—said from behind him. "If we told you now, you would undoubtedly be tempted to act too soon, and that would change everything." John turned and faced the Being of Light, suddenly ashamed of his lack of faith. "I'm sorry," he said contritely.

"I know what you saw is difficult to understand," Jesus told him. "And it is only natural to feel horrified and anxious about it. The path you are on will not be an easy one. But you have more courage and strength than you realize, and I will send someone to travel the path with you—the woman I showed you in the vision, Holly. Your new gift will bring the two of you together, and she will add to your strength, and you will add to hers."

Staring into the eyes that were the source and embodiment of compassion and love, John could only nod and let the Light's love and strength and reassurance wash over him. His doubts about his mission rapidly subsided, and he accepted the necessity of waiting for the information he would eventually need. No matter how daunting the task that lay before him, he now knew without question that everything he needed would be given to him in time, and that time would be the right one—not by the reckoning of human understanding, but by the omniscient wisdom of the Creator Himself. It was an inspiring, exalting and humbling experience, and John could only smile at his Lord and say, "I'm ready."

Jesus returned his smile and drew John to Him. "I'm glad," He said, and John knew that He was; he could feel Jesus' joy wash over and through him. "Your presence here is very precious to all of us, but now it is time to return to your body and complete your mission. The upheavals on the Earth have only just begun. It sorrows me to say that there are even greater trials and changes yet to come. Matt has been chosen to play a crucial role in the years ahead: he is a messenger who will be an important leader and teacher during the world's difficult transition from darkness to light. It is vital that he not be removed from that path." Jesus offered a reassuring smile and concluded, "Do not be afraid or doubt your abilities. I will be with all of you every step of the way, even when the darkness threatens to overwhelm you."

THE VISION OVER, John stared at the canyon and the world beyond with newfound wonder, excited and grateful finally to have closure on his NDE. "Thank you," he said quietly to God. Then he thanked the angel who had delivered the message. The angel smiled solemnly and dipped his head, and John broke into a grin, overwhelmed with a joy too big to contain. Even though he knew that the path he was on would lead him to a darkness blacker than anything he'd experienced before, he also knew he would not be alone, and that God Himself had put him on this path. Now that he had been given the last piece of the puzzle, John was ready to face the challenge with a new sense of purpose and with love for the boy he had promised to protect. It occurred to him that Matt must be frantic by now, wondering if John had reneged on his promise, but that, too, John sensed, might be part of the plan. He knew without a doubt they would get there in time, and that God would be with them, even if the outcome appeared unclear.

Holly's view of life, her own past and future, had also been profoundly changed by the realization that everything that had happened in the last few days—her suicide attempt, the "chance" meeting with John, the picnic at sunset, John's use of his gift and the terrifying chase—had all been leading to this incredible moment, the blossoming of her belief. She had believed John's account of his NDE, but now she embraced it. Experiencing the love and power of the Light, even vicariously, made it impossible to do anything else. For the first time in her life, she had felt absolute love, had been powerless to resist it, and that in itself was nothing less than a miracle. As she had after the "knowing," Holly stared at John (and also at the angel) with awe and wonder, saying a silent prayer of thanks for everything that had happened—including the things that had caused her pain, because those were the ones that had made all this possible. That was a lesson she would never forget.

The common thread that wove through the moment for John and Holly was, of course, Matt Dandridge. Now that the vision had ended, a voice in Holly's head warned her to be scared of what she had seen, and for a moment she listened . . . but it turned out to be the voice of the person she used to be, and it lacked its old persuasiveness. Instead, Holly thought about the look on Matt's face as he watched the troubles his family would have, and the courage he had shown by agreeing to go back. She also pondered, as did John, the surprising revelation about Matt and his greater mission in the years to come. In the last few minutes, everything had changed, and now she and John were part of a very special mission for a very special boy who needed their help. Like John, she was determined that nothing would prevent her from carrying out that mission.

Sharing the same thought, Holly and John looked at each other, both suddenly feeling the need to move on. "So we should go to Kansas City," John said to the angel.

The angel nodded. "As soon as possible," he answered gravely. "Be there by tomorrow." And then he was gone.

"DEAR LORD, I know my mom's gonna be mad about this—
    "And maybe you are too—
    "But please—
    "Help me find John anyway—
    "Please help me get—
    "To Kansas City—
    "Amen."

After four hours of riding his bike on uneven blacktop and treacherous gravel shoulders that were practically invisible in the middle of the night, Matt barely had the wind to finish his prayer. He had tried to pace himself, because he knew before he started that it would be a long night—Kansas City was clear across the state, over two hundred miles away—but he was running out of steam. And nerve. It was spooky being out here all alone, with all the creepy shadows and night-time sounds of owls and crickets and who-knew-what-else. Not to mention the glowing eyes of invisible creatures lurking in the trees and brush along the road. He had tried to ignore them for as long as he could, but now he was finding it almost impossible.

What he needed was a place to stop, someplace away from all the shadows and noises, where he could hide and catch a few hours sleep. His mom probably wouldn't find his note until morning, so he doubted that anyone was looking for him yet, but a boy riding a bike in the middle of the night in the middle of nowhere would look suspicious to a passing policeman. So far he hadn't even had a close call—Highway 94 was all but deserted this time of night, especially out here in the country—but sooner or later someone might see him.

Or he might run smack into a stop sign or something worse. Better to get some rest and head out after the sun came up, when he wouldn't look out of place. Sunrise was only a few hours off, anyway.

Before long, he passed a sign that said Jefferson City was only three miles away. He was tempted to go those last three miles and maybe look for a park where he could spend the night, but the thought of being spotted changed his mind. The bigger the town, the more police, he reasoned. Besides, he was almost halfway to Kansas City. There was no reason to take chances. He'd be better off someplace this side of the city, and the closer the better.

A hundred yards later, he came upon a crossroads that stretched into the darkness on either side of the highway. He stopped and fished his flashlight out of his backpack, and shone it on a sign that said FRE-MONT ROAD. Next to it was a smaller red-and-white sign that bore the name of the Good Shepherd Church, with the words "One-Half Mile" printed above an arrow pointing to the right. An idea blossomed in his mind and Matt peered down the road in the direction of the arrow. He saw nothing but shadows among rows of corn, and a wide strip of gravel disappearing into darkness, but decided to check it out anyway.

A short time later, he came upon a clearing in the middle of the cornfields, and a modest, white clapboard building loomed up on his right. Nestled among the treetops, an old-fashioned steeple gleamed softly in the moonlight; in the middle of the lawn, a dimly lighted brick-and-glass sign identified the structure as the Good Shepherd Church. Seeing no one around, Matt hopped off his bike and hid it in the bushes, then approached the building with a mix-ture of caution and hope. *This'll be safer than sleeping outside,* he thought, *in more ways than one.* That is, if the door was unlocked.

Surprisingly, it was. The door creaked as he opened it, and Matt held his breath. When nobody came, he slipped inside. He had ex-pected the sanctuary to be dark and forbidding, but moonlight was streaming through four large windows on one side of the church, and even though the room had its share of shadows and darkened corners, he felt a calm wash over him as he entered. The silvery illumination, so steady and pure, made everything look safe, even warm and inviting. After a slight hesitation, Matt took off his knapsack and headed for a pew at the back of the room.

He plopped down wearily on the end of the pew nearest one of the windows and began rummaging through his knapsack, looking for something to eat before he slept. After pulling out a flashlight, a map, a small compass, his wallet and a bottle of water, he finally found the candy bars that had slipped to the bottom. He unwrapped one of them and stared out the window, eating just enough to quiet his stomach. When he was finished, he gathered up his things and put them in the knapsack. He stretched out on the pew and faced the window, counting on the sunlight to wake him in a few hours. For most of his journey, he had been so busy watching where he was going that there had been little time to think about what he was doing and why he was doing it. Now, in the stillness of the empty church, it all came back to him in a flood of emotion. Sobbing quietly in between the words of a prayer for his family, he continued to cry for a very long time, until weariness overtook him and he fell into a deep and troubled sleep.

TWENTY-EIGHT

Rude Awakenings

"WAKE UP, little one. It is time to go."

Matt awoke with a start to find a man standing over him. At first he couldn't remember where he was, but it quickly came back to him. So did his fear of getting caught and being sent home before he could find his guardian angel. "I'm sorry!" he blurted out, trying to clear the sleep from his unfocused eyes. "I didn't touch anything. Honest!"

"I am not the minister of this church," the man replied in a melodic, accented voice. "You have nothing to fear from me."

Matt sat up as the man's face swam into view in the morning light. It was a rugged face with deep lines and extraordinarily calm, dark brown eyes that looked as if they saw right into Matt's soul. The stranger had long, straight black hair tied back in a ponytail, and he was dressed in old jeans, with some sort of fringed leather vest and knee-high leather moccasins. A little unnerved by the man's appearance—especially his eyes—Matt asked, "Who are you?"

"One who has been sent to you."

"Did my mom send you?" Matt asked, suddenly alarmed.

A hint of a smile crossed the man's lips and he replied in a meaningful tone, "No. I was sent by a *higher* power."

Finally, Matt began to understand what the stranger meant. But it still made no sense. "You're not my guardian angel," he said.

"Do not hold such a surprised face over you, little one," the man replied. "The Spirit Father sends many guardians to watch over His children. I have been charged with helping you on the journey you will take at a later season, but it was also deemed wise that I come to this place to watch over you as you slept last night."

Still wary, Matt said, "No offense, mister, but you talk kinda funny."

The man smiled sagely. "No offense is taken. I speak your language but I speak it as my people do. In this walk I am Native American."

"An Indian?"

"That also."

Matt nodded. "Have you been to the tunnel, too?"

The man gave Matt a mysterious smile. "We will talk of that at a later season. For now, you have an important journey to resume."

Brought back to reality by the mention of his journey, Matt hurriedly checked his watch. It was almost eight o'clock! He turned to the window, looking for the rays of morning sunshine that were supposed to have awakened him two hours earlier. Instead, he saw an overcast sky. Even worse, on the horizon was a band of approaching storm clouds, dark and angry, and promising rain. "I better get going!" Matt exclaimed, grabbing his knapsack and bolting from the pew.

"Yes. It is time," the stranger agreed. "But first, hear the words I have been given." His voice grew serious and commanding, but Matt thought he detected something else as well, sadness or maybe sympathy. It made him stop to listen. "The Creator has laid out a special path for you. It will not be an easy journey, but it will bring you much reward and contentment if you keep your eyes fixed on the horizon. Do not turn back! And do not hold a fearful face over you when the path becomes rocky and dark. The Spirit Father will be with you, and He will send others to help you carry your burdens. Will you remember?"

Matt nodded somberly, then glanced out through the windows at the approaching storm. When he looked back, the man was gone.

FEELING AS IF she had been hit by a train, Kate Dandridge woke up with a baseball bat next to her in bed. Over and over in her sleep last night, she had fended off her husband with the very same bat, sometimes bashing him, sometimes not, and she was relieved to find it was still where she had left it before falling asleep. The dreams had been bad enough, but at least they had only been dreams; Elliot had not come home last night.

Kate glanced at the clock and saw that she was late for work. She frowned and reached for the phone, but drew up short when a spike of pain sliced through her grogginess, a sudden reminder that her injured arm was still in a sling—and that one of her nightmares was all too real. Cursing Elliot, she maneuvered herself into a sitting position on the edge of the bed and used her other hand to dial the phone.

After calling in sick, she was tempted to lie back down and sleep until the nightmares and pain wore off, but her need to check on the kids made that impossible. As terrifying and painful as Elliot's attack had been, what troubled her the most was that her children had seen it. They had been exceptionally brave and supportive in the aftermath, but children thrust into the role of responsible adults always paid a price, and she was determined to minimize the impact. Getting out of bed and restoring at least the illusion of normalcy, if only for a few hours, was an important first step. Since the upheaval in their lives was about to get worse when she left her husband, it was more important than ever to reassure her children they could count on their mother and that life would continue.

With a heavy sigh, Kate eased into her slippers, grabbed the nightstand with her one good hand and got to her feet. Her lower back complained, still smarting from the encounter with the dining room chair, but she stood very still and waited for it to pass. Moving carefully across the bedroom, she opened the door and called out Matt's name. Getting no reply, she started across the hall to look in his room, but stopped when she stepped on a sheet of paper lying on the floor. She bent down to retrieve it, then hesitated when she saw the words "Dear Mom" at the top. Not knowing why, she felt a stab of apprehension. After reading the note, she understood completely.

TWO HOURS LATER, Elliot awoke hungover in his hotel room a few miles across town. This morning was much the same as any other morning over the last few months—with the exception of the hotel room—but it was different in an important way. He usually woke up simmering with anxiety and anger, but this morning those feelings had grown sharper and deeper. Kate had threatened the unthinkable last night, and now, as he pondered the possibility of being alone, the hangover was but a speck on an angry horizon.

On the plus side, Kate evidently had not called the police. Even though he hadn't told anyone where he was going when he left the bar last night, a man as drunk as he was doesn't get very far before he crashes for the night; if the police had been looking, they probably would have found him. But they hadn't, and he was grateful that his wife had shown some mercy. It gave him hope that forgiveness might actually follow.

On the other hand, it could also mean she had made up her mind to take the kids and leave.

The thought made his insides go cold with fear, the same fear that had driven him over the edge last night. But now he was sober and knew exactly what to do: he would go straight home and set things right. Facing his family wouldn't be easy—he felt sick to his stomach just thinking about it—but the alternative was to spend the rest of his life alone, and that scared him even worse. Yes, he would apologize to Kate—grovel if he had to—and ask her forgiveness. He would make her understand that he couldn't live without her, and that from this day on he would turn over a new leaf. He would also tell his daughter how sorry he was for what happened last night. And, if it looked like it was necessary, he would even bite the bullet and apologize to Matt.

"JOHN, WAKE UP! Our flight's here!" Holly shook him again. "Come on, John! *Wake up!*"

Emerging from a deep and dreamless sleep, John looked sheepishly at Holly. "Sorry. Guess I must have dozed off."

"I took a nap myself," Holly replied, talking fast. "But our plane's here now. And it's a good thing I woke up before it left without us."

They were sitting in the Denver airport, waiting at the gate for the connecting flight to Kansas City. Outside, the sky was gray and overcast. Inside, it was bright and cheery, but after all the excitement and physical strain of the previous night, nothing short of a nuclear explosion could have kept John awake. Having been told by the angel that they had less than twenty-four hours to reach Kansas City, they had driven back to Las Vegas and taken a red-eye flight to Denver. After a layover of several hours, the plane that would take them the last leg of the journey had finally arrived.

John was grateful for the rest, and only mildly surprised that his sleep had been dreamless; at a level similar to the knowing, he understood that the dreams and visions were finally over. Ironically, now that he understood their origin and purpose, the thought of continuing without them was a little unsettling. But from this point on, he and Holly were on their own, so to speak. Well, not really on their own. His faith had grown tremendously over the last few months—especially the last few days—and he knew without a doubt that God always answered his prayers. Sometimes, though, he just couldn't help holding his breath while he waited for the answer. This was one of those times.

He knew they would get to Kansas City, but it was difficult not knowing what would come after. It had occurred to him on the flight to Denver that even though they had been told to go to Kansas City, they had not been told where to find Matt once they arrived. When he had voiced the fear that they might not find him, Holly had quickly admonished him to have more faith. Now, looking into her tired but determined face, he felt a resurgence of confidence, and he began to understand why Holly was with him. No, they didn't know how to find Matt once they got to Kansas City, but they would deal with that at the appropriate time. Thanks to Holly, he put the doubt behind him. "Okay," he said, grabbing his bag. "I'm ready to go."

WHILE JOHN AND HOLLY were boarding their plane, Matt was riding his bike on the shoulder of a two-lane highway near Sedalia, Missouri, about seventy-five miles outside of Kansas City. Ever since leaving the church, he had pondered the mystery of his second guardian's sudden appearance and disappearance. But now he had other problems to think about. The sky had continued to grow more ominous the farther west he went, and now it looked like it was about to storm. That was the last thing he needed. "Dear God, please don't let me get caught in the rain," he said, continuing to pedal as he glanced upward in the direction he imagined heaven to be. "*Please* help me get there, and help me find John." Then he squeezed his eyes shut for a second or two and finished the prayer with a fervent "Amen."

Already feeling more confident, he smiled to himself and opened his eyes—just in time to see a possum lie down in the path of the bike. The animal rolled over and pretended to be dead, and Matt yelped in surprise, then wrenched his handlebars hard to the right to avoid running over it. As his tires hit the band of loose dirt and rock between the shoulder of the road and the field beside it, he went into a skid and plunged down a shallow, grassy slope, where he crashed into a fence post as tall as the bike.

Shaken but not hurt, he angrily untangled himself from the twisted bike frame. "Stupid possum!" he screamed, turning to glare at the unmoving creature. "Look what you made me do! How am I ever going to get to Kansas City now?" He looked back at the bike, its tires flat and rims bent beyond repair, and glanced up again at the lowering sky. He suddenly wished it would rain after all, if for no other reason than to hide his tears. He wished it would storm, with thunder and lightning and blinding rain, and he would stand all alone on the side of this road and let it do what it would, because he couldn't feel worse than he felt right now. His last chance of finding his guardian angel while he still had time had just slipped away, and all because of a stupid possum.

He started toward the creature—not intending to hurt it, but to coax it to leave and get out of his sight—then stopped. He turned to his bike and kicked it instead. As the irony of having wrecked so soon after saying a prayer started to hit him, a small red pickup truck pulled onto the shoulder a few yards behind him. A tall, beefy teenage boy got out and walked over to the spot where Matt was standing.

"What happened?" he asked, shaking his head at the twisted wreckage.

Matt scowled and pointed at the shoulder. "That stupid possum. I wrecked trying not to hit him."

"Tough break," the teen commiserated. "The bike looks trashed."

Matt stared at it forlornly. "It is."

"Where were you headed?"

"Kansas City."

The teenager's eyes widened, then narrowed in suspicion. "On a bike?" he asked. "What, are you running away or something?"

"No," Matt answered a little too sharply. He forced a smile. "I'm working on a merit badge for Scouts," he lied, hoping he sounded believable.

The teenager didn't look totally convinced, but he shrugged and said, "Whatever . . . I'm headed to Kansas City, myself. You're welcome to ride along—but this better not get me in trouble."

"It won't," Matt replied, suddenly excited. "I swear."

"Okay. Want to put the bike in the back?" the Good Samaritan asked, indicating the truck bed.

Matt thought about it for a moment. He felt bad about leaving it lying there, a big hunk of litter, but he couldn't exactly cart it around once he got to Kansas City either. "No," he finally replied. "It's history. Just leave it there."

"Suit yourself," the teenager replied, and headed for the truck.

As they pulled back onto the highway, the teenager gestured toward Matt's black eye, and casually remarked, "Looks like you got yourself a shiner in the wreck."

Matt's hand automatically went to his face. He had almost forgotten about the black eye. "Guess I did," he replied, frowning.

"You need to do something about it?"

Matt smiled sadly to himself and shook his head. "No. That's okay. I already have."

TWENTY-NINE

Convergence

THE FLIGHT FROM DENVER took less than two hours, and John and Holly arrived in Kansas City a little after noon on Tuesday. Since no dream or vision or obvious sign had come to John on the plane, they still didn't know how to find Matt, and John felt his anxiety creeping back as he walked down the runway toward the gate. Catching himself slipping into his old frame of mind, he made a conscious effort to push the fear away, but it wasn't easy, because the clock was ticking—ticking toward the showdown he had seen in the tunnel.

He kept his eyes peeled for any sign of Matt as they walked through the terminal. Holly did the same. Each time they spotted a freckle-faced, blond-haired boy they held their breath until they got close enough to see that it wasn't Matt. When they finally reached the

Budget car rental counter without having found him, John turned to
Holly and asked, "So what do we do now?"

Holly thought about it for a minute. "Why don't we look for
Dandridges in the phone book?"

John nodded. "That way we can get an address, too—assuming
they're listed." He paused, then said, "I'm not so sure about calling
ahead, though. How would we explain who we are or why we want
to see them? From what I know of Matt's father, it might not take
much to set him off. I think we should just show up in person instead."

Their course of action settled, John turned to the rental agent
standing behind the counter. "I need a car, a phone book and a street
guide if you have them," he said, smiling. The pretty young woman
behind the counter had all three. Ten minutes later, John and Holly
were on their way to the first Dandridge residence they had found in
the phone book.

"THIS IS AS FAR AS I go," the teenager said, pulling into the parking lot of a shopping mall just off the highway. "My girlfriend works
at the music store here."

"Okay," Matt responded in a tentative voice. "Thanks for the
ride." He was excited to have arrived in Kansas City but unsure what
to do next. The only clue he had about where to find John was his
dream of his guardian angel standing in front of a police station
marked "17th Precinct." Somehow he had to find his way there, but it
didn't seem prudent to ask the driver for directions. As he climbed
out of the truck, he decided to look up the station in the phone book
and hitchhike there instead.

After finding a phone booth and looking up the address, he
headed back to the highway. The thought of standing by the side of
such a busy road to hitch a ride from a stranger was more than a little bit scary, but the thought of going back without his guardian angel

was even scarier. So he took a deep breath, stepped onto the shoulder and stuck out his thumb.

Much to his dismay, the first car to pull over was a white-and-blue cruiser marked "Kansas City Police." Matt's first thought was to run, but before he could make up his mind, the policeman was out of his car. The uniformed man that walked toward him was tall, stern-looking and had a gun on his hip. Matt was almost too intimidated to breathe, much less move.

"Son, aren't you a little young for this?" The cop's voice was stern, matching his face.

"I guess so. Sir."

"Do your parents know what you're doing this afternoon?"

Matt looked down and scuffed the ground with his sneaker. He thought about lying, but decided on a compromise. "Sort of."

"Uh-huh." The policeman cocked an eyebrow and said, "You wouldn't be running away from home, now, would you?"

Matt couldn't help but cringe a little. He thought once again about making a run for it, but the cop came closer, as if reading his thoughts. Trying not to sound nervous, Matt cleared his throat. "No, sir," he croaked.

The officer scanned the highway and gave Matt a sidelong glance. "Uh-huh," he said again. His eyes locked onto Matt's and seemed to bore right through him. "What's your name, son?"

Matt hesitated, and answered slowly, "Matt Dandridge." He held his breath, waiting for the policeman to recognize the name as that of a runaway, but the officer's expression didn't change. After a few seconds, he pointed to the car and said, "Why don't you come get in the car."

His heart sinking, Matt did as he was told. Now they would find out who he was and send him home, and he would never reach John before it was too late. He had let down his family, especially his mother. And he couldn't help feeling like God had let him down. It was a hard thing to understand. All he had prayed for was help in finding his guardian angel. It wasn't like he had asked for a million dollars or something. . . .

But as they pulled into the police station ten minutes later, it looked as if his prayer *was* being answered, and it was all he could do not to whoop for joy. As it was, he let out a laugh and pointed with glee at the sign on the building. "The Seventeenth Precinct!" Matt shouted excitedly, half bouncing up and down on the seat of the car. "This is the place I was trying to find!" He turned to the cop. "Do you think you could get me inside?" The policeman regarded him with a bewildered look and said sardonically, "I think I can arrange it."

IT WAS ONLY two o'clock in the afternoon, but it had already been one of the longest days of Kate Dandridge's life. Not knowing where Matt was or if he was okay was almost more than she thought she could bear—especially after almost losing him a few short months ago. All she knew was that he had run away to find his guardian angel; where the "angel" lived, she hadn't a clue. Lori had spent most of the morning searching for her brother, but with no success. Since then, they had passed the hours waiting by the phone, worrying and praying and blaming themselves—and more often, Elliot—for the latest disaster.

When they heard the front door open, Kate and Lori looked at each other with sudden hope and ran into the living room to see if their prayers had finally been answered. Instead, they saw Elliot. Looking thoroughly pathetic and wearing the same disheveled clothes from the night before, he stopped just inside the doorway and started crying as soon as he saw his wife and daughter. He was completely unaware that the previous night's disaster had taken a turn for the worse, so the tears weren't for Matt, and Kate knew it. That, coupled with his obvious intention to ask for forgiveness, made her all the more furious. She could have forgiven him eventually for her own physical wounds, but there was no forgiveness left for what he had done to Matt.

While Elliot was still trying to find his voice, Kate launched into him with all the volatile emotions that had mushroomed that morning. "Well, the prodigal drunk finally returns! I'm glad you managed to pull yourself out of your bottle for a few hours, because I've got some news I want to share with you, Elliot. Some good news and some bad news. First the bad news: Matt's run away. After that little show you put on, he took off on his bike in the middle of the night—he left a note saying he had to find his guardian angel. We don't know where he was headed, and no one has seen or heard from him since. I hope you're happy." She paused to take a breath, fists clenched at her sides. Her eyes locked on Elliot like heat-seeking missiles and she added acidly, "The good news is that when they find him—and you better hope he's all right—I'm taking the kids and leaving for good."

Stunned, Elliot remained mute. He had come home intending to make peace. Instead, he realized everything was slipping away even faster than before. With an imploring look, he started toward Kate with outstretched arms.

"Stay away from me!" Kate screamed in a shrill voice. Fear flickered on her face and she recoiled a step. "There's nothing you can say that I want to hear! I know you're sorry—today. You're always sorry. But things just keep getting worse. Now your son is off traipsing around God-knows-where trying to find someone who probably doesn't even exist. If *anything* happens to him, I swear you'll *really* have something to be sorry about! So don't come back here all meek and mild and weepy-eyed, and expect me to say everything's forgiven. Because it isn't. You've gone to that well once too often!"

Before Elliot could reply, the phone rang, a sudden, shrill alarm that shattered the moment of angry silence. Kate and Lori immediately ran for the kitchen. Elliot stayed behind, too devastated to move.

Two minutes later, Kate and Lori returned; Kate carried her purse, and Lori the car keys. Both were smiling with immense relief, but the smiles all but faded when they faced the man who had caused the ordeal that was now almost over. "That was the police—the

Kansas City Police," Kate said, her fury returning. "They found Matt hitchhiking on the highway. He's all right, thank God! We're going to get him." Not allowing her husband the chance to reply, she added with a coldness that chilled his heart, "I want you out of here when we get back, so we can pack in peace. After we're gone, the place is all yours. At the rate you're going, it's only a matter of time before they repossess it, too." Then she turned on her heel and left the house, with Lori right behind.

SOME TIME LATER, Elliot finally moved from the spot where he had stood throughout Kate's tirade. Grim and defeated, he relinquished his fantasy of reconciliation and turned his attention to the last remaining option. He had come here ready to get down on his knees and beg Kate's forgiveness, but she hadn't even given him the opportunity to say "I'm sorry," much less beg. If she wouldn't give their marriage another chance, he decided, neither would he.

But that doesn't mean I'm going to let her leave, he mused, uttering a dark, humorless laugh. *That* was definitely not an option. The .38 Smith & Wesson a guy had tried to sell him a few days ago at the bar, now *that* was an option. . . .

MATT SAT on the edge of the bunk in his jail cell and stared miserably at the floor. After the call had been made to his mother, he had been left in the care of the desk sergeant—a big, poker-faced, soft-spoken man named Sergeant O'Reilly—but Sergeant O'Reilly had put him in this cell when the front desk had gotten busy. Afraid he'd miss John, Matt had protested, but to no avail. Since then, he had spent the last few hours waiting for his mother and wondering how his plan had gone so wrong.

He had been so sure he would find John here. This was the place the dreams had told him to go, but so far there was no sign of his guardian angel. Not out front, like he'd seen in his dream. Not in the squad room. Certainly not back here in the jail. Matt had described him to Sergeant O'Reilly and the other cop, but they didn't know who he was talking about. Now time was running out and he was beginning to get desperate. He knew he'd never get another chance to come to Kansas City, not after this.

I should've asked John where he lived when I had the chance, he thought bitterly. *Or at least got his phone number.* He kicked at the floor in disgust. *I didn't even ask him his last name,* he thought. *How stupid can you be?*

Pretty stupid, he answered. Not only had it been dumb to run off to Kansas City and scare his mom half to death, but he hadn't even had a backup plan in case something went wrong. And it had, big-time. *You should've known better,* he chastised himself. *It was a stupid idea.* But then the vision of John standing in front of the jail came back to him, and he shook his head. No, it wasn't stupid. He was supposed to be in Kansas City. And John *would* be here, sooner or later. The only question was: Would John get to the jail before his mom took him home?

Matt closed his eyes and started to pray. *Dear Lord,* he said silently, his inner voice a mixture of worry and faith, *I don't know where John is, but You do. Please bring him here before it's too late. And please hurry up, God, because my mom is already on her way.*

AN HOUR AFTER Matt had finished his prayer and lain down on the bunk to wait for an answer, his guardian angel was driving a rental car only a few miles away.

John Creed was as anxious to find Matt as Matt was to be found, but for the last few hours he had met with no success. He had no idea how close Matt was or that the boy was fervently praying for his arrival. Instead, he and Holly were on their way to the fourth Dandridge household they had found in the phone book. The first three had been in various parts of the Kansas City metropolitan area, and it had taken a couple of hours just to discover that they were all dead ends. With only two leads left, John was getting anxious. Holly, on the other hand, was serenely confident with the unshakable conviction of her newfound faith, and each time John gave vent to his doubts, she quietly reassured him with a pat on his shoulder or an "It'll be okay," or "We'll get there in time—have a little faith." After a lifetime of turmoil, serenity and confidence felt strange to Holly, more dreamlike than real but they also felt right, at a level deeper than she had ever experienced before.

John was bemused to realize the student was already teaching the teacher. Deep down, he knew she was right, that everything would happen the way it was supposed to. But the memories of Will and the mad dash to Las Vegas just wouldn't let a part of him rest until they finally found Matt. The heavy rush-hour traffic they were in didn't help either. It seemed to him as if everyone on the highway—with the notable exception of the driver in front of them—was driving seventy or better. With each passing second of being trapped in the slow lane, John grew more and more impatient, afraid that precious time was slipping away. "The drivers here are just as bad as they are back home," he groused. He glared at the car in front of them, which was going so slow that John couldn't get up enough speed to merge into the other lanes, and honked his horn in frustration.

Holly smiled neutrally, trying to think of something that would soothe John's nerves. Before she could say anything, he spotted an opening in the lane to their left, stomped on the accelerator and shot into the gap. As soon as he did, a Kansas City Police cruiser parked on the shoulder turned on its lights and pulled into traffic. A short time later, the cruiser and John's car were parked on the shoulder as the rest of the traffic slowed down to gawk.

John fumed as the policeman's image grew larger in his sideview mirror. He checked his watch and slammed his hand angrily on the top of the steering wheel. "I don't believe this!" he snapped for the third time since realizing he was being pulled over. His voice was more panicked than angry.

"It'll be okay. Just calm—" Holly started to admonish him. She left the rest unsaid when John cut her off with a warning look.

"How can I calm down?" he half shouted as he rolled down the window. "This is the last thing we need! Out of all these people, why did this moron have to stop me? I wasn't going any faster than everybody else!"

"Good afternoon to you too, sir," the policeman said wryly as he stepped in front of John's window. He wasn't smiling. "Would you show the moron in question your driver's license and registration, please?"

John winced and said in a voice that was more impatient than apologetic, "I'm sorry, Officer. It's just that we're in a hurry."

"I can see that."

"I know I was going a little fast," John said defensively. "But I was only keeping up with the flow of traffic. I thought that was what you were supposed to do."

"Nope. You're supposed to obey the speed limit. License and registration, please."

John sighed and turned to Holly. "Would you get them out of the glove compartment, please?"

Holly searched through a short stack of maps and papers but came up empty. She turned to John with a flustered look. "They're not here."

"They have to be. I watched you put them there when we left the airport."

"I know," Holly replied guiltily. She looked again. "But they're not there now."

John frowned, searching his memory. He had tossed his driver's license and the rental agreement on the dash in his haste to get going, but then he had asked Holly to put them in the glove compartment as they pulled out of the parking lot. He was pretty sure he saw her do it.

He hastily scanned the dash again, then checked the floor of the car and the backseat. There were no papers in sight. "Check your purse," he suggested to Holly and turned to the officer with a tight smile. "Bear with us for a minute. This is a rental car, and we're trying to remember where we put the papers."

When Holly failed to find them in her purse, John closed his eyes in frustration and turned to the cop. "We don't seem to be able to find them," he said, not quite succeeding in hiding his aggravation. He couldn't stop thinking about the time they were losing. "But I swear to you my license is valid and so is the rental agreement—if we could only find it. Can't you just cut us some slack this once? We're really pressed for time." Before he realized what he was saying, he added, "We just flew in from Las Vegas, and we're trying to find a young boy who may be in trouble."

The policeman's attitude underwent a subtle change. "What kind of trouble?"

Realizing he had said more than he should, John hedged: "Family problems."

"There are all kinds of family problems, and I can't think of very many that would warrant the speed you were driving," the cop replied. "Are we talking domestic violence? Child abuse?"

John glanced at Holly, not sure what to say. Both of them were keenly aware that if they told the truth they would look like crackpots or worse. Holly leaned across the seat and looked up at the policeman. She forced a smile. "Nothing that serious, Officer. It's just that we're supposed to pick up a friend's son at the mall before it gets dark, and we don't want to be late."

"You came all the way from Nevada to pick up somebody's kid?"

John uttered a short, nervous laugh. "Hardly. When we called our friends from the airport to tell them we'd arrived, they asked if we'd pick the boy up on our way to their house."

"I see," the policeman responded. His scowl deepened. "Well, if the boy is old enough to go to the mall by himself, it won't hurt him to wait." He looked at John and motioned for him to open the door. "Step out of the car, please."

"Why?" John demanded. Holly placed a hand on his leg and gave it a warning squeeze, but John ignored her. "If you're going to give me a ticket, then just hurry up and get it over with."

Now the policeman was angry. He glared at John and jerked his thumb over his shoulder. "Get out of the car. *Now*." He touched his hand to his holster and added, "It isn't a request."

Reluctantly, John did as he was told. All he could think about was failing to find Matt because of the cop. "Look," he said hotly, completely beside himself, "I already explained about the license and registration. Maybe I should put it in simpler terms—"

The cop got in his face and hissed, "Don't patronize me! I heard your excuse just fine. Now it's your turn to listen to me—and I'll try to use words *you* can understand. Okay?" His voice was low but fierce, and for the first time John began to realize how badly he had handled the situation. "First of all, when someone can't produce registration papers, I have to assume the car might be stolen. Second, it's against the law to operate a vehicle in this state without carrying a driver's license. And third, I've had just about enough of your attitude. You and I are going to take a little ride so I can check out your story. You can come with me quietly, or I can cuff you if you want. It's up to you."

Now furious with himself instead of the officer, and realizing it would be useless to say anything else, John simply clenched his jaw and nodded.

The policeman put his charge in the back of the cruiser and returned to the rental car to speak with Holly, who had remained inside. She met his gaze sheepishly and said, "I'm sorry, Officer. I've never seen him like this before. Really. The only excuse I can give you is that it was kind of a rough trip getting here. For what it's worth, we really did rent this car at the airport. And I could have sworn I put the papers in the glove compartment. They must have blown out the window."

The officer rubbed his chin and gave her a tired smile. "I believe you. But I'm going to take him in anyway, and give him a chance to cool down while I check out his story. I'm sorry, ma'am, but I can't just let him go on his merry way after the show he just put on."

Holly felt a flare of irritation at John, and then a stab of panic, wondering how much time his antics had cost them. But she silently gave herself the same pep talk she'd been giving to John all afternoon, then nodded at the officer. "I understand," she said.

"Do you have a driver's license on you?" the cop asked.

"Yes." Holly fished it out of her purse.

The cop looked at it and nodded. "I want you to follow me back to the station. As soon as everything checks out and Mr. Hothead cools down, you can be on your way. Just stay behind me and you won't get lost—but in case you do, just ask for directions to the Seventeenth Precinct."

THIRTY

A Complicated Plan

"DID YOU HAVE to lock him up?" Kate asked. She had already been upset before arriving at the Seventeenth Precinct; once she knew Matt was safe, the three-and-a-half-hour drive to Kansas City had offered plenty of time to work up a good case of maternal anger to take the place of maternal fear. Now the sight of her eleven-year-old son sitting in a jail cell upset her even more.

"Sorry, ma'am," the cop who had taken her back to see Matt replied. "But we're not a babysitting service, you know." He leaned closer and whispered, "Besides, it might make him think twice before running away again."

Kate scowled at the policeman and held out her uninjured arm to Matt. Mother and son stared at each other for a heartbeat that was filled with racing emotions, then Matt ran to Kate with tears in his eyes. "Are

you all right, honey?" she asked fiercely, hugging him as hard as her injuries allowed.

"Ye-es," Matt stammered, his voice heavy with sadness. Now that
his mother had come to take him home, his failure to find his guardian
angel loomed certain and final, a huge, dark cloud that filled him with
fear and bitter disappointment. "But I didn't find John," he sobbed.
"He was supposed to be here. . . ."

Kate stiffened and stepped back. She took Matt's arm and looked
at him sternly. "I don't want to hear another word about 'John.' No
more wild goose chases! I'm taking you home—don't you know how
scared I was?"

"But, Mom—" Matt began as the policeman led them away from
the cells.

"Don't 'But, Mom' me!" Kate cut him off.

Matt did it anyway, because he had to. "But what if John shows
up after we leave?"

Kate gave him an exasperated look that was tinged with sadness.
Lowering her voice so the cop wouldn't hear, she answered, "If he really is your guardian angel, he'll find *you.*"

WHEN HE ARRIVED at the Seventeenth Precinct, John was even
angrier with himself than before. He couldn't believe he had turned a
fifteen-minute speeding ticket delay into a total fiasco that would
probably cost him the rest of the day—including the last few remaining hours to find Matt. It was a bitter pill to swallow. He had no one
to blame but himself—but Matt and his family were the ones who
would ultimately pay the price. For once, he had been given a chance
to change what could happen, and he had blown it. Even Holly's attempts to encourage him couldn't lift his spirit, which was sliding
into a darkness of recrimination and despair that felt only fitting for
what he had done. Or not done.

He was led to a long, high desk at the front of the squad room, where the arresting officer introduced him, after a fashion, to the sergeant behind it. Holly held back, waiting in the middle of the busy room. "Got a speeder with an attitude who doesn't have his license or registration," the cop announced. He frowned at John. "I'm going to check out his story and see if he merits one of our suites for the night." John looked away, shamefaced, and as his gaze fell idly on a door across the room, a policeman, a woman and a blond-haired boy came walking through it.

WITH MATT IN TOW, Kate headed straight for the front door, moving quickly and purposefully through the crowded room. Another reminder that her life was disintegrating unchecked, the day's events—which included having to convince the police that Matt had not run away because of abuse—made her feel increasingly vulnerable, frustrated and scared. She was also ashamed, ashamed that she had failed to protect her own children, as well as herself. To preserve what was left of her shaky self-control, she focused instead on just getting outside and taking Matt home.

But the last thing Matt wanted was to leave the station. Even though he knew better than to cross his mother at such a time, he couldn't shake the feeling that leaving right then would be a big mistake. Hope stirred once again in his desperate heart, and while allowing his mother to lead him through the room, he shut his eyes tightly and prayed one last time that John would show up before it was too late.

When he finished his prayer, he muttered a barely audible "Amen," and smiled to himself, suddenly convinced that John was nearby. Opening his eyes, he looked at the front door. No one was there, but the feeling persisted. It was a sensation like none he'd ever had before, and as his mother pulled him across the room, alarm bells began going off in his head. Suddenly excited, he stopped to look behind him.

Kate immediately barked his name and pulled him back around. "Come on, Matt! I already told you, this guardian angel of yours is not showing up. So get a move on! It's going to be late when we get back to St. Charles, as it is!" Seeing the panic in his eyes, she softened her voice and added, "It'll be all right, Matt. I promise." Then, ignoring his protests, she dragged him toward the door.

HOLLY COULDN'T HELP but notice the woman with the bandaged arm, and the boy with the black eye she was dragging behind her. Not recognizing Matt at first, she frowned as they passed, disturbed by their visible troubles. But something clicked when she heard the woman call the boy Matt.

No! It couldn't be! Holly thought, staring as the pair quickly walked away.

But the boy was the right age. He was blond. His name was Matt. And now that she thought about it, he looked exactly like the boy the angel had shown them. A police station was the last place she would expect to find him, but stranger things had happened over the last few days, things that had taught her that coincidences were never as innocent as they seemed.

LIKE HOLLY, John didn't believe his eyes at first. *It can't be!* he kept thinking. *After all the searching and worrying about finding him before it was too late, he was here all along?* He looked again and his heart leaped in his chest. Yes, it was definitely Matt! He recognized the boy's face, and even more than that, his spirit. He also recognized his mother from the vision in the tunnel. Overwhelmed with relief, he broke into a grin and shook his head. God really did work in mysterious ways.

No sooner had the thought passed through his mind than he was shown just how mysterious those ways could be. Matt and his mother walked past the end of the desk where he was standing, and then kept on going. Matt's mother was obviously reading him the riot act, and not once did either one of them look in John's direction. A few seconds

later, the boy stopped and looked around, and John raised his hand
and readied a smile, but it died on his lips as Matt's mother interrupted him and propelled him toward the entrance.

By the time John realized what was actually happening, they were
gone.

HOLLY RUSHED OVER and grabbed John's arm. "Did you see that
woman and the boy? Was that Matt?" she asked excitedly.

Still in shock, John could only nod.

"His mother said she was taking him home to St. Charles," Holly
said. "Do you know where that is?"

With a look of surprise, John nodded again.

"I'm going to go talk to the cop and get us out of here!" Holly de-
clared. She squeezed John's arm and added sternly, "This time, don't
screw it up, you hear?"

While she tried reasoning with the officer, John tried to reason
with himself. Why did God go to so much trouble to orchestrate
events to bring them here and then let Matt slip away? It was obvious
they had been led here, but the rest of it made no sense.

It was tempting to blame himself for screwing up the plan—if he
hadn't given the cop so much attitude he wouldn't be stuck here. On
the other hand, if he had not lost his cool he would never have wound
up this close to Matt in the first place. So there had to be a reason why
it had turned out this way—and why Holly had heard Matt's mother
say they were going home to St. Charles. That was certainly too much
of a coincidence not to be a sign; John had lived in the very same
town for four years while attending college. The more he thought
about it, the more he realized that all was not lost—tricky, but not
lost. His confidence renewed, he made peace with what had happened and concentrated instead on helping Holly gain his freedom.

Half an hour later, after apologizing, begging—and an agoniz-
ingly long conversation between the policeman and a Budget rental

car employee who kept putting him on hold—John and Holly hurried to the parking lot and jumped into the rental car.

"St. Charles, right?" John said as he started the engine. He was tense but confident, energized by the knowledge that Matt was less than an hour ahead of them.

"Yes," Holly replied, opening her purse. "I've got the map in here."

"That won't be necessary," John said, smiling. "I know how to—"

"What in the world?" Holly exclaimed, cutting him off. "Where did these come from?" Looking stunned, she pulled the missing driver's license and rental agreement from her purse and held them up. "I swear to you they weren't there when I looked for them before. You saw for yourself!"

John gave her a wry smile. "You're right, they weren't. We were meant to wind up at that station, one way or the other, so we could run into Matt." He gave Holly's hand a squeeze, shook his head in wonder and pulled out of the parking lot. "Now all we have to do is catch up to him again—but this time we've got to do it by staying within the speed limit."

TWO HUNDRED MILES AWAY, Elliot Dandridge was waiting in his kitchen. His eyes were dead, devoid of all light. His hand held a fresh beer that was already half-empty. And the .38 Smith & Wesson he had bought two hours earlier was safely tucked away on the top shelf of the pantry.

THIRTY-ONE

Prelude

BY SEVEN O'CLOCK, Kansas City was an hour behind them, and John and Holly were heading east across the middle of Missouri. St. Charles was still more than two hours away. It had been slow going at first because of rush-hour traffic, but now they were on the open road and making good time. Even so, John gripped the steering wheel with a tense determination. His eyes, like Holly's, were constantly searching each car they approached or passed on the road, looking for the boy whose destiny had been interwoven with the fabric of their own. Far ahead in the distance, lightning flashed against a black expanse of rolling clouds that grew darker and more ominous with each passing mile. Neither Holly nor John said a word about the approaching storm; the symbolism was too potent to require comment.

SIXTY MILES AHEAD of their pursuing angels, the Dandridges were passing through Columbia, Missouri, little more than halfway home. Lori was driving; Kate sat next to her and Matt was in the back. The mood in the car was as bleak as the sky overhead; the only sounds were the splatter of raindrops on the windshield and the hum of the tires on the increasingly wet pavement. After leaving the police station, it had taken Kate another half hour to finish venting her displeasure with Matt, but since then she had ridden in silence, staring blankly out the window at the passing farms. Lori was lost in thought, too, wondering what would happen when they finally got home. The heaviest heart among them belonged to Matt, who was not only terrified of seeing his father but deeply disappointed and increasingly perplexed that his guardian angel had failed to keep his promise.

BY EIGHT O'CLOCK, as John and Holly neared Columbia, it had begun to rain. It came down lightly at first, then more steadily as they drove through town, passing the hotels and hospitals and fast food restaurants that lined the interstate. Traffic grew heavier, brake lights flared, cars slowed down. John frowned at the speedometer; the speed limit was fifty-five but they were managing only forty, forty-five at best, and he knew in his heart they were losing more ground. Even Holly, who had been upbeat and positive the first half of the trip, was starting to get tense.

As soon as they cleared Columbia and the landscape returned to fields and farms, the deluge began in earnest. Both of them started at the sudden change and cried out in dismay as wind-driven sheets of thick, heavy rain suddenly slapped against the windshield and pounded noisily on the roof of the car. John set the windshield wipers on high, but the highway remained all but invisible.

John slowed the car but refused to stop and give up one more minute or one more mile in the distance between themselves and Matt. Leaning forward in the seat, he scowled at the rain and gripped the wheel tightly, straining to see the taillights of the truck in front of him and praying that the driver would stay on the road. Holly prayed, too, but she was praying that John would have the good sense to stop.

When the big rig in front of them finally pulled over, John had no choice but to do the same. There was simply no way to distinguish the road from the solid wall of rain. Angry and frustrated, he cursed under his breath and inched the car over to the shoulder of the road. He shared a frown with Holly, then glanced at his watch and shook his head.

When ten minutes had passed, John lashed out at the steering wheel. "Enough already!" he shouted. He gave Holly a frustrated look and started the car. "This isn't letting up. We have to get going!"

Holly disagreed. "We don't have a choice!" she insisted, raising her voice above the din of the rain drumming on the car.

"But we can't just sit here!" John shot back stubbornly, reaching for the gearshift. "We're falling father and farther behind!"

Holly reached across the seat and placed her hand firmly on top of his. "I know!" she agreed with frustration in her voice. "But it can't be helped. There's no one on the road, John. Think about it—nobody's passed us since we pulled over, not even a truck! They're all stuck like us." She caught his gaze and held it firmly. "I want to get going, too, but we can't help Matt if we drive head-on into a concrete abutment. Don't make this worse than it already is." She offered him a small, encouraging smile, adding, "Have a little faith. They probably had to pull over, too."

John returned her stare, his mouth a thin, intractable line. With a frustrated sigh, he finally agreed and shut off the car, turning his face to the rain-obscured window. Any illusions he had harbored about catching the Dandridges before they returned to St. Charles had been washed away by the flood of water pouring from the sky. But he also realized that Holly was right—he had been too quick to panic. There had been a good reason for everything else that had happened, so there had to be a reason for the delay as well.

Even so, he had to struggle to leave it in God's hands. What awaited the Dandridges would happen after dark, and because of the storm, night was falling almost an hour early. John couldn't help but feel anxious—and he knew that in spite of her words, neither could Holly—not with ninety miles still left to go.

The next twenty minutes, as the storm raged on, were the longest of John's life.

HAVING PASSED THROUGH Columbia before the downpour began, the Dandridges were less than an hour from home. The wind was gusting and the sky continued to darken with an unbroken cloud cover that stretched up ahead as far as they could see, but for now the rain was more a nuisance than a threat. Only Lori, as the driver, paid any attention to the rain; Kate and Matt had more important things to worry about.

For the last two hours, Kate had put off breaking the news to Matt that she was definitely leaving his father. Now she decided it was time. Forcing herself to face him, she turned around and gave Matt a serious but loving look. "Matt, honey," she began. "There's no easy way to say this. . . ." She paused, drew in a sharp breath and said, "I don't think we can live with your father anymore, not while he's like this. You and Lori and I are going to move in with Grandma."

Matt searched his sister's face in the rearview mirror, but found no sign of hope, only ready tears. He looked at his mother and asked softly, "When?"

"As soon as possible," Kate replied, staring fiercely at the highway that was taking them home. "Tonight, if we get back in time."

Having hoped it wouldn't happen that soon, that there still might be time for John to show up and make everything right, Matt was devastated by the news. It was the final nail in his waning hope's coffin.

"I'm sorry!" he blurted out in an anguished voice. His eyes were suddenly glassy with hot, salty tears. "I didn't mean to mess everything up by running away!"

The words cut Kate to the quick. She grabbed her son's hand and squeezed it. "No, honey! You didn't mess anything up!" Matt's running away had been the final straw for her, but it distressed her to hear him blame himself for something his father had caused. "It's because of what your dad did last night—and all the other nights over the last few months. This is *not* your fault!"

"But Dad started drinking more because of my accident. And all the bills . . ."

Until the previous night, Kate had never knowingly discussed Elliot's drinking when Matt was within earshot, and it almost killed her to realize that he blamed himself for that as well. It made her even angrier at her husband. "No!" she said sharply, squeezing his hand again. "You shouldn't blame yourself for the accident. That's all it was—an accident." She took a deep breath, trying to compose herself. "Your dad is sick, Matt, and that is definitely not your fault. He needs help but he's too proud to get it. And until he does—" She started to say that it wasn't safe to live with him but caught herself, explaining instead, "I think it's best if we moved out. I hope it will only be for a few days. I don't know. . . . I'm hurt and angry at what he's done, but I want you to know I still love your father." She gave him a sad smile. "And I hope we can work this out. But it's up to him. The best thing we can do right now is pray for him. And, please, *please*, don't blame yourself. It is *not* your fault."

Matt wiped at his eyes and slowly nodded his head, trying to accept his mother's words. But he still couldn't escape the crushing conviction that he had doomed his family by failing to find his guardian angel. And the thought of going home—even if only long enough to pack some things to take to his grandmother's—filled him with dread, because he knew, deep down, that his father would be waiting when they finally arrived.

~

IT HAD BEEN eight-thirty before the rain eased up enough for John and Holly to get back on the highway. Now it was nine. They only had sixty miles left to cover, but each one seemed to be crawling by, even at seventy-plus miles per hour. It felt as if they were racing in slow motion, caught in a dream where the scenery whizzed by but left them with no sense of significant motion.

John glanced forlornly at the rain-soaked road. *Matt's probably almost home by now.* He looked at the dash clock and amended the thought: *Maybe he's already there . . .* Reflexively, his guts clenched and the muscles in his back tensed even more.

A minute passed. His eyes flicked nervously from the odometer to his watch to the never-ending road. Another minute passed, and another long mile. He glanced at Holly but said nothing; the atmosphere in the car was charged but quiet. With each passing mile, his sense of frustration and uncertainty grew as he wondered where Matt and his mother were now, wondered what was happening or about to happen. Before long, the frustration grew unbearable and he was overwhelmed by the obsession to do something more—anything besides sit and watch the miles drag by.

"Dammit!" he exploded, looking at Holly with an anguished expression, unable to keep his thoughts to himself any longer. "They're probably home by now. . . ."

"I know," Holly agreed softly. Her voice was as heavy with worry as John's.

John stared at her for a moment and shook his head bitterly. "We have to *do* something!"

"But we *are* doing something," Holly reminded him gently. The reassurance sounded as if it were meant as much for herself as it was for him. "We're doing as much as we can—what we're supposed to. We have to trust that they're still okay and that nothing will happen before we get there."

"But what if it does?" John countered, unable to stop thinking of the last two times he'd been in this type of situation. Even though he knew in his heart he hadn't been meant to prevent Will's death or stop Holly from trying to take her own life, he still hadn't been able to let go completely of the residual guilt of having failed them somehow. This felt too much like those situations—no, it felt worse, because this time the outcome *did* depend on him.

He stared at his traveling companion for a moment longer before returning his attention to the road. He knew she was right, and he desperately wanted to believe her words. *God has everything under control,* he reminded himself for the umpteenth time in the last few hours. *The Creator of the Universe wouldn't let something as controllable and puny as a lousy rain storm ruin His plans. . . .* The thought calmed him a bit, but he still felt the need to do something more, and to do it now. God *was* in control, but He also depended on Holly and him to do their part. It was an agonizing dilemma—knowing when to act and when to simply wait—especially when Matt's welfare, and maybe his life, depended on how he resolved it.

With great effort, he stilled his mind and asked for guidance. Almost immediately, the answer came: It wasn't necessary—or even possible—to understand God's plan or know for certain what was happening right then; what was required of him was to do what he was told to do and leave the rest up to God. That meant getting to St. Charles as soon as they could *and* (he now understood) doing something else as well—although he still wasn't sure what that something else was.

A brightly lighted Citgo station appeared up ahead, a solitary beacon at the top of the exit ramp they were already passing. It was the first place they'd seen open in quite a few miles, and as soon as John saw it he instantly knew what else they were supposed to do. At the last possible second, as the ramp veered off from the highway, he swerved to the right. The tires caught briefly on a V-shaped patch of gravel and mud between the shoulder and the exit, and the car roared up the ramp, throwing Holly against the door with a startled cry.

"*What are you doing?*" Holly's eyes went wide and she wrestled with the door handle, trying to sit up.

"Calling ahead to warn them."

"*Warn them?*" Holly's tone made it clear she didn't exactly think that was a good idea. "What are you going to say? They probably don't even know who you are."

"I know," John replied in a thoughtful voice. He rolled through the stop sign at the top of the ramp and headed for the service station. Scanning for a phone booth, he prayed the Dandridges' phone number wouldn't be unlisted. *No, it'll be listed,* he corrected himself. *No need to worry about that.* He knew that much, even if he didn't know how to explain why he was calling. "I'm not sure what I'm going to say," he answered, spotting a phone booth at the edge of the gas station's lot. "I guess I'll know when they answer the phone."

ELLIOT SET DOWN his beer and glanced up sourly at the clock on the kitchen wall. It was a little after nine. He had called the Seventeenth Precinct of the Kansas City Police an hour ago and had been told that Kate had left with Matt around five. "What the hell's keeping them?" he complained to the clock. He glanced out the window. It was dark outside and thunder sounded off in the distance. *They should've been here by now—unless they went to Kate's mother's.* Elliot sneered; the possibility was offensive for a variety of reasons.

A few minutes later, he was considering calling his mother-in-law when the phone suddenly rang. *That'll be Kate,* he thought. *No doubt calling from you-know-who's.* An icy smile spread across his face, and he lurched from his chair and crossed the room. When he reached the phone he hesitated, then picked up the receiver. "Hello," he said in a chilling voice.

Except for the sound of steady rain, he was met by silence on the other end. After a few seconds, a disconcerted male voice said, "Sorry. I guess I dialed the wrong number."

Elliot immediately wondered if Kate had a boyfriend. That would explain a lot. He felt a spike of jealousy, then it fell into the pit where the rest of his emotions had gone to die. It didn't matter anyway, not anymore. He uttered a chuckle that sounded off-kilter even to his own ears, and glanced out the window. Kate's car was just pulling into the garage out back. "No problem, pal," he replied with a smile and voice that were darkly agreeable. "All the numbers are coming up wrong tonight. No way around it." Then he hung up the phone.

UNNERVED BY ELLIOT'S tone and the not-so-subtle implications of his words, John stared at the receiver for almost a full minute before finally hanging up. His mind was racing furiously, imagining all kinds of frightening scenarios and frantically searching for a backup plan since warning Kate was no longer possible. It didn't take long to come to the conclusion that there was only one option.

He made another quick call to directory assistance, then one to the St. Charles Police Department. "I'd like to report a domestic disturbance," he said as soon as he was connected.

"What's your address?" the woman on the other end asked in a routine voice.

"It's not at my house," John answered quickly. "It's across the street at the Dandridges'. The guy likes to knock his wife and kids around when he gets drunk. It sounds like that's what's going on now."

"What's their address?"

John consulted the soggy slip of paper in front of him and repeated the address he had gotten along with the phone number from directory assistance.

"Okay, we'll send someone over," the woman responded. "And what is your name, sir?"

"I'd rather not say. They're neighbors, you know."

"I understand. But we need a name to put on the complaint."

"I'm sorry," John replied nervously. "I just can't say. But this isn't a crank call. I think you better get over there as soon as possible. The guy can get violent." Knowing he had done all that he could, he hung up the phone and raced to the car. What he didn't know—and wouldn't for at least another long hour—was if he had made the call in time or not.

"WELCOME HOME," Elliot said as Kate walked through the kitchen door, followed by Lori and Matt. The words were sarcastic, more a challenge than a greeting. He glanced at his daughter and glowered at Matt, who averted his face. "I see Indiana Jones is safe and sound."

"Yes, he is—no thanks to you," Kate replied sharply.

Elliot turned his drunken, stony gaze on his son again, and Matt, having dreaded this moment all the way home, retreated behind his mother. "It's not like I kicked the kid out," Elliot said acidly, looking at his wife. "He left of his own free will, remember."

"Because of you!" Kate retorted, shocked by his attitude. She reached for Matt's hand and faced her husband with a look of profound disappointment. "I guess I'm naive," she said sadly, and with more than a little bitterness. "I thought you would at least be relieved that your son is okay. I guess I should have known better. . . ."

"Oh, give me a break!" Elliot shot back. "Why is it I always wind up the villain?" The sneer returned to his face and he added, "Of course I'm glad he's okay. But if you want my opinion, you baby him too much. Hell, he found his own way to Kansas City—I would have let him find his own way back, let him find out what the real world is like! But, no, you go racing off to get him so he won't get traumatized or stigmatized or some such crap. A little tough love would do wonders around here." He looked at all three of them, one by one, with an unnerving gaze and added, "For everybody."

His children stared back with undisguised shock, then hurt and fear. Kate regarded him with a look of contempt. *"Tough love?"* she retorted in an incredulous voice. She cupped Matt's face and turned it toward Elliot, exposing the black eye he'd given his son. "Like this? And this?" she said, raising her own bandaged arm. "This is what your 'tough love' did to us, Elliot—and for your information, love's got nothing to do with it! It's called *abuse!* And I'm not going to let you abuse us anymore. From now on, if you want to try tough love, you'll have to practice on yourself. Like I told you this afternoon, we're getting out of here!"

Surprisingly, her husband backed down. His aggressive posture and hateful expression slowly crumbled. In the ensuing silence, the old Elliot seemed to peek through and a guilty look flitted across his face, followed very quickly by a look of desperation. When he spoke, his voice was mild, almost plaintive. "Isn't there some way we can work this out?"

"Yes," Kate replied, her own voice softening but still edged with anger. "You can get some counseling to help you stop drinking and get back on track. That's all it will take, Elliot. And you don't have to go alone. I'll go with you."

As quickly as he came, the old Elliot slipped away. The volatile stranger who had taken his place over the last few months returned, his demeanor as hard and scornful and intimidating as ever. "Back to the blackmail, I see. I already told you I wasn't going to do that. And even if I needed a shrink—which I don't—we couldn't afford it. So forget it. It's not going to happen. Period."

Kate started to point out that therapy wouldn't cost as much as his drinking, but realized it would be fruitless. Instead, she sighed and shook her head. "If that's your decision, we have nothing more to say to each other. The children and I will leave."

The silence returned, charged and uncertain, and Elliot stared at his wife with an inscrutable expression. The clock ticked audibly on the wall at his back as everyone held their breath and waited for his response. The silence stretched out for almost a minute. Thunder boomed again, a little closer this time. Finally, Elliot's eyes flicked to the pantry where he had hidden the gun. He looked back at his wife. "Fine," he said coldly, taking a step toward the pantry. His gait was slightly drunken, but his words were clear. "That's *your* decision. I can live with it, but I doubt you'll be able to." Dismissing her with his eyes, he crossed the room and reached for the pantry door. As he started to open it, the doorbell rang.

Elliot froze in his tracks and Lori ran to get the door, grateful for the interruption. A few seconds later her voice rang out, "Mom? Dad? The police are here. . . ."

Kate glanced at her husband with a questioning look, but Elliot refused to meet her eyes, staring guiltily instead at the knob in his hand. Even though he knew the police couldn't possibly know his plans, his paranoia said otherwise. When Lori called out again, he let go of the knob as if it were on fire. After toying with the idea of bolting out the back door, he reluctantly followed Kate into the living room instead.

FIFTEEN MINUTES LATER, the police apologized for having disturbed them and headed back to the cruiser parked in front of the house. They seemed reluctant to leave, not quite convinced the call was a mistake, but Kate had truthfully (if not altogether convincingly) assured them that nothing was going on that required their services. What perplexed her was who had called them in the first place. An anonymous call from a neighbor didn't make sense, especially since it was placed before she arrived home. But someone had made the call. Standing in the doorway, she pondered it briefly and gave up. She was too tired to puzzle it out, especially since nothing had come of it.

As the squad car left she felt a stab of panic, suddenly wondering if she had done the right thing by sending the police away. At one point, she had almost told them they were a day late, but she had resisted the temptation. Now it occurred to her that Elliot might think she was the one who had called them, and if he did, the thought might very well trigger another violent outburst.

Wondering if they should leave, she checked her watch. It was almost ten, too late to call her mother, especially with something as upsetting as the news that she was leaving Elliot and wanted to move in for a while. And she and the children were completely drained, physically and emotionally, too exhausted to go anywhere unless it was absolutely necessary. Warily, she looked at her husband, trying to gauge his mood.

Elliot had turned away from the door and was staring pensively at the row of family photos on the living room wall. He had seemed cowed and embarrassed while the police were in the house, saying very little except to answer their questions with monosyllabic answers. Now that they were gone, all the fight seemed to have gone out of him. As Kate closed the front door, she told herself that maybe it would be safe to stay the night after all.

But maybe it isn't, a voice whispered in her head. *You better think twice before making a decision.*

She cast a glance at her children, thinking of the trauma they had already been through, determined not to let it happen again. Then she regarded Elliot across the emotional and physical distance between them, searching for clues that he might turn his anger into violence once more. His face was haggard, his shoulders drooping, his hands hanging open and limp at his sides. If he was ready to explode, he was doing a good job of hiding his feelings, something he had never been good at before. And he seemed oblivious, or at least indifferent, to her presence. Considering how long the day had been, it was tempting to stay, especially since the police were only a phone call away.

But the cautionary voice in her head wanted more proof. Kate stared at the empty spot where the sofa used to be, the sofa that of late had been her husband's bed. Gathering her nerve, she tried one last test. "Elliot?" she said softly, trying not to provoke him. "The children and I are too exhausted to go to Mother's tonight, so we're going to stay here. Are you going to be able to find a place to sleep?"

His back to her, Elliot's reply sounded halfhearted, resigned. His voice was heavy but with no detectable sarcasm or rancor. "Don't worry about me. The bed's all yours. I doubt that I'll sleep tonight. . . ."

Kate gave a small nod of relief but her heart was overcome with bittersweet sadness. The man across the room seemed light-years away from the one who had knocked her around last night, but he was even farther removed from the man she had married. Once he had been someone she loved and trusted, unpredictable but passionate; now he seemed a hollowed-out shell of the same man. In spite of everything he had put her through recently, she couldn't help feeling at least a little bit sorry for him. In her pity, she decided they had nothing to fear if they stayed one more night.

It would prove to be a fateful and tragic decision.

THIRTY-TWO

Empty Frames

As the wind began to howl around the corners of the house, the first few drops of rain plinked against the kitchen windows. A single light burned dimly above the porcelain sink, barely reaching the table where Elliot sat; he was indifferent to it, surrounded instead by his personal shadows. He also failed to notice the rain, as well as the crack of approaching thunder. Elliot was too busy nursing another beer—as well as the rage he had lived with so long.

Soon, the sound of weary footsteps from the upstairs bedrooms died out and didn't resume. Kate and the kids had finally gone to bed, and a pall of silence fell on the house, blanketing the simmering turmoil with a deceptive peace.

It was time.

With a grim smile, Elliot finished off his beer and walked

unsteadily to the pantry. He opened the door and groped in the dark among the boxes and cans on the top shelf for almost a minute, but didn't find the gun. Just when he began to fear that Kate had found and hidden it somewhere, his fingers brushed the barrel of the Smith & Wesson. He smiled—deeply, perversely—and took down the weapon, then grabbed another beer and moved to the living room.

This part of the house was even darker than the kitchen, touched by just a hint of the corner street lamp and the promise of lightning from miles away. The edges of the room were lost in shadow and the empty spots where furniture had sat were now taunting specters; everything was gone but the row of family photos above the sofa's ghost. With a grunt, Elliot settled cross-legged in the middle of the floor. He cradled the gun in his lap and looked up at the photos. Before long, he was lost in a maze of his own design, going deeper and deeper, turning corner after corner until the safe way home was but a distant memory, buried in a tangle of bitterness and despair.

All he could think about was Kate's irrational anger.

Her shrieking accusations.

The look in her eyes as she told him she was leaving.

He knew she was serious this time. Matt's little stunt had chased away any second thoughts she might have had, and now she was as immovable as a block of granite.

And so was he—there was no way he would do what *she* wanted, either.

They were truly at an impasse. They were truly at an end. . . .

Another wave of rage and disbelief washed over him, and then one of great sadness and loss and hurt at the thought that his wife wasn't alone in her treachery. Lori—*his* Lori, Daddy's little girl—had turned on him, too, casting her lot with Kate's betrayal.

And Matt . . . he had done more than simply go along with the plan. For reasons that were still a mystery, Matt had stoked the fire from the very beginning. In some ways that hurt worst of all.

Try as he might, he couldn't understand it. He just couldn't wrap his mind around the impossible thought that his wife and children were preparing to leave him all alone in the bleakest, most trying hour of his life. It was just too unreal, too painful, too . . . *unacceptable.*

But they *were* ready to leave him. And since all his appeals to their reason and love had utterly failed, the time had finally come to give up the fight.

But that did not mean he would let them go. He could *never* do that.

A tear spilled onto his cheek, and another and another. He inhaled sharply, then deeply, mourning the loss of the ones he had held precious, and who, once upon a time, had regarded him the same way. Suddenly angry, he batted away the tears and turned from the photos. He stared bitterly instead at the gun in his lap. He had lost his nerve after the police showed up, but only for a while. His father had always told him, "A man's got to do what a man's got to do. Take charge of things, Elliot. And don't put up with any crap!" The first two instructions had turned out to be more easily said than done, but he had successfully embraced the third piece of advice. He had never, never taken any crap from anyone in his life. And he wasn't about to start now, especially not from his own wife and kids. Shaking his head angrily, he went over to the family photographs hanging on the wall, took them down and one by one removed each picture and ripped it to pieces.

When he was done, he hefted the gun once and checked his watch. It had been fifteen minutes since they had gone upstairs, and almost that long since he had heard anyone moving. They were probably sound asleep by now, but he'd give them fifteen more minutes, just for good measure.

And then he'd make sure they never woke up.

∼

HOLLY POINTED OUT the window at the road sign they were passing. "St. Peters!" she exclaimed. Almost immediately, she frowned. "Oh, it's St. *Charles* we're looking for, not St. Peters."

John turned to her with an anxious smile. "Yeah, but St. Charles is the next town. The exit we want is only five miles away. We're almost there. . . ."

~

"AIN'T GONNA HAPPEN," Elliot kept repeating in a voice like the knell of a funeral bell. His eyes kept flicking from the ruined photos to the gun in his hand and back to the photos as the rain came down harder in advance of the storm. "I'm sorry, Kate. But it ain't gonna happen. . . ."

Upstairs in their bedrooms, Matt and Lori were lost in the safety of a deep and dreamless sleep. Kate was sleeping almost as soundly, as soundly as her injuries would allow. Her face was turned to the window and her bandaged arm lay across her chest, rising and falling with the gentle rhythm of her quiet breathing. Her other arm was draped over the edge of the bed, her fingers lightly brushing the handle of the baseball bat propped up against the nightstand.

~

ELLIOT CHECKED his watch. Fifteen minutes were up. He took one last look at the empty frames and torn-up photographs that littered the floor, lingering over each with an uneasy mixture of emptiness and sorrow. As he did, a flash of lightning arced across the sky, illuminating the picture fragments with a stark white light. It flickered and died as fast as it came, and a muffled crash of thunder followed a few seconds later.

Slowly, he got to his feet. He stared at the Smith & Wesson in his hand as if it were a stranger yet his oldest friend. He shook his head grimly, glanced out the window at the volatile sky and headed for the staircase.

~

FINALLY, John thought, seeing the St. Charles city limits sign on the side of the highway. *We're finally here.*

He turned to Holly with a nervous smile and nodded in response to her unspoken question. "The next exit is the one we want," he said softly, trying not to sound as tense as he felt. "Just a few more minutes." Then he added to himself, *Just a few more minutes, and we'll know if we got here in time or not. . . .*

For the next few miles, he kept praying they had.

THERE WERE FOUR DOORS at the top of the stairs. Straight ahead was the upstairs bathroom. To the left was the bedroom he had shared with Kate until recently, and on the right were Matt and Lori's bedrooms. The doors were barely visible in the near-total darkness, but after years in this house, he could find them all blindfolded. His tread was heavy on the hardwood floor as he turned toward Matt's room, the gun held tightly but pointed down at an angle. When the floorboards squeaked midway across the landing, Elliot froze. He and Kate had often been awakened by the same squeak when the kids had tried sneaking in or out past their bedtime, and now he held his breath, momentarily panicked that he might have woken one of them.

By the time he realized his fears were groundless, he had changed his mind about which door to open first. *No,* he thought, a twisted smile coming to his lips, *I'll think I'll save Matt for last. Let him see what he caused. That'll wipe the fake little innocent smile from his face.* Nodding with perverse satisfaction, he wagged the gun at Matt's door and continued down the hall.

He paused outside Lori's room for almost a minute before quietly opening her door. His daughter was little more than an amorphous shape in the middle of the bed, her face obscured by shadow, her body silent and unmoving save for the gentle but regular sound of her breathing. Leaving the door open, he took a step toward the bed and stopped as his eyes were drawn to the window. An oversized teddy bear sat perched on the sill, framed by frilly curtains and the weak light drifting in from the street lamp. The bear seemed to reach out to him with its overstuffed limbs and goofy grin, the bright red ribbon around its neck turned crimson in the night. He had bought it for Lori on her thirteenth birthday—had picked it out himself, something he rarely did—and the sight of it brought back a flood of memories. Memories that were at once precious and painful, disconcerting as he stood with a gun in his hand.

The weight of the Smith & Wesson brought him back to reality and he shrugged off the memories, stepping closer to the bed. Lori's thirteenth birthday was an eternity ago, and the memory of it tarnished. The world and the daughter he had once loved were gone, and everything that had made his life bearable had been cruelly taken from him. . . .

With a heavy heart, he raised the gun.

Just beyond the window, the wind began to howl, and Lori stirred in her sleep but did not wake up.

At the edge of the howling came the long-promised downpour, and the sound of it pounded in Elliot's ears along with his blood. Soon the pounding became a roar, and obliterating all but his most tortured thoughts, it both screamed for him to shoot and filled him with dread, demanding a decision, demanding a release. His finger touched the trigger, preparing to squeeze, but as soon as it did, his arm began to tremble.

Elliot closed his eyes and shook his head.

I can't, he thought.

"I have to," he croaked and pointed the gun.

Lightning flashed, immediate and blinding, blasting the room with electric white. Elliot's eyes flew open, and in the second before the clap of thunder followed, he found himself gazing at the sleeping face of his once-beloved daughter. Even in the harsh light her face was sweet, a slight smile resting on her barely parted lips, her blond hair a halo on the pillow beneath her head. Elliot's resolve began to waver again, and he strained through a haze of alcohol and pain to recapture the feelings that had brought him this far. The vein in his forehead stood out from the effort, angry and red. The muscles in his back, his chest and arms grew unbearably tight, and his arm began to shake, more violently this time. But the finger on the trigger was perfectly still, poised or paralyzed, depending on the signals being sent from his brain.

When the thunder did come, rattling the house with a powerful *boom,* even as the next round of lightning began, a different signal was sent from Elliot's brain, one that had little to do with his will. Lori's eyes opened, sleepy and confused, at the very same moment when Elliot was jolted by the deafening thunder.

His arm jerked.

His finger twitched once.

The gun went off.

Lori uttered a small, plaintive cry of surprise, and turned to her father with questioning eyes. A look of pain contorted her face. . . . Then her eyes grew vacant and she slipped away.

Elliot stood by the bed and stared in shock, stunned by the thunder, the sound of the gun, the dark spreading stain on Lori's sheet. Stunned by the emptiness in his daughter's eyes.

Then he fled the room.

BY THE TIME he reached the landing, his resolve was firmly in place. There were no lingering doubts, no regrets or emotions other than resignation and escalating rage. The decision had been made for him, and now there was no turning back.

Kate was next.

A FEW MINUTES EARLIER, the familiar sound of squeaking floorboards had set off an alarm in Kate's brain. In a matter of seconds, she was wide awake and her fingers had reflexively tightened on the bat handle. Then a great blast of thunder had shaken the house, followed by a series of lesser shocks. In between, a different explosion had reached her ears, the backfiring of a car or something else. It had been difficult to make out because of the thunder, but it made her uneasy, triggering another alarm in her brain. She had just decided to investigate when her bedroom doorknob began to turn.

Kate gripped the bat tighter, keeping it out of sight at the side of the bed. She held her breath, waiting to see who would come through the door.

It opened slowly. Her husband stood in the doorway, his face a terrifying mask of madness strobed by the lightning that flickered outside. When she saw the gun that dangled from his hand, a chill ran through her. *A gun? What was Elliot doing with a gun?* It was an image her conscious mind did not want to process, but on a deeper level, it began to sink in. Then she knew what the other sound had been.

He had already used the gun. . . .

On who?

Suddenly, Kate felt as if she were going to be sick. She clamped her teeth against it, and against the shriek of horror that came right behind. Instead, she screamed in her mind as the bottom fell out of everything she knew. Thoughts that were too painful—too horrifying—to accept bombarded her brain, but no matter how hard she tried to dismiss them, they refused to let go. The gun in Elliot's hand wouldn't let them.

He wouldn't hurt his own children, she kept saying to herself.

He wouldn't! He couldn't . . .

But deep in her soul, she knew that he had, and the only thing that kept her from leaping from the bed and beating Elliot bloody was the overriding need to find out for sure. So she held in the rage and terror and sickness with every bit of control she could manage to find, and waited instead for her husband to come closer.

Praying that he hadn't noticed she was awake, Kate lay very still and watched through slitted eyes as Elliot ventured into the room. The summer storm was fully upon them now, and as it raged outside, it filled the room with furious sounds and the wildly twisting shadows of wind-whipped trees. Elliot moved slowly but steadily across the floor, the gun in his hand glinting in the erratic bursts of light, a little closer each time.

Fifteen feet.

Ten feet.

Five feet away.

As he crept up to the bed, Kate prayed for a miracle. She wanted to scream and wake up from the nightmare or leap from the bed and flee the room—anything but die. But for the sake of her children—

Please let them be alive, she prayed, *oh God, please let them be alive!*

—she lay very still, fighting back the shock and mounting terror. When Elliot finally stood at the other side of the bed, staring down with a look that chilled her blood, a part of her still refused to believe this was happening, was afraid to acknowledge it and make it true. But when he raised his arm and pointed the gun, she reacted swiftly.

In one fluid but frenzied movement, Kate brought up the bat from her side of the bed. She rolled onto her side, ignoring the pain in her injured arm, and swung one-handed with every ounce of rage that coursed through her body. "*What have you done?*" she screamed as the bat smashed hard into Elliot's shoulder and glanced off his jaw.

Elliot collapsed with a look of surprise and a cry of pain, falling facedown with the gun underneath him. Kate scrambled from the bed and stood over him, wild-eyed, chest heaving, the bat wavering above her head, poised to strike again. Through her own ragged breathing and the cacophony of thunder and driving rain, she shrieked again, "*What have you done?*"

Slowly, Elliot raised his head and met her eyes. "Don't worry," he gasped. His eyes were glazed but his grin was sickening. "She never knew what hit her."

Kate staggered back a step. Her shoulders sagged and her whole body began trembling violently. "No," she whispered in a stricken voice, shaking her head slowly from side to side, then shaking it faster. Her keening wail rose above the crash of thunder: *"No!"*

Elliot's grin only widened, and Kate stared in disbelief, too stunned to think of anything except smashing that look from his hideous face and obliterating the words that still burned in her brain. With another strangled cry of anguish and rage, she raised the bat high.

Before she could bring it down, a sleepy, troubled voice from the doorway stopped her: "Mom?" Kate wheeled around to look. Matt was there, still dressed in the clothes he had worn for two days, his hair disheveled, with a look of confusion giving way to horror. *"Mom? What's happening?"* Kate stared at him for a moment with relief, then guilt and finally fear. Dropping the bat, she ran toward the doorway.

She was halfway across the room when Elliot pulled the gun from beneath his body. As Kate opened her mouth to warn Matt to run, Elliot rose up on one elbow, aimed and fired.

Kate stumbled as the bullet slammed into her back, but she kept on going, carried forward by momentum and a driving fear. She looked at Matt with panic in her eyes, her right arm outstretched, waving him away. *"Run!"* she gasped raggedly. *"He already shot Lori! Get out of the house, Matt, and call the police!"* She heard Elliot rasp coldly, "It's already too late," and she stumbled again, falling as the second bullet ripped through her back, burrowing past ribs and piercing her heart.

She felt a sudden bloom of pain and a moment of pure panic . . .

A gentle tugging from a spot somewhere deep in her chest . . .

And then she was free.

~

MATT STOOD in the doorway, wide-eyed and petrified, his mother's last words burning in his ears. He didn't know what to say. He didn't know what to do. He didn't even know if he should believe what he'd seen. He just couldn't grasp it—refused to grasp it. Everything was blurring, growing fuzzy at the edges, and he felt as if his brain were about to explode. He wanted to run to his mother, but he knew in his heart it was already too late. He wanted to run at his father and make him take it back. More than anything, he just wanted to run or shut down, to curl up on the floor and close his eyes, and hope that when he opened them everything would be different.

All of that changed when his father called his name and struggled to his feet, brandishing the gun. In an instant, Matt's fuzziness and weakness were replaced by a single, overpowering thought: *Run!* With a last, tortured glance at his mother's still form, he slammed the door shut and pounded down the stairs with his father's crazed shouts ringing in his ears.

When he reached the front door, he threw it open and raced outside. Standing on the walk in the pouring rain, he was immediately faced with a life-and-death decision. Where should he go? Where would he be safe? Should he run to a neighbor's? He glanced at their houses. That wouldn't work. All of them were dark. His dad would probably catch him before he woke anybody up.

Matt looked around frantically. "*Where are you, John?*" he said faintly to the night, wiping a mixture of rain and tears from his eyes. "*You promised to be here!*" His voice was desperate, tinged with disappointment and a budding bitterness. If there was ever a time when Matt needed a guardian angel, that time was now. He had never felt more alone or more scared in his life.

A brilliant flash of lightning exploded in the sky. Night turned into day and the *boom-boom-boom* of deafening thunder followed in its wake. Matt yelped in surprise, feeling threatened and exposed in the sudden light. Automatically, he turned to look at the open front door. His father had nearly reached the bottom of the stairs, and he was yelling out Matt's name and screaming angry oaths with the gun in his hand. That was all it took to get Matt moving. After casting about in panic for a few more seconds, he decided to hide in the crawlspace under the front porch.

Praying that his father hadn't spotted him, Matt headed for the only opening at the corner of the house. As soon as he scrambled inside he heard his dad step out onto the porch about twenty feet away. Matt immediately froze and cocked an ear to the floorboards overhead.

Maybe he'll leave and go looking for me, Matt thought. *It might not be too late to get help for Mom and Lori if I can get back inside and call the police.* He turned the thought into a hasty prayer, and waited to see what would happen. Then, another thought occurred to him: *What if Dad comes down here to look for me instead?* Reflexively, he turned around and peered into the crawlspace, hoping it wouldn't be necessary to go farther inside. This had long been his special hiding place, but usually only on bright, sunny days. Now it was pitch black and the air was heavy and thick and still. It was also wet, with water seeping in beneath the slats of the porch and dripping from the cracks between the boards overhead. Matt shivered and made up his mind. It was scary to think about venturing into that darkness, but the thought of his dad standing in the opening with a gun in his hand scared him even more. Without a second thought, he crept farther under the porch.

As soon as he did, he heard Elliot's footsteps above him, coming in his direction. They passed directly overhead and went all the way to the end of the porch, stopping above the spot where Matt had cowered only seconds before. When Elliot spoke, his voice was almost casual but had a maniacal edge that made Matt's heart beat even faster. "I know you're down there, son. I'm not blind, you know." His next words were drowned out by a clap of thunder, then Matt heard him say, "—be all right. I don't want to hurt you. Honest." He barked a dark, bitter laugh and added, "I just want to take you upstairs to show you something."

A chill raced through Matt's already shivering body. Thinking of his mom and Lori, he choked back sobs and screams of rage and instinctively retreated even deeper into the crawlspace. *Why was this happening? Where was John?* He couldn't understand it, couldn't help but wonder if God had turned against him. . . . Still, the only thing he could do right now was pray. It was his only chance—if he could make God listen.

Matt knelt down in the mud, clasped his hands together tightly and drew in a hitching breath. The smell of his own fear was strong in his nostrils, mingled with the smells of sweat and rain and pungent mud. *Dear God, are you mad at me? Did I do something wrong?* He faltered for a moment and began to cry, quietly but with so much pain and desperation that it seemed as if his body would come apart at the seams. *If I did, I'm sorry—really, really sorry! Please, dear God, please send my guardian angel—or any angel you can—before it's too—*

Crack! came the sound of splintering wood. Something slammed into the ground right next to him, and a small spray of mud splattered Matt's folded hands. Elliot's disgusted, taunting voice followed: "I'd rather do this face-to-face, but I guess that's too much to expect from a momma's boy." His voice came closer. "If this is how you want to play it, that's fine with me—it'll be as easy as shooting fish in a barrel."

Matt scampered, wild-eyed, farther under the porch. Almost as if he could see through the floorboards, Elliot followed. After a moment of silence, he blurted out accusingly, "You're the one who turned Lori against me!"

There was another *crack!* above Matt's head and a splatter of mud a few feet in front of him. He jumped and screamed, and screamed again as his father laughed and lightning flashed, filling the crawlspace with pale white light and rolling thunder. Praying and sobbing, Matt scrambled forward on his hands and knees, farther away from his father and from the flickering opening that was his only escape.

Elliot followed and stopped once again a few feet shy of where Matt was cowering down in the darkness. When he continued his list of grievances, his voice was on fire with blind hatred. "And thanks to you, you're mom was going to leave me!"

A third shot rang out. A third hole was blown in the porch's floor and another bullet slapped into the muddy earth, closer than the last one. Matt shrieked hysterically and lunged deeper into the darkness. When he collided with something solid he shrieked once again, realizing he was trapped against the closed-off end of the darkened crawlspace.

Now there was nowhere left to hide and the only way out was forty feet behind him. In between was his father standing above him with a gun. Matt's heart sank, and wave after wave of painful emotions washed over him. It wasn't so much that he was afraid of dying, but he was terrified at the thought of dying like this. As the grief and fear became too much to bear, great wracking sobs shook his body suddenly, violently, and then just as suddenly he was completely still, too paralyzed to do anything but collapse in a corner of the smothering darkness and whimper as his father's footsteps closed in.

They stopped right above him. For a moment, everything was silent, including the storm, until the boards above Matt's head squeaked one last time. Elliot's breathing sounded nearer now, loud and ragged, as if he were squatting on the floor, trying to get as close as possible to Matt. His voice seemed closer, too, unnervingly close, as he talked to himself with a series of muttered oaths and strangled cries. When he directed his words to Matt once again, he sounded cold and crazy, like the killers Matt had seen in dozens of movies. The voice might as well have been that of a total stranger—a deadly stranger. The father he had known was lost and gone, Matt suddenly realized with fresh despair, as lost to him now as his mom and sister. . . .

"Nowhere left to go, is there?" his father taunted. He let loose a chuckle that made Matt flinch, then his voice turned serious. "I don't know why you did this. . . . But you left me no choice, Matt, no choice at all." He uttered a mirthless laugh and added, "You could say you backed me into a corner—I imagine right now you know what that feels like." The boards groaned again, and Matt cringed, knowing that his father had stood up and was at this very moment aiming the gun.

"I'm sorry, son," the voice drifted down to him with an awful finality, "but you made me do this."

Matt drew in a deep breath and squeezed his eyes shut so tightly that for a moment he thought he was seeing lightning again. His whole body shook with dread anticipation, and his heart jumped wildly, lurching in his chest. Bracing himself against the rough, damp wall behind him, he quickly began to pray for his father and himself, expecting to feel the bullet slam into his head or his back or his chest at any second.

From above came the click of the trigger being pulled.

Matt froze and the words of his prayer suddenly vanished.

But instead of hearing the bullet explode from the barrel, instead of hearing the wood crack open above his head, instead of hearing his own final shriek of pain—he heard his father curse that the gun was empty.

Not waiting to see what would happen next, Matt bolted from the corner with a hasty, heartfelt *Thank you, God!* and scrambled frantically through the mud on his hands and knees. When he reached the opening, he took off running.

THIRTY-THREE

Crossing Over

AFTER STOPPING at a 7-Eleven for directions, John and Holly had driven the last five blocks in utter silence, the knots in their stomachs growing steadily tighter as the numbers on the houses counted down to the one they had come so far to find. They both spotted it simultaneously and Holly shouted excitedly, "There it is!" As she pointed at the house, a young boy who looked like Matt shot out from under the front porch and raced across the yard. In the open front door stood a man whom they immediately recognized as Matt's father; as Elliot turned to go back into the house, John thought he saw the glint of a gun in his hand.

John jerked the wheel hard and headed for the curb—and then slammed on his brakes as Matt fled blindly into the path of their car. He was muddy and wet and looked absolutely terrified. The squeal of tires froze him in his tracks, and John and Holly jumped out and ran to him, calling his name.

Matt looked shocked to see them. "John!" he cried hysterically, trying to catch his breath. "He shot my mom! *My dad shot my mom!* And I think he killed Lori, too. . . ." He burst into tears and sobbed in a voice that was heart-wrenching to hear, "He was trying to shoot me, but he ran out of bullets. . . ."

Holly gasped. She stared at Matt in disbelief, horrified at the thought that the woman she had seen only that afternoon was dead, and that Matt—like her—had lost his mother far too soon and in a violent way. John was horrified as well, and the relief he had felt briefly at seeing Matt alive was immediately marred by the prospect of having arrived too late to save his mother and sister. Unwilling to leave without making sure there was nothing he could do for them, he took Matt's arm and handed him over to Holly. "Stay with him while I go inside. If anything happens, get in the car and go get help." Before either of them could stop him, John raced toward the house in the pouring rain.

Holly called after him, but held on to Matt, who struggled and screamed for John to come back. As John bounded onto the porch and disappeared through the doorway, the boy tore free and ran back into the yard. "Matt, wait!" Holly screamed. She immediately started after him, but Matt was too fast and disappeared behind the house in a matter of seconds. Her heart pounding, Holly glanced briefly at the empty front doorway and hurried around back in pursuit of the boy.

ELLIOT FOUND John before John found him, and now the two of them faced each other in the Dandridges' kitchen. Elliot stood in the middle of the room by the dimly lit sink, his back to the hallway. His newly loaded gun was trained squarely on John, whom he had forced to sit down at the kitchen table. John was trying to talk Elliot into putting down the weapon when the screen door banged open and Matt flew into the room.

When he saw what was happening, Matt lurched to a stop just inside the door and stared at John with a look of dismay and returning terror. John's heart sank. Of all the scenarios he could possibly think of, this was the worst, with Matt leaving the relative safety of the yard to come back inside to warn or help him. If things had been bad before, now they were ten times worse. Quickly, he shot off a silent prayer for help.

As John prayed, Elliot trained the gun on Matt. He appeared ready to fire. "*Don't!*" John shouted, jumping from his seat.

Elliot pointed the gun at him. "Stay where you are." John reluctantly sat down, and the gun swiveled back to a spot midway between the table and its former target. Elliot frowned at John. "Who are you?"

Before John could answer, Matt blurted out, "He's my guardian angel!"

Elliot snorted and looked John over. "So, he really does exist, huh? He doesn't look like much of an angel to me." He turned his gaze back to Matt and said, "I thought you came up empty when you ran off to Kansas City."

"I did," Matt replied heavily. "But God sent him to help me anyway."

Elliot uttered a short, derisive laugh. "I see. Well, he's a little late. God must have sent you the second string, kid." With a note of bitterness he added, "Looks like you got your old man's luck."

"Mr. Dandridge—Elliot," John interrupted, resuming the conversation that Matt's sudden appearance had cut short earlier, "why don't you put down the gun? Let's talk about this. . . ." His voice was urgent but soothing, with a calm that belied the rush of fear he was actually feeling.

"There's nothing left to say," Elliot replied flatly. "The time for talking is long gone."

"*Please.* I don't believe you really want to do this."

"What would you know about it?" Elliot replied sharply. Despite his tone, he lowered the gun slightly.

John thought about what he'd been shown at the end of his near-death experience, then shook off the memory. "Look," he said earnestly, "I know you've had a rough time, but we can work this out. It doesn't have to be this way. . . . Let me call an ambulance for your wife and daughter—let's get some help before somebody dies."

"It's already too late for that," Elliot said coldly, and John reeled as the words sank into his brain. Glancing at his son, Elliot added with a weariness that could almost have been mistaken for sadness or grief, "It's too late for all of us." He raised the gun and pointed it at Matt.

John shot to his feet and threw up his hands. "No! Wait! He's just a boy—your son, for God's sake! If you have to shoot somebody, let Matt go and shoot me instead!"

Elliot lowered the gun again and stared at John with an incredulous look. "Why in the world would I want to do that? This has nothing to do with you—unless you keep insisting on making it your business. As a matter of fact, why don't you leave now, while you still can."

"I can't do that," John responded stubbornly. Hoping his refusal would buy them some time, he stared defiantly at Elliot, desperately racking his brain for something he could say to reach through his madness, something to connect him to reality once again. A tense silence filled the room, and John continued to stare at Elliot's bleary-eyed face with a burgeoning intensity. Before long, he felt a surge of powerful emotion that wasn't his own, a powerful mixture of hatred and despair and terrible loneliness. With a jolt, John realized he was knowing the man—as he had Ruby and Will and Denton and Holly—only this time no physical contact was needed.

Time slowed to a crawl and he tasted Elliot's madness as the connection deepened. Turbulent thoughts and emotions and memories washed over him, looking for escape, validation, release—

Shoved onto a path of deep-seated fear by a shocking and ever-expanding loop of video: airplanes plowing into buildings filled with people, leaders of nations exacting mutual retaliations, and the ever-present threat of the next unknown . . .

The termination notice, the sense of frustration and continued failure—and heightened fear . . .

Matt's accident and recovery, the relief giving way to a looming specter of economic disaster . . .

The debilitating cycle of booze and despair . . .

Feeling guiltier as Kate's disappointment grew . . .

More nights at the bar, feeling helpless to do anything but slide farther in.

The feelings of shame and utter humiliation brought to a head by Matt's Sunday surprise, the explosion of rage he couldn't contain . . .

The look on Kate's face as she lay bleeding on the floor at the foot of the china cabinet, the look of shock and horror on his children's faces . . .

Kate saying she was leaving, a mother—his own—who left when he was young and never came back, the growing panic and lonely fear.

The gun . . .

Lori's face as the shot rang out . . .

The gun . . .

Kate's body as it jerked and fell.

The gun once again . . .

Shooting up the porch with the hope and the fear he would kill his own son.

John struggled with the memories, and struggled to defuse them, but the pain and rage in Elliot's heart was stronger than anything he had experienced before. In the past, the process had always been mutual and without resistance, but this time it was fierce, because Elliot was in the thick of an interior battle, determined to force himself to finish what he had started.

The experience was intense and at times almost unbearable as the darkness flowed into John's heart and mind, but he steeled himself against it and redoubled his efforts, conjuring up the memory of standing in the Light. The effect was immediate. Indescribable love and joy welled up inside him, surging through his heart and body and mind. When the energy expanded until he could no longer contain it, he saw as well as felt the light leap across the space between himself and Elliot. It completely engulfed Elliot, pushing at the madness and straining to reach the goodness that still remained in his heart.

The madness fought back, and the struggle continued for what seemed an eternity. The light grew brighter and brighter still, and finally the darkness began to retreat. But just as John sensed the light would win out, just as they were reaching a critical point, the madness suddenly flared in Elliot's mind and a single, volatile, powerful thought came blazing through—

Now, the gun!

John's eyes went wide. Elliot was going to shoot—now, and at Matt!

"*No!*" he roared, and with a sudden epiphany that this was the moment that had brought him to St. Charles, he lunged from the table and shoved Matt aside.

He heard the gun fire—

Felt a thud in his chest and a burning sensation . . .

Then staggered back with a hole in his shirt—a hole that immediately began to turn crimson.

As he fell to the floor, John saw Elliot point the gun at Matt once again—and then he saw Holly appear in the hallway with a car jack in her hand.

Elliot opened his mouth and uttered Matt's name, but before he could say or do anything else, Holly clubbed him squarely in the back of the head. He collapsed in a heap with a look of surprise and a grunt of pain. Holly glanced at him just long enough to make sure he was out, then ran to John with an anguished cry.

She kept saying his name, over and over, in between sobs and cursing Elliot, but John's eyes remained fastened on Elliot's face. The connection between them had gone dark and silent when Holly struck him on the head, but John could feel him drifting back to consciousness; the connection was still open. Thoughts and emotions were emerging again, but this time they began whirring and flying and ripping jagged holes in the fog of madness surrounding Elliot's mind, as if Holly's blow and the ensuing pain had sharpened their edges and set them in motion. Soon all that was left was the naked truth, and the truth was more than Elliot could bear. Horror and remorse and crippling self-loathing followed in its tracks, and then a painful decision was made and accepted as the only resolution. Elliot's mind grew dark, darker than the madness had ever made it, and the connection snapped, leaving John with a memory of utter despair that was as frightening as anything that had come before. He knew what Elliot had decided to do—and he also knew he would not be talked out of it. . . .

Elliot began to stir; a hand moved slightly, a foot twitched once. John glanced up at Holly, who was yelling at Matt to call 911. The boy was in shock, staring at John's wound with abject horror. "No!" John rasped through gritted teeth. "Get Matt out before Elliot wakes up!"

"I think he's dead," Holly croaked, casting a half-apologetic glance back at Matt.

"No," John responded, giving her a meaningful look. His breathing was labored and each word was an effort. "He isn't. . . ."

Holly's eyes went wide with alarm. She glanced over her shoulder at the gun peeking out from beneath Elliot's body, and started for it.

"No!" John gasped again. He coughed once, weakly. "No time . . . Just . . . get . . . *out!*"

Holly stopped and gave him a meaningful look of her own. Her response was final: "Not without you." Ignoring John's protests, she took Matt by the shoulders and stared intently into his eyes. She shook him, gently at first, then more insistently when he failed to respond. "Come on, Matt . . . We've got to get going. . . . *Matt, come on!* You've got to snap out of it! Grab one of John's arms and help me get him out of here!"

Across the room, Elliot moaned. John cast a quick, worried glance in his direction, then looked up at Matt. As he did, the edges of his vision began to grow dark, and he suddenly felt faint. "Matt," he said weakly, in little more than a whisper, "do . . . what she says. . . . Got to go . . . *now!*"

Matt blinked once, twice and shook his head, as if suddenly awakening from a very bad dream. He looked over at his father, and stared back at John. Finally, he nodded.

Moving quickly, Matt took one of John's arms and Holly took the other. As they lifted him, John moaned, and the stain on his shirt grew slick with new blood. His vision grew darker, and cold beads of sweat broke out on his forehead. His legs felt too weak and wobbly to move, but for Matt's sake he managed to stay upright as they led him to the door and out to the back stairs. Behind them, Elliot began to whimper, and the whimpers turned to sobs, great wracking sobs that in turn became wails of unimaginable anguish.

John held his breath as they staggered outside. There were only three stairs, but each one was torture—any movement at all, even drawing a breath, made him weaker and fainter, and seemed to ask more than it gave in return. Praying for Matt and Holly—and Elliot—he let himself be jarred and jostled and carried, all the while listening for the gunshot from inside that he knew would be the last.

It came when they reached the final stair. One shot rang out, clear and deadly, and the wailing stopped. John looked at Holly. Holly looked at him. They both looked at Matt. John's connection with Elliot suddenly reopened, but this time John felt no pain or confusion or searing remorse, only a yearning for what John had shared with him before . . . and Elliot's yearning to see his son's face once again. After only an instant, it went dark, and John knew the connection was severed forever. Elliot was dead. It was finally over.

A sadness washed over him, for Elliot, Kate, Lori and Matt—especially for Matt, who was just a little boy and had lost so much—and he sent off a prayer for Elliot's spirit, that God's love would heal him and bring him home, and that Matt would find the healing and love he would need to deal with the tragedy. Matt was so special, so innocent and sweet, and he had been through so much, that John couldn't help but feel a great surge of love and compassion as he looked at the boy's face. He reached up to squeeze Matt's hand, to give him a little comfort and needed reassurance, and as he did, a fresh bolt of pain shot across his chest and down his left arm. Almost immediately, he felt as if his upper body were in the grip of a vise, a grip so tight that it took away his breath and doubled him over. He sagged to his knees and cried out in pain, then slipped through the arms of Holly and Matt and collapsed on the ground.

Matt burst into tears and began shaking his head slowly from side to side. John looked up at him. "I'm sorry . . . I couldn't . . . get here sooner," he said raggedly and tried to smile. He turned to Holly, who knelt by his side with an expression that said she was trying to be brave but losing the battle. John attempted to smile again. "It's okay," he said faintly and drew a shallow breath. "It's okay . . . Really." The vise tightened again, and a burning sensation spread through his chest. He felt the last of his strength begin draining away, taking the burning along with it, and in their place came a familiar peace that soothed his body as well as his mind.

He smiled up at Holly with no pain this time.

He squeezed her hand weakly.

And then he crossed over.

THIRTY-FOUR

Parting the Veil

ONE MOMENT HE WAS STARING up through the rain at the traumatized faces of Holly and Matt, and the next he was looking down at his own dead body. It lay on the wet grass, eyes still closed from his final prayer, and a large, dark stain on his rain-soaked shirt. The sight of his lifeless form didn't bother John in the least—he had died once before, after all—but he was greatly distressed by the timing of his passing. Watching Holly shake him and beg him to come back nearly broke his heart, and seeing Matt's horror and shock and disappointment filled him with a painful sense of frustration that bordered on failure. *No! Not now!* he prayed fervently. *Please send me back! I can't leave them now!* Expecting at any moment to hear the tinkling of bells and to be borne away by a rushing wind, he desperately tried to will himself back into his body, but nothing happened.

"It won't work," a familiar voice said from behind him. John turned around and saw Will Gibson. He was standing with an angel. Like the messenger who had appeared to him yesterday at the Grand Canyon, the angel was very muscular, although he was slightly shorter and wore a different robe. His hair was golden. Will looked much the same as the last time John had seen him, except that the light emanating from inside his body seemed brighter than before. His gentle smile was a welcome sight, and the presence of the angel was intrinsically comforting, but John remained agitated about Holly and Matt.

"I told you I'd be waiting when it was your time to come home," Will said warmly. As had happened in the tunnel, the communication was telepathic, not vocal. "I just didn't know it would be now."

"But it's too soon!" John replied.

Will gave him a kindly smile. "No, it isn't, John. This time it really *is* your time."

John shook his head and addressed the angel. "This has to be a mistake. Can't you send me back, like the last time? Matt and Holly need me now, more than ever before! You know what just happened. They're going to need a lot of help to get through this. . . ." John looked down at them, then turned to the angel with a frown on his face. "I'm supposed to be the boy's guardian angel—I can't abandon him, not when he just lost everyone he loves! And what about Holly? She tried to kill herself only a few days ago! This is the worst possible time for me to leave them alone."

"They won't be alone," Will responded. "They will have each other now. You brought them together."

John was not persuaded. "But what Matt just went through could ruin his life! It would devastate a grown-up, much less a little boy! What about his mission?"

"What happened tonight will not ruin his life," the angel said firmly, but in a loving voice. "It will define and shape it, but it will not destroy him. God will make sure of that. And because he endured such suffering and tragedy, many people will be blessed."

"You can only do so much for them, John," Will joined in. "The rest is up to them, and up to God."

"But I was told to be Matt's guardian angel—and God sent me to Holly, too! I have a responsibility to them. They were counting on me. . . ."

Will gave him a reassuring smile and took his hand. "You will still be able to help them whenever they need you. Just like when I was sent to warn you at Hoover Dam. But your earthly mission is done."

The angel nodded. "This is a pivotal time in human history, and the Earth is fast approaching a day of reckoning, a time of upheaval and transformation that will bring about great changes in the way humans live and what they believe. As you have been told, the boy for whom you gave your life will play an important role in the healing that comes after. He will touch many lives and bring them closer to God. That is why you were sent to him. That is why, when you chose your life's mission, you volunteered to help at this critical time in his earthly life—and in Holly's. Her mission is to help Matt, too. And his is partly to help her." The angel regarded him with an expression of great love and approval, and concluded, "Your earthly mission has been completed, and you have done what you promised. The love you have shown by your care and sacrifice will ripple out to more people than you could ever have imagined. God is very pleased."

"I'm not sure I understand. . . ." John responded.

The angel nodded and said, "The knowledge of your own part in choosing your mission was erased from your memory when you were born. But your spirit has always known everything, even if your mind only remembered some of it." He pointed to a spot in front and above them, and the night scrolled back as if a window had suddenly opened onto another world. "It pleases God that you care so deeply for Holly and Matt," the angel continued. "But He wants you to know they will be fine without you, and that now your place is back in heaven."

With Will and the angel standing by his side, John watched as the future—Holly and Matt's, and even his own—unfolded before him, much like the events in his life review. The experience was at the same time sublimely surreal and intensely real, and John was instantly transfixed:

He saw Holly staying by Matt's side in the coming weeks, forging a bond that was destined to be.

A few months into the future, and a year or so hence, a gradual end to their pain and sorrow; lazy days and happy days when sunshine and laughter held old memories at bay.

Holly content, a loving adoptive mother, fulfilling the role that only she could play in Matt's new life.

Another few years, Matt growing tall and handsome, growing happy, making friends, and thirsting for answers and a closeness with God.

Holly healed also of her longtime pain, growing confident, unafraid, learning what it means to love and be loved.

Matt as a young man, wise beyond his years, coming to understand and accept the tragedy and trials in his life as positive forces for growth and change; being prepared and strengthened for his coming mission by profound and powerful spiritual encounters that would leave him with great insights and extraordinary gifts.

And throughout it all, from this day forward, Holly and Matt would never be alone; his involvement in their lives would not end with his death, and he would be at their side when they needed his help, sometimes unseen, at others only sensed; more help would come, too, from angels, Matt's mother and others who would bring comfort, protection, a whispered word, a coincidence arranged . . .

In glimpse after glimpse, he saw that Holly and Matt would be all right without him; more than that, the deaths of Kate, Lori, Elliot and himself—as tragic as they were—would be used by God to shape Matt's future in a positive way, not because God was cruel or indifferent to the deaths of His children, but because the four of them had finished what they had come here to do . . .

The night sky scrolled back even farther, and the portal grew brighter, and brighter still, until it was filled with a glowing, vibrant light that made the darkness all around them completely disappear. John felt a sense of heightened anticipation, a wave of love and indescribable joy, and new images began to shimmer and emerge from the light:

A shining city of gleaming gold and purest white, a vast city of light with no discernible end.

Closer now, within its towering walls of layered gold: soaring spires and majestic arches, pools and courtyards and colorful terraces of indescribable beauty.

Awe-inspiring temples and towering cathedrals, magnificent buildings of every kind, each of them breathtaking in scope and design; their walls were glowing, as if fashioned from materials more precious than anything ever seen on earth, or from pure light itself.

Just beyond a line of ancient trees that rustled gently, moving without wind of their own accord: undulating meadows of amber and green, and gently rolling hills, inviting and tranquil, stretching out as far as the eye could see.

In another direction, off in the distance: majestic mountains, treelined and snowcapped, glorious and reaching toward an endless sky.

And in another, not far: lush, tropical growth, pulsing with energy so real he could see it, and teeming with creatures of every size and shape and conceivable color; in its center, an incomparably sublime and sparkling waterfall, hundreds of feet tall, its cascading waters vibrating and singing with a living voice that filled his spirit with peace and awe.

A garden appeared, the most fabulous, enchanting and splendid garden in heaven or on earth, and his spirit soared at the explosion of color and fragrance and energy; now the garden was all around him, the most beautiful blossoms of the most luxuriant blue, the deepest red, the most dazzling yellow, the creamiest white and the most glorious purple he had ever seen; each bent to greet him with a loving song as he passed among them.

There were people coming and going, strolling through the gardens and courtyards and lawns singly or in pairs or accompanied by animals, running through the meadows or sitting on the banks of a winding river, or striding between the buildings with a purposeful gait; each of them was glowing with the same inner light, but it varied in intensity and size and color, like auras of happiness or purpose or peace that flowed from a core of unwavering love.

There were angels as well, resplendent beings who moved among them, some dressed in robes of shimmering white with blue or red or amber trim, and others in thick, white garments of wool; some appeared young and others ancient, some with wings but many without; some were short but many were tall—some of them as tall as eight or nine feet—and each of them radiated great love and purpose and incredible strength.

All in all a multitude of spirits, and he saw—and began to remember—that heaven was an exciting, bustling place, a new, full life, not just somewhere to go after death, or a permanent vacation of eternal rest; it was a continuation of life, with work and friends and spiritual growth, but without the hindrance of fear and a physical body; it was the life he had known before coming to earth, the life he was destined to lead once again, and it filled him with a powerful, irresistible yearning for the only true Home he had ever known.

He saw it all again, the city, the gardens, the mountains and forest, the people, the angels, wonder upon wonders upon indescribable wonders, and then a wonder even more astounding crystallized before him.

A great throng of people and all manner of angels were gathered together before a glowing platform in a vast, light-filled hall; on the dais was a throne of incomparable majesty and indescribable beauty, surrounded by thick but luminous fog; the throne was empty, and more spirits rushed in and joined the crowd, until the space in front of the dais was filled with a sea of glowing beings.

There was an air of excitement and great celebration, then, in the sweetest, purest voices he ever heard, the angels began to sing. . . . Their song washed over him, and over him again, until he suddenly realized with a profound sense of gratitude and humility and belonging that the song they were singing was intended for him! They, and the spirits gathered before the throne, were rejoicing at the successful completion of his mission, praising God's plan and welcoming him home.

A hush came over the assembled spirits, anticipation rippled through the mighty hall and the angels' song ended and another began; their voices soared, ever higher and sweeter with words and feelings of great reverence and praise, thanksgiving and love; the glow around the throne, in the dais, the walls and within the spirits themselves, grew deeper and more radiant, until suddenly the throne was ablaze with light, the brilliant, glorious, eternal, energizing and life-giving light of God Himself.

John's eyes could only see the hem of a garment, but his spirit thrilled as feelings of approval and peace and joy rippled from the throne; a mighty hand emerged from the light—a hand that pointed in his direction—and a white-gold beam reached out and touched him, enveloping him in a flood of divine, paternal, unconditional love. Then, the Father spoke and the vision ended. . . .

When the night sky returned, John looked at the angel with wonder. For a long time, he was speechless. Then, with profound gratitude, he said, "Thank you . . . for everything." The pull to leave the Earth and experience the events he had just seen in the vision was almost overwhelming. Still, there was one last thing he wanted to do. "I have a favor to ask before we go."

The angel smiled knowingly. So did Will.

"I would like to say good-bye to Holly and Matt," John explained with an earnest smile. "I'd like to let them know everything will be all right. And that I'm all right. It just might give them the comfort they need to get through the next few months."

"Yes, it will," the angel replied, giving John a look of approval. "As you saw, you will have many opportunities to visit them in the coming years. Tonight is the first. So, go," he said smiling, gesturing to the place where Holly and Matt bent grieving over his body. "Offer them comfort and encouragement. But do not reveal the details of the future you were shown."

~

"DON'T BE AFRAID. It's me."

Holly and Matt glanced at each other, and looked up. In a matter of seconds, the expression on their faces went from stunned disbelief to exultant joy and back to grief. Matt spoke first in a cracking voice: "You died?"

"Yes," John answered, giving him a gentle smile.

Holly closed her eyes and moaned softly, but Matt's face suddenly lit up with hope. "But you're coming back, right?"

John smiled regretfully and shook his head. "No. This time I won't be coming back."

Matt's face fell, and Holly opened her eyes and stared at John with a stricken expression. Tears streamed down her cheeks, and her voice trembled. "But you can't die now! Not now, for God's sake, John! Not like this . . ."

"It's my time, Holly," John said tenderly. "Try not to be sad. Be happy for me. I'm going Home."

"I know," Holly croaked, shaking her head. "But still . . . I don't want to lose you so soon."

"You haven't lost me. I'm still alive—and I'll still be with you."

"But it won't be the same!"

John started to answer, but Matt let out an anguished groan and great wracking sobs began to shake his body. John looked at him and knew that not only was he devastated by his parents' deaths, but he also felt responsible for John's as well. He also knew that Holly was wrestling with guilt. John's heart went out to them, and he prayed for the right words to ease their pain.

"I know you're both hurting and scared," he began. "Angry, even—at Elliot, me, with yourselves, maybe even with God. I wish you could have been spared what happened tonight. It was terrible, unthinkable. . . . But you need to know that none of it was your fault. *None of it!* And don't grieve for me. It was my time. I'm happy and very much alive! And I've seen where I'm going, and words could never begin to describe how wonderful and beautiful a place it is. So, please, don't feel sorry for me, and above all, don't blame yourselves."

"But I failed at my mission!" Matt sobbed inconsolably. "Everybody's dead. . . ."

"No, Matt, you didn't fail," John said sharply. "Your dad was responsible for everything that happened, not you. You've got to believe that, because it's the truth. He forgot to trust God, and gave in to despair, and it twisted everything until he didn't even know what he was doing anymore." He paused and added, "God has already forgiven him. In time, I hope that you will, too. It wasn't your mission to save your family. You did as much as anybody could have done, Matt, but it was out of your hands. Your real mission is just beginning."

At first, Matt's reaction was almost imperceptible. His breath still came in hitching gasps, but his sobs grew softer, and as he stared at John with glistening eyes, John knew he had succeeded in giving him at least a small measure of comfort. "I can't tell you what it is, but you have an important mission ahead of you, Matt. Very important. Both of you do, as a matter of fact," he said, glancing meaningfully at Holly, whose eyes went wide and suddenly thoughtful. "You may find it hard to believe right now, but you have an exciting journey ahead of you, believe me. And God will bless both of you in tremendous ways."

Matt stared at him for a moment with a puzzled expression, and John knew he was struggling desperately to believe his words. "But who's going to be my guardian angel?" Matt asked doubtfully as the wail of police sirens started in the distance.

"I will," John said, smiling deeply. "And so will your mom and a host of others who were helping you long before I arrived. Even if you don't see us, we'll always be there when you need help." He looked at

Holly. "And Holly will be your guardian angel now, too. And you will be hers. From this time on, you have each other. Both of you are valiant spirits and special in God's eyes, and He brought you together for a very special purpose." Seeing self-doubt in Holly's eyes, he added, "I'm not saying that just to make you feel better, Holly. God has shown me what a brave and precious spirit you are. You have so much love to give. And so do you, Matt. That's why God wants you to take care of each other.

"I know this still hurts. It will for a long time. But one day it won't hurt quite as much and you'll go on with your lives—and they will be rich, rewarding lives. God can bring great good from even the most senseless tragedy, and He will bring great good from this. I know. I've seen it."

John fell silent, realizing it was almost time to depart. It was a bittersweet moment and he felt great sadness at leaving, but also excitement for what lay ahead for Holly and Matt, as well as for himself. He was overwhelmed by a rush of great love for this boy he had managed to save, and for this woman who had unselfishly joined in the mission, and the love filled his being and leapt through the air as a stream of light flowing straight to their hearts. For the first time that night, Holly and Matt smiled, if only briefly, and John knew that although they had not seen the light, they had surely felt it.

After a moment, Holly looked at John and said in a soulful voice, "I'll miss you, John. . . . And I love you."

Even though he no longer had a physical body, John reached out and embraced her with his spiritual body. "I'll miss you, too." Then, he hugged Matt also. Will and the angel stood to one side, visibly moved. "I love you both with all my heart," John continued. "Remember what I told you, and hold on to your faith. Never forget that God is with you, even in the darkest, most desperate hour! All you have to do is ask for help." He moved back and smiled deeply, lovingly, knowing he had done what he had come there to do: tell them good-bye and offer some comfort and hope for tomorrow. "Always remember that God loves you," he said. "And so do I."

John looked at Will, and then at the angel, who gently smiled and held out his hand. John nodded. He glanced back one last time at his friends, and reached for the angel's waiting hand.

AUTHOR'S NOTE

For more information about the spiritual subjects explored in this book, the author recommends:

The Celestine Prophecy, by James Redfield. New York: Warner Books, 1993.

The Celestine Vision, by James Redfield. New York: Warner Books, 1997.

Closer to the Light, by Melvin Morse, M.D., with Paul Perry. New York: Ballantine Books, 1990.

Conversations with God (Books 1–3), by Neale Donald Walsch. New York: Putnam, 1995–1998.

Embraced by the Light, by Betty J. Eadie. New York: Bantam Books, 1993.

Marianne Williamson Audio Collection. New York: Harper Audio, 1993.

A Return to Love, by Marianne Williamson. New York: HarperCollins Publishers, 1996.

The Soul's Remembrance, by Roy Mills. Seattle: Onjinjinkta Publishing, 1999.